THE STEALER OF SOULS

Marge flew down to treetop level. The yacht was there, well concealed under a lot of brush and natural camouflage. The central cabin was large enough to have portholes, and she landed on the deck and looked in.

All her companions were there: Joe the barbarian, his mate Tiana, the little thief Macore, the mermaid Tura, and Captain Bly. They were sitting around a table as if about to eat, but none was moving.

The Master of the Dead had already stolen their souls, and they were nothing but zombies now, responding only to his orders. Their souls were imprisoned in little bottles, hidden somewhere in his secret horde. And there was nothing Marge could do to save them.

All she could do was scuttle the ship to prevent their being taken away—and pray that Throckmorton P. Ruddygore would arrive in time!

By Jack L. Chalker
Published by Ballantine Books:

THE WEB OF THE CHOZEN

AND THE DEVIL WILL DRAG YOU UNDER

A JUNGLE OF STARS

DANCERS IN THE AFTERGLOW

THE SAGA OF THE WELL WORLD
Volume 1: *Midnight at the Well of Souls*
Volume 2: *Exiles at the Well of Souls*
Volume 3: *Quest for the Well of Souls*
Volume 4: *The Return of Nathan Brazil*
Volume 5: *Twilight at the Well of Souls: The Legacy of Nathan Brazil*

THE FOUR LORDS OF THE DIAMOND
Book One: *Lilith: A Snake in the Grass*
Book Two: *Cerberus: A Wolf in the Fold*
Book Three: *Charon: A Dragon at the Gate*
Book Four: *Medusa: A Tiger by the Tail*

THE DANCING GODS
Book One: *The River of Dancing Gods*
Book Two: *Demons of the Dancing Gods*
Book Three: *Vengeance of the Dancing Gods*

Vengeance of the Dancing Gods

Jack L. Chalker

A Del Rey Book
BALLANTINE BOOKS • NEW YORK

A Del Rey Book
Published by Ballantine Books

Library of Congress Catalog Card Number: 85-90649

ISBN 0-345-31549-9

Manufactured in the United States of America

First Edition: July 1985

Cover art by Darrell K. Sweet

Map by Shelly Shapiro

To Erica Van Dommelen,
of the Dawntreader Cattery;
the best proofreader in or out of the business

TABLE OF CONTENTS

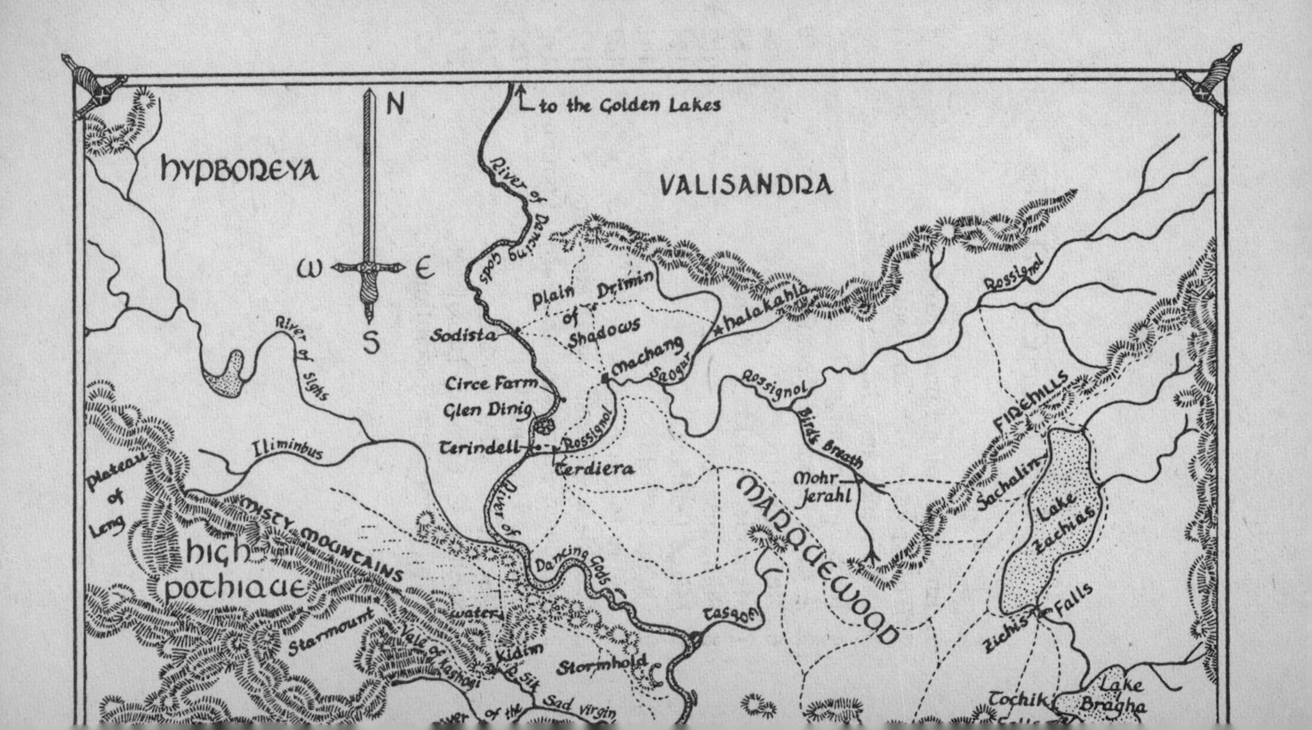

to the Golden Lakes
N
W
E
S
HYPBOREYA
VALISANDRA
River of Dancing Gods
Plain of Shadows
Drimin
Halakahla
Sodista
Machang
Saogur
Circe Farm
Glen Dinig
Terindell
Rossignol
Terdiera
River of Sighs
Iliminbus
Plateau of Leng
MISTY MOUNTAINS
High Pothiaue
Starmount
Vale of Kashogi
Water
Kidim
Sit
Sad Virgin
Stormhold
River of Dancing Gods
Tasgof
MANQUEWOOD
Mohr Jerahl
Bird's Breath
FIREHILLS
Sachalin
Lake Zachias
Zichis Falls
Tochik
Lake Bragha

River of the Sad
Valley of Decision
Lake Ogome
Gorge
Corbi R.
River of Sorrows
Sorrows Gorge
Dabasar River
River of Dancing Gods
Witchwood
River Morikay
LEANDER
ZHIMBOMBE
Zhafqua
FLOOD PLAIN
Rombi's River
Lake Ktahr
Castle Boquillas
Wolf Island
Khafdis River
Quoos
Clidrum
Yingling
Marahbar
Codra
Shelly Shapiro '83
HUSAQUAHR

CHAPTER 1

ENCOUNTER ON A LONELY ROAD

If a worshipped idol has power, it shall always emanate from the eyes or the navel, except for golems, in which case see Vol. XCVIII.

—The Book of Rules, XCLV, 194(d)

IT WAS THE BEST OF TIMES; IT WAS THE WORST OF TIMES. In point of fact, Husaquahr had been blessed now with good government—as good as it was going to get, anyway—and peace for several years.

In other words, it was pretty damned dull in Husaquahr.

Oh, there were the usual quotient of crimes, magic spells, occasional irritating *geases*, and a number of black-art wizards and witches lurking about, and the general population was oppressed by a ruling class of one sort or another as usual, but it was minor, petty stuff. There'd be no great new warrior kings to fear and celebrate in song and story through the generations, no wondrous battles, the tales of which would thrill the newer generations for centuries, no epic quests or bold adventures that would make this a time to look back on. Since the defeat and subsequent exile of the Dark Baron and the dispersement of his armies, even those who were most evil in Husaquahr seemed willing to compromise with the good and just have a comfortable old time.

The rider on the black horse was almost invisible in the dusk, wearing as he was a tight black body stocking, black belt, and worn riding boots. He was a small man, both short and slight, and wore only a small dagger for his defense. He looked elfin, although he was of totally human blood, and somewhat boyish; yet any who looked into his cold, penetrating eyes knew both fear and respect. They were dark eyes, as black as his garb, and they were very old eyes as well. They said to one and all that this was a dangerous man and not ever to be taken lightly.

It had been seven years since he'd stood with the greats and fought with the best of this world the forces of evil and darkness brought forth from Hell itself by the Dark Baron. He had killed many men then and a few since, but never without cause.

It was cool in Husaquahr right now; the gods of the north wind breathed down deeply this year into the southern lands and refused to take their rest, even as the days grew longer. He pulled his cloak a bit more tightly about him to ward off the stinging fingers of wind and saw in the waning light of the setting sun the signs of an approaching stormfront. There was no question as to what sort of front it might be—soon snow would be all that would be possible out here. It was already far too late for snow, but someone had forgotten to tell the snow that this was so.

Only an idiot would be out in wastes like this with weather like that coming on, he told himself sourly. There seemed little hope that he could outrun the storm, less hope that there was any place along this route where he could find shelter for the night or the storm's duration, and it was much too far to turn back to the last settlement. He knew what was behind him; what was ahead certainly offered more hope, since he was ignorant of the details, although perhaps not anything better.

He had taken this ancient road primarily to avoid uncomfortable pursuit. A slight smile came to his face and he reached down to his belt and into a small pouch and brought forth a giant emerald, as large as a lemon and alight with an inner green fire. He would have given it back, having proved his point and met the challenge, but the priests of Baathazar weren't the sort to be forgiving just for that. He had no use for the thing—he had long ago amassed more money than he knew what to do with and he had the most powerful friends and allies in all the world to bail him out if need be.

Necessity had made him a thief; but once he'd chosen his profession, he'd been bound by the Rules concerning thieves, and the occupation had both shaped and gotten along famously with his personality. He was a thief, and he'd always be one—the greatest thief in all Husaquahr, perhaps the world. The profession was the grandest one offered someone of no means and little magic, for each theft was a challenge, each caper a unique puzzle to be solved. The more impossible it was, the more he was drawn to it as a fly to honey. He had stolen this, the jewel in the navel of the great idol Baathazar, in full view of ten thousand pilgrims and half a dozen high priests with great powers of wizardry. It had been easy—but only in retrospect. He was quite certain, without being egotistical, that no one else could have pulled it off.

Still, he would have returned it to them—sent them a note telling them where to find it, perhaps involving them having to lower themselves to a great indignity to get it; but they would have retrieved it. What was the point? The thing was worthless to him now.

They had not, however, a true appreciation of his skill and, yes, his integrity as well. They didn't really care if they got the stone back, so long as they got the "desecrator" of their sacred idol. It wasn't even much of a god, as these things went—one of those left over from the bad old days, supported by a decreasing number of followers.

That, more than anything, was what had made them bad-tempered fanatics. Priests used to all that power now had to undergo a lot of belt-tightening, and they didn't like it one little bit. He was a handy person to take all that frustration out on. In a way, he'd known it from the start and had taken steps to counter it, steps which included this escape route. The one thing he hadn't counted on, though, was snow.

It began soon and quickly built up into an uncomfortable blinding world of white flakes. Within minutes he was no longer certain that he was still on the road, or in which direction he was going, and he knew he'd have to stop soon or perish. This was no weather nor fit place in which to be stuck, whether man or beast. His horse was already complaining and it had no place to go, either.

Chance would not save him now, nor all his skills, and he knew it. Only magic would get him out of a fix like this, and he had very little that really mattered. He wished, at least, he had some power to dry up the snow or conjure a nice inn with good ale and a warm fire. Damn it, he wasn't even dressed for this weather!

At the thought, the jewel in the pouch seemed to hum and throb, slowly at first, but with a building force that could no longer be dismissed as mere imagination. He stopped in the midst of the storm and removed it once more, noting its unnatural fire and glow.

Why did a god have a navel to begin with? He wondered about that idly, knowing that he was trying to take his mind off his impending doom. He stared deeply into the jewel's throbbing fire, and suddenly it seemed to him as if the wind were calmed and the storm silenced. There was, all at once, a deathly hush about him and his mount, and he knew in a moment that he was not imagining things. This was indeed magic, dark magic of the blackest sort, the kind of magic that he would never touch in any other case but this. He didn't know whether or not he'd sell his soul to live—he frankly wasn't certain it was still his to sell—but it was better than the alternative.

He hopped down off his horse and looked around. There was still near total darkness; yet where he stood no wind blew and no snow fell. There was, in fact, an unnatural warmth which was already melting the snow that had fallen upon the ground on which he stood, turning it to mud.

He placed the stone on the ground and drew a pentagram around it with his dagger. It wasn't a very large pentagram, but that which he expected to occupy it would fit one the size of the head of a needle if need be. He stepped out of the pentagram and then closed it.

"All right, green fire," he called aloud to the thing, "if indeed you are a gateway to elsewhere, then I hear your call. Whoever is bound to you should come through, so that we may discuss things."

There was a sudden hissing from the stone, which flared into extraordinary brightness, and then the sound of escaping steam as a thin plume of smoke rose from it until it was perhaps shoulder-high. The steam, which gave off an uncomfortable heat in spite of the raging snowstorm all about him, widened into a turnip shape, expanding to fill the entire area. When it contacted the boundaries of his crude pentagram, it ceased growing and instead solidified.

The demon who showed up was something of a turnip itself.

It seemed to be all face, a comical, Humpty-Dumpty sort of thing whose waist was its mouth, above which sat two huge oval eyes. The head rose into a point, at the top of which was just a shock of purple hair. Below, the thing sat on two huge clawed feet, but seemed to have no legs to speak of. Its arms, coming out of its body just below that tremendous mouth, were short and stubby things of misshapen crimson, ending in long and mottled hands with great black claws at the fingertips. It looked around, spotted him, opened its mouth, and licked its lips with an enormous black tongue. The inside of the mouth was lined with more teeth than a shark's, all pointed and sharp, and beyond those teeth seemed to be a bottomless hole.

This, then, was the source of the priests' powers and the reason why they were nearly frantic to get back the stone.

"You're not one of those mealy-mouthed priests," the

demon croaked in a voice so deep and reverberant that it moved the very air. "That means that either their silly faith is overthrown or you're a pretty damned good thief."

"The latter, Sir Demon," the little man responded, bowing slightly. "I could not resist the challenge, although, to be sure, I had no idea I was stealing more than a great gem."

"All great gems have demons assigned to them. You should know that. Otherwise, where do you think all those curses came from?"

"Good point," he admitted. "However, this, I suspect, is a different sort of gem."

"In a way," the demon agreed. "I can certainly see that you've mucked up your getaway. This is no curiosity call."

"Quite right, sir. I need a service, it is true, if the price be not too high."

The demon studied him. "What could you offer me, thief? Those in your profession tend to wind up with us anyway, so your soul isn't much of a deal. Still, you never know. What's your name?"

"I am Macore of the Shadowlands," the thief replied.

"Macore, huh? Seems like I heard the name. Hold on a moment while I check."

Instantly the demon vanished, leaving Macore alone once more. No, not quite alone—from the center of the pentagram came forth the lush sounds of massed violins playing a rather pleasant if monotonous melody. It was very nice at first; but as time wore on and both he and his horse began to get very impatient, the strains of the music began to irritate him.

Suddenly the music stopped. Just as abruptly the demon was back. "Sorry to keep you on hold so long, but his Satanic Majesty's filing system is lousy. We have so *many* customers and prospects these days that he really should automate it, but that would make it too easy for us." His voice took on a mocking tone. "It's supposed to be Hell, remember that!" He sighed, and the sound of it went right through the little thief.

"Still," the demon continued, "I did find the file. Thought your name was familiar, too. One of the minor demon princes got sent all the way down to the dungpits a while ago and he ain't stopped wallowing in more than just dung, if you know what I mean. All the time, this self-pitying wail about how he was gonna deliver this world on a silver platter and got cashiered instead of rewarded for it. What's he expect, anyway? It's Hell, after all."

Macore thought a moment. "His name wouldn't be Hiccarph, would it?"

"Yeah. That's the one. So it *is* the same Macore. Okay, that simplifies everything. What do you wish, thief?"

This was suspiciously too cooperative. "And what is the price?"

"First you tell me what you want, then I'll quote you the going rates. That's simple enough. You keep it simple, I'll keep it cheap. Fair enough?"

"I can ask for no more," Macore responded. Already the temptation was there to ask for whatever he wished, to go for it all, but he knew that this was the trap of demonic bargains. He had no intention of delivering himself totally, now and forever, as a slave to this creature. "Naturally, I wish safety and security from this storm and from my pursuers. Of course, I mean this in the way that I am thinking it, without loopholes or various things I did not think of when requesting it."

The demon nodded. "All right. What else?"

"That is it," the thief told the creature. "That is all I want from you."

The demon sounded slightly disappointed. "Nothing more? Great wealth may I bestow upon you. I could make you irresistible to women of any sort. I could give you immunity from all spells, or give you many of the powers now reserved for wizards who must suffer to gain what I offer."

"Suffer now or suffer later," Macore responded. "That is of no concern to me." He admitted to himself that the sex appeal was quite tempting, but he had never really had much trouble in that direction. "I have all the wealth I need—I steal for the sport of it. Women and I get along quite well without demonic spells. I have great protections against much of the spells of this world, and I have enough magic to get along. No, I'll seek the price for what I asked and no more."

"You are hardly in a position to bargain," the demon pointed out.

"Nor are you," the thief responded confidently. "I know enough of the laws of magic to know that one such as you has but one door into the world, and your door is obviously that gem. Were I to die here, that gem might well be lost in this wilderness for generations, perhaps forever. You would then have no outlet to relieve your own tedious existence in Hell. My passing over to your plane is not nearly as terrifying to me as your being cut off over there is to you, and I know this. Now, quote me fairly."

The demon spat. "Bah! Ones like you are pains in the ass! However, I'll quote you fairly. You actually desire three things, then. You wish to survive and again take up your life. You wish to elude your pursuers. And you wish it straight, with no tricks or loopholes. Very well. For your miserable life, you must agree to give this stone at the first opportunity to one who can and will make use of it. Agreed?"

"That is simple enough. Agreed."

"For security against the priests and their followers, you must accept a mark that I will place upon you, so that all of Hell shall know that you have dealt with me and will recognize you at once."

He was a bit nervous at that. A demon "mark" could be anything from a small scar or birthmark to something quite extreme and quite hideous. "I will not agree unless I know the nature of the mark."

The demon didn't like that. "The priests will know your identity and they will hunt you down eventually. I promise only no physical deformity or infirmity. Take it or leave it."

He sighed, knowing that he'd gotten as much out of the demon as he could expect, and knowing, too, that the demon was right. He had struck at the core of the priests' cozy racket and stolen the base of their power. They would never rest until they got him, unless called off by supernatural means more powerful than any in Husaquahr. "All right—agreed."

"Finally, you can see the potential for traps and loopholes in the first two agreements. I could turn you into one of the faerie, an unpleasant sort of one, or make you a lover of other men, or perhaps a plain woman, or thousands of other possibilities. To gain it gently and without loopholes, I require that you freely accept a *geas* from me, one which you will not know but will be compelled to carry out."

"I must know the nature of that *geas*, demon," the thief told him. "I would rather you changed me into a monster than perhaps to kill a friend."

"Admirable. However, you must understand that any *geas* of which you have knowledge will be readable by wizards, and that is unacceptable. No, even this much will be taken from you if you accept. I will go this far. The *geas* is a single task, it involves no one's death or in fact even harm to anyone, friend or stranger, nor will it in any way alter the social, political, or military fabric of Husaquahr as it stands. The consequences do not, in fact, really affect Husaquahr at all. There is risk to the task, but none that you are not up to facing."

"You wish me to steal something, then."

"Sort of. The task is that, although you do not actually have to steal the object, you must reach it. That is all I can tell you, for anything more might render the *geas* useless."

"It does not sound too bad. Will I know at some point what the *geas* was?"

"You will know—when it is done."

"Then I will accept."

"Done!" cried the demon.

Macore was slightly disappointed. "No blood contract? No terrible oaths?"

"Don't be ridiculous. We save that sort of stuff for the psychos and fanatics. Your word is bond, as is mine. I return now to my dwelling place and expect to find at least one new sucker very soon, as per our agreement."

"But—our bargain! How will I survive the wastes in this storm? And what mark have you placed upon me?"

The demon chuckled, not only at the question but at the fact that Macore had already had all memory of the third bargain and *geas* wiped from his mind. "As for the first," it said, "the storm has already abated, and the town of Locantz is but a half-hour's gentle ride in the slush. You will be able to see the lights of it when I leave. Just head for them. As for the second—no shadow or reflection shall you cast, no matter how polished the mirror or bright the light. That should actually come in handy to one like you. I will take my leave now."

Macore felt more than a little relieved, but he was a bit suspicious. "Now that the bargain is done, can you tell me, before you leave, Sir Demon, if that town was there at the start of this business?"

"Of course it was. Fun's fun, after all. . . ." And with that, it vanished, and a sudden cold blast of air hit him. He had been perspiring from Hell's heat—not that Hell was actually flames, but there was some strong reaction, some sort of friction, created when one from the netherworld projected into this—and now it seemed to turn into tiny icicles as he stood there. He erased the pentagram and picked up the gem, which was still quite warm to the touch, and placed it back in his pouch, then climbed quickly back upon his horse and looked around, finding the lights of the town in a moment. He kicked his mount forward, anxious to reach an inn and a warm fire.

No shadow and no reflection. Not a bad mark, as these things went, and, as the demon said, possibly quite useful.

He'd have to find some convenient explanation for it, though, as it was going to be a bit obvious to his friends. A curse, perhaps, for stealing the gem in the first place. That sounded right. Considering what the demon could have done, it seemed a small price to pay. Perhaps in the town just ahead he could fulfill his end of the bargain and get rid of the damned stone. He certainly wanted no more of it or Squatty Bigmouth, either. He had had enough adventure to last awhile, he told himself. Perhaps it was time to take a little time off and see some of those old friends again.

Terindell, he thought longingly. *I shall visit the great old wizard at Terindell.* He suddenly very much longed to see the place, although he hadn't given it a thought in over five years. He did not, however, wonder why.

CHAPTER 2

THE TROUBLE WITH GODHOOD

Barbarians may make effective monarchs, but will be unable to reconcile their civilized duties with their inner natures.

—Rules, VI, 257(a)

THE TWO WOMEN COULDN'T HAVE BEEN MORE DIFFERENT in appearance. One was small, dark, and incredibly voluptuous, almost in a state of undress, more of her body covered by her long brown hair than her clothing; the other was tall, chunky, with short hair and a stern face, dressed in leather jerkin, trousers, and slick black boots. The contrast was only accentuated by the fact that the one in leather had a toad on her head.

"Oh, Djonne!" the looker wailed. "Things just haven't been the same in Raven's Lair since little Alee fell into the giant dough mixer while competing in the Grand Husaquahrian Bake-Off!"

"I *know*, dear," the tall one in leather consoled. "Just think of my poor Hanar here, turned into a toad just because he left out one little teensy clause in his contract with the demon!"

"*Hmph*! You think *you* have problems? I mean, if Alee had just stayed dead instead of returning as a spirit to this house, that might have made it bearable! Now, though—it's dough, dough, dough, all over the place. You can't sit or walk without stepping in it; and, if you manage for any length of time, she *throws* it at you. It's gooey and sticky and *hell* to get out of pile carpeting!"

"Not to mention those creepy cannibals stalking the place," the one with the toad responded.

"*Wark!*" croaked the toad perched atop her head.

"Oh, don't you worry, *dahling* Hanar," the big woman consoled it. "They've only eaten humans so far. You're safe as long as you remain a toad."

The small pretty woman sighed. "Yes. They were reformed cannibals who had been strict vegetarians for years, but they liked the taste of poor Alee so much while judging the contest that they can't rest until they've sampled the rest of the family!"

"It was silly to enter the bread after the—ah, accident," Djonne told her friend. "I mean—it was *that* which turned them on."

"But what were we to do? Without the money from the Bake-Off we would have lost the house, the toadstool groves—*everything* that makes life worth living! And we won, too! If only Master Gwelfin can duplicate the taste, without having to throw people into the mixing batters, we'll be richer than any in the land!" She paused. "Perhaps it wasn't Alee after all. Perhaps it was the forty-day-old dried mermaid's scales. . . ."

"Oh, enough of this, Moosha!" Djonne cried. "What's done is done!"

"You know they say I pushed her in! Always coming around, asking questions! They say that's why Alee's come back with her abominable doughballs!"

"I know, I know. It's true the top rung of the ladder over the vat was sawed almost through, but I know you weren't the one."

The pretty Moosha stopped and stared. "You do? Why?"

"Because during the only time when the rung could have been sawed through, I know you were making it with your brother Mischa. I—saw you."

"You were peeking into windows again?" Moosha was aghast.

"It's a hobby. Besides, I know you were only trying to console your brother because of his curse."

That sobered Moosha. "Yes, yes! That was it! How horrible to have to go through life with a curse like that. You see, someone started to play music outside, and the only way to save him was to involve him so much that he could not hear it."

"Compulsive tap dancing is a horrible thing," Djonne agreed.

"Particularly when there were taps in the room but no shoes!" Moosha responded. "Think of the *pain*! Besides—it was safe. I knew even then that I was pregnant!"

"What! But—who? You're so chaste that the two-headed dragon went after you a few months ago!" Djonne paused. "Oh, my! It's not . . ."

"Yes—he caught me. We've been having an affair ever since. Little did I guess that I had enough fairy blood in me to make something else happen!" She sighed. "Bowser has been *so* jealous."

"Your *dog*?"

"No, silly—my horse."

"Will it be a dragon or a human?"

"Who can say? Oh, Djonne! I'm so alone and afraid!

Haunted, stalked by cannibals, pregnant by a dragon! To whom can I turn?"

Djonne got up, came over, and hugged her. "Moosha, I made a sacred oath when Hanar got turned into a toad that I would love no other man and I have kept that oath. But you I love, my darling Moosha, and I always have loved you."

They embraced and kissed. At that moment there was the sound of smashing glass. The couple broke and stared into the darkness in panic.

"It's *them*! The cannibals! They've found me at last! Oh, what will we do?" Moosha cried.

"There's no way out!" the other told her. "We must make our stand here for better or worse!"

"Oh, Djonne!"

"Oh, Moosha!"

"*Wark!*" said the toad.

All went dark. There was sudden, stunned silence.

And then the audience rose to its feet and clapped and cheered so loudly and so long that it seemed like the very theater would collapse.

High in the royal box, two giant figures, looking like massive statues, sat and watched impassively. Both were easily ten feet tall and as white as the purest marble, with matching white hair and white robes. Now and then, though, the curious onlooker could see one or another of the pair stir and know that indeed these were great statues come to life. One was a woman of tremendous proportions and radiant, idealized beauty; the other was a man with the face of a stern yet achingly handsome man and the body of all men's dreams.

They stood suddenly. As the cast came out for their final bows and stared at the great figures in awe, the entire theater fell silent. Then the goddess gave a smile of favor and a nod to the company, and the audience gave an audible sigh of pleasure and relief. As the two gods turned and left the box, the roaring cheers started again.

"You did quite well, my love," the Goddess Eve said

to her companion. "I could tell what torture you were going through."

"I never liked this god business much anyway. You know that," the God Adam responded sourly. "But when it makes me sit through that maudlin soap opera . . ."

"Come, come!" she consoled. "This is only every two years!"

"Well, that's part of it. I mean, they left a hundred more threads dangling this time than they did before. It never ends. And we have two years until the next chapter, while they play the cities and the boondocks!"

"Oh, come! Come! It gives the peasants something to talk about during the interim. As for us—well, it is one of the obligations we have in exchange for running things."

"*Huh*! I don't see old Ruddygore showing up at these premieres, and he's now Chairman of the Council of Thirteen."

"He probably writes them. I have heard it said that he has an entire group over on Earth doing nothing but tape-recording daytime serials for him. Still, it's over now. We can become ourselves once more and not have any further ceremonial appearances until the temple rites on Mid-Day."

"Yeah. Three whole days. Not long enough to go anywhere or do anything, except get cooped up in that ivory tower of a castle."

They reached and entered a small dressing room that was strictly out of bounds to anyone, even theater staff, on nights like this. There the Goddess used a now familiar spell to change them both back into their human selves once more.

They were still both quite attractive and quite large. Joe de Oro was six feet six and two hundred and seventy pounds of pure muscle. Tiana was just a half inch shorter than he and proportioned accordingly. Both were actually classified as barbarians under the complex Rules that governed this strange world. In human form they tended to dress minimally in rough-cut furs and preferred going barefoot. Although they still bore a striking, if less perfect, resemblance to the God and Goddess whose nude statues were everywhere, no one ever made the association when they walked the streets as ordinary folk. The resemblance was occasionally noted, but only that. Part of the reason was a spell, of course, that prevented anyone from making the logic leap, a spell put on by the whole of the Thirteen and thus literally unseeable and unbreakable, despite the powerful wizards who roamed the land, but another part was the fact that they were imposing but, quite certainly, humans; with black hair, brown eyes, and bronze, weathered complexions, they hadn't the supernatural aura of gods.

Nor, of course, were they gods, although the majority of the people of the nations of Husaquahr thought they were. The evil Kaladon had kidnapped and bewitched Tiana and made her into the Goddess in a plot to take control of the whole of Husaquahr. Joe and others, including, ironically, his sworn enemy the Dark Baron, had disposed of Kaladon, but the old wizard had been clever enough to spread the power about among some of the others of the Thirteen who lived in Husaquahr. They found the legitimacy that their roles as anointed high priests and priestesses of the new cult gave them quite satisfying. Neither Tiana nor Joe liked the deal, but they were not really offered another one. Even a good wizard like Ruddygore had found this new religion a culturally unifying force and supported its continuance. To be sure, it made the emergence of another Dark Baron quite unlikely.

"I'm just plain *bored*, that's all," Joe grumped. "I mean, I was always on the move, always going someplace else. I wasn't forced into trucking—I chose it for its freedom, such as it was. Over here, they held out the idea that, once I did a few things for them, I'd be free to roam and see this crazy place. Instead, what do I find? I'm a damned god who has to wait an hour just so he can ride his horse out without getting stuck in traffic!"

"Do you regret it, then?" she asked him. "It was I who

had no choice, not you. You know that you still don't have to do it. You could walk out now, and we'd find some stand-in to pretend to be you during public ceremonies."

He grew irritated. "Oh, come on—you know better than that. I knew the price coming in, or at least I thought I did. Sure, I'd like to go roaming around and finding adventure, but not alone. Without you, it just wouldn't be any fun. It's just, well—so damned *boring*! Worst of all, there's really no end to it. All this luxury and power is okay, I guess, but even gods need a vacation once in a while."

"We can't do much right now, I suppose, but let us talk to Ruddygore. He is due in near the end of the week, anyway. Let us take some time off and go down to the island and get away from it all. Discuss it with him there. He always seems to know when something has to be fixed and how to fix it."

"Yeah, well, maybe. He hasn't been exactly chummy lately, either. Just ducks in and out every once in a while with a new script to fit something or other he and the Council are doing. I guess that's the other problem. We're the only two friends we got. None of the old gang stops by anymore, not even Marge, and it's been years since we heard from Macore or even Grogha and Houma. No battles, no adventures, no big travels, and no social friends. Who can be comfortable being friends with two folks who are worshipped by a few million people?"

"I know. Something must be done. I will admit that on more than one of these occasions I have had the urge to say something silly or screw up the ceremonies. The cost, however, would be great to us both, and very unpleasant, as you know. Ruddygore chairs the Council, but he could neither contain nor control them if we messed up their little racket."

He sighed. "Well, I guess the island's as good as any for a little relaxation, anyway. It's the full moon on the sixteenth through the eighteenth, you know."

She nodded. "I know."

The full moon was quite important to both of them. Joe had long ago become the rarest of transmuters, a pure were, condemned on the nights of the full moon to turn into whatever animal or fairy or other nonvegetative creature was nearest. Nor was he alone in this curse. It was inevitable that sooner or later, if only in the intensity of their lovemaking, Tiana would come to be bitten and also get the curse. She had known this before and had accepted it.

In point of fact, what Joe had originally seen as a terrible affliction now provided both of them with their only diversion. They had the power and authority pretty much to arrange what they wanted to be, and they had been a lot of things—human, animal, and fairy. It also meant that as the fairies feared only iron, they feared only silver, and Tiana, whose magical powers were quite strong, had learned first of all the spell for transmuting silver into some other substance when it was too close to her or to Joe.

She reached over, took his hand, and squeezed it, smiling. It was surprising to both of them, but without magic, at least as far as either knew, after all this time they were still very much in love with each other and very devoted as well. It was strange, really, but they both still felt like honeymooners. Even stranger was how so nearly perfect a love could still leave them both unhappy.

"Perhaps it would be different if we could have children," she said softly.

"Forget that!" he snapped. "You and I know that must never happen!"

There was, in fact, a curse that went down through her family, a curse levied perhaps a thousand years before on the females of her line. It was said that one of her distant ancestors was a great and powerful sorceress. The details were unknown beyond that point, except that this sorceress in some manner either made a bargain or attained a powerful curse that she would never die. Instead, she would die at childbirth with her firstborn girl, and her soul would then enter the body of the newborn, and so the cycle would continue forever. It was, of course, roughly even odds, boy or girl baby, but that was a pretty severe step to take. Joe wasn't at all certain about the soul business, but he knew that Tiana's mother had indeed died in childbirth while giving birth to Tiana. She had always thought the curse a local one on her own mother, and while she was convinced she had her mother's soul inside her, Tiana had not at the time realized just how continuous this was. Now, with the records of Castle Morikay, her ancestral home, at her disposal and more time than she liked to have, she found just how far back the curse went.

Both of them did want children, but there seemed no safe way to get them. Her love was strong enough that she was willing to take the risk for him, but his love was strong enough that he would in no way allow it, no matter what his desires.

There were, of course, magical ways of determining the sex of a child; but when dealing with a curse as ancient and as powerful as this, such spells could not be depended upon.

"I think it's clear enough to leave now," he told her. She got up and put on her fur cape, and the two of them quickly left the room and walked down toward the stable area. It had mostly cleared out by the time they got there, and there was no trouble finding their horses.

He still felt a lot of tension and frustration within him and had no desire to go quickly back to the castle that dominated the city. "I feel like getting rip-roaring drunk and maybe taking apart a bar," he growled.

She laughed. "Count me in! Lead on!" They galloped off down the street to find a likely victim.

The riches of Castle Terindell were legend, but few tried to gain them, for Terindell was the home of Ruddygore, his current name of his more than three thousand identifiable ones, and Ruddygore was the Chairman of the

Council of Thirteen, the strongest of the strongest among wizards. The great vaults below were made of solid iron, enough to kill any of the fairy folk, save the dwarves, with nothing else added. For humans and dwarves, who had no such weakness, there were other traps, both mechanical and sorcerous. None who had ever tried for those vaults had ever been seen or heard from again.

Still, more had tried since the war than had ever tried before, and some of them were the very best. Ruddygore believed that it was the peace and quiet in the land that caused the increase. He well understood that, to a master burglar, the challenge was irresistible. There were things in those vaults, however, that no human or fairy should ever have, things even he wished he did not have to have, and the penalty had to be severe and permanent for that reason alone. He almost never went down there himself, except to check that none had indeed been successful and to reinforce the spells and traps.

The thief's name was Jurgash, and he considered himself, as did all good thieves, the finest at his craft in the world. Also like all great thieves, he was very rich and also knowledgeable in the magical arts. Unlike most, he was also a powerful practitioner of those arts, although he used that power, other than for gratification and amusement, only to combat such power in his objectives.

Like almost all the great thieves, too, he was a small, wiry, slightly built man, in the peak of physical condition. He had entered Terindell through the front gate, in the guise of a man who had been set upon and robbed on the road and who needed help. He was a convincing liar, so much so that he often believed his own lies while he was telling them.

Ruddygore, as he well knew, was not at home, nor was his adept and very dangerous companion, Poquah the Imir. This had left mostly the staff, which were a few humans, some elves, and various and sundry other creatures—even one ogre, Gorodo, the trainer of the wizard's small but powerful private army. Jurgash dealt mostly with the elves though, as he expected, and they had believed every word of his story, fed him a fine meal, and put him up for the night in a luxurious guest suite. In fact, he had the virtual run of the place for the night, which was even better than he had hoped, although it showed just how dangerous the vaults might be. If the old and powerful wizard could in fact leave his castle in such gullible hands, then all that was truly worthwhile was so well guarded he believed none could get to it.

The door down to those vaults looked deceivingly simple, with a huge basic key lock that any amateur could pick. Of course, that was how it should be. The first traps would not be on the outside of such an entry, but just inside. The only advantage he had as a thief was the knowledge that Ruddygore himself had to go down there once in a while, so there was a way around every trick and trap, every spell and danger, if he could spot them all in the proper order and solve their riddles.

An experienced hand with a probe revealed the first one right away. The big wooden door, in fact, was not locked at all, and any attempt to fiddle with the lock mechanism meant instant activation of alarms. Examining the door carefully, he saw that it was, in fact, not a normal door at all. The hinges, for example, were false. The door, in point of fact, appeared hinged in some way from the bottom. Try and pick that lock and the entire door, built of heavy wood and probably reinforced with iron or lead, would suddenly and quickly fall outward, crushing the would-be thief like a rat in a trap.

He had his kit with him; from it he took a small handle that was actually a magnet. He placed the handle as far up on the door as he could and then, holding his breath, he pulled gently. The door, which was clearly iron-cored, gave, coming forward as he pulled. He stopped as soon as he dared and examined the small, dark area he had revealed. As he had suspected, there were two alarms, one mechanical and one magical. The mechanical one, nothing more than a pull-string, proved easy to bypass, but the spell was enormously complex and took some time to understand and build onto enough to bypass its trigger.

Removing his door block, he continued to pull down until he was satisfied that there were no more traps, at least on the door. No alarms that he could sense were sounding, and he felt reasonably satisfied that he was safe. He carefully stepped inside, then used his handle once more to pull the door back up to its closed position. He was now totally in the dark, and knew he would have to risk some light. He brought forth a small torch and lighted it with his flint, not wishing to try any spells in this place until he could see just what he was dealing with.

The torch flickered and then burst into life, and the thief gasped. In front of him was a great hole, a bottomless pit of blackness. The floor did continue, but it was a good twenty feet to the other side, and no ladder, rope, or other way to bridge the chasm was evident. He shifted his sight to the magical bands and saw a criss-crossing network of complex red and blue strands across the whole of the chasm. He realized quite suddenly that the spell was so complexly woven that it would take hours to unravel enough even to guess its nature. He ignored that as impractical; instead, he looked for loose ends and found none. The spell was a complete one, then, not an interactive type wherein he or another intruder would provide the additional mathematics to enact its horrors.

He wondered, in fact, about that chasm. Nothing in his research indicated that Ruddygore ever brought with him a great bridge or ladder, and he could hardly see the huge fat man going hand over hand on a rope. Clearly one could cross this without apparatus, but to do so would have required at least one loose end in that spell to which a small solidifying spell could be tied, sufficient to allow someone simply to walk across on thin air. This was a spell of concealment or revealment, then, not a true trap in and of itself. That meant that either it hid something that was actually there or showed something that was not there.

Could the chasm be false? He gingerly tested, and found his foot going down off the edge without finding any support. No, at least some sort of depression was there. But if the chasm was real, how did Ruddygore cross it? By added spell? If so, what was the purpose of this one? He doubted the added spell anyway; it was somewhat complicated, and he had many timings from his spies and paid informants. Ruddygore went in and rarely spent more than fifteen minutes inside; the longest time known was just over half an hour, which included the time going to and coming back from the vaults. He did not cast and uncast spells in that period of time.

Could the spell, then, conceal a bridge? One could not simply cast for it—that would break that fine spell there and send up an alarm, at the very least, and perhaps something fatal. A bridge, then—but perhaps a bridge that did not start at the edge and was barely wide enough for one of Ruddygore's bulk? Anyone testing the edge would find space, but if he knew where the bridge was, he could just blithely step across it.

But where would such a bridge be? On one side or the other, certainly, and not anywhere in the middle. Ruddygore would not risk a misstep, nor make it so complex that he couldn't get anywhere here in a hurry. But which side? If Jurgash were the wily wizard, he'd have that bridge on one side and a very ugly surprise on the other. There was no way to test it without possibly triggering an alarm, so the only solution here had to do with psychology. Ruddygore was right-handed; right-handed people tended to move to the right, which would place the bridge on the right-hand side. However, the wizard would know that this was an elementary trick.

Taking a deep breath, Jurgash the thief picked up his bag, sighted the left, ran to the edge and jumped off into what seemed to be open space.

He came down hard on a stone surface and fell forward,

skinning his hand and knee. His kit flew forward out of his hands, but hit some sort of stop and halted. He felt the thrill of confidence, although it still looked to him as if he now sat on thin air. He reached over and retrieved his kit, then got carefully to his feet, feeling a surge of exhilaration and confidence. Not easy, no, but this was a challenge worthy of him for certain!

He did not, of course, fall for the gap further on in the bridge; it was almost inevitable, and only an amateur or a fool would be so thrilled at solving the bridge that they would not expect it.

At the other end, things changed once more. A tunnel made a sharp turn and then led to a deep descending stairway. The steps were of stone, but obviously could not be trusted and had to be examined one by one. Several proved to be booby-trapped, but the trap he appreciated the most was the invisible wall that moved down when one skipped over an obviously booby-trapped step, setting him up for a very close shave. He barely missed it, and redoubled his caution.

So far, most of the traps were mechanical. Fine, effective puzzles, but far below Ruddygore's skill as a wizard. When he reached the bottom of the stairs, though, he turned back around and saw that the whole series of forty stone steps were now ablaze with ribbons of red, yellow, and blue magic, tied in complex patterns. He immediately guessed the purpose—the same traps were there, but now all of them were reassigned, perhaps even reversed. Going up would be a totally new challenge. Still, it told him something more, something which sobered him a great deal. He had passed the point of no return, the place at which the amateur would either be discouraged or easily fooled. Anyone getting this far would be a pro of the highest order. When a defender started blocking exits it meant that the thief must now win or die. He already now knew too much of the defensive system to be allowed to live.

He, however, had no intention of going back out.

Everyone knew that Ruddygore had in his vaults the magic lamp that granted wishes; it had been stolen once by the Dark Baron and then back from him, and had been used in plain sight. It would wish him out of here safely with whatever loot he wanted.

The tunnel had no more evident traps for about ten feet, although it still angled down, but then it emptied into a small chamber that was lined with mirrors. There seemed no way out—there were three reflections of him in front, two more on each side. The floor was still solid stone, with no signs of magic, and the ceiling was also featureless stone and a good fifteen feet up. Clearly, then, one of the mirrors was itself an illusion of a mirror, or was in some way hinged and trapped.

He stood there, in the center of the room, contemplating the new puzzle, when suddenly a ghostly, reverberant voice spoke to him. It was Ruddygore.

"You are to be congratulated, thief, for getting this far," the voice said. "Now you stand, however, in the primary trap, the one that cannot be passed by any other than myself. For the record, you are now twenty-six feet from the vault doors, and there are seven doors there, six of which, when opened, contain horrors more terrible than you can ever imagine, and only one of which contains what you seek. Don't worry. This is the end for you."

He knew that the voice was part of an activation spell now, and that in fact Ruddygore had no knowledge that he was here. It was a generic taunt, meant to discourage and unnerve.

"If you wish to halt things now, I give you ten seconds to turn and walk back through the tunnel to the base of the stairs. There you will find a recording of the one spell that will allow you to pass easily upward and back out into the castle. It will also, of course, turn you into an ogre and make you my absolute slave forever afterward, but that's the price you pay for staying alive. Fail to take this and you will die, and your soul will be consumed by these mirrors and used to feed their powers."

He looked frantically around. Ten seconds! He would not be panicked, but he knew enough not to take the threat lightly. He had triggered a spell for sure, and it was certain not to be a bluff. But how had the spell been triggered? With a sinking feeling, he thought he knew. The mirrors. The spell was triggered if they reflected any form but Ruddygore's!

He stared in horror at the mirrors, then watched as his own reflections seemed to take on a life of their own, then *step out of the mirrors and come toward him*, daggers drawn.

They were upon him before he could even take the offer to be an ogre.

CHAPTER 3

OLD FRIENDS AND OLD ENEMIES

Neither friendships nor relations shall be anything but subordinate to one's true nature as established by these Rules.

—Rules, III, 27(c)

THE FACT THAT THROCKMORTON P. RUDDYGORE LOVED to travel by ship was well known, so his arrival at the island castle retreat in a sleek racing yacht was not unusual. The fact that the lake in which the castle sat had only one outlet, the Khafdis River, which was not navigable made it a bit more unusual. Ruddygore's ships did not travel in conventional places or along conventional paths.

Lake Ktahr was broad and enormous, although quite shallow in places. From no point on Wolf Island, even the highest tower of its castle, could any land be seen beyond the waters, which made it ideal for Joe and Tiana. Beyond its cliffside castle and outbuildings, the island was still wild, although no wolves were known to be there. The island had received its name ages before because of a peculiar, wolflike prominence jutting out from the high cliffs. The vegetation was lush, the climate generally warm, and there were a few small white sand beaches accessible by steep trails from the high island floor.

Once, not long ago, this place of secluded beauty had been the center of Husaquahr's evil and the site of an epic battle between Ruddygore and its previous owner, the Dark Baron, Esmilio Boquillas. The castle itself had been expropriated by the couple regarded by many as gods and had been redone and staffed with Ruddygore's loyal servants, or "employees" as he always called them—mostly elves and other fairy folk whom he trusted over humans.

It was a bright, warm, sunny day when Ruddygore arrived, and Joe and Tiana went down to meet him personally at the only anchorage on the island, a mile or so from the castle itself. No matter how many times they saw him, the old sorcerer made an impressive sight.

Ruddygore was not merely tall—almost as tall as they were—but he was *big*, and with his long white hair and flowing white beard he looked very much like what the real Santa Claus should look like, complete with a rough, reddish complexion. Although he'd been known, in private moments, to dress quite informally, he was now dressed in his normal public attire—striped pants, morning coat, formal shirt with vest, bow tie, and top hat. He seemed not to notice the heat and humidity.

Ruddygore, of course, was not his real name. He had, it seemed, thousands of them, and probably more that were still not traceable to him. He was quite old—thousands of years old at the very least—and his past made up a considerable body of both Husaquahrian history and legend. To know a great sorcerer's true name was to have some magical power over him, and it had been so long since his own name was uttered by anyone or anything that it was said that even he had forgotten it.

His comical name and appearance belied his tremendous power, which was the strongest known in this world where magic ruled—at least the strongest known human. In addition, he had one other skill, one piece of information no other wizard knew, and one which gave him a decided edge in a world where magic worked and technology was virtually unknown. He alone knew how to cross the Sea of Dreams between his own world and Earth, and he alone was privy to the secrets of technology that Earth had.

He came down the gangplank like some great king, clutching his cane with the golden dragon on its hilt, but he warmly shook Joe's hand and hugged and kissed Tiana with evident real affection. "How good you both look!" he said enthusiastically in his great booming voice. "It's good to be back home and among friends once more. Come—let us go up to the castle. Poquah will see to our things."

Poquah was the thin adept of Ruddygore's, an *Imir*, or warrior elf, by birth and training. His race had but one innate power, but it served them well. No one, not even their closest friends, even noticed their existence unless they wanted to be noticed. It was often spooky or even irritating to have him seemingly pop up from nowhere and vanish just as quickly, but it was very handy for a warrior. Like humans, though, any powers of wizardry had to be learned by hard study and apprenticeship, and he was the first known of his race to have both the talent and the desire.

Ruddygore's great bulk looked unmanageable, but the old man was really quite spry. He mounted the horse they'd brought for him with a single easy motion and managed to look both comfortable and, considering his garb, ridiculous at one and the same time. The couple mounted their own horses, and they started off up the winding, switchbacked trail to the top and then to the castle.

"I can tell that something is amiss with you," Ruddygore noted as they rode. "Excuse my prying, but are you two having—difficulties?"

"Not in *that* way," Joe responded. "Frankly, we're just bored to death and sick and tired of all this."

"With your support, we are the richest and most powerful in all this world," Tiana added, "yet we are no more free than the lowest serf in the fields."

"Well, everyone's trapped in one way or another," Ruddygore replied. "No one is ever really free to do whatever he or she wishes, I fear. Still, if one has to be trapped, it's far better to be trapped at the top of the heap than at the bottom. Believe me, any of the peasants putting in eighty-hour weeks and going home to a mud-and-straw hut would trade places with you in a minute. It *is*, however, both ironic and unfortunate that the higher one climbs, the less freedom and more responsibility one finds. In that sense I am no more free than either of you."

"But you *are*," Joe retorted. "I know you're busy and have little time, but you can occasionally manage a break, a vacation, and you can do it on another world, where no one knows your identity or powers."

Ruddygore thought about it a moment. "Well, that's not really true. When I'm on Earth I manage mostly to get away for an evening here or there, but in general I'm quite busy. What happens there affects what happens here, as strange as that sounds. I'm not going to explain it to you, since it's somewhat mystical and technical, but let's just say that the greater Hell's power on Earth at any given time, the greater its power here."

"And how is Hell doing over there?" Tiana asked him, only half serious.

"Quite well," he responded. "Better than here, which worries me a great deal. The threat of nuclear war grows greater each day, while crime runs rampant. The human genius for killing other humans has developed whole new and massive ways of waging war without Armageddon, but that won't last forever. Repression and terrorism are up all over, and the true measure of Hell's success, the amount of fear injected into the daily lives of the most inconsequential of people, regardless of nation or ideology, is way up. The tides this causes in the Sea of Dreams are large and dark, and they are washing up on our shores as well. I do my best to build the dikes to keep it from engulfing us, but I fear it is a battle that cannot be won for long. The effect is not as strong the other way, alas—our defeat of the Dark Baron lowered tensions somewhat on Earth, but not nearly enough. They are back even now to their prewar levels."

That was depressing, but not something they either understood or could do anything about. Joe said, "Well, I don't want evil or another war or anything like that, because it would kill too many people, but frankly I'd do almost anything to relieve this boredom. We need a break, Ruddygore." He sighed. "You know, I felt sorry for Marge, but the fact is she's getting to see this place while I'm stuck on a damned false throne as some kind of monument. We can't even really enjoy *this* place. We're due back in only four days. That's just not enough."

"Don't feel sorry for Marge—ever!" Ruddygore admonished him. "She's really happy for the first time in her life."

"You've seen her, then?"

He nodded. "Yes, about a year and a half back. She's still much the same, but she's fully accepted and adjusted to her faërie* nature now and she seems to be fully enjoying life. The fairy folk have a far greater joy in life, even the smallest and most ordinary things, because, while ageless, they are no less mortal than we, but unlike us, if they die before the Last Trump is sounded, they die the

***Faërie* refers to the heritage, magic nature, power, and "realm" of fairies in general; it has a connotation of that which is withdrawn from human ken. *Fairy* refers in more specific manner to individuals, races, traits, and abilities of the fairy folk; its connotation is more that of a normal, day-to-day existence.

real death. It makes them appreciate things more and cherish every moment. It's one reason why fairy folk in the main seem childlike, although you know that they aren't."

"You make the threat of true death seem like an asset," Tiana noted.

"Oh, no! It just makes the outlook different, that's all. You see, deep down, no human really believes that he or she can die until it happens. The fairies, whose power is partly based upon belief, know the truth of that and its finality. Because of that, you either go nuts or you live every moment of life to the fullest. Whole races of fairy folk have gone in both directions." He paused a moment, then continued.

"However, as to your holiday problem, we might be able to solve it. I agree that you need a break, if only because of the boredom. Both of your natures are free-spirited, and that's part of the problem. Me, I could use a little boredom now and then. Let me think on the problem for a day or so. Perhaps we could invent a new holiday, one in which the two of you would supposedly go back to Heaven for a few weeks or something. I've never really been comfortable with this idiotic theology, but it *has* been convenient in many ways and it's no sillier than ninety-nine percent of the religions and cults in this world or on Earth. So long as it emphasizes Heavenly values and virtues, it doesn't serve Hell's ends, and that's more than can be said for most of them."

They arrived at the castle, where elfin grooms took their horses, and they entered and went to the Great Hall. They settled down in comfortable, fur-covered chairs, and a servant brought them a tray of delicacies, and another brought drinks. Ruddygore, still formally attired but with hat taken, settled back and looked somewhat relaxed.

"I can tell that you have been arguing over children again," he said casually.

They both jumped. "*What!*" Tiana cried. "How did you know?" She had visions of spies all over the place.

"Because it's something that would happen if boredom weighed heavily upon you. I know you both too well."

"Well, it's out of the question," Joe growled.

"Why?" the wizard asked him. "Oh, I agree when it comes to Tiana, but you're both weres. You can become each other. The genes would be the same."

"You mean *me* have the baby?" Joe was aghast.

"Certainly. Oh, at thirty-six hours a month I fear the pregnancy would be about fifteen or sixteen years to term, but what of it? A simple spell would continue you every were-period until it happened, although you'd have to make certain that you did in fact become Tiana each time or heaven knows *what* you'd give birth to in the end, but it's possible."

Joe shook his head in wonder. "No, I don't think so."

"Well, perhaps there are other ways. We'll see."

"It is the first night of the full moon tonight," Tiana reminded him.

"Oh, yes—I know. Don't mind me. I'm here for a brief rest and to do some studying anyway. Something is up. I can smell it. Something that I feel both here and on Earth, and that means something big. I want to find it and nip it in the bud before it bites all of us."

Macore was a small man dressed in a dark gray tunic with an integral hood. The hood, of course, was down now, in the bright daylight and in the company of familiar friends, and revealing a darkly handsome man with an angular face, always clean-shaven, and a nose perhaps a bit too big but of which he was inordinately proud.

He was not surprised to find Ruddygore away, although his usually reliable sources told him that the old boy was due back almost any time now. Macore was one of the few who knew where Ruddygore went on these frequent and sometimes long business trips, although he'd never been to Earth, and all he knew about it was what he'd learned from associating with Joe and Marge in the old days.

The old days, he thought sadly, sitting in a small reception hall and picking at the fine meal Durin, Ruddygore's elfin master chef, had prepared for him. How quickly the time passed, he reflected, and how much older he felt. Not that he wasn't physically as good as he ever was, but now more of that speed and quickness came from spells and elixirs, dearly bought, instead of through natural training, as it had been not too many years ago.

He wondered, sitting here, why he felt so depressed. Things were not, after all, that bad, and he really had no complaints. The life of a thief was a lonely one, but he had chosen it, rather than being forced into it. Those who were forced into it were amateurs and tended to remain so. He had only sympathy for them. He, now, was different. He was rich, he was famous—or infamous, depending on who heard the name and under what circumstances—and he had the friendship of the head of the Council and the two demigods who dominated life, particularly in the area of the river. Few had ever caught him and none had ever held him; he was getting into his middle forties now, pretty old for any sort of thief.

He loved a good roll in the hay with a willing wench, but there was no end of those, and he wished no lasting commitments to anyone. To make such a commitment was to make him eternally vulnerable. He was, in fact, at the top of his profession and he had achieved everything in his wildest dreams—plus a lot more.

And that, of course, was the root of the problem. When one has broken into dark towers ruled by witches and ancient gods and stolen their treasures, picking the unpickable locks and breaking the unbreakable spells, what was there left for him? He could, he reflected, do no better than to equal himself in the future, and one of these days even he would make a fatal mistake, borne of carelessness or age. No human being was perfect. It was this knowledge—that he should quit now, while well ahead, or inevitably die—that was eating at him. He was the gambler who was now ten thousand ahead, able to support himself forever, who knew that if he played long enough he'd lose it all, but could not stop playing because, really, he didn't want to do anything else.

And what challenges were left? What had not he or one of his colleagues never failed to crack that was worth cracking?

With a start, he thought of one. One right below him, in fact, and the best guarded of the lot. He could recite the names of two or three dozens of the finest who had tried it. He'd never seen them again, and probably would not, in this life. It had never occurred to him to steal from Ruddygore. Mooch off him, certainly, and use his name and political influence where it was advantageous—but steal from him? The man was the most responsible for elevating him from petty con man and minor crook to the king of thieves he now was.

But did he have to steal—or merely solve the problem?

He dwelt on the idea that evening as he put away his things and made ready for bed. He looked at his shaving gear and then stared into the mirror and scowled. Nothing, no reflection at all, stared back. It was as if he were invisible; yet, of course, he was solid and real. He'd been cutting himself shaving for several weeks and still hadn't really gotten it right. He would grow a beard and to hell with it, except that trimming a beard was just as difficult. It hadn't seemed much of a curse, and it really wasn't, considering the alternatives, but that demon sure had one hell of a nasty sense of humor.

He'd traded the jewel off quickly, as agreed, to a young and ambitious black magician with some useful spells to trade. He hoped the kid thought fast. He kind of suspected that the other part of the deal, that the priests not catch up with him, had been handled by them blaming whoever had the gem. If so, the twerp better grow up real fast.

Throughout the next day the problem of Ruddygore's vaults haunted him, and he really had the urge to give it a try. He milked the staff for all the relevant details, which weren't much, but helped more than they knew, and mapped out a rough idea of what was down there. Naturally, there'd be mechanical traps, and ones with fixed spells—those were rather simple. He didn't fear those, although they'd be formidable indeed, so much as he feared electrical traps—the one kind of guard that no thief in this world would expect or understand. They had used a few such in the war, and of them all the ones he feared most were those which transmitted and those which took a code to turn off.

With a start, he realized that energy was energy, whether it was magical or electrical. One of the spells he'd gotten from the young black magician was in fact an energy-damping spell, although of course the fellow hadn't seen it that way.

He decided to give it a try. What the hell. This would surely make him the king of thieves if he did it; if he didn't, at least he wouldn't have to worry about his future careers.

CHAPTER 4

INVITATION TO DANGER

There is no puzzle so complex that it cannot be solved.
—Motto of the Thieves' Guild of Husaquahr

NONE IN THE LONG AND VARIED HISTORY OF HUSAQUAHR had ever seen Throckmorton P. Ruddygore move this fast or be this angry. He had spent four days on the island recovering and relaxing from his unknown ordeals, then had headed off for his great castle Terindell in Marquewood as Joe and Tiana ruefully headed back to their own duties elsewhere.

As usual, Ruddygore always checked the seals, and when he discovered that no less than three attempts on the vault seemed to have been made in his absence, a new record, and one of them by Macore, he blew up. Of course, the staff was only guessing at this—they knew that all three had entered, two who thought they were surreptitious and Macore through the front gate—and that none had emerged again, but none could be absolutely *certain* that the vaults had been the cause of it.

Ruddygore was certain, taking only a cursory glance at the front door of the vaults and taking a reading from the memory in the wood. "How *dare* they!" he stormed to Poquah. "Particularly Macore! Well, they all got what they deserved. Let's go down and see what damage is done."

What had taken hours for the greatest of thieves to figure out Ruddygore did in a quick series of motions, so automatic that one would not have even guessed the traps were there. He pulled down the door, stepped in, went immediately over the bridge that seemed not to be there, then down the stairs, rapidly, skipping just the right steps and ducking at just the right points. Poquah, who knew the route as well as his master, did likewise, at least until the hall of mirrors. The mirrors would attack anyone without Ruddygore's full reflection in all of them, so the sorcerer had to wait a moment there until Poquah was with him and under his protection. He took the opportunity to read the walls, and found signs of two thieves gone to Hell in there between checks. Poquah was the only one of faërie, other than the dwarves, who would not be instantly killed by the iron in the vault, and that was only because of a spell that interacted with Ruddygore only when Ruddygore was present.

Two thieves. That worried him. Two, not three—and neither of the two were familiar.

"I don't like this, Poquah," he muttered darkly. "It is

absolutely impossible for any, be they human or fairy, to pass this point unless with me. Even a false visage won't do it, since the mirror sees and recognizes such spells. About the only type of creature capable of passing through here would be some sort of vampire, and Macore is not one of those. Well, come on. Let's see just how far he got."

The Imir walked before him now and through the center mirror as if it wasn't there, as indeed it was not. It was an illusion, reflecting the others. An immediate bright, searing light hit them, hot and intense, but there was no sign of any remains or essence to show that anything had ended its life here.

"Definitely no vampiric spirit," Poquah noted. "It would have been destroyed at this point."

Ruddygore again took the lead, pressing the keystone in the wall that was invisible in the brightness of the light to ordinary eyes, insuring that the spring-loaded, stake-filled walls beyond would not close on them. Down another few stairs and around a curve, they broke through a complex sonic pattern that was impossible to avoid and well above the threshold of even an animal's hearing. The sorcerer went up to a small wooden box, flipped it down to reveal a numeric keypad, then pressed a nine digit combination that prevented the alarm box from going off, triggering all sorts of signals above and even nastier traps below.

They entered the main chamber and faced the seven identical doors, like those to bank vaults. Each had different and complex spells and locks on them, and there was no way to tell which one was real and which were the decoys.

Ruddygore and Poquah stood there, puzzled. Still none of the signs showed any trace of a recent visitor. This wasn't unusual if one just passed through, but death imprinted the inanimate objects surrounding it with a specific and retrievable set of signals.

"Clearly, either Macore did not come down here, or

he succeeded in entering the vault," Poquah noted in his dry, flat tone.

"No, if Macore had succeeded in getting all the way, he'd have returned upstairs, either to prevent any suspicion from coming his way or simply to taunt me about his feat in breaking my elaborate system," Ruddygore responded.

The Imir walked over to the second door from the right and examined its spells and locks. "Nevertheless, someone not only was here but managed to choose the correct vault. It is an amazingly skillful job, but the seals have certainly been tampered with."

Ruddygore strode quickly over, looked, and saw that it was true. He frowned worriedly, not liking this at all. "Not even the Dark Baron and his demon prince succeeded in breaking into these vaults. I don't care *who* it was, Macore is simply not this good. This is serious indeed, Poquah. I smell the hand of Hell in all of this, for only they would know enough of these vaults to bring someone this far."

"Still, the doors are scrambled randomly every few hours. How could even Hell know the correct one at that particular moment?"

"I don't know. But all these attempts by all these master thieves in the last couple of years, which I'd foolishly taken as just chance and the wages of being famous in dull times, I now suspect is more than that."

It would have taken the best of wizards many hours to unwork any of the spells on any of the doors, which were at the heart of the final security system. The true vault shuffled magically between the doors randomly, but at least once an hour; none could undo the spells and pick the locks in less than two, not even a member of the Council itself, which meant that even someone who got this far would be forever picking the lock to what would be the wrong door.

The only one who could undo the spells in sufficiently fast time to get into the right one was the maker of the spell, and it still took Ruddygore better than ten minutes. He rarely visited the vaults, or even checked them. He only checked to the last point where the thief was destroyed.

The spell undone, he had effectively frozen the vault shift and now took a great key from his waistcoat pocket and placed it in the lock, then turned it in an elaborate series of moves. The lock was, in fact, a nine number combination lock, and it had to be done just right, including removing the key before attempting to open the door. He did so, then pulled up on the handle and the great metal door swung away.

The vast treasure trove of Ruddygore's went back for what seemed to be miles, but he didn't try and walk the corridors and check every little thing. It was all keyed to him and to a personal inventory spell, and it took him almost no time at all to determine that the only things missing were fifty-one pounds of gold—real, not fairy, although the fairy gold would have been a better prize—and one of his American Express cards. The gold one, naturally.

There was, of course, only one way to get someone and that much gold back out, and he immediately walked far back along the corridors of the vault until he came to the Lamp. He was more than a little surprised to find it still there.

The Lamp of Lakash had been formed in the earliest days of Creation by the great powers who created the world. It looked, in fact, the way it should have—an ancient oil lamp that had once reminded Joe of an antique gravy boat with a top on it, sitting atop a rounded stand. It was originally designed as a fudge factor by the early Creators, since it could, within some strong limitations, violate or alter the laws of science and magic and grant a wish. Hell had made a stab for it, and it had been lost in the turmoil for eons afterward, even existing at various times on Earth as well as here, and giving rise to both worlds' legends of magic wishing lamps and genies. Ruddygore picked up the lamp and rubbed it gently, trying to remain calm and mark his words well while he held it. No matter what legend said, none were entitled to more than one free wish on the Lamp. Make two and, while the second was granted, the wisher changed places with the genie, becoming the slave of the Lamp in place of the one now there. Ruddygore had no desire to pay the price he would have to pay if he, even inadvertently, made a wish.

When it had been recovered by Joe and Marge, it had contained Dacaro, the evil wizard and former pupil of Ruddygore's, who had taken refuge in it against the demon prince Hiccarph.

The genie of the Lamp appeared, and Ruddygore sighed as he saw who it was.

"It's not my fault!" Macore the genie protested.

"I should have known," Ruddygore said disgustedly. "First tell me why you did it, then how."

"The why of it I only now fully understand," Macore replied, and proceeded to tell the story of the gem, the snowstorm, and the demon. Now that he had completed the *geas* the demon had laid upon him, he remembered all the details.

"So, anyway," Macore continued, "I was set up to do it. I had lots of information from the demon—he ducked down You Know Where and talked to Hiccarph, who, it seems, is currently shoveling shit and hating it. With the information he planted, added to my knowledge of you and my own skills, I did it. I can tell you, it wasn't easy, even with that."

"I can see getting to the mirrors. Many have done so. But how did you get past them?"

"Simple. The mark the demon laid on me was to have no shadow or reflection. The mirrors saw nothing. I, of course, saw the mirrors and deduced the gimmick, so that meant you had to have something to kill vampires beyond. Way back when, I lifted one of those pairs of sunglasses you had made for Marge, on the idea that it might come in handy, so I put 'em on and saw the keystone plain as day."

"But the sonic alarm—that's battery-powered! Earth technology! How did you come up with the combination?"

"I didn't. The young punk of a black wizard I traded the gem to gave me several spells in return, one of which was a blocking spell. Allowed me to go through spells that only activated when you broke their web because it kept the spell's energy lines intact as you passed through them. I figured that spells are just energy, and so is an alarm system, so I cast the spell several times, including there, as a precaution. I broke the sonic beams, sure—I didn't know about them until you just told me—but the spell kept the signal from being transmitted back to your box."

Ruddygore nodded gravely. What happened when the sonic beams were broken was that a simple transmitter was interrupted, causing it to send a strong signal to the alarm box. Macore's spell simply kept the current stable even when he passed through, so the box received no wrong signal. "And how did you guess the correct door and pick it in so short a time?"

"Oh, I'll admit that took me the better part of a day, and I damned near died of thirst and starvation taking all that time, even with my supply kit. I sensed the movement and figured out the gimmick, so the first problem was deciding on how to figure out which door held the vault at any given moment. You have a lot of fairy gold in here and every decent thief who's any sort of a pro has a diving spell for fairy gold. The iron in the doors was a big problem, but I've practiced at finding an ounce or less in some dutchess' necklace, so with several tons to work with even the iron couldn't block it out. Once I figured that part, I had to work on undoing the spells on the door, and that took damned near forever. Eight, maybe ten hours at least. It was hard to know just how much time had passed. Picking the combination was a piece of cake—

it's my job, after all, and these are commercial vault doors, even if they are antiques."

By this time Poquah had joined them, and was listening intently. "I can follow this far," the Imir commented, "but I cannot understand how you could pick the lock and know that the vault would be beyond when you opened it."

Macore laughed. "See? That's how thieves make their living. Even the best wizards think like wizards, not like thieves. You see, once I figured out that the thing moved around every hour or so, *it didn't matter which door I cracked*! All I had to do was crack it but leave the key inside the lock and then sit back and wait until my spell for the gold detected that the true vault was behind the door I'd already opened. Then I just took the key out, opened the door, and walked in. Simple."

"Simple," Ruddygore repeated glumly. "Yes, when you had Hell's knowledge of the map of the place, a good knowledge of my habits and electronics, and when you cast no reflection and have all the right spells to counter these things! This is far more serious than simple robbery and escape. This was plotted and planned by Hell, with the plot coming from Hell's highest level and through official channels. When the Demons saw that they had *you* in their power, they set it all up, having failed with their own thieves. The young black magician certainly was expecting you, and was certainly told just what spells to provide you. So, come—give us *all* the bad news. You are the genie; hence, you made two wishes."

Macore sighed. "You're not gonna like this. . . ."

Macore had rubbed the Lamp, and a rather surprised Dacaro, still darkly handsome and in the black leather uniform of the Baron's forces, had appeared. As a practiced wizard, it was quickly clear to Dacaro that the thief who'd freed him was not wholly himself.

"I must make my wishes to free myself of the *geas*," Macore told him, somewhat woodenly.

"I am bound to obey you, as you are to obey whoever sent you, but if you can, will you first tell me of what has happened since I was imprisoned in the Lamp?"

Macore nodded, and proceeded to tell the wizard how the Dark Baron had lost the battle, both on the battlefield and in wizardly combat with Ruddygore, causing an uneasy stalemate. He told of the return of Tiana, the unmasking of Boquillas, the great turnabout that Ruddygore had played on the Baron and his demon ally, the great face-down, and how Hiccarph had been yanked back to Hell while Boquillas had been stripped of his powers and eventually exiled to Earth after he helped defeat Kaladon and then tried to double-cross everyone.

Dacaro listened intently, but only when Macore had finished did he ask, "So who sends you now to this place, thief?"

"I am sent by Hell, by commandment of a demon whose name I know not."

"Very well, then. I am more than weary of the djinn. What a poor, miserable rattrap of a place, inhabited only by magical creatures who can do nothing *but* magic yet to whom nothing is real without mortal wish! It was, however, an education in magic that might prove more than useful, so discharge your *geas* and command me and the Lamp."

"First, I wish that no wizard of Council rank, be they on the Council or not, shall be able to cross the Sea of Dreams to Earth until bidden to do so by name by a wizard of such rank on Earth."

"It is done," Dacaro intoned.

"I also wish that when you are human again you be transported to the presence of Esmilio Boquillas on Earth, and be bound to his service, to materialize only when he is alone and unwatched, along with as much true gold as you can carry with you, stating the words '*Hutsut Ralston on the rillorah*' when you are ready to go."

"Done!" Dacaro cried, and suddenly became solid flesh once again. Macore, looking as if he were awakening from some sort of sleep, faded into insubstantiality and found himself drawn to the Lamp and pulled into it. He knew no more, until Ruddygore called him out.

"I should have guessed as much." Ruddygore sighed.

"I do not understand why he didn't simply wish the Lamp over there if he had this much latitude," Poquah noted.

"No, he really couldn't. Neither Boquillas nor Dacaro can use the Lamp, and he knew we'd be able to trace it through the djinn, anyway. The Lamp was more danger than asset to him. For the same reason, he took no fairy gold, since its atomic weight and structure varies enough that it might not be accepted on Earth as real. However, the real gold he took will net him a rather large sum, I would say, sold judiciously. Also, thanks to some prior wishes and some strong limitations, the Lamp is of far less effectiveness there than here. It takes one of our world now to do much with it, and even then the Rules governing its use on Earth are extremely restrictive since the Compact limiting direct conflict between Heaven and Hell to mortal intermediaries."

"But what can Boquillas be up to?" Poquah wondered. "He has no power, and is, after all, on Earth."

"Yes. On Earth, thanks to my muddle-headed compassion. On Earth, where Hell's real battles are waged, no holds barred. No, he has no power himself, but he has vast knowledge, perhaps nearly equal to my own, of magic and its usage—and now he has a sorcerer powerful enough to use that knowledge."

"Surely that will not avail him much on Earth! The Rules do not apply there!"

"Ah, but magic *does* work there, as you should know, my friend. It has simply been forgotten by most and disbelieved by the vast majority of people intelligent and dedicated enough to use it. And, you are right—there are no Rules there. I would never have sent Boquillas there if he had even a hair of his power, or if there were any formidable professional wizards still living and operating there. Now, though—he has found the way. And this time with Hell's full cooperation and blessing!"

He sighed. "And the worst part is, I can no longer even get over there to stop him."

She was a creature of the night and the fairy light and she loved it. She had been across the length and breadth of Husaquahr, and she had been the consort of kings and wizards, rogues, thieves, pirates, and mercenaries, and had to a degree shared their adventures. For one so tiny and delicate, she was a creature of great power, both known and unknown to mortals and other fairies.

She did not choose this life or this existence. It was forced upon her, as it was forced upon her sisters who were born to it. But she had not been born to it; she was a changeling, a human who had become a fairy when taken to the land where faërie power still held sway, and while she was totally what she now was, she was also the one she had been.

She was four feet ten inches tall, with a skin that was a soft burnt orange. She was humanoid, but not human. Her fingers, far too long for a woman's, ended in clawlike nails; so, too, her toes, and all digits both fingers and toes were webbed. She had a cute, sensuous face with enormous, sad, dark eyes and a playful, sensuous mouth, flanked by short, thick, blue-black hair shaped something like a pageboy with bangs over her forehead. From either side of her head protruded erect, shell-like pointed ears. Her body matched her face, and was both sensuous and perfectly proportioned.

But the most striking feature was the wings, sinister and batlike but somehow less threatening in deep crimson than in demonic black, although from the back the wings were a deep purple. They were not merely attached to her but seemed almost woven into and between her arms and body, so that, if an arm moved out or forward, the membranes fluttered and acted something like a natural cape, when not extended for flight.

She was of the race of Kauri, an all-female race with a very special place in the interrelated and complementary nationhood of faërie, a race numbering only a bit over three hundred, one of the most ancient and most primal of faërie types. They all looked exactly alike, but by a faërie sense of reading what was truly important about an individual as easily as humans might notice superficial surface features and blemishes, they all knew just who each was at all times.

To the Kauri, the whole world was magic and they alone were born just to enjoy it. In the sanctuary of their home at Mohr Jerahl, they flew and played tag and acted like small, uninhibited children without any self-control, having not a care in the world. Part of their job was removing from men, both human and otherwise, the heaviest emotional burdens inside the men's souls. They took it within themselves and fed off it, but they also acquired in this way more than they could consume. To cleanse themselves fully, they had to return quite often to Mohr Jerahl, where the Earth Mother who bore them lived in the heart of volcanic fires and could cleanse in those fires the stains they had removed from the souls of others.

Marge had often reflected how ironic it was that her Kauri powers grew enormously the more of that guilt and fear and loneliness she ate, yet the less fun it was when she had too much. She had returned to Mohr Jerahl only the previous night from a trip to the north, where she had participated in an ancient and colorful barbarian rite. When a chief or warlord married, there were three days of celebration, feasting, dancing, and all the rest, but on the wedding eve it was traditional for a Kauri to visit and service the groom, to take away that which might harm the relationship and make his soul pure for the wedding. While this involved, among other things, incredible sex, the Kauri even took away the guilt. Nor was there much in this case—there was a male race which was the counterpart of the Kauri, the Zamir, and they, too, were hired to service the bride.

Marge had always wanted to meet a Zamir, but she'd discovered long ago that it was simply not possible. Even when brought face to face, Zamir and Kauri could neither see, hear, nor feel one another, or in any way sense one another's presence. Each was nonexistent to the other—although not to everyone else.

Marge was unique in several ways other than being the only known changeling among the Kauri. She was from another world; she had vast experiences beyond the comprehension of a Kauri; and she was highly educated. She was also, of course, the only Kauri, and probably the only one of the fairy folk, to have a west Texas accent.

The barbarian wedding had taken its toll on her, and she was glad to be back at Mohr Jerahl and to have dipped into the fires of the Earth Mother and be cleansed once more. She was prepared to remain quite a while now and just relax and play.

She was content, really, with her lot in life, and the most important thing was that she had learned the faërie way of not looking ahead or anticipating, but living each moment to the full and making the best of whatever the situation was. She had meant to visit Joe, Tiana, and old Ruddygore; she still intended to do so, but she did not plan nor have any sense of time as humans did and she simply hadn't gotten around to it. Time was measured by day and night and nothing else; she had no idea how long it had been, except that it didn't seem very long at all.

It was, then, with some surprise that she received a summons to return to the Earth Mother only one night after coming "home," as she thought of Mohr Jerahl. The summons was internal, and it was obligatory. The Earth Mother was rather direct and, well, earthy; subtle was not something she understood.

Marge flew in toward the small hissing spatter cone in the center of Mohr Jerahl and unhesitatingly flew into its crater, oblivious of the heat and of the red bubbling lava. Instantly, she was one with the Earth Mother.

"I come in answer to your call, my Mother," she said, projecting her thoughts into the swirling mass of reds, oranges, and blacks.

"You bet your ass you do," the Earth Mother responded curtly. "A problem has come up which resulted in a request for you specifically. You've been out quite a while and I'm generally inclined to ignore such requests, but this one seems different."

Marge didn't really feel like going back into the world right now either, but she had no choice in the matter and said nothing.

"It appears that the forces of Hell are once more on the march, not in the old army sense, but in the way they are most effective," the Earth Mother told her. "As a rule, we're neutral in such matters, but this is an unusual situation. It involves the Dark Baron and others whom you know well."

She was startled. "But the Dark Baron is not in this world any longer!"

"That's true—but his influence pervades the world still, for his darker employer is not limited to merely one world or one place. This appears to be something so big it involves both worlds, and as one of both worlds it has been requested that you join the company formed to counter the evil. How do you feel about it?"

"The third adventure," she responded, suddenly remembering. "Oh, yes, my Mother. I will go."

"If I decide it, you'll go. I am hesitant. There are no signs or signals I can read on the course and outcome of this, since it involves Earth. There is great danger and possibly death in this. There is a great possibility that you will have to go to Earth to get this resolved."

"To Earth!"

"Yes. And if you do, it will not be as you were but as a Kauri you will go. Your powers are sufficient to mask you from ordinary folk, but none with the sight, including those from this world, will be fooled. Worse, Earth is a place terribly in need of Kauri, so the pressures on you will be enormous to help all that you find, and you must resist this. There is no way while there to cleanse yourself. Half of Earth is made of iron, which means it will be uncomfortable at the very least, and while there are spells to protect you, they offer only a very limited protection. It will be arranged so that you can handle small amounts without more than slight discomfort; but if you are injured by iron, it cannot be healed, and if you are killed, it will be the true death."

"I'm not afraid of that. I longed for the true death once, and was only saved by providence from taking my own life. All that I have done since has been the only truly happy time in my life. If the bill must be paid for that, then it must."

"Good girl! I'm proud of you! Very well. You will go to Castle Terindell, arriving on the night of the new moon, and from that point you will be in the hands of Ruddygore and his company. Just remember at all times that you are Kauri. Your will is strong. Control yourself and place the mission above all else." The Earth Mother hesitated a moment. "If you don't come back, I'm going to be really pissed off."

It was the closest thing to affection the Earth Mother had ever said to her, and she was touched.

"As a Kauri, I would not want to do anything to cause you anguish."

"Go, then! Before I change my mind!"

And, with that, she found herself flung from the top of the volcano back out into the open night air.

The moon was a thin crescent in the sky, telling her she had but three days to make the castle. It would not be difficult.

CHAPTER 5

A LONG-EXPECTED REUNION

The Council is absolute in all matters of adjusting or supplementing the Rules. Council members may not like or be allied with one another unless they so choose, but must be civil when meeting in session. This Rule should not be taken as a constraint against assassinations.

—Rules, II, 77(a)

IT WAS A SOMBER PARTY, BUT, NEVERTHELESS, THROCKmorton P. Ruddygore was a good host. There was gourmet food of every kind, fine wines and even champagnes, and the best accommodations. It was, in fact, a historical meeting at Castle Terindell; short of the convention of the Brotherhood, it was the first time anyone in living memory could recall that all thirteen members of the Council were in the same place at the same time.

Of course, they and a few others knew of the one other time, when these same men and women faced down the Dark Baron in his castle and stripped him of his membership and his powers, but this sort of gathering was unprecedented.

There was Ruddygore, of course, now Chairman of the Council and host to the gathering, still taking some delight in showing off his priceless collection of pink flamingos and plaster-of-paris statues gleaned from Earth; and the lovely and two-faced queen of the witches, Esmerada, who'd only survived the Baron by switching sides. Here, too, was Fajera, the huge black-robed figure from the continent of Murrl far to the south of Husaquahr, and the scholarly Docondian, the lean and dangerous Sargash, the ancient gray-robed Mathala, and all the others—the thirteen most powerful men and women of their world, and, perhaps, of any world.

Joe and Tiana, too, were there, along with many others both human and of the faërie. All had great power in the world of one sort or another.

Of all those invited, Marge was the last to arrive, circling the great castle and remembering all that had happened to her since arriving here. She took a turn over the great River of Dancing Gods which here joined with the Rossignol and widened into the greatest moving body of water any had ever known, yet still a thousand miles from its mouth. It was nostalgia and the beauty of the scene that made her hesitate; she no longer could even understand shyness or other social inhibitions.

Finally she dipped down, flying over the moat and outer castle and then into one of the brightly lighted windows fronting on the reception.

"Ah! A Kauri!" someone commented. "The old boy spares nothing."

Joe was polishing off a glass of good dark ale when he heard the comment, and he turned and saw her. It was impossible for him to know if this was just any Kauri or Marge—they all looked absolutely identical—but she spotted him, smiled, and winked, and he felt pretty certain. Tiana had always been uncomfortable with Marge around, but she knew better than to be anything but calm and gracious now.

Joe walked over to her, towering over the tiny fairy form. "Hello, Marge," he said a bit uncertainly. "It's been a long time."

For the first time Marge realized that it *must* have been a long time. Although Joe was still strong and in the best of shape, she noticed now a few gray hairs among the black and a certain etching of lines in the face. It shocked her a bit, since she was coming from a place where time meant nothing and the only close friends she had never aged.

"Hi, Joe. I guess it *has* been long. You lose track of time after a while. You're still looking good, though."

"I'm getting bored and lazy," he told her. "You got the best of the deal, believe me." He paused a moment. "I'm sort of surprised to see you here, to tell the truth. The old man asked for you specifically?"

She grinned. "He couldn't help it. The Rules guaranteed three adventures, and we've only had two. But if this involves Earth, it's something the two of us are best able to handle anyway."

"Maybe," he responded hesitantly. He still had trouble reconciling her fairy nature with anything practical. The Kauri were enormously powerful but only in defense. None could so much as stick out a foot to trip someone or slap a face or stick a pin in somebody's rear. Not that they had to, so great were their defensive powers, but those powers defended only them, not anyone they might be with.

"Do you know the details of this?" she asked him.

"Not much. Ruddygore's supposed to brief everyone at a meeting here tonight. All I know is that Dacaro's free because of some demon and he and a fortune in gold have gone to Boquillas on Earth. The Baron has as much knowledge of magic as Ruddygore, and Dacaro has the power and strength to use it. Imagine that team set loose on Earth with no scruples, Hell's help, and a population that doesn't even really believe in magic."

She nodded, but said nothing, just looking around at the assembled dignitaries. "Looks like a rogue's gallery, if I ever saw one, right here. Two-thirds of the people here are more in Hell's grasp than Boquillas."

And she wasn't wrong in that. The fact was, the ruling powers were a mixed bag of personalities and many, if not most, were magicians of the blackest sort—the kind of folk who'd cheerfully torture small children and kill and maim whole populations of innocents without losing a moment's sleep. It was thought that no one, not even Ruddygore, could reach such a height of power and position without a driving egocentrism that surpassed all normal human understanding.

In fact, the only thing any of the Council really feared was that Heaven and Hell would come together for the final conflict, the Armageddon that would settle forever the fate of all the universes. Until then, unless they were careless, as Tiana's father had been, or upset the balance of power among the wizards, as Boquillas had tried to do, they were incredibly powerful and nearly as immortal as, and far less vulnerable than, the fairy folk. It was a Heavenly attack they feared, which would end their power and perhaps bring them the true death, and so the more evil they were, the more they feared the final conflict. They liked things just the way they were and wanted the due bill as far down the road as possible.

Those who were not wizards generally stuck to themselves, feeling somewhat uncomfortable around such true power, and bided their time until Ruddygore was ready for them.

He entered with a flourish, in full flowing robes of sparkling gold, and was instantly the center of attention, greeting everyone with friendly informality and the usual banalities and acting for all the world as if this were a happy and well-planned occasion. It was only when he got to Marge that the act seemed to slip a bit.

"I'm quite happy to see you, Marge. I hope this won't interfere with your new life too much."

"Don't worry," she responded lightly. "Every once in a while it's good to have an adventure."

He winked and was off again on the rounds of the room. Finally winding up at the pastry tray, he took seven or eight and a half-bottle of vintage champagne and settled down in his big, plush, oak chair, which he'd cleverly managed to place on a slight riser near one end of the room, so that it not only gave him a total view of the occupants but also somewhat resembled a throne. Everyone quieted down rather quickly as it was noticed that he was now simply sitting there and examining them thoroughly. In a minute or so, there was silence.

"Most of you know the reason we're here already," the big sorcerer said at last, "although perhaps not all the details. We are faced with a minor crisis and a major decision and we'd better get to it. This is an informal party, not a formal Council meeting, and I hope to gain a consensus rather than force through any record votes."

That was clever, Tiana thought. It meant that they might well vote to go against Hell, while being able to deny that they were on Ruddygore's side later on if things went wrong.

"You all are the ranking wizards of this world of ours, such as it is," Ruddygore continued, "and the leaders of some of the most powerful of fairy races who still have some membership on Earth. Also here are some with long records of service against the Baron and whose help we might need, depending on what is decided."

He paused a moment and took a drink of the champagne, then went on.

"Now, as you all know, Esmilio Boquillas was sentenced to a total loss of power by the Council, and that sentence was carried out in accordance with the Rules. When, afterward, he continued to present a threat to us, the Rules called for a duel to the death with him; but, as we had stripped him of his powers, this would have been murder. As you also know, the Rules specifically forbid that sort of thing when a ranking wizard is rendered powerless by an action of the Council. This left me no choice but to exile him to Earth, feeling that there, where technology rules and there are no really major ranking magicians, he'd no longer be any threat to us. As it turned out, this was a mistake, but it was a mistake made *because of mandated Rules*. In other words, we are responsible, as Rule makers, and so we have both the authority and the ethical imperative to act in this matter. What we must decide first is whether or not we have the duty to do so and the will."

"Perhaps you'd better first give us your idea of what he's up to," the witch queen Esmerada suggested.

"Well, I have no clear ideas on that. We now know that he retains some sort of organization here, on this side, and that he can somehow reach them, perhaps through Hell and perhaps through magical means. This matter of the Lamp was carefully planned down to the smallest detail, and it had to have been planned from this side, if only because a number of traps in my vault chambers have been changed since anyone was in there who survived. Someone recruited top thieves and somehow forced them or convinced them to try, and each one had some sort of spell or charm that fed data back to a master wizard here. They all failed, but the information got out, and each one got farther than the last. The fact that the Baron still has powerful allies even in Husaquahr, along with a means of communication, means that he is a direct threat. The fact that his ally must be a wizard of the top rank makes it our concern directly."

They didn't like that, none of them. The implication was clear that one of the very wizards in the room was in fact in league with the Dark Baron.

"Still, what concern is that of the Council?" the dark wizard Fajera asked. "Boquillas is powerless and cannot cross the Sea of Dreams any more than we can, wish or no wish. What damage he will do is on Earth, which is outside our province."

"Perhaps not," the huge wizard responded. "First of all, Boquillas now has a wizard close to top rank, if not equal to us, at his beck and call, and the Baron retains his tremendous knowledge of magic and spells. This is a two-pronged attack, but it is not aimed necessarily at Armageddon on Earth, although that might well be its result. Earth is well nigh defenseless against our kind of power as we are against that of Earth. Were it just Earth, I wouldn't have called this meeting, but it's not. The workings of Hell set up great storms across the Sea of Dreams, and those storms are lashing out at the breakwaters of our own world. Hell is doing so well, in fact, that Earth is in an incredible mess. It will take very little to push down our barriers so that the evil washes once more into our lands and lives, but even that is not a real concern.

"The real concern," he added, with menace in his voice, "is that this is being waged on both fronts with Hell's cooperation. Armageddon is but a single decision away on Earth. So far they have resisted all pressures and provocations, but it might not take much to tip the balance."

"But the Baron would be as unlikely as any of us to cause it!" the fat Careska protested. "He has as much to lose as we, particularly now that he has access to some power to protect himself!"

"Perhaps, but you forget that our Baron is an idealist and easily swayed," Ruddygore responded. "I assure you that the injustices of Earth make us look like a chorus of angels in the earliest Garden. He and his allies here might well be fooled into thinking the objective is more limited. He is also, of course, a failure, an agent of Hell who totally failed at his objectives and caused great embarrassment and trouble to the powers that be down there. This is a way to rehabilitate himself, get back in their good graces. Certainly Hell is not going to press for the final battle unless it thinks it can win, and the signs are now quite favorable for it. It doesn't matter—the danger is there and it is real, and we, by our actions and our Rules, set it up. The only thing that remains is what we do about it. We can wash our hands of it and do nothing, in which case our nice little system is doomed to crack and fall, and armies will again march and destroy—and we might turn around and find Armageddon at any moment. Or we can act now, preemptively. I say we can't take the chance nor shirk our responsibilities. I say *act* and now! What say you?"

There was dead silence for a moment, although each

of the wizards seemed to sink deeply into thought and occasionally make side glances at the others.

"I take your silence for consent. The next question is what to do about it."

A regal-looking but ancient dwarf none had even noticed spoke up in a deep, rumbling voice. "Go over there and kill the bastard. He is mortal now."

Ruddygore nodded. "Thank you, King Ewedol, for saying the unspeakable. I concur. Boquillas alone is a defenseless human being. He must be killed, and without mercy. Without him, Dacaro will be formidable but manageable as he will not have that vast store of knowledge and experience the Baron brings. With Boquillas dead, I will once again be freed to cross the Sea of Dreams and deal with that slimy little bastard personally."

"So whom are you going to send over there to do the deed?" the red-robed Sargash asked him. "It is one thing to say that you will kill him, but he is certain to be better protected than your vault! Those from here will remain bound by the Rules, while his Earthly allies and demonic friends will not, and none may be wizards of the top rank."

"Quite true," the Council leader agreed. "I am aware of the problems. I am also aware that any we send will be known as soon as they arrive, if not before. For that reason, the Company I shall form for this task will be done entirely by me. Some of its members will be obvious to any here, but some will not."

"Why not just take your damned Lamp and wish him dead?" the dwarf king growled.

"A good question. The Lamp is old, and of limited effectiveness, although it is still quite powerful. Unfortunately, its reach will not extend across the Sea of Dreams in either direction. To be used against someone or something on Earth, it must be on Earth, and that presents even greater problems, as it really wasn't designed for there. On Earth it is erratic, unpredictable, and very limited. To be useful at all there, the Lamp would have to be no more than a few feet from the object of the wish.

Did you not all wonder why Dacaro didn't just take the Lamp? It's because the thing can no longer travel by its own power across the Sea of Dreams, and to carry it over the Sea would have put him at risk to my own powers and agents." He looked around. "Are we agreed, then?"

Again there was dead silence, which pleased the big sorcerer.

"All right, then. In the meantime, I intend to find and stop the wizard on our side and put an end to him—or her. This person is no less dangerous to us and the future than was Boquillas, and will remain no less dangerous, even if we deal with the Baron. I do not intend any more loose ends. Had Hell not interfered, I would have crushed the Baron on the castle walls. Hell will not save this person this time!"

By the next evening, all had left to return to their own domains, leaving only Joe, Tiana, and Marge as outsiders in Castle Terindell. Ruddygore had spent the day seeing the others off and consulting with the rulers of the fairy races who had also been present, the latter because he feared their use as hostages or pawns by the Baron. He seemed well satisfied.

Now, in far less formal company, they sat around the same great room with its walls filled, floor to ceiling, with the red-bound volumes of the Books of Rules, waiting for the signal to go. Poquah joined them, as silent and impassive as usual. The Imir was a wizard probably equal in strength and power to Dacaro, but he was of the faërie. In an otherwise equal contest between him and a human wizard, however, he would lose. That was the way of magic.

Ruddygore entered, looking tired and drawn, but he seemed far more relaxed with just Joe, Tiana, Marge, and Poquah about. "It's been a difficult time," he told them wearily. "Still, it's nothing compared to the tasks laid out to accomplish. This will be far trickier than outwitting an army or even fighting a demon, which you might have to do."

"When do we leave?" Tiana asked him.

"*We* do not," the wizard replied. "The Company must be carefully balanced, using a number of complex factors. Certainly it is necessary that Joe and Marge go, as they are originally from Earth. They know how to cope there, and will not be taken aback by the cultures and technology there. Also, at last report the Baron was in the United States, which makes it even more imperative. Unfortunately, the Baron knows this as well as I do, and Joe, you will never be an invisible sort. Remember, too, that the Baron knows of your were nature. He will know how to kill you and he'll not make any mistakes on that score again."

Joe nodded. "I'm ready for that. He still has to fear every living thing during the three nights of the full moon while I'm there, and if he has to steal that much gold for a bankroll, he can't arm everybody working for him with silver bullets."

"I agree. But that suspicion factor will make it triply difficult to get to him during those periods. Still, it's a massive psychological factor. He'll never hide so well that he won't quake in terror at every fly on the wall or spider in the woodwork."

"Yeah, but what about Marge? I mean, she's pretty much of a standout in the good old U. S. of A. Very few girls there have wings, for example."

Ruddygore grinned and looked knowingly at Marge. "I gather you have never actually sampled the joys of Kauri."

Joe flushed and Tiana gave a real hard look to both him and to the wizard. "Of course not!" the big man growled.

"Then you don't know that the Kauri work their magic by appearing to their—client—not as themselves, but as the idealized woman of his dreams. They do not change, but to everyone else they *appear* to be someone else, and they can do this at will. Right, Marge?"

"That's about it. That's what makes this sound like fun."

"Well, it isn't!" Ruddygore snapped back. "This is deadly and serious. The odds are very much against any of you surviving, let alone accomplishing this mission."

She shrugged. "One thing at a time."

Ruddygore sighed, accepting her faërie outlook because it was useless to change it. "There are, of course, a few problems with you, Marge. For one thing, none of the fairy folk photograph at all. Any of the Baron's agents who takes a photograph of you, or looks at a video image, will not see you and will immediately know that you're one of their quarry. For another, your guise is transparent to any wizard or anyone else with very strong second sight. Fortunately, few have the sight on Earth and many of them only have it when they're drunk or on some drug or other. But Dacaro will certainly not be fooled for an instant, and we can assume Boquillas has made provision by this time not to be fooled, either. And don't ever forget that both know you, Boquillas in particular, and know the powers and limits of Kauri."

"I understand. Don't worry. The Kauri are nothing if not careful about such things."

"Well, it only takes one slip and the tremendous power you'll feel over there, as you are, may blind you to your dangers and limitations. I can give you, and Poquah as well, spells to protect you against the routine iron of Earth, but it is only limited protection and iron will still burn, scar, and even kill if it penetrates your skins. So much contains iron there that you'll have to be on constant guard."

Joe's eyebrows rose and he looked at the Imir. "You're coming, too?"

"I am a wizard of considerable strength who has spent some time on Earth," Poquah replied calmly. "My powers are more than sufficient for concealment and will also aid, I suspect, in locating and penetrating the plot. I am just below the power threshold established by the wish. Why? Do you object?"

Joe remembered the Imir's courage and dedication in their previous bouts with the Baron. "No, of course not. Glad to have you."

"I assume that what goes for Joe goes for me as well," said Tiana, feeling left out.

Ruddygore sighed. "No, my dear, I'm afraid it doesn't. You can't go."

She stood up angrily, a very formidable sight. "I am going!"

"You cannot. Even if we could find some way to fake the Goddess's departure for what might prove a great length of time, and even if we could convince the Council to allow the risk of your not getting back, it still won't work."

"I was born here, yes, but I was raised and educated in Europe! I am as much of Earth as these two!"

"Not quite, but, yes, I'll grant you that you would be a valuable addition; but, you see, it just isn't possible. The wish Dacaro used against wizards blocks *power*, not skill. You are over the wizard threshold, my dear. You are too powerful. The wish prevents you, not I."

She looked at Joe, stricken, and Joe looked back with equal anguish. In more than five years they'd been an inseparable team. "Then I won't go, either," Joe said flatly.

The anger and frustration seemed to subside in Tiana. "Yes you will, my love," she responded with a wistful sigh. "You must. Not only is this far bigger than just the two of us, but I think the Rules and your own nature command it. If you could go, and did not, it would eat at you forever. If none of them came back, you would not be able to live with yourself, wondering. I could not stand to see that happen to you. You will go."

Joe still looked uncertain. "We'll see," he muttered under his breath.

"There is a gray area here that must be addressed," Ruddygore told them. "The Rules apply here, and they apply to all of us, but they do not apply to Earth. That means we won't need an unwieldy seven or more for our company, but it also means that Marge will remain a Kauri, bound by Kauri rules as well as her own nature, and the same for the others. This is also true, to a degree, for Dacaro and Boquillas, particularly when interacting with ones from here. I would not be too concerned about it, though. It certainly will not be Marge who takes on Dacaro in the end."

"Yeah, well, that's the point, isn't it?" Joe snapped. "I mean, you're gonna drop us over there cold, at which time we somehow have to find out where in a country three thousand miles wide and two hundred million strong they're hiding, then take on a super-powerful wizard with no wizard to match, all without being picked up and locked away in some looney bin by the cops. It's crazy!"

"Actually, it's more like two hundred and fifty million people," the wizard replied casually, "but I think we can narrow down the odds a bit. I am not without resources and an organization of my own there, although I will admit it's weaker in the United States than in Europe. You will have help, anyway, and money—as much as you need. I admit, however, to not having a good plan on how to face down Dacaro. That is why I think you and Marge should take a preliminary trip down the River of Dancing Gods. I think we should have a consultation with the Oracle of Mylox, which will accomplish two purposes. First, it will tell us if this deed is possible. That much of a straight answer we can expect, anyway. Beyond this, we might or might not learn more. Oracles are always right but they aren't very dependable and are always obscure."

Joe looked at Tiana, then at Marge. "Oh, great. Just where is this Oracle, anyway? I never heard of him."

"Oh, he's quite famous, but, alas, a bit expensive and somewhat inconvenient to reach. He lives on a small tropical island about a hundred miles or so due south of the river's mouth, and it's difficult to get to and often difficult to return from."

"If it's that bad, I could fly down alone," Marge offered.

"No," Ruddygore replied, "that won't do. For one thing, it's too far out for you to fly without a rest stop. The sea's rough from the bottom of the continent to there, and the only bit of rock is quite hostile. More compelling, however, is that the Oracle's predictions are only truly reliable when requested by a mortal, not one of fairy blood. Someone must go who is not of the fairy races and who is also going on the expedition. I think that pretty well singles out Joe as things stand now."

"There is more to it than that," Tiana noted. "You said there were two reasons, and I suspect I know the second. Joe is bait."

Ruddygore nodded. "I'm afraid so. Whether one of those in this room last night is in league with Boquillas or whether it's someone of rank not on the Council is irrelevant. The Baron knew who would be sent against him from the moment he put this plan into operation. The fact that Macore was chosen to do the deed tells us that whoever we're dealing with on this side knows us rather well. There were spies on you, probably from the moment Macore freed Dacaro, Joe, and once they see you heading south, it will be no puzzle at all to them where you're going and why. Sooner or later they will make an attempt at you both, and then we'll either have our villain revealed or we will be able to trace the attackers. You must appear in every way to be alone, but they will not be the only ones keeping a sharp eye on you. When they strike, help will not be far."

"Then I will at least go with them to the Oracle!" Tiana proclaimed.

"No, my dear, you will not, even if you must be prevented by spell from doing so. I have been forced into an agreement with the Council that both of you shall not be put simultaneously at risk. Don't worry. Joe can take care of himself, and you will be reunited before the Company leaves for Earth."

"Yeah, sure." Joe sighed, secretly relieved at this. He wouldn't like to have her there to be used as a threat against him in a fight, he knew. "Don't worry. Hell, maybe the Oracle will tell us it's a waste of time."

Ruddygore stood up and looked at them, grim-faced. "If so, a darkness will fall over this land which will make us yearn for death or even Armageddon, to gain some release."

CHAPTER 6

NOSTALGIA TRIP

Anyone bound by these Rules of magic and behavior shall remain bound to them, even if in a plane where the Rules do not apply in and of themselves. This Rule is mandatory until death. After death, it is optional.

—Rules, III, 106(d)

TIANA WAS WORRIED, BUT SHE HAD HER DUTIES AND SHE was stuck with them, and so she reluctantly returned to Castle Morikay, there to prepare for the opening of the vitally important Lavender Festival, after a long and tearful farewell to Joe. He, at least, knew that some of those tears were less from separation than from a desire to chuck it all and go with them, no matter what. It was clear, not only to the two of them, but to Ruddygore as well, that the demigod situation simply could not be tolerated much longer. Something had to be done to get rid of the need for that.

Poquah best knew and understood Ruddygore's Earthly organization and he also knew Earth. He was, therefore, sent on ahead to set things up and ease the transition of the others when they arrived. The Imir believed with Ruddygore that the faster this was done the better, and so the preliminary detective work and evaluation was under his direction.

He hoped that the rest of the Company might be determined by what the Oracle had to say, although, if not, he had a few ideas in reserve. What he did not like was too much delay. He had no idea what grandiose scheme had been hatched by his old enemy, but he did not underestimate him.

So it was that Joe and Marge were pretty much alone as they walked down the long path from Castle Terindell on the bluff to the small dock just down from the junction of the river Rossignol with the great Dancing Gods. Marge needed no baggage, of course, but did wear a belt hung loosely on her hips which supported a small leather case. In it were two pairs of the sleek but gogglelike sunglasses Ruddygore had ordered made for her long ago so that she could remain awake and alert in daylight. Even with them, her daylight vision was quite poor, since her eyes were those of a nocturnal creature, but at least she could function and not become comatose.

Joe, too, traveled light, although not quite that light. It was now spring, and they were heading south into subtropical and even tropical climes, so he felt little need for heavy furs and boots, preferring to stick to his ornate sword belt, which held his great magic sword in a snug but easily reached scabbard, and a simple brown loin cloth. With his long, straight, black hair and reddish brown skin, he looked very much like an idealized version of his Apache ancestors.

He stopped and looked over and down at Marge. "Seems like old times again, doesn't it?"

She smiled. "Yeah, it does that, all right. I still can't help thinking like a target, though. I heard of these oracles, and even if any of 'em can really predict anything, you never can figure 'em out until it's too late, anyway, so what good are they?"

"Well, the old boy seems to think that this will be different. Anyway, it feels good just to have a little action again. I've been bored to death."

The boat was a small luxury sailing vessel that could operate well both in shallow and deep waters. Ruddygore had described the captain as an old water rat, but they weren't prepared to be greeted by a creature who stood nearly six feet tall and looked for all the world like a giant brown rat with broad, flat feet and tiny humanlike hands. The giant rat wore a blue and red jacket on which epaulets had been sewn at the shoulders; in between its huge rodent's ears perched a small sailor's cap with polished bill. If the thing weren't so imposing, and if it didn't smell, close up, like twenty gallons of stagnant water, it would look almost comical, Joe thought.

Marge whispered, "He's a Fahadur. Be polite."

"He's not of the faërie, is he?" Joe whispered back.

"No. Just one of the several hundred nonhuman races around."

Joe could only feel upset at his shock and his ignorance. He'd seen a number of nonhuman races, and even fought a few, but his real knowledge of most of this world and its creatures was abysmally poor. For all the perspective Morikay and Wolf Island provided, he might as well have been in Philadelphia.

The captain had a gritty, rasping, unpleasant voice that came from somewhere far beyond the snout, deep in the throat.

"Welcome aboard the *Piebald Hippogryph*!" he said. "I'm Captain Bly." He stuck out a small, gray-pink, taloned hand.

Joe took it without hesitation. He wasn't used to shaking hands with giant talking rats, but he'd been several years now in the social and diplomatic circuit. "Glad to meet you."

"I'm glad the ship's not named the *Bounty*," Marge mumbled.

"Is this your ship, Captain?" Joe asked, either not hearing or ignoring the comment.

"No, it's actually owned by a bunch of little old ladies who had to invest their quilting money in a tax shelter, but for all intents and purposes it's mine. We run charters to various points up and down the river system. You don't get luxury like this on the average vessel," Bly bragged.

And, in fact, he wasn't kidding. There was far more room below than either of them would believe—two very well-appointed staterooms with large beds with feather mattresses and a dining and lounge area off of which was a well-designed galley. The area was presided over by a very beautiful young woman whom Bly introduced as Audra. Only the fact that not only Audra's eyes were green, but her skin and hair as well, suggested that she was something other than human.

"I can see your question, and it's a common one," she told them without it having to be spoken. "I am a wood nymph. I had just lost my tree in a fire and had switched to another when they came to lumber the area. I was in hibernation at the time and wasn't marked or registered, so they took the new tree and used it in building this boat."

"You mean you're stuck, attached to this boat?" Marge asked, a bit taken aback by the comment.

"Oh, yes, at least until it is totally destroyed. I don't mind. At least it gives me some chance to see the world and earn my keep, and I meet a lot of interesting people. It could have been worse. I mean, they could have used only *half* of the tree."

Marge shuddered. The idea of severed limbs appearing all over the place was unnerving.

Bly took them back topside. "She literally lives inside the ship itself, or in its timbers," he told them. "Makes it easy, considering the limited crew's quarters, and real convenient. She's happy, and we get free maid service.

Only trouble is, she's a lousy cook, since she just sits up here and takes in the sun for a couple of hours and gulps down some water. She tries following recipes; but if you've never eaten food, how the hell can you ever learn how to do it right?"

"You won't need much on my score," Marge told him. "I eat fruit and take juices now and then, maybe even some wine, but nothing else."

"Well *I* eat, and a lot," Joe noted. "However, I'll take your advice and do my own cooking, if Audra will let me in the galley for it."

"Oh, sure. She's used to it. She'll stand there and take all sorts of notes trying to figure it out. Ah! Here's our pilot!"

The face and form of yet another pretty young woman appeared; she was holding onto the side of the ship, apparently just back from a swim. When she hauled herself aboard, though, and sat on the rail, a long, fishlike tail, cream-colored like her skin, extended down from her waist. Joe had seen mermaids before in Husaquahr, but never this close up. He had always imagined the tails as dark and scaly.

"Tura, meet our passengers," Bly called to the mermaid.

"Hi! Glad to know you!"

There were introductions around, and Joe began to wonder just what sort of cruise this was going to be. Certainly he was glad that Tiana was off at Morikay. What would she say on discovering that he was to be in close quarters for several days with a Kauri, a wood nymph, and a mermaid, with his only competition a giant rat? Mermaids, he knew, were always female, but mated solely with human men—but only at one time in the year and for the duration of getting pregnant.

This, then, was the crew of the *Piebald Hippogryph.*

"Anything to report, luv, before we get under way?" Bly asked the mermaid.

"No, it's pretty clear. Steer forty degrees to the main channel, then follow it. There was a herd of wild hippocampus grazing on the river bottom about nine leagues south, just off the main channel, but I wouldn't worry about them."

Bly looked at his two passengers. "Very well, then. Any luggage or other gear to be stowed?"

"We're clear," Joe told him. "We tend to travel light."

"Very well, then. It's a pretty easy trip going downriver. The current's strong and gets stronger from here south, and I use the sails more as a brake than as power. We'll run until dusk every day, then tie up at a settlement, if it's convenient, or along the shore, if it's not. Barring bad weather or unforeseen accidents, we should hit Marahbar in about ten days."

They mostly got out of the way as the mermaid again went over the side and Bly cast off the lines fore and aft, then went leisurely to the large wheel located in the rear. As he said, he didn't even bother to set any sail at this point, although it was clear from the look of a forward line that something or someone was pulling the ship away from the dock and pointing it in the right direction.

As soon as they got into the main channel of the Rossignol, the line went suddenly slack, and Tura hauled herself back aboard, looking a little winded. She glanced over, saw Joe and Marge sitting on deck, and smiled.

"In main ports they have trained hippocampus to do the tug work, but out here it's just little old me," the mermaid said, between deep breaths.

She didn't look that strong, but Joe reminded himself not to underestimate a mermaid's strength or power in the water again.

Tura was well accustomed to moving along the ship, using the rails and other projections. She sat down near them and stretched out her long tail. "Fish out of water," she commented apologetically.

"You stay on board when not working?" Marge asked her.

"Sometimes, yes. Everybody thinks of us as related

to the fish, but we're air-breathing mammals, just as humans are."

"But don't you—dry out—after a while?" the Kauri asked.

"Oh, sure. Don't you? But this is skin, not fish. I've got layers of protection underneath it that you don't, so I don't have to worry about water temperatures and the like, at least not much, but the skin's the same. I'm pretty awkward out of the water, but there's no harm in it any more than with Joe, say. Worst problem up here in bright sunlight is that it's so bright I don't see as well."

Marge, who had her goggles on, chuckled. "I know what you mean. Maybe you ought to get a pair of these made. Without them, I'm totally blind and out like a light up here in the day."

"Say! What *are* you, anyway? I don't think I ever saw somebody of your race before."

"I'm a Kauri."

The mermaid stared at Marge, then looked at Joe, and gave a knowing smirk. "Oh. . . ."

"Hey! It's not that way!" Joe protested. "We're old friends and partners, that's all."

The mermaid looked startled. "Why not?"

"Huh? What do you mean?"

"Why *not* that way? You one of them muscle boys who only likes other muscle boys or something?"

Joe flushed. "Of course not! I'm happily married!"

Realizing that the mermaid would never let Joe off her hook and that he was incapable of getting off it gracefully himself, Marge intervened. "I'm a changeling. We're from the same place and knew each other before I changed."

Tura sighed, and Marge knew that she'd put it down as a case of fate stepping between two old lovers. Wrong, of course, but unrequited love was a more convenient explanation than the truth.

They were now well past Castle Terindell and out into the River of Dancing Gods. The Rossignol and the Dancing Gods met rather gently, but did not immediately mix.

It was fascinating to see the difference in coloration as the two rivers flowed side by side without any barrier between them except speed and density. When these finally equaled out, perhaps a few miles south of the junction, there was a gradual merging into one body.

Marge yawned as the sun took its toll on her. Finally she said, "I'm going to go down and get some rest. Considering everything, I think it'll be a good idea if I keep my usual schedule for this trip. Somebody with good night vision should be awake while we're tied up."

He nodded. "Go ahead." In point of fact, he thought, it was a very good idea all around. He wondered if the crew had been told anything about the possible dangers, and, if so, just how much of a fight they would put up. He decided not to press the question now, but to ease into it. Marge went below, and he and the mermaid just sat there and enjoyed the nice day for a while.

"I hear a lot of birds," Tura said suddenly, frowning. "I can't see them, but my hearing and sonar are pretty good, even up here. It seems as if they're staying directly over the ship."

He looked up and around, only now aware of it as well. The birds were pretty high up and both overhead and a bit behind, but they were only dark shapes at this distance and under these conditions. "Do you have a telescope or something?" he asked her. "I'd like to know what kind of birds those are." He was suddenly quite tense. If those were ravens . . .

"Sound like eagles to me," Tura said. "Funny that they'd be around these parts."

He relaxed a bit. "That's okay. I think that they and we have a mutual friend."

In about an hour they came upon a herd of wild hippocampuses, whose horselike heads and forequarters blended into huge, mermaidlike tails. They were far larger than horses, and they looked meaner than hippopotamuses, despite colors ranging from pale blue to passionate pink. It didn't look as if it would take too many of them to sink the small ship, and that worried Joe.

"Oh, don't worry so much," Tura chided him. "They're peaceful vegetarians living in the shallows and feeding off bottom plants much of the time. The only problem we ever have with them is a stampede, when they'll panic and instinctively head for deep water. It mostly happens during sudden thunderstorms, and the weather's clear and sunny."

"Yeah, just the same I—"

At that moment, a tremendous explosion seemed to go off right over the herd of more than thirty of the huge creatures. There was no flash or blast or any other sign of its cause, but the tremendous *boom* it created was so strong it could be felt as well as heard.

The great animals panicked, launching themselves straight toward the boat in a strange mixture of gallop and smooth, almost snakelike motion. Except for the fact that they all seemed to be rushing straight for the *Piebald Hippogryph*, however, no two were moving exactly alike or in a predictable manner, and all were making low-pitched, grunting sounds that filled the air.

Bly had been taken as much by surprise as had the hippocampuses by the explosion, but he acted almost instantaneously, bringing the ship around hard and pointing it, it seemed for a moment, directly at the oncoming stampede. Then the bow came around some more, and not only Bly's hands and feet but even his long tail seemed to be working one control or another. There was no time to unfurl sail and try and get past them; instead, what he appeared to do was somehow put on the brakes and stop dead in the water.

It was a long swim to shore, and Joe braced himself for the crash.

Bly had done all he could with the ship; holding the wheel and rudder fast, his tail snaked into a small locker and picked up some small objects with the skill of a tentacle. The huge creatures were now almost upon them, and it seemed inevitable that they would strike the *Hippogryph* and overwhelm it, crushing at least the bow.

Bly had been smoking a long, thin cigar, and now coolly touched it to the objects he'd snaked from the locker. The tail then hurled whatever it was forward with great strength, then immediately returned to the locker for more.

A series of small, staccato explosions went off between the ship and the hippocampuses. They weren't in the same league as the great noise that had stampeded the herd, but from the viewpoint of the animals they went off right in front of them. The tail tossed another smoking bundle, and again the *rat-a-tat-tat* of the explosions came. Joe had hit the deck and was clinging to a rail for dear life; he felt the ship suddenly shudder and heave and knew it was all over.

There was great splashing about, water washing over the side and onto the decks, and more violent thumps. It seemed as if the *Hippogryph* was being flung in all directions at the same time, but suddenly things calmed down, and the noises and splashes receded.

It was about half a minute before Joe realized that he was still on deck and that the ship was still afloat.

"Bly's the best captain on the river, that's for sure," Tura said calmly.

Slowly, the big man picked himself up off the deck and looked around. There seemed no sign of the terrible horde. All was calm and bright once more. "Wha—where'd they go?"

"Into deep water, but they won't stay there long," Bly's strange, rasping voice responded from the rear. "That's why, as soon as I get us straightened out and back where I'm sure of my markings, we're gonna drop sail and run like mad. Having survived 'em on the way out, I sure don't want to be sunk by them on the way back in!"

Joe was confused, and looked to the mermaid for help.

"He brought us about and dropped the centerboard, among other things, bringing us to a temporary halt and aiming us in at the stampede. That made us a smaller target," Tura explained. "It wouldn't stop us for long, but it was enough to allow him to break out and toss some fireworks we keep on board right in front of them, and that turned them just enough. A couple of them grazed us, but I won't know the real damage until I get a chance to go down and take a look."

Joe looked around. All was peaceful once more, although he could see some debris sticking up from the side of the ship near the bow. There was no question that they had indeed been hit, and his respect for Bly's abilities, no matter what his appearance and manner, went up enormously.

He stared at the far horizon, where the shore was barely visible, and said, "You know, there was something very fishy about that stampede."

"No, they're mammals, too."

He gave her a sharp look of disgust. "It's not bad enough I have to put up with one Marge, now I got two," he mumbled. Louder he said, "No, I mean the explosion. We have to face facts here. There was no natural cause for that explosion, and it's timing was perfect. Somebody waited for us to come by and then blew it, hoping we'd be trampled—and it almost worked."

They were soon well past the danger area, and Tura was able to go over the side and check things out. Audra had already merged with the wood and reported no damage to her areas, but she could sense only that part of the ship made up of wood from her own tree. Certainly they were not taking on water, which was a relief.

"You know," Bly commented, coming back on deck, "that girl of yours can sleep through anything. If they'd split us open, she'd have gone down with the ship."

"It wouldn't matter," Joe told him. "As long as she wasn't hurt, she's as comfortable in water as anywhere else, or so I'm told. Otherwise fairies that fragile would all be dead. Still, somebody's out to get us, that's for sure."

Tura suddenly broke through the surface and leaped

up to grab the rail, then hauled herself aboard. "Not too bad," she told them. "Some outer planking is pretty messed up, but the inner hull's sound. The only puncture is a few inches above the waterline and it's not very serious."

"We'll make Harmatuu tonight," the captain responded. "If we're lucky, we can get her patched enough there to take us all the way." He paused for a moment. "It might take a couple of days, though. Sorry, sir."

Joe thought it over. "I'm not too broke up over the delays, but I'm not sure—well, maybe I'm just suspicious. Captain, is there any other town where we could make repairs other than Harmatuu?"

"Not safely. The next town south with a shipwright big enough to work on the *Hippogryph* is better than two days sail. Why?"

"Well, a stampede's a good threat, but not really a killer. The odds are that whoever started it was aiming at damage rather than anything else. If it sunk or killed us all the better, but damage is all he could count on."

Bly thought it over. "A trap, then? You think they wait for you in Harmatuu?"

"I think I'd better think that."

"Well, she's not handling very well, and I'd hate to try her for any length of time under full sail, but if we take it slow and mostly drift down with the current we *could* skip the town and continue south."

Joe went over to the rail and looked out at the broad river, whose multicolored patterns showed deeps and shallows and which seemed now so serene. "No," he decided. "First of all, this isn't your fight. If we continue on down, crippled, it means we'll be easy to stop and maybe be sunk next time. If they strike, let it be soon, and on land, at a place where we're expecting it. Make for Harmatuu, Captain. I'd rather face a horde of sword-wielding demons than mysterious explosions from on high."

* * *

It was well after dark when they reached the small town on the Marquewood side of the river, which meant, at least, that they were still theoretically in friendly territory. It wasn't much of a town—a small docking facility, a main street, and two parallel streets were about it. It was actually just a place for local farms to bring their produce down to ships and pick up supplies ordered from elsewhere; it wouldn't really exist even for that if Marquewood's road system reached this area of the country.

However, because it was halfway along a deserted stretch of the river, there was enough minor barge repair business to maintain a small repair yard. It was, of course, closed when they got there, but it was hardly a problem finding someone with authority in a town this size, and Bly was soon able to make arrangements, with suitable extra payments, for a quick fix. The fact that his charter was Ruddygore's made a big difference in Marquewood, which both loved and feared their most illustrious resident. Bly was rather evasive about whether or not the sorcerer was actually aboard, and that helped matters more.

There was a small inn with a bar-restaurant and four sleeping rooms upstairs, two of which were taken. Joe took one of the spares and Bly the other; Tura pulled out a wonderful wheelchairlike contraption and had no trouble getting around town, but decided to stay in the river itself; and Marge, after hearing about all that had happened and understanding the dangers, decided it would be better for her to stay outdoors, Kauri-style. Audra, of course, had to stay with the ship, which was fine as well, since it guaranteed a friendly person on board at all times, especially during the repair phase. It would be very difficult for anyone or anything to sneak on board, and just as difficult to leave any ugly surprises there.

There was a small square in the middle of Main Street, with a huge marble statue before which was a flame-lighted altar. It was a statue of two enormous figures, one male, one female, perfect in physical form, much overendowed sexually, and quite naked.

"It doesn't look much like either of you," Marge noted critically.

Joe flushed. "Come on! I'm embarrassed enough about this sort of thing as it is. I mean, look at this! Offerings!"

"Well, take heart. Your feet are almost black from the flame and the heads and shoulders of you both are covered with bird droppings. At least they aren't all that religious around here."

"I don't know whether to be grateful or insulted by that," Joe grumped.

There wasn't much else to do, so they joined Tura and Bly at the inn. Tura wore a black pullover sweater and had a blanket wrapped around her lower part; it was difficult, although not impossible, to tell that she was in fact a mermaid and not simply a pretty paraplegic.

Marge drifted away from them and they soon lost sight of her in the small but loud gathering in the bar. Bly proved that his eating habits were fairly disgusting as his form might suggest, but he was quickly through his meal. "I'm going to turn in," he told them. "I want to be there first thing tomorrow to make sure everything's done just so. I've asked around, though. The other two rooms upstairs are taken by folks who are regulars through here. One's a farm-implements salesman and the other's a mate on a barge on layover here. Strangers stick out in a town like this, so maybe we're home free. Still, watch it anyway."

"I will," Joe assured him, and the strange ratlike creature left.

Joe found Tura both charming and interesting, even if she did eat everything raw. He found that the three shipmates knew that they were on a potentially dangerous mission and what the ultimate destination was, but that they didn't know anything about Joe or Marge personally.

Tura talked about the life and attitudes of her race and its ways, with some wistfulness. She was, it seemed, more at home in the ocean than in the rivers, and she was here and doing what she was doing basically because she had been exiled.

"My people all belong to clans, which are more than that—they are distinct tribes, with their own coloration and markings. You can't change your clan—you are what you are. But if you don't go along with whatever the clan leaders demand, you risk banishment. Our territories are sacred and are tightly controlled. All who use them must do so with the approval of the clan, and, of course, clans often fight over territory with each other. I simply grew sick and tired of it. I just couldn't do what they ordered."

"So you disobeyed and they threw you out?"

"It was more than disobedience, really, I—I refused to kill someone they ordered me to kill."

Joe was shocked. "They actually do that?"

"All the time. Usually it's killing someone randomly from another tribe that killed one of us, either accidentally or on purpose; but sometimes it's land-people who won't pay tribute or show the leaders proper respect. It doesn't take many of us to sink a ship, you know."

Joe just shook his head in wonder. Somehow, he had never thought of mermaids as being like the Mafia. He could see the racket, though. He'd been a truck driver, after all, and not everything and everyone that he'd worked with during his career had been legal and aboveboard. There were routes and cargoes where protection had to be paid, and territories that were reserved for certain companies and owners. Here everything of importance moved along the great river system and across the broad ocean, and the ones who controlled their territories would indeed have enormous power.

He felt sorry for Tura. Because she'd been banished, she couldn't go home or she'd be killed, but the other clans had different colors and markings and wouldn't accept or trust her. She was an outcast from her own kind, in her own way as torn from her world as he'd been from his.

She liked the land—a forest had the same mystery and

romance for her that the bottom of the sea would for him—but she needed to be near water much of the time. She was good for extended periods, but eventually her skin would dry out and crack or break out painfully if not fully immersed for quite some time. The sun also caused discolorations after a while that carried the threat of skin cancer.

"I've always wanted to go up to a mountaintop," she told him, "and feel the cool snow and look down on the world. It's silly, I know, but it's something of a dream."

"It's not silly," he assured her. "Not at all."

The place had thinned out, and it was clearly near closing time, which was still early in a place like this.

"Come on," he said. "I'll walk you back to the ship."

She smiled and nodded, then suddenly shook her head. "Ugh! I think I overdid the drinking. I never drink, much, and I feel—dizzy."

He was concerned. "Are you gonna be all right? I mean—tonight?"

"I—maybe not. I don't know. I guess I have to, though."

"No, no. You can stay here. It's a fairly large room."

She looked over at the wooden stairway leading up. "I don't think I could manage that, at least not in my condition."

Joe grinned, got up, went around to her, and picked her up. She was heavy, but she was no Tiana. By this time, only the proprietor was in the place, and he paid no notice at all.

He got into the room, put her down on the bed, then went back down to get her wheelchair. As he was going back, the proprietor called to him.

"Your finny lady's got a load on, huh?"

Joe shrugged. "That's about the size of it."

The man reached under the bar and took out two small corked bottles. "This one is for the lady. You sleep nice but you don't get sick and you don't have much of a headache in the morning. The other's a little good-night drink for you—on the house."

Joe noted which was which, then nodded. "Thanks."

"Any friend of Ruddygore is a special guest here."

Joe went back up to the room and stowed the wheelchair to one side. She was lying there, looking through the pictures in a small book that was on the nightstand. Joe knew by the cover photo that it was the biography of J. Millard Harrilot, the founder of the largest chain of inns in Marquewood. Joe hadn't noticed that even this little one was part of the chain until he saw the ubiquitous paperback.

At least all the beds were king-size in Harrilot inns, and never did Joe need that more than now.

He sat down, took the bottles, and uncorked them. "The barkeep says this stuff will give you a good night's sleep with no hangover," he told her. He sniffed it. It smelled like cherry brandy. His smelled much more pungent and powerful, with a trace of anise.

She smiled, and they touched bottles. "To the mountains!" he said, smiling.

"To a good day," she responded, and they both drank.

The stuff was smooth but strong going down. He went over and blew out the light and returned to bed. Suddenly, he felt a little dizzy, too.

"Hmph! Must have been a real kick in that," he commented and lay down.

Almost immediately he felt as if he were floating—not awake, but not asleep, either. It was an odd but euphoric dreamlike state and it felt far too good to fight.

Tura, too, lapsed quickly into the same sort of state, and they lay there, eyes closed, hardly aware of anything, and particularly not aware of the door to their room opening and a black shape entering.

The newcomer quickly examined the two of them for spells and curses. Tura had a few minor charms, probably purchased from some river wizard, but was essentially clean. Joe was not quite as clean, however. Not only did he have a lot of strong magical protections bearing Ruddygore's unmistakable stamp, but there was something else there, too, something infinitely complex and dark. The man carried within him an incredibly powerful curse, one that was of the blood. The stranger hadn't expected that, but couldn't divine its exact nature.

He was himself an enormously powerful wizard, but it hardly seemed worth it to undo all of Joe's protections methodically. With the potion they had both taken, it was far easier just to go around them.

He could do little about the Kauri and even less with the nymph, and Bly didn't matter all that much in this, but these two he could affect now. He knew better than to challenge the big man directly with some sort of armed force; he had a charmed sword, and that curse looked as if it gave him some strong measure of protection as well as cursing him. Well, he had lives to spare—when the time came.

For now, a little monkey-wrench was in order, nothing more. Something to keep them off-balance until the time was right.

The potion would do most of the work. All he needed to add were a few more practical "suggestions."

CHAPTER 7

MEMORIES ARE MADE OF THIS

The following shall be taken as the only legitimate purposes for messages from beyond the grave: (a) warnings; (b) prophecies; (c) curses; (d) related grave matters. All other motives should be suspected.

—Rules, CVI, 201(b)

"IT'S A GOOD THING I STAYED UP PAST SUNRISE," MARGE told Bly as they walked back to the inn from the boatyard. "I really can't believe this. How could it have happened?"

"Deliberately, you can be sure," the ratlike creature responded. "It had to be right in the inn. There's no evidence that either of them left that night."

They approached the inn at a brisk clip. "The inn is still closed to the public?"

"Oh, yes. I had enough influence to handle that, which is a very good thing, as you'll see."

They entered through the rear door, walked past the small kitchen and into the main tavern area, and then froze.

Joe had apparently moved all of the furniture back from the center of the serving floor and set up several cushions. He sat there now, stark naked, an equally but more naturally naked Tura on his lap, and the two were alternately laughing, giggling, and making out like newlyweds. They seemed oblivious to the newcomers, occasionally breaking and feeding each other small morsels, mostly bread and fruit bits.

Marge, who did some of this sort of thing as a business, was nonetheless disgusted by the display. She cleared her throat several times, and, when that produced no reaction, she said, rather loudly, "AHEM!"

They both turned, big grins on their faces, and looked at the two interlopers. "Oh, hi!" Tura called with a giggle.

"Joe! What the hell *happened* to you?" Marge demanded to know.

Joe had a puzzled expression and then looked at Tura. "Who's Joe?" he asked her, and she shrugged.

Marge frowned. "*You* are! And you're Tura. Don't you remember your own names?"

"I never heard of no Joe," the big man responded. "You?"

The mermaid shook her head. "Nope. And who's that other one you said?"

"See?" Bly whispered. "Bewitched for sure. Both of 'em."

Marge nodded. "I wish I could see the spell, but in daylight and with these glasses on I'm as spell-blind as you are. Joe's pretty well protected against spells, though. I smell a potion in this." She turned her attention back to the unlikely pair. "So if you're not Joe and Tura, what *are* your names?" she asked them.

"I dunno," Joe responded, then looked at Tura. "You?" The mermaid shook her head, but it was clear that this lack didn't bother them in the least.

It took quite a while for Marge to get the whole story out of them, what there was of it. Clearly neither of them had any memory whatsoever of their past or their identities, nor did they wonder about this or even care about it. They had awakened together upstairs in a bed and it was like being born at that moment. They had no idea where they were, or why, and no interest in such things. They only had eyes for one another. They were passionately, madly in love, and the center of the universe was the other one and absolutely everything else was irrelevant. In point of fact, it hadn't even occurred to them that Tura had a fish-like tail while he had legs; it seemed the most natural thing in the world for them.

"Definitely a whale of a love potion," Marge told Bly. "I'm something of an expert in these things. It's tied to an uninhibitor of some kind. It's a really primal potion, too. Joe doesn't even know he's naked, or care. I doubt if either one of them knows the difference between good or evil, for that matter."

"So they are in some ways like small children," the captain replied. "But what are we going to do? The ship's repairs are minor and will be completed by late this evening. We can sail tomorrow—but with them like *this*. . . ."

Marge thought a moment. "If they were slipped a Mickey, the odds are it was done here after everybody else left. It would have taken a small gang to have gotten them both upstairs when they were out, and I don't think it's that elaborate, or we'd have noticed something. That leaves the one man who was here for certain last night. Where's the proprietor?"

"Still asleep, I think. His daughter runs the breakfast part and she was the one who discovered them—like that—and awakened me."

She thought for a moment. "I'm a lot weaker in the day, but I might be able to manage enough for this. Do you have a way to contact Ruddygore in an emergency?"

"I have some pigeons aboard, yes."

"Well, send him a message now—this morning. It shouldn't take more than half a day, considering how little distance we've traveled. Tell him basically what happened and request his help or an antidote, then meet me back here."

"All right, but what then? I mean, he's an awfully *big* man for us to handle, if he doesn't want to be handled, and Tura's no lightweight—most of that tail is pure muscle."

"I know. We'll cross that bridge later. Get that message off. I'm going to find out why and at whose order this was done and, hopefully, find out the potion."

She left him and walked to the back, meeting up with a thin, nervous-looking girl of sixteen or so. "You the innkeeper's daughter?"

The girl nodded.

"Where is your father now?"

"In back—but he's sleeping. He doesn't like to be disturbed at this hour."

"I think maybe we should wake him, don't you? Or don't you want to open today? Suppose they decide it would be fun to smash chairs and bottles?"

The girl nodded, looking both scared and glum, and led the Kauri back to a large wooden door. Marge looked up at her. "Your mother in there, too?"

"No. My mom died a few years back."

"Uh-huh. No brothers or sisters?"

"No."

"Is this door unlocked?"

"Certainly. Why should it be otherwise?"

"Well, I'll wake up your old man. You just go back and keep our two lovers happy and make sure they stay put inside the inn."

"I don't think he—"

"Just do it, girl!"

This was more than the innkeeper's daughter could handle, and she left.

Marge gently turned the knob and entered a hallway. At the end was a stairway going down to the cellar, and she realized that they lived down there with the potables and other stored items. That was perfect for her.

She lighted no light, although it was very dark at the bottom. All this suited her just fine. The walls were stone, it was somewhat cool, and there seemed no sign of a window. Taking a chance, she removed the goggles and found, to her relief, that the cellar blocked out the radiation that would affect her. In fact, in a place this dark and this well insulated, it was almost like being in night, and she felt her powers grow to near normal.

Most of the cellar was still devoted to storage, but one

area had been divided into three small rooms. It was pretty clear which one held the proprietor; he snored like a dragon.

Although her motivation was different, she automatically drew on her powers as needed, taking in the impressions from the sleeper beyond the wall and using them without even thinking about it.

The Kauri's power over men was great, in part because it drew upon the man to supply what was necessary and most appropriate. She opened the thin door to the proprietor's bedroom and saw him instantly, sleeping sprawled across a bed much like the ones upstairs. He was an unassuming, dark, chubby man with a close-cropped beard and thin mustache.

"Wake up," she said softly, but it was no request or timid attempt. It was a command with fairy power behind it.

The man stirred, shifted, then frowned, and opened his eyes. She reached up and found a candle, then willed the energy to flow from her to it. The candle flickered into life, lighting up the entire small room. He saw her in an instant, and his mouth dropped. "Umora?"

"Yes, my darling," she responded, knowing that he was seeing not a Kauri but the image of his dead wife, not as she was but as he remembered her.

He yawned and sat up. "But—you should be at peace now! I did what you asked of me." He paused a moment. "You are not like you were. You are beautiful and radiant once more."

"I have not returned before, my love, for it is generally forbidden. I was sent back because I was told you had committed a grave evil. Are you saying you did it in my name? For me?"

"But—you were here! Cold from the grave! I saw you!" He shuddered.

So that was it. "Someone made you believe it was me, but it was not. You were fooled by a very evil one, my darling. Who was it?"

He shook his head, trying to take it all in. She could see he was struggling, but she presented the preferable vision of reality, even if the false one. Bit by bit, he told her the tale.

She—or one who'd looked like her—had come to him in the early morning, as she did now. But that one was not beautiful as she now was; no, she'd been only a terrible shadow of her former self, a recognizable but horrible corpse, partly decomposed. She—his wife's corpse—had told him that her soul was trapped and could not go on, held by one who was the Master of the Dead. The Master had sent her to request a small task of any who came, and had agreed that, if he performed that task, she would find eternal peace. Her voice and horrible appearance had haunted him and filled him with pity. When she'd piteously complained of the cold and the worms, he could do no more than follow orders. To free his beloved wife from such a fate, he would have committed mass murder; this was merely to slip a potion, which he'd been assured was not lethal, to a couple of strangers.

"Who gave you the potions?" she asked him.

"You—she—did. Left them here."

"Then you never saw this Master of the Dead?"

"I—well, sort of. He was here, last night. Where I don't know, but he was here. I was to leave the keys available and then come down here. I did, but not all the way. I heard him moving about and heard him mount the stairs. When he came out, I peeked through the eyehole in back—you remember when and why we put that in."

She nodded and let him continue. Best not to get trapped into details she couldn't possibly know. This thing had its limits, and she was no mind reader. Irritated, she realized that she hadn't asked, nor did she know, his name.

"All I can say is that he was a big man, dressed all in black robes. His face I didn't see, or any particular features. Just a large man dressed in full robes and hood of solid black, that's all."

"It was definitely a man, then, my love? No woman or another sort of creature or fairy?"

"No—it was a man. A wizard for sure. He went out the front door, and I checked; all was quiet, so I just came down and went to sleep." He hesitated a moment. "Those two were a strange pair, even for an inn. What did the potion do?"

"You will see. I must go now, but do not feel guilty. You did what you thought you had to do for my sake. Other powers far greater than me will deal with this Master, and I will return to the peace and joy I left. Goodbye, my darling."

The candle winked out, and for a while he just sat there on the side of the bed in the dark shaking his head and looking very guilty indeed. She had become as nothing to him, and she was able to exit and climb back up the stairs without his even noticing that anyone was opening and closing the doors. She hesitated, almost forgetting to replace the goggles, but did so just in time.

The daughter was waiting hesitantly in the hallway near the door.

"Your father was not awakened by me," she told the girl. "Don't worry. He may be up shortly and acting a little strange, but don't be afraid for him." She then walked past the girl and back to the inn proper.

The Master of the Dead. . . . An animated corpse of the innkeeper's wife. . . . This was power indeed, but at least the bastard lived up to his name. Her thoughts went back to the male wizards on the Council. She found she wouldn't put it past any one of them, Ruddygore excepted.

One thing was certain, though. She and Joe had certainly underestimated their foe here in Husaquahr, expecting as they did more of a frontal attack or at least a good stab in the back, with her as the more vulnerable target. With this one simple gesture, the enemy had halted this expedition at its beginning, with minimal exposure, and taken out the best sword in the bargain.

The two were still there, but not for long, it appeared.

"I am water," Tura said, "and you are Earth. I feel like an early morning swim."

Joe got up, then scooped up the mermaid as if she were a feather. "Anything you want, you get." He started for the door, which was locked; when it didn't move at his prod, he stood back and kicked it hard. The lock splintered and the double doors swung open, one hanging by only a part of a hinge.

Word, of course, had gotten around the little town already that morning, so they were more curiosities than shocks to those who were already out on the streets. Joe went to the center of the street, looked up and down, and spotted the mast of the ship at the far end, and headed for it. Tura lay in his arms, giggling and laughing all the while.

Marge took flight, knowing she couldn't stop it and just determined to shadow them and, if need be, beat them to the river. There was nothing she could do; anyway, they were going pretty much where she wanted them.

They reached the bank and then went out on a small pier. Joe didn't stop, walking right off the end with Tura still in his arms and hitting the water with a big splash. For a moment Marge felt fear, wondering if Joe could swim; but as she flew over them she found that he seemed to swim quite well, although not nearly as well as Tura.

There was little she could do except hope they'd play and stay nearby. She looked around and saw the eagles circling lazily in the air high above, then headed up toward them. It was quite an ordeal and she was extremely tired and weakened by the sunlight, but she was determined to make it.

Fortunately, one of the eagles noticed her, sensed her weakness, and descended to her level.

"What brings you to us, Kauri?" the eagle asked somewhat menacingly. In many cases, eagles were not adverse to attacking fairies if they appeared weak and out of their element.

She was banking on them being on the same side. "If

you please, great lord of the skies, we need to contract the wizard Ruddygore at once and it was hoped by me that one of such grace and mastery could aid in this."

"What's the problem? Were you attacked while we roosted?"

Quickly, Marge sketched in the problem and pointed out the swimmers far below.

The eagle snorted. "Surface grubs," it murmured derisively. "Wait here, if you can, on these currents. I'll have to take this to a higher-up."

With that, the eagle climbed. He related the story to the second level above, which in turn relayed it to the third, which finally dispatched someone to the highest eagle in the bureaucratic and physical pyramid. Marge only hoped that the message didn't get garbled in the translation.

Finally the word came back down, and the lowest eagle approached her once more. "You sent the pigeon this morning with this news?"

"As much as we knew at the time. Not the details I gave you."

"Well, we can beat the pigeon if we have to. Get on below, and we'll take it from here. You should hear something in a couple of hours at most. How are you going to keep them handy, though?"

"We'll think of something," Marge replied, more in hope than with any concrete idea. She wearily descended and looked for the pair of potion-induced lovers. They were on the bank, in very shallow water and mud, and both of them were apparently dismembering and eating a live fish.

She found Bly looking over the repair work, which did indeed seem more inconvenient than serious, and sent him to the inn for Joe's sword. She was determined to try every trick available to her to get Joe under control, but she badly needed some rest. It was going to be a busy evening.

Finally, she went down to the galley and saw Audra.

"Have you any booze on board other than the usual ale kegs?" she asked the nymph.

"Yeah, I think we have some." The nymph rummaged around to the resounding sound of hammers and saws, then brought up two bottles of what looked to be decent wine. "This do?"

"Maybe," Marge said hopefully. "Just keep them handy while I make a quick visit to the village apothecary shop."

"Yeah, okay, I—*yeow*!" The nymph jumped a foot and whirled around, looking very angry. "Those bastards just *goosed* me in the deck planking!"

The fact that the apothecary was a small room in the back of the public stables was not encouraging, but Marge looked around anyway in hopes something could be done, at least temporarily. When, after a while, no one seemed to notice her, she called out, "Hello! Anybody here?"

A strange head suddenly popped up from below the double-doors leading to the apothecary storage room. She jumped, startled, then stared, not sure if she was looking at a fairy or a human face. It was round and rosy-cheeked, surrounded by snow white hair the thickness and consistency of sheep's wool, with a bulbous nose and tiny, squinting eyes. "Yes, my dear?" the stranger asked, in a voice that sounded like a very old man speaking falsetto. He seemed to have difficulty with his vision, and certainly did not see her clearly, judging by where he was looking.

"Over here," she told him. "You the apothecary?"

"Oh, my yes! Phineas T. Harbottle, at your service, m'um. What seems to be the problem?"

"I have a male, six feet six and all muscle, who's been slipped a love potion that apparently also has induced amnesia. He's cavorting around naked in the mud with a mermaid, who got the same stuff."

"Well, at least it's mutual," Harbottle commented. "Last few times I've had to deal with such potions, the devotion was strictly one-sided. Makes for a messy thing, you know."

"I've sent off a message for help to Terindell, but I need something to keep them under control until that help arrives."

"Oh—slip 'em a Mickey, huh?"

"Well, it worked to get them into this mess. Say! How do you know the term 'Mickey' anyway?"

"Oh, I know all the great Irishmen, Mr. Michael Finn in particular. We do some business around here with some emigré leprechauns, you see, and they love to tell stories. Unfortunately, they love to tell the *same* stories. I'm afraid I'm the only one they can pin down who'll still listen to them. Only the Americans believe in 'em anymore, you see—the Irish are far too practical these days—and it's far too fast a culture in America for them. Also, it seems, these Americans who think of themselves as Irish are ten times more Irish than the Irish, so the little people tend to wind up coming over here."

Marge decided not to go into her own origins right then. "Can you help me?"

The strange little man scratched his head. "Well, I don't know. You don't happen to know which potion, do you, or have a residual sample from the bottle?"

"The bottles were gone when the couple was discovered, and with them the brand name."

"Well, describe the symptoms—fully."

She did so, sparing no detail.

Harbottle just listened, and when he was up-to-date he said, "It has to be a very old formula. I haven't heard of this combination in—must be seven, eight hundred years, at least. You've a very old-fashioned wizard here, or he's got one devil of a cellar. Still, wait a few moments and I'll see what I can do."

He seemed to disappear again behind the dutch door. She wasn't tall enough to see much of what was inside, but he must not have been too tall himself to vanish so completely from sight—from sight, but not hearing; the noises that began coming out of the stall were incredible.

It began with the simple clinking of glass and then the

sound of mortar and pestle, but soon all sorts of things started happening. Once it sounded as if a whole barnyard was in there, and once a huge cloud of foul-smelling purple smoke arose from the floor and she heard Harbottle say, "Oops! Oh, dear!"

Finally the strange head popped up again, and a chubby arm held up a vial of a swirling orange liquid that seemed to smoke a little. "I had to compromise a few ingredients," he told her, "because some of the better stuff just isn't made anymore. Here—take it."

She reached up and took it; she found it warm but not too hot to hold. She sniffed it, and turned up her nose. "*Phew*! Smells awful!"

"Tastes worse," Harbottle assured her. "That's one of the Rules, you know. Poisons and potions all taste wonderful, while treatments and antidotes taste like mildewed, broiled swampwater. You should feel lucky. Many of them are far fouler than that one, and are nearly impossible to administer."

"It's going to be a good trick just administering this stuff. How much should I give to them and what will it do?"

"Damned if I know, actually. I'd say divide it roughly equally and get them each to drink as much of it as possible. The more they get inside them, the more complete the results will be. And because of the substitutions, there may be some odd side effects, or it might not be totally effective. He has a wife and magic sword you say?"

"Yes. I have the sword, anyway."

"The wife would also be handy. However, the sword has its own life and identity, and it can aid its owner in many ways. If he takes it, the sword will at least weaken the spells that may go along with the potion. There may also be physical side effects because of the cross-racial nature of the romance, as it were, but most should be temporary."

"Um—thanks a lot. Any ideas on how I get them to drink this?"

"You came for a Mickey and I gave you a treatment. I can't be expected to come up with *everything*."

She was grateful to the strange little man, no matter what, and she suddenly became acutely aware of just how distant she'd become from the real world. "I—I'm afraid I haven't anything to pay with right now."

"Oh, that's all right—I'll just put it on Ruddygore's tab. If you see him, however, you might remind him that I haven't seen a payment in almost a hundred and seventy-eight years, and I could use a bit. I've been building a cyclotron in the basement bit by bit by mail order and I'd really like to get module number 1068."

She stared at him. "I beg your pardon?"

"A cyclotron. It's a device for shooting atoms—"

"I know what it is. I just never expected to hear of one in Husaquahr, let alone the power to run it."

"Oh, one problem at a time. I'll work on the power later. Right now it's so nice and long and complex it's sort of a work of art. Well, good luck."

Marge was feeling a bit dizzy. "Yeah—thanks." And, with that, she walked back out of the stable and into the morning sun.

Bly lured the potioned pair onto the ship with an offer of food and a very large bed, which they took. The ratlike captain seemed confident that he and some locals could contain the pair should they emerge, and urged Marge to get some sleep. There was no chance right now to get them to take the potion, nor any plan to do so, so the captain assured her that he and Audra would work on the problem while she slept. If they were lucky, or smart, it was possible they'd come up with something.

Dead tired and knowing she'd gone about as far as she could, Marge went to the other cabin and went to sleep.

Marge awoke to the smell of fresh paint and a general quiet, and she didn't know whether this was a good thing or not. She quickly left the stateroom, entered the galley, and found Audra there.

"Hi!" the nymph greeted her. "Well, things should start popping around here soon, I guess."

"How's that?"

"We managed to keep our lovers pretty well happy here, with a few minor incidents—old Ruddygore's not going to like the town's damage bill, I'm afraid—and then this real *creepy* guy and this strange-looking girl came down a couple of hours ago with a note from Ruddygore. They zinged 'em cold with a wave of the hand and then examined them real careful, you know? Then the guy looked at the stuff you brought and said it might work, might not. Anyway, they're waiting up on deck for you now before trying anything."

"And our lovers?"

"Still out cold in the other cabin." She walked out from behind the counter; as she approached the left cabin door, it opened for her. It was pretty clear what parts of the ship were, in a way, parts of Audra.

With the sun down, Marge's fairy sight and powers were at their full potential. Both Joe and Tura were out cold, as advertised, and kept that way by a strong local spell that was easy to see. Below it, their bodies seemed to have a reddish-brown glow of a kind she had never seen before. This, then, was the potion. Below that, she quickly sorted out the older spells and Joe's curse and noted, with some amusement, that Tura now had deep and complex black spell bands as well. Sometime during the day, Joe had bitten her for sure.

Interlaced, though, were newer bands that bore a far different signature than any of the others. These, then, were what the Master of the Dead had added, and what were, in fact, the greatest potential threat to undoing the harm.

Nodding to herself, she went back out and up on deck.

Bly was there, looking pretty tired. He'd had a very busy day that had started early, and she felt sorry for him. With him were the pair that Audra had told her about, dressed in long, black cloaks and hoods. For a moment she wondered if she could trust a mere note. The Master of the Dead had been described as looking not too dissimilar to the larger one.

They turned and put down their hoods when they heard her, and she gasped. "Tiana! Macore!" The larger one she'd thought of as being the Master of the Dead had been Joe's wife.

Both were grim-faced, but managed smiles at seeing her.

Marge stared at Macore. "I thought you were stuck in the land of the djinn for the duration."

"No, the old boy has some other uses for the Lamp," the thief replied. "And some other uses for me, too, I'm afraid. I'm gonna be his meat for a while, until we solve this whole business or I die in the attempt."

Marge turned to Tiana, who towered over her. "I—I'm sorry this happened."

"Something like this had to." The big woman sighed. "I am afraid this world is not safe when one goes adventuring. When word came, I could not be restrained."

"Ruddygore suspects that this is a trap to draw him into a compromising position—a fight on the enemy's timing, terms, and turf," Macore explained. "He'd rather pick his own point for a showdown."

"I can understand why Tiana's here, but why you?"

"Because I'm a thief—and a damned good one."

"How's that again?"

"Look, the potion's bad enough. Why lay that crap on them as well except to lock them in, antidote or not. This Master of the Dead had to know that a potion's not necessarily permanent, so he tied it to some spells there, and five will get you fifty that what they mean are booby traps. Undo 'em any way but perfect and they'll reach out and get you and maybe everybody else in the immediate vicinity. Tiana's got the power, and I'm pretty good at traps."

Marge nodded, feeling relieved. At least she wasn't going to have to go through this alone. "So when do we start, and what do we do first?"

"You do not have to do anything, dear," Tiana told her. "You have been more than enough help this day. It is for me and demon-brain here to take."

"I'll stay," the Kauri told them. "I've got very good defenses and I'm not as easily affected by spells as humans are; also, this is partly a spell of passion, on which I'm something of an expert."

"All right, then. On your own head be it," the big woman replied. "Let's go down and take a look at our sleeping beauties."

Bly opted out of the session, not only because he wasn't being paid to take risks like this, but also because he was too tired to do anyone any good. Still, that left the three of them very crowded in the cabin with the two sleeping beauties.

"She is quite pretty," Tiana noted. "What sort of person is she—normally?"

"She seemed nice enough," Marge told her, "but I really didn't have much of a chance to get to know her. There was something inside her, though, something melancholy, that I sensed. She was not happy."

"I ask because Joe was in fact attracted to her, and without any spells or mermaid tricks. Joe is simply one of those men who loves women. All women. If she also had a sad story to tell, it would get to him. Even as insulated as we have been these past years, I have seen it happen before."

Marge looked at Tiana strangely. "You mean he cheats? And you know it?"

Tiana shrugged. "So do I—and he does *not* know it." She sighed. "Well, let us get to work."

Like surgeons studying a wound before operating, the three examined all of the newer spells. That was the only real advantage they had—that each spell cast by anyone bore a distinct signature. It could be disguised, but no two wizards' spells were ever exactly alike—like fingerprints. The spells, then, could be sorted out—but not necessarily deciphered.

It took some time to fix both the start and the end of the complex colored bands of the spells, but this was absolutely necessary to dissolving them. Once the route was traced, they could begin. Fortunately, the wizard had not wanted to spend a great deal of time inside the inn room and had come with the spells prepared. As he could not know who the partner would be, the spells were essentially identical except for sexual identity diacriticals, and this meant that if one were solved, the other could also be. More difficult would be further down, where the spells reached out to both of them with common threads. The spell had to be unraveled in the exact same order as it had been cast. Anything else would do no good and would simply backfire on the unraveler.

It was easy going at first, but then they ran into a knot of finely woven yellow and red threads crisscrossing in all directions. The first trap. Tiana looked at the little thief. "Macore?"

"Oh, it's a boomerang spell, all right," the little man responded thoughtfully. He followed beyond the trap to the next junction. "The trouble is that he's got something innocuous running across something nasty, using the same color and pattern. We have to get only the continuing threads of the spell and none of the obscuring one."

"The progression seems obvious enough. Six to twelve to twenty-four, with the last making a right turn at the junction."

"Ah, but that's what he wants you to see. But, here—six strands become twelve become seventy-two straight on, then back to twelve beyond the next junction. That's also symmetry. I'd go straight. The odds are he's much more concerned with the spell than the trap. In any event, I'd go for the more complex pattern as being the spell itself in this case."

"All right. Here goes." Tiana concentrated and dissolved the threads running through the junction and into a braided pattern. Nothing happened, so she continued on to the next junction, then took the turn again to go back to the six.

Marge could do nothing but watch their operation. She could follow it, but not the complexity of the spell removal that Tiana was doing, and she certainly had a great deal of respect for Macore, who seemed to think like a thief all the time. It took about an hour to follow the pattern all the way down, and then they shifted to Tura. Macore had guessed right on the matching spells as well; this Master of the Dead had been in a hurry. Even so, he was a real pro.

It was, Marge understood, something like unknitting a complex quilt with little bomb triggers set to go off if you lost the thread. Soon, though, there remained only the simple binding spell connecting the pair, and both Tiana and Macore grew confident and more relaxed. They were almost done when suddenly a snakelike coil of pure energy leaped out and engulfed everyone in the room.

"We really blew that one," Tiana sang, in a lusty operatic soprano.

Macore and Marge both looked at her and then at each other.

"We have a real comedian here," Macore sang, in a low tenor that was slightly off-key.

"It sounds like grand opera," Marge sang to them.

Audra suddenly came through the door singing, "Would anyone like some wine—and cheese?"

"Oh, this is terrible, terrible, terrible!" Tiana sang.

The others chorused back, "Terrible, terrible, terrible!"

The spell's simple bands were still connecting them and clearly visible, and Tiana, putting a finger to her lips for silence, proceeded to unravel each of them in turn and roll the thing back to the two unconscious forms. It was not much of a spell as these traps went; more a thumbing of the nose at the one who sought to undo the Master's work.

Being careful not to make the same mistake twice, since a trap sprung more than once became more and more complex and, after a while, became impossible to unravel, she removed the last of the spell.

Macore let out a deep breath and turned to Audra. "I'll have that drink now, lass." He beamed. "Ah! No more singing!"

"I thought you had a lovely voice," the wood nymph told him.

Macore beamed. "We'll have to talk this over later, my dear. Business first." He turned back to Tiana. "Now we've still got that stupid potion to deal with."

She nodded, but, before she could say anything else, Marge put in, "The alchemist said that the sword might help, and that each should get an equal dose of the antidote."

"Let us try it," the big woman said. "Can you get the sword?"

"I can't touch it. You know that. Macore? It's next door in my cabin."

Macore nodded, smiled, and blew a kiss to Audra, then went out and was quickly back with the sword. It had begun to hum discordantly when Macore had picked it up, but now, in the room with Joe, it seemed to give off a small but pleasant electronic sort of whine. Tiana took it, placed it in Joe's hand, and closed his hand around the hilt. The sword began to hum a strange tune, which startled them. Marge frowned, then said, "I think it's something by Ferlin Husky."

"Huh?" Tiana asked her, looking confused.

"Don't worry about it. It knows it's home."

Macore looked at them. "Can we force that vile brew down them while they're out without choking them or losing it?"

"We will see. Bring it here," Tiana commanded. Audra exited and returned with the bottle, which was still smoking slightly. With Macore's help, they propped up Joe's upper torso enough to get his head only slightly leaned back. His mouth, fortunately, was somewhat open. Holding the head and mouth, Tiana poured just a little from the bottle into his mouth and held it closed. Joe coughed, but didn't otherwise react.

The glow around his body diminished slightly.

It was a slow and somewhat messy business, using it bit by bit until the glow seemed to vanish completely. The rest they tried with Tura, whose mouth was closed and had to be pried open, but eventually it worked. It was, however, a good thing that Tiana was so big and strong herself, Marge reflected.

At last, the potion was gone, and they stood back. "Time now to wake them up." Tiana sighed, sounding tired. She removed her spell quickly, and they waited. When nothing happened after a little while, the big woman said, in a loud voice, "Joe! Wake up!"

Joe's eyes opened, but they were vacant and staring.

It was the same with Tura. No matter what, they could get no reactions out of them at all.

"What's wrong with them?" Macore asked, irritably. "Did we blow something or what?"

"I don't think so," Marge responded. "But, you see, I can feel and see emotions. They are tangible things to me. There's nothing there. No feeling at all."

"Joe—sit up in bed!" Tiana commanded, and the big man did as instructed, staring vacantly ahead.

"I was afraid of this," the big woman said hesitantly. "When I saw the reactions, I knew. We have been wasting our time, my friends. Now we know what the Master of the Dead took away in those two little potion bottles."

"You mean—he took their essences? Their souls?" Marge breathed, shocked.

Tiana nodded. "I fear so."

"But—they were animated lovers, playful innocents today!"

"It was the spell," Macore told her. "They were playful lovers, yes, but they were simpletons, too. It was a mask, an act, to deceive us while the Master made a clean get-away. So much for Ruddygore's plotting. All we've got here now are two animated corpses that will dance a jig if we tell 'em to but don't have a thought in their heads."

Marge threw up her hands in disgust. "Oh, great! *Now* what do we do?"

"We must track the bastard to his lair and reclaim them," Tiana said determinedly.

"Oh, sure," Macore agreed sarcastically. "That should be a snap."

CHAPTER 8

SOUL SURVIVORS

All castle and fortification wells in disuse for more than three centuries are declared as homes for monsters.

—Rules, LXXI, 207(c)

A DETAILED MAP OF THE REGION AROUND THE TOWN WAS spread out on the galley table as they gathered around to try and figure out where their quarry might be. Macore was certain that this Master of the Dead had to have a base not far from the town itself, because the wizard was able to take some time to research the innkeeper and his personal life in order to get a hold on him; also the Master might have determined where they would stay, but would have no way of knowing what day or week they would set off on their journey. He also obviously had to have access to the local graveyards in order to pull his animated corpse routine, assuming it was, indeed, no illusion.

"I'd say south," Bly commented, looking at the map. "And certainly on this side of the river. North of here are some rolling hills and plains that are good farm country but not much on concealment. Old Harbottle has considerable power, and all the folks around here know and trust him, and he's seen no strangers with this kind of power. Now, look—about twenty miles south of here starts a swamp and marsh area that extends for the next sixty miles downriver and inland a good twenty-five."

"The Holimau Swamp," Macore said. "Everybody in these parts is scared stiff of it."

"Exactly," the captain agreed. "Makes it the perfect place to hide out if you've got real power and still want to be close enough to sneak into town, maybe transformed as a bird or animal as need be. I know the region pretty well. I have some relations from that part of the country."

It was the first time Marge realized just what kind of place somebody who resembled a giant bipedal rat would find most comfortable.

"Any ideas?" Tiana prompted him.

"Well, there are a lot of old structures and ancient ruins in there, mostly reclaimed by the swamp, but I'd guess he's using one of them. He's human, I think, and likes his comforts. He could have ravens or some other birds as his spotters, but he had to get into town from there, I'll bet, and fairly quickly. That limits it to just five possible spots where it's easy enough to get in and out quickly but far enough in to stay concealed. They'll have to be checked out, somehow, tomorrow, maybe by the eagles, if they're willing to do it."

Marge looked it over. "Why wait? Just mark the places on there. I can fly, and I have power and some advantage in the dark."

They all stared at her. Finally Tiana said, "All right—if you're certain. But be very cautious. He's bound to be expecting us sooner or later, and if he captures your soul, which is faërie in nature, your body will become nothing but stone, an ornament for his door, subject to damage, wear, and breakage which would be permanent, even if you were sometime freed."

Marge's eyebrows rose. "I didn't know that—but I'll

be careful." And, with the marked map, she was off to the south.

Flying a thousand feet above the treetops and following the bends of the great river, Marge was struck, as always, by the great beauty of the night world.

Once over the swamp, she headed inland, descending and taking out the map, looking for whatever landmarks she could find and trying to judge distances from a height. She found the first two—cold, forbidding places overgrown and almost invisible, if not looked for specifically—with little trouble, but quickly dismissed them as lost to everyone, even the Master of the Dead.

The swamp was alive, not only with plants but with a tremendous variety of animals and insects; but, while some seemed threatening and some downright scary, they really didn't bother her too much. Creatures of the night knew how to survive in the night.

The third place she did not find, in spite of being certain of her location. It had apparently been so reclaimed that it had ceased to exist. The fourth was in remarkably good repair, and gave off emanations of great power, but this power was not human nor was it faërie—it was something far stronger and older and, well, *evil*. Whatever it was, though, was wedded to the building and the swamp, and would not be likely to trouble itself with the affairs of their tiny ship, no matter what its mission.

The fifth, however, was another matter—an ancient keep of some kind, partially overgrown but showing signs of much recent activity. The short trails to and from it had clearly been recently cut and well maintained since, and it sat on a small island. The water there was quite shallow; far too shallow for the *Hippogryph*, but not too shallow to permit a small, flat-bottomed boat from being poled in and out to deeper water, where something better might await, hidden from sight. The boat—really nothing more than a raft—was there and securely tied to a tree.

The place itself was dark, but she sensed a fire somewhere within, and felt a *presence* there, a human presence but one not to be trifled with. It was also, oddly, somewhat familiar, but she couldn't place it, nor did she expect to. There were other presences, too—but of a different sort. The place was well guarded, both inside and out, by figures that appeared human from a distance but gave off no sense of warmth or life at all.

The dead guarded the Master of the Dead.

He had been here some time, that was clear. How long it would be impossible for anyone but him to tell, but certainly it was long enough to have captured the souls of the newly dead and dying. She wondered how many of the family, friends and associates of those who lived in the region he had under his complete control? How many were being blackmailed with the souls and corpses of their deceased loved ones?

This was a wizard with a hell of a skill, and it gave him increasing temporal power. As Ruddygore's skill in traveling between here and Earth gave him power and knowledge, so the ease with which the Master bottled up the souls of his victims gave him a different and darker, but no less powerful, domain.

It was, however, pretty boring company.

She swung back around and headed for the ship, after scouting the most likely approaches and methods of reaching the place. Without a raft, it would be a bitch getting into there, and if they got one from the town or built one, it would certainly telegraph everything.

She had been gone several hours, and it would be dawn in perhaps two more. She felt as if she'd already put in a good night.

She circled the ship, then landed on the afterdeck. It was oddly quiet, and she grew immediately suspicious. Surely after all this, they would have posted a guard, she thought, and slept in shifts.

"Hello!" she called out. "Is anybody here?" She walked around to the bow and back again, seeing no one and finding no lights. Carefully, she opened the double-doors leading below and latched them open, so she could have some sort of getaway. She did not go all the way down, however, instead using her powers to sense what life there was.

Nothing. She registered no life below at all. That was particularly odd, since, even though both female and a fairy, she still should have gotten something from Audra, who could not leave the ship.

Suddenly the cabin doors slammed open and a host of horrible-looking creatures burst out. They were loathsome, grotesque versions of human beings, bodies with skin hanging and parts of skull and bone protruding, dressed in decaying rags. She quickly discovered, however, that zombies could move damned fast.

She turned, but tripped on the top step; by the time she'd scrambled back up, the leading one was almost on top of her. She pushed off into the air and felt a cold, dry, horrible hand grab her right foot. Twisting in the air, she felt resistance suddenly cease and she was up and away, just avoiding the outstretched arms of the rest of the terrible creatures.

She was five hundred feet in the air before she looked back and saw, to her disgust, the zombie hand still clutching her foot. It had been in such poor condition that she had managed to wrench it loose with her twist.

She felt horrified and repulsed by it, but actually crossed two-thirds of the river before daring to land on a small island and pry the grisly thing off with sticks. She then jumped into the river to remove any last traces of the horror from her body.

Finally feeling a little cleaner, she rose back into the air and headed south once more. Later she would have the luxury of screaming, crying, and maybe fainting; now she had to be clearheaded and absolutely perfect.

It was clear what had happened. Knowing that they would soon come for him, the Master of the Dead had decided to jump the gun. It was possible that he commanded Joe and Tura to do it, for those with the souls had the power—or perhaps they were merely overwhelmed. At any rate, it must have happened shortly after she'd left. She thanked providence that she had insisted on going out that evening; the Master had obviously counted on their deciding on a morning search.

The fun and games were over. The Master had ceased toying with them and now had all but one of them in his power, that was clear, including the two who represented a strong and Council-backed theocracy. In a sense, he'd been shrewd with his fun, gambling a little that all of his antics would not attract someone truly able to challenge his power and so gathering even more into his net. Now he had not just the voyagers, but Tiana and Macore as well.

She knew she was racing against time. Within a half hour of sunrise it would be clear to the eagles that something was wrong and they would investigate. Within an hour after that, they would be reporting to Ruddygore on the one hand and launching their own search on the other. She doubted that the Master would remain at the swamp base much longer than he had to; he had accomplished his mission in spades. Not only would any expedition to Earth now not contain those most threatening to Boquillas, but he had under his complete control the bodies of the demigod and demigoddess. If he were a member of the Council, he would have wrested temporal control from Ruddygore without a wizard's battle and he would be supported by the other members, as long as he kept them comfortable and protected. If he were not a Council member, he was in a good position to make a deal with them, no matter what Ruddygore might say.

But the rule and the religion would take on a far darker coloration under him. Ruddygore had been right to worry; with the Baron and Dacaro doing something terrible on Earth and the Master assuming control here, Hell might well be in the driver's seat, no matter what the outcome of Armageddon was supposed to be according to the script.

She was certain he would return first to his redoubt. If he'd lived there a fair amount of time, as she surmised, he wasn't going to leave without checking under the bed to see if he'd left anything, particularly anything incriminating.

Still, she wasn't sure what she could do. She was no match for a wizard of his powers and she knew very little about the process he was using. She knew, of course, that souls could indeed be extracted and captured in sealed vessels, such as bottles, but she also had been taught that such rituals were complex, fairly long, and involved invoking a particular kind of demon. The Master had apparently no need for any of this; he'd taken, by the innkeeper's account, no more than a few minutes to do his dirty work to Joe and Tura, and certainly seemed to have moved fast in the case of the rest of them. Tiana, in particular, was untrained and undisciplined, but had a lot of raw power and a lot of protection, yet he'd apparently taken her as easily as he had the others.

She circled in and dropped to nearly treetop level, slowing and checking the most obvious route in and out. Obviously she had missed them being moved south only by a freak of perfect timing—on the Master's part. Entirely too much was going that bastard's way so far, she decided angrily.

She thought she spotted something, then dipped down and perched in a tree. Yes—there it was. A sleek yacht even larger and more luxurious than the *Piebald Hippogryph*, well-concealed under a lot of brush and natural camouflage. She decided to have a look, and cautiously drifted down until she was on deck. There seemed to be no one aboard, but that was by no means certain, considering the nature of the enemy's troops.

Someone had been here, though, and recently. She could see the fresh breaks in the vines on which the concealing camouflage was hung, including some fresh enough to be still oozing their acidic sap. They had brought them in, where they'd been met by the raft, probably. Someone had gone aboard, possibly to check for last-minute readiness, then had continued on, back to the swamp base. Hanging on the stern of the ship, held by pulleys, was a small, sleek little sailboat that might well be the lifeboat. It showed signs of use, and, in fact, was still dripping water.

When you had zombies to row if there was no breeze, or you didn't want to be noticed, you could go twenty miles up the coast very nicely in that thing.

The central cabin of the yacht was large enough to have portholes above the deck, and she looked in. It was pitch dark, of course, but that didn't bother her.

They were all there, just sitting around a central table as if about to eat dinner; only none were moving, or even doing more than blinking and breathing. Joe, Tiana, Tura, Macore—even Bly. In the center of the table was a life-sized statue of a woman of unnatural beauty, formed in travertine marble. With a shock she realized that it was Audra.

Joe, she saw, was wearing his sword, and the others seemed armed as well. She guessed the trap. The Master needed no zombies to guard them; they would guard themselves. They did not think, however, and so would be quite literal in their orders. They would not have curiosity and would not be likely to investigate strange noises outside.

She went to the rail and looked down, praying that there were no fearsome creatures below to attack her. Then she jumped and slipped into the water and swam underneath the craft.

The Master had cut it close. There were only two feet or so of draft between the ship and the bottom at this point, although it deepened quickly only fifteen yards or so in back. It was chosen for maximum concealment from ground and air and a quick getaway, but that wasn't what she was looking for. She spotted what she hoped was it, cursing the fact that somebody born and raised in west Texas knew very little about boats of any kind, and then came back up and landed on the deck. There was a forward hatch with several clamps, and she undid them, not without difficulty, for her strength wasn't all that great, and then she swung the hatch cover open, praying to the Earth Mother that no corpses leaped out at her.

They didn't, and she went down and into the blackness. She was instantly relieved to find some water down there, and began quickly searching for its source. This was, or had been, a smuggler's craft, and it had some very efficient means of scuttling in a hurry if need be.

The valve wheels and clamps were iron, and it took her several minutes to find something of wood so she could manipulate them from a distance. Once the stick broke and she actually had to leave and find another; but eventually she managed to turn the rusty wheels enough to open the valves much further than they should have been. Water was not entering in torrents, but enough was coming in, she hoped, to sink this boat two feet in the swamp mud.

She flew out, knowing she could do no more, and closed the hatch, refastening the wooden pegs that secured it. She could only hope that she had opened the ports enough to sink the ship, yet not wide enough to attract attention. There was a gurgling sound below, but it was quite faint through the hatch cover.

She heard someone coming, the sound of pole hitting water and the creak of timbers, and rose up into the trees to see. Suddenly she was worried that her timing had been off; if so, the Master would be able to take his ship out into the main channel, but it would then sink like a stone in twenty or more feet of water, drowning those aboard.

It was not the Master, however, but some of his zombies, carrying neatly stacked boxes sealed with ropes. She felt great relief at seeing the horrible creatures, for it meant the Master was still up at the redoubt and that, perhaps, he was making his first mistake. He would not risk taking any of his captives if he were forced to use the small boat, and even that would be slow and conspicuous. She suspected that, come morning, it was going to get very hot for the mysterious stealer of souls around here.

She decided to go up to his fort and see what other mischief she could accomplish to slow him down. Kauri were not ones for revenge or other petty emotions, but this guy deserved all she could do to him.

A false dawn was already permeating even this remote place, and she knew that very soon her powers would begin to wane and she'd be forced to wear the glasses, putting her at a great disadvantage. Still, she had to see what she could and do what she was able to foul the wizard up. Dawn would also mean the start of the process to nab him.

Torches had been lighted now from the small raft landing to the trail up to the ancient building, the light flickering ghostlike against the moss and lichen-covered walls. The corpses guarding the way seemed now almost to fade into the swamp growths themselves, although they made no real effort at concealment. She flew over them and checked in the window openings of the stone structure which was three-tiered with three squares atop each other, each slightly smaller than the one below. At one time, this had probably been a temple. To whom or what, she preferred not to know.

She was surprised to find, in the large lower chamber, what looked like living men and women working, packing up and stacking boxes. She realized with a start that their silence and their mechanical movements indicated that they were of the living dead. Scattered around the walls were numerous statues of various kinds of rock, like a museum exhibit to the races of faërie in this region.

There seemed little she could do here, but she had a thought about the raft. The odds were that of the four zombies riding it out, two at least would remain on board the yacht to stow the stuff while the others brought it back for the next load. The lack of the raft wouldn't stop the Master, but it sure as hell would slow him down even more.

She couldn't carry much of anything and fly, and she didn't weigh an awful lot, but there was something to be said for speed and momentum, and she was too determined to be repelled by what she was thinking of doing.

She waited until the raft was away from the yacht, perhaps midway back to the redoubt, and saw that there were two of the creatures polling from either side. She arose high in the air, came down as fast as she could and still maintain control, then struck one of the zombies in the back with her feet.

The collision unbalanced her for a moment and she fought to stop a tumble before she hit something, but the animated corpse had fallen face first into the swamp.

Something told the other one it was under attack, but it really didn't have the ability to figure out by whom or what, nor how or why. She managed to pull the same trick on it without any real additional danger. There was a price to be paid for using automated labor, she thought with satisfaction.

One of them picked itself up from the ooze and started doggedly toward the raft, which was now hung up against a clump of vines. As the first rays of the sun broke over the River of Dancing Gods, it was making a determined effort to get back up on the raft. Putting on her goggles, feeling her strength ebb a bit and her powers wane, she continued the rather easy job of knocking the thing back off.

Suddenly there was a great disturbance in the water, and she turned and saw a huge number of the walking dead treading forward through the swamp, carrying boxes. These were more than she could handle, although she had an idea to make for the first one or two and have the others trip over that one.

She rose up and then dived on them; but as she approached, she felt a sudden numbing paralysis. Incredibly, she seemed to stop in mid-dive, just a few feet above the heads of the army of the dead, and remain suspended there, unable to move.

Behind the zombies with the cartons came the living dead, carrying a large, dark, figure, hooded and robed, in a raised sedan chair. The zombies continued on, but the ones with the chair did not. From the folds of the cloak a hand gestured, and she felt herself gently lowered and moved forward, almost in front of the figure.

Inside the hood were two glowing eyes that seemed to have their own inner luminescence. Although it should have been clear, no face, no other details, could be seen.

"Well, the set is now complete," a voice said from under that hood, a voice that seemed somehow familiar. She had met this man, heard that voice, somewhere before—but she couldn't place it, nor was it one she knew she would be expected to recognize. Someone she'd met, but not someone she knew.

"You will make a fine addition to my sculpture garden, my dear," he commented with self-assured good humor. He was clearly pleased with himself. "Perhaps I'll place you on one side of the walk entrance and the wood nymph on the other. Yes, that would be pleasant indeed."

She found that she could speak. "The Earth Mother's strength is beyond any human's," she warned him. "You will incur her wrath at this."

"Probably, but she really can't do much so long as you're not dead, and you won't be dead, just bottled up for a time."

She trembled at this, both in anger and fear, knowing that his confidence was not misplaced. He knew the Rules and the ways of all the faërie, that was for sure.

"Come. We will go to my ship together, and I will reunite you with your friends."

She floated just ahead of him as the marchers continued on toward the yacht, frustrated that she could do nothing and feeling even more frustrated that her efforts hadn't counted for much against a really major wizard. Hell, even if the ship had sunk by now, he could probably refloat it with a wave of his hand.

But there were some things even a wizard had problems with. As the yacht came into view, it was clearly down and on its side, settled in the mud. Worse, because it had rolled slightly on its side it had pulled down much of the camouflage that concealed it from both ground and aerial surveillance. Overhead there was the loud screeching of birds that might have been eagles; certainly there was a strength and urgency to their cries. Marge felt somewhat better. Even if the Master of the Dead could easily refloat it, he didn't dare sail such a conspicuous barge, now that there was a strong chance it was known to his enemies. For the first time, things were going against him, and it gave her a feeling of real accomplishment. She had nothing to lose by taunting him.

"So what do you do now, hot shot?" she jibed. "*You* can still take it on the lam, but your boxes and your zombies won't move so easily."

The Master stood up in his sedan chair, shaking with anger as he stared at the crippled craft. "*You* did this!"

"Serves you right for buying a smuggler's craft. I think maybe you'd better decide what you can carry with you and get out of here, unless you're ready right now for a face-down with Ruddygore. I assure you *he's* ready for *you*. The whole point of this was to draw you out!"

Now, from the direction of the river, they could hear a chant that could only mean oarsmen working at great speed.

"O-re-um! Row, rum! O-re-um! Row, rum!"

"Ruddygore loves a grand entrance," she told him. "After all, he knows he's not going to catch you unless you want to fight."

The Master of the Dead seemed to hesitate, as if weighing his alternatives. Finally he said, "All right, then! Ruddygore's day is coming, but it will be at a time and place of *my* choosing, not here and now."

"O-re-um! Row, rum! O-re-um! Row-rum!" It sounded much closer now.

"I'll grant you a round, but only a round," the Master continued. "You will yet grace my garden walk, and your friends will slavishly clean and protect your image by my commands! I will not forget you, Changeling! I grant you your temporary freedom now. Have your companions and welcome. They will not be good company!"

Suddenly the force holding her in the air ceased, and she plunged into the water. When she came up, she found the zombies still standing there, like some inanimate statues. The sedan chair, however, was empty.

The sight of the undead horde still there unnerved her, though; she had no idea how far the Master had fled or whether he was sticking around to see if perhaps he *could* surprise Ruddygore. She took off immediately and went out to the river to greet and brief the great wizard.

The source of the chanting was a large galley, all right; but even as she cleared the trees, she saw that it was already well past the only possible landing to enter this area and continuing south at a steady pace.

Ruddygore had not yet arrived. Without knowing it, she'd bluffed the wizard out!

She grew suddenly paranoid. Just how far had she bluffed the man, and was he now on the run or waiting to see how bad the damage was? If he had remained anywhere nearby, it wouldn't take him much longer than it had taken her to discover that the Marines weren't landing after all.

She decided to play it safe, at least initially, and flew up to intercept the eagles.

The great birds, she discovered, were merely hunting breakfast in the river and still hadn't much idea that anything was wrong. There were no clear signs of violence aboard the *Hippogryph*, after all, and it was still far too early to expect the humans on board to be up and about.

She quickly pinpointed the danger spots and filled them in on the situation. While Ruddygore was absolutely opposed to the introduction of Earth technology into Husaquahr, he was not above using it himself whenever it would give him an unfair advantage. The chief of the eagles had a small, battery-operated device around his neck; through a chain of such devices, his voice could reach all the way to Terindell.

The great leader was imposing, fully the largest bird she had ever seen, but he was not one for her to fear. After all, if you couldn't trust an eagle scout leader, who could you trust in this world?

"We have failed to contact Ruddygore directly," the great bird told her. "There was some serious trouble far to the west that drew him. A feint, I suspect, but it causes a few problems. It may be another day, perhaps two, before we can get him here. There is a force with two fairly strong wizards at our disposal on a ship not far from here, but it may take two or three hours for them to get here and get in the area."

She thought for a moment, still too charged up to feel tired. "We can't afford to wait. If the Master is still anywhere nearby and sees that Ruddygore isn't here, he'll return and remove their souls at the very least."

"You are certain he did not already take them?"

"He was too confident and in no particular hurry. But he might well return for them at any time. I must go back and find them before he gets his chance. Signal the force to come in, but we can't afford to give the Master the hours."

"What makes you think you can find them, Kauri?"

"I believe I can—smell—them. That's the best I can come to it. It's best done in the dark, when I have my full powers, but I think I can find them. There are only a few places they might be. Just give me cover if you can."

"It will be done. Go."

She headed first for the yacht, the most likely place. She was a bit upset to find that her friends had toppled over, but relieved to see that, at least from her vantage point, Audra hadn't broken, nor was there any sign of blood or other injuries. However, with the Master's control gone, they were no longer a threat to her, which counted for much. Still, they would starve or otherwise die of a number of things if she didn't restore them soon.

She was none too confident that she really *could* smell out captive souls, but she knew that the zombies gave off no real emotive life-force sensations. She was betting that the souls would.

The boat, however, proved barren. The next step was the unnerving one of flying low over the zombie army, still holding boxes high over their heads in a frozen processional. Again, she could not sense what she sought and she began to fear that the souls were undetectable to her.

In a little over an hour, she'd methodically traced the trail back to the ancient redoubt. She had no desire to go poking around inside; the Master had shown himself possessed of a ghoulish sense of humor and a love of booby traps. She perched on a tree limb and tried to think it out.

Think the way Macore would think, she told herself. So far, beyond the obvious, she'd been looking in the places where *she* would hide them.

Suppose now, just for a moment, that he never had any intention of taking the souls with him. He would have to be dependent on the ship to move any cargo, and the chase would be on, no matter whether his pursuers knew who and what they were looking for or not. Counting the zombies and his living dead assistants, he'd have far to much to carry with him while traveling by spell. What sneakier place to leave them than right here, where he knew their location and could return after the heat was off?

But that posed another problem. The redoubt, trapped and guarded or not, was sure to be eventually vanquished and searched almost stone by stone, by a force including wizards powerful enough to detect such things. That meant no hidden panels in the walls or the like. Oh, there might well be; but even if there were such things, they'd be poor hiding places.

Where, then? She took off and slowly circled the place, keeping fairly low and trying to be careful not to fly into any low-lying branches, mosses, and vines. Someplace secure and protected, but not a part of the building itself.

The second time around, she began carefully to study the ground. She had seen from the yacht the kind of camouflage the Master liked, and now she looked for signs of it.

And she found it—a matlike covering well in back of the main building and so well done that one could walk right over it and not know anything was beneath. Only the telltale outline of regular yellowing of dead vines and leaves had given it away, and even then it was only because she was specifically looking for it, and the darkness of the swamp had aided her limited day-eyesight.

She removed the matting with a great deal of effort that exhausted her. The thing was *heavy*. Still, she managed to uncover enough to see that it hid the remains of an ancient well that must have once served the site in its glory days. She looked back at the old ruins and judged the distance at about three hundred feet. Not bad at all if you have a zombie army. A horizontal tunnel leading from beneath the redoubt to the well itself would have been easy, and would also have provided a slick emergency exit.

She could not, however, do any more. The telltale yellow and orange bands dimly perceived deep within the well told her that the cache might be there; but, if so, it was well guarded, both by spell and perhaps by entities of some kind. All she could do was keep a watch on it, and wait for Ruddygore's wizards. She hoped they were good ones.

The wizards sent with the force shadowing the party were not what anyone expected. Their names, they said, were Agie and Magie, and they were identical twins. They were also in every sense of the word little old ladies with high-pitched, tremulous voices and thick gray hair, neither taller than Marge. They doddered and twittered about like two elderly grandmothers on a picnic and were very hard to take seriously, particularly since each of them had the annoying habit of repeating some of what the other had just said.

Captain Kolos was an officer in the Marquewood militia directly attached to the river defense forces. He looked, sounded, and acted like a professional military man, but he treated the two little old ladies with some deference and respect.

Marge was now feeling dead tired, but she wouldn't miss this for the world. "You mean *those two* are going to tackle whatever's in the well?"

"Don't sell them short. I admit they are—uh—eccentric, but no more than a fat old man running around these parts in a top hat and silly-looking clothes."

"Good point," she agreed. She watched as the two doddered over to the well, which had now been completely exposed by the troops, and seemed to study it. Marge and Kolos went over to them.

"What do you think?" the officer asked them.

One of them turned and put a finger to her lips, then turned back, as the two continued to circle the opening. Finally they nodded to each other and came together.

"A dirty set of spells," one said.

"A dirty set," the other agreed.

"But can you remove them?" the captain asked.

"Oh, yes. In fact, we've already done most of it."

"Done most of it," the other agreed.

"Well—can we get in?"

The nearer one nodded. "Yes, you can go in. However, I'm afraid that if you do, you'll have to clear away an obstacle."

"Clear away an obstacle," said the other.

"Huh?"

"There is a guardian held by the only remaining spell.

Once we remove it, it will be instantly freed. You must remove it to go down."

"You must remove it," the other emphasized with a nod.

"It is mortal? It can be killed?"

"Oh, yes. But it is quite large, and you will not meet it directly with swords or arrows. The only way to be certain is to burn it out."

"Burn it out," said the other.

The officer thought about it. "Well, if we do that, and the souls are in fact down there, won't we risk damaging or harming them?"

"That is a risk. If the souls are freed by melting the cork or glass, then they will not return to the body but will pass on. Fairy souls will become disembodied spirits, doomed to wander."

"Doomed to wander," agreed her sister.

Marge thought a moment, then said, "Why not use electricity?"

They all stared at her. "It is a natural phenomenon, not something that can be used like a sword or tar pot," the captain noted.

"Perhaps it can, if the kind wizards here can help. Copper is one of the best conductors of electricity. If we can get a large amount of copper wire, then a fierce thunderstorm overhead, we might be able to get the lightning to strike the wire." She suddenly stopped. "No, forget it. The thing isn't going to sit still with copper wire shot into it while we wait for a strike."

"Oh, I think this can be arranged," Agie said calmly.

"Yes, this can be arranged," her sister agreed.

What they finally settled on was a mesh net made of copper and connected by a pure copper lead to the highest point on the old ruins. The net was quite nicely woven and even somewhat flexible, primarily because it was transmuted from some of the Master's camouflage netting by the sisters.

When all was ready, the troops were positioned around

the well, but not too close, and the sisters simply stood there, a bit to one side, eyes closed, hands linked. Almost immediately, it grew darker and there was a sudden chill in the air. Above, where there had been a nearly clear sky, clouds swirled in a frenzy of agitation, looking almost like paint in water. Then the very ground began to shake and tremble with the fearsome sound of thunder. Lightning licked from the clouds to the ground and danced in pencil-streams just above the treetops. Suddenly, Marge saw, one of the sisters took her mind off the storm and threw a basic nulling spell back into the well.

Almost immediately there was a roar like the sound of a rogue elephant, and from the well suddenly sprouted great squidlike tentacles, waving around and lashing out both at the air and at the ground around. The troopers tensed as a sudden violent rainstorm struck, but the sisters and the troops held their ground.

The creature in the well pushed upward, clearly striving now to get out, and the copper mesh lifted as the start of the body emerged, revealing two gigantic and evil-looking but unnaturally human eyes.

Suddenly there was an enormous flash and a bolt came from the terrible storm and struck the rod atop the ancient ruin. The charge was enormous, and was instantly carried along the line to the mesh.

The creature was suddenly thrashing about in agony, engulfed in a swirl of crawling electrical energy. It flashed and flailed against the mesh, but this only got it more snarled in the thing.

A second great bolt struck the rod and led to the creature, and this time there was a horrible smell of burning flesh mixed with the strong scent of ozone. Now yet another bolt struck, and another, and the great squidlike creature leaped up from the well until its massive body was clear and rolled on the ground. They retreated before it, but while the tentacles continued to lash out, and it continued to hop around, one look at the eyes and the senseless motions told them it was in its death convulsions.

Now the troopers poured spears and arrows into the creature; as soon as the rain stopped, brave teams with buckets of foul-smelling liquid ran out, trying not to get trapped in the death-throes, and threw the contents of those buckets onto the creature wherever they could.

At least a dozen buckets were unloaded before the thrashing of a tentacle killed one man and wounded another, and Captain Kolos signaled for a halt and nodded to bowmen, who lit flame-tipped arrows and shot them into the mass.

The creature burst into flame, and for more than a half an hour they watched as it continued to burn and seemed almost to melt down, until, finally, it was nothing more than a bubbling mass.

The two sisters looked very tired, but also smug and satisfied.

"It's clean now, in the spell and creature sense of the word," Agie told them. "You may go down now."

"Yes, go down now," Magie echoed.

It took another hour to explore the three hundred yards or so of the tunnel, and to find the cache hidden in a small chamber off to one side, almost in the center of the tunnel. The opening had a simple door, obviously rather recently installed, and a lock that didn't take much force to break. It was made primarily to keep the pet watch-squid from fooling around with the merchandise.

Inside the chamber, lighted by torches and lanterns, they gasped at the contents. There were cartons upon cartons of bottles, each marked with a symbol code with some sort of crayon.

"It will take forever to figure out who these all are," Marge said, feeling hope fade. "How will we ever break the code?"

There was a box that hadn't been sealed or labeled yet, and Kolos looked at it, reached in, and removed a bottle. "Well, maybe it won't be impossible. These bottles seem to have labels with names on them, although a few have been screwed up. Looks like some water got into here today. See?" He took them out one at a time. "This one says Lucas something or something Lucas. This one says Jones. These two have been water-smeared. Kaz something on this one, and something 'berg' on this other. With any luck we might get many of them matched. It's a good bet that most are dead, anyway, so we're just freeing them, but I hope we can find the ones for those six living assistants out there. They may know just who this fellow is."

There was a small group of bottles off by themselves on the floor near the door. Marge went over and saw that the water, or humidity, or whatever had caused the labels to drop off, but the corks, at least, looked new. She nervously reached down, picked up the labels, and handed them to the captain. "What names are these?" she asked him.

He looked at them. "Joe O," he read, "T of M, Cap, MM, MCR, and WDNYM," he read. "Not very helpful."

"Well, it is and it isn't," she responded, her heart sinking. "I think I can take a guess at them. Joe is the big barbarian and my old partner. T of M is probably Tiana of Morikay, Cap is Captain Bly, MM is perhaps 'mermaid,' MCR is Macore, and the last probably stands for 'wood nymph.' Captain, I'm afraid that those bottles contain the souls of my company."

He looked at them, then at the labels. "Which is which?"

"I haven't the slightest idea. The labels had fallen off, and apparently our opening the door caused enough of a breeze to mix them all up. We know which bottles, but not who's in what!"

CHAPTER 9

MIXED DOUBLES

Anything that can go wrong will. It's more fun that way.
—Sayings of Murphitus, ancient Husaquahrian philosopher

THEY ASSEMBLED THE FIVE BODIES AND ONE STATUE IN the cabin of the *Piebald Hippogryph*, and the six bottles were set on the table in front of them. Agie and Magie, although very tired and looking very frail, had consented to advise on the restoration, but they really could help only with the technical procedures.

"One soul is identical to another in the pure state," Agie told them. "Only when it is mated with the body does it become distinctively individual, although, of course, it contains the coded information on memory and such, which will reorganize the brain when it enters. The trouble is, we can't tell one from another unless they're in bodies and can tell us for themselves."

"Unless they can tell us," Magie agreed.

Marge and Kolos both frowned. "So," the Kauri said, "it's strictly luck in this case, and the odds of getting them all right are impossible." She had a sudden thought. "What if they *are* wrong? Can't you unmix them when we know who's who?"

"Oh, my, no," Agie said worriedly. "Once the soul and the body mate, we know of no way to undo them except through the same sort of process that caused this in the first place, and that requires a demon and a very serious bargain."

"Very serious," Magie repeated ominously.

"What about transmutations, then?" Marge suggested, trying to figure a way out of this. "I mean, I've seen people changed into animals and vice versa."

"People into *animals*, yes," Agie replied. "That's no problem. But people into other people—that is different. One can take on the *appearance* of another, but it is all illusion. Sorry—it's the Rules, you know."

"It's the Rules," Magie echoed.

Marge knew about the Rules all too well, but she wasn't ready to give up yet. "When Joe and I first came here from Earth, Ruddygore did something to change our appearance. That didn't mean much to me in the end, because I was a changeling, but Joe didn't look much like the man you see here."

"Oh, yes, but, you see, that was in the process of binding you to the Rules. Even then—was not a demon directly involved?"

She nodded. "I'm afraid so," she responded. "I'd forgotten."

"Then your only hope is for Ruddygore to call in some of his debts and get a demon to help them again, if Hell will do so. If the demons are directly involved in this plot, they will not be likely to help in any case."

"Not at all likely," Magie agreed.

Marge turned to Kolos. "You've reached Ruddygore?"

He nodded. "The problem was relayed to him. He said, in effect, that he was reasonably satisfied with the outcome and not to bother him unless either this Master struck again or you'd seen the Oracle. He seemed to regard this problem as a minor matter, I'm afraid."

Marge whistled. "It won't be minor to *them*. Still, that sounds like a go-ahead to me. We certainly can't keep them like *this*.

"Can we do it one at a time? At least we'll have a chance that way to get *some* right," she suggested, knowing she was clutching at straws.

"Oh, they'll be out cold for a day or so," Agie told

her. "It takes more time to write information in than to remove it and erase it, particularly if it's going into a different body. Don't worry, though. The longer they're in a new body, the more they'll adjust to it. Hormones and such, you know, and the animal parts of the brain and all that."

"Hormones and animals," Magie repeated, sounding a little eager.

"You mean—if they're in new bodies long enough, they will become so wedded to them they won't want their old selves back?" Even Kolos was shocked at the idea.

"How—long before this happens?" Marge asked hesitantly.

"Oh, it varies tremendously. A few days with some, a few weeks with others, even longer with some—depends on the personality."

"It depends," Magie added for emphasis.

Marge looked at the bottles, then at the reclining bodies. "Well, it has to be done. They can't do anything as they are. At least, Audra's won't be a worry. That's a fairy soul."

"Makes no difference," Agie told her. "A soul's a soul to this sort of thing."

"A soul's a soul," Magie agreed.

Marge took a deep breath. "Well, let's get this over with."

The process turned out to be something of an anticlimax. A spell was placed on the cabin interior blocking exit by literally anything, so that the souls could not escape and perhaps find refuge in that zombie army still frozen out there. The four inside the room who already had souls were safe; given a choice, they were assured, freed souls always went for vacant bodies, if such were handy. Only when there was no alternative present was there a chance of possession.

Agie stepped forward, took the first bottle, asked for a corkscrew, found one at the rather nicely stocked small bar, and opened the first bottle as if opening a bottle of wine.

Literally nothing could be seen, even on the fairy bands, but Marge felt a sudden added *presence* in the room, a presence very much alive and with an overwhelming feeling of confusion. It seemed to fly about the room, then settle on the forms and then sink into one, almost as if the body had absorbed it. Marge sensed that it had entered Joe's body.

One by one the process was repeated, with nearly identical results. It was interesting to note that none of the first five had gone to the pretty statue of the nymph Audra; all had gone into the still living bodies. That left Audra's form for number six, whoever or whatever it was. Marge hoped that it was in fact the nymph, and that at least a small percentage were correct from the start. Unfortunately, here, as on Earth, she knew that Murphy's Law seemed supreme even over the Rules.

Audra's statue shimmered, then changed color, and the rock seemed to fade into a pleasant green complexion. For the first time in almost a day, her leg was down and her body in a totally relaxed position, with a peaceful expression of sleep replacing the slightly surprised look she'd had frozen onto her.

"Well, that went well," Agie said, satisfied. "I don't believe we will be needed anymore, Captain. Oh—this process has effectively divorced the nymph from her boat, by the way. She should be independent, at least until and unless she mates with another tree."

"Can the bullshit and let's blow this joint," Magie said suddenly. "I need a belt."

And, with that, the two ambled out.

Marge took the opportunity to sleep the rest of the day, knowing that the sleepers wouldn't awaken any time soon, perhaps not until late in the next day, and knowing, too, that Kolos's crew was busy both at pumping out the water to refloat the yacht and going over everything with a fine-tooth comb for any clues to the one who'd bought or chartered her.

By the time Marge awoke, somewhat after sundown, the ship had been refloated and was actually underway back up the river to the small town from whence they'd come.

Marge allowed Captain Kolos to take advantage of her, and in so doing she fed and renewed her strength. She had a strong feeling she'd need it when those folks finally woke up.

Through the next day, the troops came to several conclusions: first, that there was nothing clearly identifiable with any specific individual aboard the Master's ship itself; and, second, he had both good and expensive taste. They would trace the registry, of course, but it would have been through so many blinds that the actual identity of the Master might not be known by even the one who eventually turned it over to him. It would take many long days just to catalog the boxes taken from the swamp redoubt, and weeks before anything concrete could be gotten from them.

They had been told that the longer it took for the restorees to awaken, the more likely it was that they had been badly mixed up. When night fell for the second time and none had yet awakened, Marge and the others feared the worst.

About two hours after nightfall, Joe stirred, rolled slightly, then opened his eyes, and looked very confused. Suddenly he got up to a sitting position, looked around, and saw Marge sitting there. Just from the expression and the carriage, Marge had a sinking feeling.

"Hi," Joe said, in a soft, effeminate voice.

Oh, boy!, she thought, her heart sinking. "Which one are you?"

"Why, I'm Audra, of course. Who did you think I was?"

Marge pointed, directing Audra's eyes to the end of the sleeping figures. Eyes followed, and the former nymph gasped. "If that's *me*, then who am *I*?" She looked down at her body, then stood up and kept staring. "Oh, oh, *oh*!"

"I'll explain it all when the others wake up," Marge told her. "That'll save time and maybe my sanity. You won't be the only one."

After a while, Audra seemed to be able to think about other things and came over and sat in a chair at the table. It was really strange to see that huge, muscular figure swiveling its hips and walking almost daintily.

Finally, though, Marge got the story. She had been gone barely half an hour when the Master's forces came. There must have been many of them, but Audra saw only the Master of the Dead, who'd apparently been nearby much of the evening. Marge suspected that he moved when he did because he saw her take off; he was worried about her destination, and also concerned that he was going to lose his prey one by one. It had been simple, and quick. Bly had been taken while asleep topside; Macore when he went on deck for some air. Then the Master himself had burst into the cabin below, where Audra and Tiana had been talking, and had held up his hand before the big woman had been able to do anything at all to counter him and all had gone blank—until the awakening here, on the ship.

Tura suddenly stirred, opened her eyes, and sat up, wide-eyed. "It is a wizard!" she screamed. "It is the enemy! Take—"

Suddenly she seemed to realize that this was somewhere else, and she saw the pair at the table. "Joe! Marge! Thank heaven! What . . . what has happened? Why do you stare?"

The accent was unmistakable, slightly Germanic. "Tiana, I presume," Marge said disgustedly. "Take hold and prepare yourself for a big shock."

Tiana took it quite well, certainly. She took her own metamorphosis into mermaid, in fact, far more matter-of-factly than she accepted the very swishy and effeminate Joe.

One by one they awakened, and a pattern emerged. Macore and Bly had changed bodies; Tiana and Tura had changed bodies, and Audra and Joe had changed bodies. The sight of the beautiful but delicate nymph walking and talking like a—well, a male truckdriver—was almost as incongruous as the reverse.

Tiana stared at the nymph. "Joe? You mean I am now married to a *nymph*?"

"Yeah, I got the same problem *being* one," Joe grumped.

"Oh, I don't think it's so bad," Audra commented. "It's the first time I've ever been able to see myself, and I wasn't bad at all, if I *do* say so."

Macore's tail knocked over an empty chair. "You think *you* got problems!"

"What's wrong with that body?" Bly demanded angrily. "It's a hell of a lot more versatile and tough than *this*."

They all started talking and yelling and complaining at the same moment and it took some time with Marge yelling at the top of her lungs to settle them down. Even so, they kept getting each other confused, and that took continual correction and adjustment.

Finally, Marge was able to send for food for them, since they were all starving and also tremendously thirsty—the wine was going fast—and then to explain to them the events that had brought them to this point and the news about their present conditions.

"I'm convinced that Ruddygore can unmix you all," Marge told them, "but he seems tied up at the moment. One thing is clear—he won't talk with us again until and unless we see the Oracle, and the longer you all stay that way, the worse it will be. That means we should proceed downriver with all speed and get to the Oracle as fast as possible."

"I agree," Bly added. "However, this will take some getting used to for all of us. I still have hands and feet and I can still sail anything that floats. For organizational purposes, I suggest that certain duties are essential. We need a pilot, and Tura is no longer able to do the job as fully as it can be done. That means you, Madam—" He gestured to Tiana "—must do the water work while under Tura's direction. Tura knows how to handle the boat; she'll be able to spell me, allowing us to travel both day and night, if we have adequate river conditions and reports. We will stop only for supplies, and just long enough to take them aboard, providing we need no more repairs. Marge, you will have to fly ahead to make these preparations and do some night time lookout work as well."

It sounded reasonable. "What about me?" Macore asked.

"I will find a lot of work for you to practice in that body. I know that body and its capabilities well. Everyone will do his or her part, because we all have a strong stake in getting this done and over with. Audra, you're going to have a hard time getting used to that body and that freedom, but we'll find uses for you. No one knows every inch of the ship better than you."

"That leaves me," Joe noted. "What can *I* do in *this* body?"

"Somebody," replied the captain, who was still the captain no matter what body he wore, "has to do the cleaning and cooking."

Joe looked horrified.

"When do you intend to get underway, Captain?" Marge asked him.

"As soon as we can reprovision the entire ship. I trust neither water nor wine nor anything else. Not a moment longer, though. If things start going our way, which I tend to doubt, we could easily make three hundred miles a day. That will put us in Marahbar in four days, perhaps five, depending on weather and currents. From there it is a day's sail over open ocean to the island we must reach. Hopefully, Ruddygore will reach us upon our return to Marahbar. If not, sailing upriver is far slower than sailing down. Four days down is easily thirteen days back, with optimum conditions."

That was almost three weeks, not counting the time

spent on the island, Marge noted. And that was if everything was perfect.

The first two days and nights were slower than expected, as they tried to ease their way into their new tasks. Tiana, in particular, was critical to Bly in spotting ever-changing hazards, and while she took to the water as if born a mermaid, thanks to instinctual skills and reflexes that came with the body, she had a lot to learn about hazards, and particularly what was and was not important to the captain.

Bly, for his part, seemed more than mollified despite his body switch. Before, he was simply getting paid a big bonus to deliver his passengers; now he was told that, by the laws of Marquewood, the Master's former yacht, after it was tracked down and registry cleared, belonged to the victims of the man who had owned it. The others quickly agreed to give their shares to him in exchange for limited use. Bly stood, in a few weeks, to become a very wealthy, independent businessman.

Late in the morning of the third day, however, the wind picked up radically and began blowing almost due north, making progress nearly impossible; soon after the skies darkened and they were in the midst of a strong and terrible storm that forced Bly to put in along a sheltered part of the riverbank and wait it out. Marge suspected more foul play, but Bly dismissed it. "These storms are not uncommon this time of year," he told her. "The trouble is, they can last a long time as they sweep in from the ocean and across the flood plain and then strike these mountains."

Tiana, for her part, seemed to be relishing her new freedom after more than five years as a pampered symbol and believed a mermaid's tail was a very small price to pay for it. The rain and wind hardly bothered her. Marge had been both careful and curious in talking to each of them, looking for how things were or were not changing. Certainly, the first day or so, they had all gone crazy addressing each other by the wrong names, but that seemed to have quickly passed as the *personalities* inside the bodies tended to dominate.

"It is most interesting," Tiana told her. "My wizard's powers are way down from what they were, yet my new abilities, particularly the sonar, are amazing. I have also been looking at myself and the others, and have discovered some very strange things."

The storm tossed and battered the small boat in spite of the shelter. "Like what?" Marge asked, a bit nervous at this acceptance.

"Curses. The were curse remained with the body, as I suspected, as it is a physical curse, which means that I, Tura, and Audra now have it, but not Joe. On the other hand, some other curses, such as my own curse of death in childbirth, are also basically physical, although linked to the metaphysical. It seems to have remained with my old body as well."

For Tura's part, she was relishing the fact that she was human and that she had legs. "I was an outcast to my people," she told Marge, "and now I can walk, freely, on dry land!"

"You don't miss the water world?" Marge asked her.

"It's odd, but I don't. I keep dreaming of—mountains."

Macore now managed to get around without being clumsy, and had even begun to practice a bit with the prehensile tail, but he still clearly called his form his "rat suit" and had no use for it as a permanent thing.

The storm dragged on for three more days, and it seemed that, each time they slept and then awoke again, the victims of the Master seemed more and more at ease with what they were, although the two most extreme cases, Joe and Audra, were unmistakably mismatched.

Joe, however, found that, rain or not, he needed to lie out on deck at least a few hours a day. The nymph needed water and light and very little else to survive.

"How do you feel, Joe?" Marge asked him.

"I'm going nuts," he complained. "I've been turned from a king into a slave at one swipe of a spell. Everybody demands I do all the cooking for them on their different schedules, then they complain about what I cook and how I cook it—as if I wanted to eat it. Food just sort of, well, turns my stomach or whatever's in there. Then it's always change the beds, clean and polish the insides, dump the garbage. It's boring, demanding, and it never ends!"

"Welcome to the wonderful world of being a housewife," she commented. "I did it for years, you know. Maybe this will give you an appreciation of what the people who do the work have to go through."

"Yeah, I guess, but it's a pain anyway. Poor Irving's having an identity crisis as bad as ours, too. The sword can't decide if Audra or me is really me. If it comes to a fight, I hope it picks Audra, though. That sword has a life of its own in a swordfight so it won't be a slaughter, but I couldn't even *lift* it."

"You'd have more trouble than that. Irving is of an iron alloy. It would kill you. Still, more is troubling you than that. I can sense it."

"Yeah, well, it's the dreams and funny feelings."

"How's that?"

"A wood nymph's half plant, half teenager, it seems. Something inside keeps nibbling at my brain, keeps telling me not to fight, to let go. I can handle it okay, but every night it gets just a little bit stronger. I found myself daydreaming today, looking at Audra over there in my body and getting slightly turned on, for instance. I only really cried twice in my life before, but now I seem to bawl at every little thing that goes wrong. And when Macore told that crazy joke of his, I got the giggles and couldn't stop. The *giggles*! I've swapped with Tiana as a were, and even you, and never felt anything like *this*."

She sighed. "Poor Joe. The trouble is really that you've become a fairy and a nymph. The races of faërie are more primal, more elemental than humans or other thinking races. We don't have as much self-control, and we tend to experience everything larger than life. It's in our nature. I should know! And nymphs are seductresses not known for clear thinking or intellectual abilities. It's not like humans, who learn. It's more instinct, a way you *have* to be. We can only make do and hope that Ruddygore will bail you out in the end, as usual."

"Yeah. Why is he so insistent about our seeing this Oracle, anyway? And what's more important than us?"

She shrugged. "Maybe a lot. I have an idea that he spends a good deal of his time fighting evil on a plane we can't see or imagine, and in that kind of fight we're sort of secondary. You know what's not far over the cliff walls on the other side over there?"

"Huh?"

"The Valley of Decision, where we first turned back the Dark Baron."

"Huh. I'll be damned."

"When we're underway again, we'll be passing the Zhafqua which leads to Morikay, and then the Khafdis which begins in Lake Ktahr. It's our own recent history we're passing through. Keep that in mind."

"I'll try," he assured her. "But this storm better break soon, or by the time we get through this I may not be able to fight off going nymph anymore."

There were still light showers, but the wind had shifted and Bly decided to get underway. The resumption of the journey brightened all their spirits and, as they proceeded south, the weather brightened. Just before sunset, the sun briefly appeared, just to give them a beautiful sunset, and things looked up once more. The ship had weathered the storm far better than the inhabitants, and they were no more than two days from Marahbar.

"We'll have to stop at the port," Bly told them, "not only because we're low on provisions but also because I'll have to get the proper clearances and briefings for the ocean hop. There are a lot of nasty things out there in the ocean just waiting for small boats, and there's no sheltered harbor, if we run into another of these blows."

"How long will this take?" Marge asked him.

"Not long, I hope, if the news and weather are good. Macore and I have been working on some fundamentals, since, due to the description and portrait on my master's license, he will have to impersonate me."

"It shouldn't cause much of a problem," Macore assured her. "I've gotten pretty used to this body now, and I've always been good at conning people. Bly'll be right there, and I've got enough of what's required to get by."

"I hope that the rest of you will remain aboard," the captain said to the others as they gathered on the deck. "However, if it is necessary for any reason to get off, or interact with any workers or officials, play the part your looks demand. We wish no complications with officials over who's who and what's what. Be who others think you are, no matter what."

For Joe, every day since he'd reawakened in this strange fairy body had been something of a nightmare, and the days mostly boredom and frustration. As Marge had said, the situation wasn't as much being someone else, even a female wood nymph, as it was the compulsive nature of the faërie as a group. His mind and memory were still pretty sharp, but the fact was that a wood nymph didn't need and wasn't designed, as it were, for such a mind and memory. The fairies, as a rule, were born with all the attributes, basic skills and aptitudes, and everything else needed to become what they were supposed to be; behavior was preordained and could not be changed. Most fairy folk, then, learned what they needed or wanted to learn and that was that.

Now he was at war with that nature, and it was a war he couldn't possibly win. Just as a cat was a cat first, and, in fact, Marge was Kauri first and Marge second, so he had no choice about being a wood nymph. If the right stimuli were present he'd have to act and react as a wood nymph would, no matter what he thought or how much he detested it.

The worst part was that Audra didn't face his problem. She was human now, and humans didn't have instinctive and compulsive behavior patterns. She was the sum total of her experience—and that was as a wood nymph. The fact that she was now big and strong and male didn't make much difference to her; it simply meant a change in technique and the fact that she no longer had to be fearful of others or apprehensive about her safety. She was also now freed from her attachment to a specific place, although Marge, who knew the laws of such fairies, assured him that this was a protective device and not truly a compulsion. If he didn't consciously wish to do it, he could retain his independence, such as it was.

He had decided to remain strictly aboard while in the port, although he was dying to see one of the great City-States. He was physically weak, and, unlike Marge, was totally defenseless in terms of powers, and yet he was a nymph and would behave like a nymph. He'd never been really scared of much of anything before, either on Earth or in Husaquahr, but he was scared now, almost frightened to death.

After Macore and Bly went ashore, the others grew restless, with the bright lights and noise of a massive and living cosmopolitan city crisscrossed with a network of canals and levees. Marge had already gone, almost at nightfall, assuring them she'd be back in a couple of hours at worst, and Audra and Tura really couldn't be talked out of it by Tiana. For the former nymph, it was her first and perhaps only, chance to see what a big city was like; Tura wanted to walk around and find what it was like to be a human rather than a mermaid in such surroundings. That meant that Tiana was more or less forced to figure out the big wheelchair, since she didn't really trust those two on their own out there.

Joe normally slept at night, but he fought sleep much of the time now, and the sun of the past two days had given him a lot of reserve energy. He still kept below, and it wasn't until boredom, curiosity, and apprehension at hearing nothing topside caused him to emerge and look around nervously. When he found no one else aboard, he nearly went into a panic. He felt suddenly very alone and very vulnerable. There was activity all around this twenty-four-hour port, with dockworkers, stevedores, and all sorts of others doing their jobs.

A young man, dressed as a dockworker of some sort and apparently on a break, saw the small figure and walked over to the side of the *Hippogryph*. "Hello!" he called, sounding friendly. "What sort are you?"

Suddenly Joe felt a tremendous rush through his whole body, and from that instant he was no longer in any way in control. He found himself walking sexily over to the rail near the gangplank and smiling sweetly at the man. "I'm a nymph," the pale green girl said in a soft and sexy voice.

"Is that right? What's your name?"

"My name is—call me *Joey*," the nymph said.

It was nearly morning and there was much consternation on the afterdeck of the *Piebald Hippogryph*.

"How *could* you be so stupid?" Marge demanded to know, sounding angry as hell.

"Look, what was I gonna do, huh?" Tiana responded, sounding angry herself. "I'm going to stop somebody intent on going who's six-six and two-sixty, all muscle? And I had my own problems, remember!"

Macore and Bly tried to make some peace between them and finally got the whole story. It was apparent now that Audra had no intention of returning to the ship; by midway through the first bar, she'd excused herself to go to the bathroom and that had been that. Once Tiana and Tura had determined that the former nymph was gone, and not apparently a victim of foul play, they decided to return to the ship and confer before notifying the authorities. It was, after all, a city of almost a million inhabitants and not familiar to either.

The bigger surprise was Tura. They'd gotten back to

the docks, and Tura had lifted Tiana from the wheelchair and carried her aboard, but then she went back, supposedly for the chair. Instead she'd looked back and said, "I'm sorry—but I have the chance to climb mountains and no one is going to take that away from me," and walked away, taking the wheelchair with her.

"I doubt if Tura intended or even thought about it," Bly said defensively, "but when Audra did it and it was clear how nearly impossible it would be to find even somebody that imposing, the impulse was irresistible."

Marge had a sudden thought. "What about Joe? He was left here all alone!" She made for the cabins below and found the form of the small, light-green nymph lying face up on one of the beds, eyes open and staring.

When Joe had no reaction to her entry, she had a sudden fear that he had been attacked again somehow by the enemy, although the body was certainly still living flesh. When Joe moved a little, she relaxed, but needed no special powers to realize that something was radically wrong.

"Joe? You all right?"

The figure sighed, then seemed to come at least partially to life. "I'm not really sure, Marge. It took control of me tonight. For an hour, I became Joey the Nymph, with all that implies, and I enjoyed every minute of it and I want more of it, lots of it."

She was shocked. "Who?"

"Nobody special, except for the hour. Oh, don't go rushing off trying to find some cad. I discovered I *do* have some powers, but they're directed to only one end and I used them. I couldn't help it. I was worse than Audra ever was, at least to me. I wasn't a thinking person anymore—I was a primal force with an irrepressible need."

"Joe, you've got to keep fighting it. Okay, it happened and maybe it'll happen again, but you've got to hold on to what's really you in there. It will only be permanent if you let it."

"It's coming after my mind now, Marge. It wants to

get rid of all that gets in the way, to push it back or wipe it out." He sighed. "What was the yelling about on deck?"

Marge felt suddenly very uncomfortable. This was not the time for such news, but there was no way to conceal it, either. She swallowed hard and told him.

He just nodded fatalistically. "Well, that's it, then. They've committed no crimes. They can't be hunted down legally or charged with anything or brought back against their will, and Audra, at least, is so naïve she'll be in thrall to somebody with power by tomorrow if she isn't already. Face it—the Master's won."

"I won't give up, no matter what you say! And don't you *dare* give up on me, either! Ruddygore has tremendous powers and can traffic with whatever powers he needs to!"

"Ruddygore's got more problems than us now," Joe responded dejectedly. "With no demigod or goddess to trot out, he can't fake it for long without the Council finding out. Once they do, they'll oust him from the leadership and start running things their own way."

"Well I, for one, am not going to give up and I'm going to fight you for your own sake as well! Things have looked pretty dark for us before and we've always pulled it out!" She turned and walked out, actually feeling as confident as she spoke. Things just *couldn't* end this way! They wouldn't *dare*!

She told the others about Joe, and Bly sighed. "Well, my charter is still to get you to the Oracle. There's a tide in just under two hours. We either take it or we face another stormfront moving in that might keep us bottled up for a couple of days. I'll do what you say, since you're the boss, but if what you say is true below I wouldn't like to have Joe stay around here."

"Sail, then. We'll leave messages. I just wish there was something we could use to get the cops looking for those two!" She had a thought. "Did Audra take Irving?"

Tiana sighed. "No. Weapons scare her. And forget about the wheelchair. Macore found it two blocks away."

"Hmmm . . . what about rape? That'll get 'em."

"One look at Audra, even in that body, and they'll laugh it away."

Marge suddenly grinned. "I know! And it will stand up to psychic examination, too! Warn them that they've got two *werewolves* loose in the city!"

CHAPTER 10

OBLIQUITY SPLIT

When chronicling great adventures, the chronicler should take pains to use words that even the most educated of readers must look up. This may make your chronicle very slow, if not impossible, to read, but it will be critically acclaimed throughout the land, for none will wish to admit that they didn't understand and relish every word. Instead, they will use the comfort with such phraseology as a litmus test for intellectual equality. No one may ever really read you, but all will be forced to purchase a copy of the chronicle to convince others that they did, and your brilliance and intellect will be permanently unquestioned.

—The Romantic Saga Writer's Manual of Style, Marahbar

"I CAN'T UNDERSTAND WHY THIS IS SUCH AN UNTRAVeled route if this Oracle is as hot as Ruddygore thinks he is," Macore said to Bly as they passed beyond sight of land and picked up a stiff breeze.

"Oh, he makes it just hard enough to get to him that you really must want to," Bly replied. "Being removed like this means you have to have some money and/or influence to make it, and that keeps the common folk away. He also charges two arms and four legs for the service—in advance—which also tends to keep traffic down."

"I thought the best oracles were ascetics," the thief in the ratlike body noted. "All the ones I've seen are."

"Were they reliable?"

"Um—no, not really."

"See? I've never been out this way before, but I'm told that he started out like the others, but slowly discovered that it just wasn't required. Now he lives like a prince on his own little island kingdom and has done so since he discovered somewhat by accident that asceticism wasn't necessary."

The sail billowed in the breeze; while the ship rolled and rocked in somewhat choppy seas, it made good progress. Bly was determined to make the island before nightfall.

"What's so dangerous about night on this route?" Macore asked him.

"Well, there are occasional krakens and other giant creatures out here, and we have to pass close to the home of a race of nocturnal sirens."

"Sirens? They sing and lure ships to the rock?"

"Oh, no, that's another kind. These are fire sirens. Wail like banshees and the sound sets your ship aflame."

Macore let the subject drop.

Marge was asleep below, and Tiana went down to see Joe. She had been warned by Bly that this area was hostile to mermaids of her markings, and she decided to forgo any chance at ocean swimming for now. She wanted to see Joe anyway. She made no real use of the rails that Tura had put in to get about better; she felt no loss of dignity crawling across the floor, pulling herself with her two arms. The hands, although human-looking, were webbed; spread out, they provided traction and even some suction.

"Hello, Joe," she said as cheerily as she could, hauling herself up and settling comfortably in a chair.

"They finally got me, Ti," he sighed.

"Me, too," she reminded him.

"No, not really. If anything, you're better off. You're still damned good looking and strong, you've got the mermaid's powers, and you're free now to wander. Maybe slowed a little on land, but you're self-sufficient and most of Husaquahr is on the rivers anyway. A mermaid who's also a were should do great."

"Marge has done pretty well in a body as pretty as yours," Tiana noted. "Even if the worst happened, it is not the end of the world."

"It's death, Ti! Death for me, anyway. Kauris are complicated. They have to be in lots of different cultures' company, they can fly, and they have great defenses. Nymphs are the least common denominator. They're built for sex and seduction and nothing else. I can take any man, no matter how celibate or faithful. Every once in a while, it all clicks, and then I deposit the issue in a tree and wait until a new nymph forms. With no real need to eat or have any of the other needs, and limited to maybe half a mile from the host tree, the only thing a nymph does when no man's around is make out with other nymphs and take the seed from trees to plant more trees and extend the forests. That's really what they're for—to keep the forests pruned, planted, and nurtured, and it's something that's needed in this world—but *it's all they do*! And they do it all by instinct. They need just enough brains to talk to humans and maybe communicate warnings to them as well, but their kind of life, alone and stuck in the wilds with no real needs, means that the more stupid, dull, and ignorant they are, the better off they are. They're fairies too, remember. They don't die unless their tree suffers some terrible tragedy so quick they can't disengage, like sawing or burning down Audra's. It's *forever*, Ti!"

She thought about it, trying to think of what to say in response. "You are certain this is true? How?"

"I just *know*. It's built into the genes or whatever fairies have in place of them. I know the whole bit—now that I've broken the ice, so to speak, and let it take control."

"You speak of 'it.' What is 'it'?"

"This body, of course! It's—well, sort of like a machine. No, it *is* a machine. That's really what fairy folk are—living machines designed to keep order in the world. That's why they couldn't continue to live on Earth, once the machines took over. Some did what they were supposed to do, and others undid what they were compelled to do faster than they could do it."

She thought about it. "Perhaps that is why Ruddygore is so intent on keeping the machine out of here, while not adverse to using it himself, yes? He has nothing against machines, but knows that, if they come here, the fairy folk have no place else to go."

Joe nodded. "I think so. It explains a lot, anyway."

"But you can exist without being stuck to a tree in a forest."

"Well, Joe de Oro, in this body, can, and the body knows it. That means that Joe's in the way, you see. Joe would also go nuts doing a wood nymph's job. That means Joe's got to go. Ti, the brain's part of the body! Every hour I lose a little something. First it wasn't much, and that was only when I was asleep, but now it's going on awake or asleep, and I think it will just get faster and faster when I *do* rest. That's what's really driving me nuts. I know things are going and I don't even know what! I can't!" Suddenly Joe burst into tears and cried for a long time. Finally he sobbed, "See? I can't even control myself this much anymore!"

"I think it has a long way to go, considering this conversation," the mermaid noted. Still, Joe was certainly telling the truth. His speech was softer, gentler, and very feminine in tone now, where before the change it had been hard. Joe got up and walked over to where there were some tissues to dry his eyes, and she saw that he now had a natural gait better than any she'd ever had. Finally, she had only one thing to fall back on.

"Joe?" she asked hesitantly. "Do you still love me? Even as I am?"

That stopped him for a moment. "Yes. Of course I do." It was said with some surprise in his tone, as if he hadn't really thought about it.

"Then hold on to that! Fight it! We are near the end of this road! Fight it not for your sake, but for mine!"

"Ti—I—" he began, but was suddenly sobbing once again.

The island was a small and probably extinct volcano, covered at the bottom with lush vegetation. It wasn't hard to find the Oracle's place on it; the island wasn't that big, and a marble palace, which Marge later would compare to pictures of the Taj Mahal set into the mountainside, was hard to miss. It was also just inland from the only decent anchorage.

A whole crowd of dark brown nymphs greeted them with joy and giggles and surrounded the party when they came ashore in the ship's dinghy. Two female centaurs had hitched themselves to a large coach, which could accommodate them all, and off they went. It was a little unnerving to be riding inside with no driver, but the centaurs knew their business.

"I wonder if he allows any other males on the island except as guests?" Bly mused aloud.

"Would you?" Macore came back.

"I just thought of a hitch in this," Marge noted hesitantly. "This only works with mortals, as I remember, and Joe's no longer one of them."

"But both Tiana and I are," Macore reminded her. "And I, at least am going along if this misbegotten expedition ever gets started."

Tiana looked over at Joe, who seemed uncomfortable. "What's the matter now, my poor Joe?"

"Those field nymphs. I felt—right at home. All I could think about when they were around was looking and acting prettier and sexier than they were."

"Almost over now, Joe," Marge consoled, as they pulled up to the great palace and stopped. They got out, and marble steps stretched up as far as they could see.

"Just go on up," one of the centauresses said to them. "He's always in, and he's expecting you."

Tiana looked at the steps and gulped. "I had enough trouble getting in this coach. There's no way I will make it up those stairs."

The other centauress laughed. "Oh, don't worry. See over there, by the waterfall? The water turns a wheel that eventually turns a belt that will take you up. You can all use it if you want. I wish *we* could."

The belt was slow but it had small wooden clamps that served to support them. It did take you up, but at a very slow rate. Tiana, not being very mobile on land, and the others, now being rather small, were carried by the belt; only Marge chose not to take it. The sun had not yet set, but Marge had her goggles on and could easily fly the distance.

Once up, they walked and Tiana crawled to the front door, which was open, and then went inside.

There were golden fountains, rich tapestries, and plush carpeting all over the place. It was, in fact, fancier than Castle Morikay, and they were impressed.

"Well," Marge said, "anybody who makes enough money to afford all this surely must have *something* on the ball!"

A far door opened and a pudgy man of medium height emerged wearing a brown satin robe. He looked like a stereotypical monk, in fact, complete with rosy cheeks and a prominent bald spot. He smiled at them and said,

"Oh, hello! I'm glad you're all here.
Just relax a moment and I'll send for beer."

"Nothing for me, thanks," Marge replied. "Anybody else?" They all shook their heads in the negative.

"Oh, I know you needed nothing this time.
It's just the Rules I must speak in rhyme.
I'm the Oracle of Mylox, you see,
And a poet is something I'll never be."

"*You're* the Oracle?" Tiana said disbelievingly. "Uh—sorry. You're just not what I expected, that's all."

"You are not what I expected either.
Fahadur, nymph, mermaid, and thief are
neither
A big barbarian strong and manly
Unless a reasonable facsimile thereof is
handy?"

Joe seemed ready to burst into tears at that; while Tiana calmed him, Marge and Bly explained to the Oracle what had happened. He nodded with kind understanding, although Macore muttered, "If he's so omniscient, why do we have to tell him this?"

The Oracle heard him, and tried to explain.

"The future is closed to an oracle, too.
I can no more see next year than you.
But when questions I'm asked by those who
come,
I have the power to answer some.
This power's much higher than me, you see,
I'm only the medium through which you'll be
Hearing from a power even wizards can't know
A power, I'm sure, which comes not from
below."

Macore considered it. "In other words, if someone asks you a question, he gets an answer from Heaven itself?"

"Not an answer, no, I'm sorry.
Heaven talks not to me, don't worry.
I have a gift with which I'm able
To tap into the great cosmic babble
Where past and future all are one
And find the clues before I'm done.

Alas, such heavenly cosmic lines
Are far too great for human minds.
You'll get the truth now, don't fret!
Making sense of it you do not get."

"Hmmm . . . that explains a lot," Macore said aloud, although he added *of nothing* to himself. "Well, okay, so through you we can tap the cosmic mind and get relationships that apply to us. What about direct questions, though? Any ideas on how we start with this? Do you need a trance or something?"

"I can give you no suggestions,
But some have gotten answers to questions.
The power's an automatic thing with me.
We can start right now if the rest agree."

Marge stepped forward. "I think we ought to, and just get it over with. I know the questions Ruddygore wanted posed, and I'm sure we'll add some. I guess, for safety's sake, we'll have to get Captain Bly to pose them, though. By a crazy twist of fate he's the only human being among us."

"Fairies get no good answers, it's true,
But any mortal among you will do.
Fahadur, mermaid, human all three
Can get some decent results from me.
Please step outside before we begin.
It's something I need to start my discipline."

They went out onto the porch and saw that the tremendous number of nymphs who'd greeted them at the dock, joined by countless others, were all gathered there at the bottom of the great stair. The Oracle smiled and then gestured, and the nymphs began to chant.

"Oracle! Oracle! You're the greatest!
With your verse you satiate us!
You're so wonderful, just divine,
Your wondrous talents always shine!

Go, Oracle! Go, Oracle, Rah! Rah! Rah!
Go, baby! Go, baby! Cha! Cha! Cha!"

He turned sheepishly to his visitors.

"I know it's false, not worth a cent,
But all great artists need encouragement."

With that, they went back inside and the oracle took the usual lotus position on the floor in front of the big fountain.

"All right, then," Macore said, feeling even more skeptical, "let's get this over and done with. I want to know if there is in fact a dangerous evil now facing Earth from Boquillas and Dacaro."

The Oracle closed his eyes, seemed to concentrate for a moment, then said,

"The Armageddon bell rings clear
Should the evil ones appear
To the millions and with one breath
Give to the west the kiss of death."

Suddenly he snapped out of it, looked around, and smiled.

"Hopefully you got some news.
I remember not my own muse."

"We got it, all right," Marge told him, "and it isn't good."

"Yeah, but what's it *mean*?" Macore asked.

Marge shrugged. "I don't know if we can figure out the specifics yet, but it's clear that Ruddygore was right. It's Armageddon if they aren't stopped."

"If they *can* be stopped," Macore responded worriedly.

"The prophecy said *if*, not *when*," she reminded him. "That means there are two probabilities and we're the other one. You seem to know the questions, Macore. Keep going. You're doing fine!"

"Okay, Oracle, then I ask this. Who will be needed to stop them?"

Again the monkish man closed his eyes for a moment, then got the message and delivered it.

> *"The two who came must go once more*
> *To the place from which they tore*
> *Their lives but not their inner souls.*
> *To this the thief must burrow through holes*
> *To set the treasure before those who wish*
> *While the demons are stopped by a pickled fish.*
> *For when evil wishes upon a star*
> *It makes no difference where you are.*
> *With Peter Pan's glow and swords below*
> *It must grant the wish or Earth will blow."*

"*Whew!*" Marge sighed. "That's a lot. Well, at least *part* of it is clear."

"Clear as mud," Macore responded.

"The two are obviously Joe and me. You, obviously, are the thief," Marge pointed out.

"Yeah, okay, I'll buy that. But where do we get the pickled fish? And it seems like I'm supposed to steal something but give some treasure away. What treasure? And who or what is a Peter Pan? It may all be true, but it makes no sense."

"I know who Peter Pan is, but it doesn't help, believe me. Maybe it will make sense to Ruddygore," Marge said.

"Yeah, well, maybe. It might also make sense to us when we see Earth blow—firsthand. I'd say that meant fire, or disaster, or war."

"Yes. The last war. And something they're going to do will cause it." Marge sighed. "We need more information, but we're not getting it here. I think, though, we ought to ask a couple of personal questions about our own situation. Considering those lines, I'd say they're critical."

Macore nodded and turned back to the Oracle. "Okay,

time for a personal question. Is there any way, other than trafficking with demons, to get back into our old bodies, and will we?"

The Oracle again closed his eyes. Marge wondered what his mind must be like if it touched, even grazed, Heaven for only an instant.

"Physical bodies matter not;
Souls are real and what you got.
All can find the way back home,
But only those that did not roam."

Marge gasped. "Poor Joe!" she sighed. "And we obviously need him."

"Well, good news for us, anyway, Cap," Macore commented. "Marge? Anything else you want to ask?"

"No more questions will I call.
Your deposit's run out and that's all,"

said the Oracle.

"Well, that's it, then." Marge sighed. "I guess we should be heading back. You know the itinerary, Captain. What happens now?"

The captain finished writing down the prophecies in a small notebook, then put away his pencil. "We go back. There's a good chance we can still beat that storm and be in before two in the morning if we leave now. We're to return to Marahbar and check into the Hotel Windjammer just up on the riverfront and wait. Ruddygore will either meet us or send for us there. That's all I know. Then I get paid, and maybe I get my old body back—if we both still want it that way. I'm getting somewhat used to this."

"Same here, but I think we're not well suited for our respective businesses, Cap. Let's be off."

They thanked the Oracle, who responded with some bad and innocuous verse and then clapped his hands. A huge, muscular satyr, the first male of any sort they'd seen other than the Oracle himself, appeared, bowed to the monkish prognosticator, then came over to them. "I will assist you in getting back to your ship," he rumbled. "I understand one of you has problems with stairs."

They went back and found Tiana and Joe, who seemed to have recovered a bit. Both looked almost awestruck at the sight of the satyr, and Joe had to be physically restrained.

"No problem," the satyr commented, and picked up Joe and Tiana, one under each arm, and began the walk down the stairs.

Marge flew along, seeing Joe's agony but knowing it was all for the best. "You're the first male anything we've seen other than the big man himself," she noted. "Did we just miss the males or am I right?"

"Oh, you're right," the satyr growled. "He doesn't like males around very long, that's true. It's just that he needs me. You see, my actual name is Porange Chilver."

She shrugged in midair. "So?"

"Think of what insanity he would endure if he ever accidentally ended a sentence in 'orange' or 'silver,'" the satyr commented.

The coach was waiting below, and the creature almost threw in the two he carried and immediately bade farewell. "Best I get away fast or that nymph will have to be knocked cold," he noted, and he was indeed away fast.

It required all of them to hold Joe down, but the centauress team was off in a flash and they headed back to the dock.

While still going along the broad avenue leading to and from the Oracle's mansion, Joe suddenly went wide-eyed, then swooned and fainted. They checked and saw signs of life, but all were clearly worried.

"He's burning up, like a fever," Tiana commented. "His head feels as if it's on fire."

Marge looked at the small figure and felt concern. "The inside is as bad as the outside. The fairy blood is telling. He's fighting it like hell, but I'm afraid we're losing him."

* * *

They beat the storm into port, but the wind was way up and it began to rain heavily while they were still on their way to the hotel. It was an old, low, sprawling structure several miles downriver from the port, but it was certainly first class in every way. That was one thing about working for Throckmorton P. Ruddygore; he might get you killed or changed into a toad, but everything was always first class.

The suites were actually duplexes around a small private courtyard and pool, which suited Tiana quite well. She had been out of the water too long; if she didn't get a good immersion, and not merely from a rainstorm, she could find herself with peeling skin and a painful skin condition. She was, of course, reluctant to leave Joe, who was still out, but Marge assured her that she'd keep watch.

The attendants at the Windjammer had certainly seen everything before; they took Joe in on a baggage cart without so much as a comment, although they did offer to fetch a healer with some expertise in fairy ailments, which was accepted.

The one who arrived in the hour before sunrise was a rather severe-looking middle-aged woman who told them that she was Auruga of the Western Wastes. She had much experience with the fairy folk and with nymphs, but she was now retired and working for the Witches Anti-Defamation League.

She listened to a general account of what had happened, performed an examination and a series of rituals, then told Marge, "There's nothing really that can be done. Whoever inhabits this body is mandated to be a wood nymph and nothing else. The body's housecleaning now, as it were. When she awakens, she'll have no memory, no curiosity, and no will or capacity to learn anything beyond what it takes to be a better wood nymph. She'll know everything about what nymphs do, because that's part of her nature, and that will be that. Sorry."

"Then—Joe's essentially dead?" Marge couldn't believe it.

"More or less. Oh, when the Final Judgment comes, assuming the body lives that long, the information and personality might be restored, but not until then."

"But, damn it, I became one of the faërie and it never happened to me!"

"That's because you're a more complex organism doing a more complex job. Many of the fairy races are smarter than people in their given areas. It neither hurt nor interfered with your function to retain your old self. Nymphs are among the simplest forms of fairy folk. They serve a function, nothing else. Best thing for her would be to take her to a nice forest and leave her. She'll mate with a tree and be happy and never know the difference."

They couldn't bring themselves to do that; but with the witch's visit, all hope was really gone, not only for Joe but for the mission.

Joe had still not awakened by early the next evening when Ruddygore arrived. He usually liked a flourish, but in this case he came secretly, in a plain brown robe and hood. Somehow he seemed to think that this effectively disguised his massive nearly four hundred pound frame and huge white beard. Without a transformation spell, Ruddygore could never be in any way inconspicuous, let alone incognito.

His usual jovial mood was gone, though. Things had not been going well for him, either, and he seemed less concerned with Joe's plight than with the contents of the Oracle's verses.

"Do you understand any more than we do?" Macore asked him.

"No, not much, but it's pretty clear the direction we must take. Things have gotten pretty nasty here, but the Earth threat still takes first priority, because, if it goes, *we* go. The two are connected in more ways than one, I fear."

"You mean our friend in black?"

"Indeed. I am no longer head of the Council. Because of his trick with the bodies and souls, which is quite good

I might add, he's effectively destabilized the religion we set up and, as such, turned the Council into acting on its own to preserve their domains and interests. He has made deals with a sufficient number of them to keep them pretty much out of the fray and he's already beginning to capitalize on it. He is coming out of the northwest of Hypeboreya with a legion of the living dead who are his slavish and unkillable troops. They're not invincible, but every casualty they inflict on the defenders becomes another of their own number. A few wizards are nervous about him, but he's working entirely within the Rules and playing very good politics with his equals. Nobody knows how strong he really is, so they are loathe to challenge him and quick to make deals. Of course, *he* doesn't know how strong he is, either, or he would have waited for me."

Macore sighed. "So it's all falling apart again. Get rid of one Dark Baron and you get a Master of the Dead."

"Well, it's pretty much the rules of the game, isn't it? Evil loses battles but never wars. I've been going crazy trying to organize and devise a defensive strategy against him. It's been difficult because he *is* as good a politician as sorcerer, and because he seems to have armies of the dead planted all over the place. We brought up massed dragons and stopped them at the River of Sighs, but another force of the same simply came marching out of the Misty Mountains to the south. No place is safe from him, but he stays in the background and relies on his anonymity to protect him from a direct challenge. It's frustrating."

"But I can't see how he could connect with this Earth business," Marge put in. "I mean, if Earth goes, he goes, too, right? So why this?"

"I doubt if he really understands the stakes on Earth. He made a deal, that's what. He would stop you from interfering in our enemy's affairs, and in exchange he was given access to ancient spells so foul and yet so powerful he could march on Husaquahr. If he were truly convinced that Armageddon was the result of the Baron's actions, I don't think he would have gone along, but they've conned him as he cons others here. I am fascinated by the fact that you found him familiar, though, Marge."

"We've met—I know that. Years ago. Maybe when I first came here. That's all I can say for sure."

"Hmmm . . . although I've never met him in this incarnation, I, too, have the feeling that I know him and he knows me, perhaps well," the wizard commented. "He certainly knows a good deal of how I think and he knows almost precisely the strengths and limits of my power. There is something familiar about the signature on his spells, but it is remote and hidden from me. It's been too long, and the level of sophistication is quite a bit higher. In some ways he reminds me of Dacaro in the old days, but we know where Dacaro is, and that's now been confirmed by the Oracle." The big man sighed. "Well, I suppose there's nothing we can do until we take out the greater threat. We've learned all we can up to now."

"How can we?" Marge asked him, sounding pained. "I've been trying to tell you since you arrived that Joe's gone—hopeless. Mostly by luck, the switch is permanent! A brainless wood nymph's no help—you heard the prophecy!"

Ruddygore allowed himself a smile and reached into his robe. "*Nothing* is permanent except the true death and Armageddon," he said softly, taking from some pocket within his robe the Lamp of Lakash.

"The Lamp! Of course!" Marge exclaimed excitedly. "If it can send Dacaro to Earth, it certainly can restore Joe!"

"We have some limits and must take some care in its use, though," the wizard warned. "First of all, it will grant no fairy wish—only mortal ones—but it's still a trap for fairy folk as for humans. In other words, Marge, you're disqualified on several grounds—and so am I, on different grounds. Macore, it would grant your wish—but stuff you back in the Lamp, so we don't want that."

"Who's in there now?" Marge asked him.

"A fellow named Jinner, appropriately enough. He was

in a spot of trouble a while back and begged me to bail him out. I did, but warned him that I would call in the price, and I did to free Macore. Don't worry—he's an aspiring magician and he's always desired to visit the land of the djinn—and he'll not be in too long. There are others I wouldn't mind filing away in there, and I'll pick one when I'm about to put it back in storage. Don't worry about that now. First, Captain, take the Lamp and wish yourself and Macore restored."

Bly took it, and for a second there was a real gleam in his eye. Then it was gone, and he sighed. "Forgive me, but temptation with it is a rather inevitable thing. Frankly, sir, had *you* not been present I might be too weak to resist."

"Don't worry—you can't succumb," Ruddygore told him. "I cast that spell before I handed the thing to you. Now—do it."

Bly thought for a moment. "I wish—that my soul was once again in the body into which it was born, and that the occupant of that body occupy the one I do now."

From somewhere a man's voice seemed to cry, "Done!"

There was no evident action, but the ratlike creature asked, "Did I say it right?"

"I'd say you did," the wizard responded, "considering you're back. Macore—the Lamp, please. All you can do is wind up back in it."

The little thief looked sheepish, then handed back the Lamp.

"Now I need to perform a slight ritual to check on a few things," Ruddygore told them, and shut his eyes as if concentrating. He did not move or even seem to breathe for what seemed like several minutes.

"But the prophecy said the others wouldn't get their bodies back," Macore reminded Marge in a whisper.

She nodded. "Let's see."

Suddenly Ruddygore's eyes opened, and his expression was grim. "I'm afraid the prophecy is correct, too. I find no evidence that either body is still alive. Either the Master found them or something untoward happened to both. I fear the former, alas. The Master would be anxious to make certain that our demigod and demigoddess could not reappear with full powers and so turn the Council back against him out of fear of me."

"Can't you just wish them replacement bodies that look the same?" Macore asked.

"Well, not really. I can turn them into lizards, yes, but I can't quite recreate them as they were—a fact that, I might tell you, they will not find tragic. Go awaken Tiana and get her in here. I'm going to give her the options, since she's the only one left right now with a clear right to a wish."

"The first priority is to save Joe," Tiana told them firmly. "All else matters little."

"Only the Lamp can convert, or reconvert, fairy to mortal," Ruddygore told her. "I can perhaps do something with you by using ordinary magic, but Joe will require a wish all his own. You will need to cascade, or string together, a series of related desires to form a complete wish we can use to accomplish our result. While we think on its wording, let's talk about you and what *you* wish that I might do for you."

"You know enough to know that I wish to go with them," she replied. "And I know enough of the Rules to know that it is in my best interest to remain as I am, as inconvenient as that would be."

They all looked at her, then at Ruddygore, puzzled by her statement.

"Tiana is simply stating a fact of mermaid lore. If a mortal man makes love to a mermaid he will always be in love with that mermaid. He might still go off and marry and have great affection for others, but he'll still be in love with that mermaid."

She nodded. "Yes, that is it."

The old wizard thought for a moment. "You know, while I was on holiday in Chicago a few weeks ago I took in a cinema that concerned a mermaid. I am a sucker for books and pictures on the fantastic, as you might understand. It gives me an idea. It has to be physiological and hold together, so it won't be quite as simple as the cinema might have it, but I think I can work a spell that will help using that idea. Indeed, I had already guessed this and worked it out on my way here."

They all stared at him expectantly.

"Of course, we can't send you over to Earth as you are. It would be too conspicuous and too limiting. We can't not make you the mermaid because of our Rules and your desires. Admittedly, the Oracle made no mention of you, but it didn't mention Poquah, either. Now, what this spell will do is basically give you legs when you are totally and completely dry and upon solid land. It will take several hours to take effect completely, and if you get wet or are surrounded by water below, it will reverse itself—and very quickly. There will be drawbacks, because you will remain a mermaid. You must immerse yourself at least once a day, perhaps before going to sleep, or it will become very painful. Also, the inner bone and muscular structure will not be well-adapted to walking, so you will have to walk slowly and will also still feel some pain, which will grow greater the more you're on them. You'll still be best off in a wheelchair or on crutches, but you will *look* human. Is this acceptable?"

"Of course. I'm no worse off than now and actually far better, no matter what the limits."

"Very well. You'll still have the webbing, and you'll still have the constitution of a mermaid, her powers, and other limitations, so be careful to observe them strictly. I'm also going to change your complexion, as I understand that your present clan has you marked for death. I'm going to give you a chocolate brown complexion, not only because it will allow you to pass as a human better on Earth but also because it matches no known mermaid clan here and as such will confuse the hell out of them."

"Sounds good. I don't mind."

"Well, *I* have a question or two," Marge put in. "First of all, how come she was too strong a wizard to pass over before but she isn't now? And second, why the hell would anybody take a vacation in Chicago?"

Ruddygore chuckled. "As to the first, mermaids are covered by a different volume of the *Rules*, and that supercedes, and limits, her powers. She still has power, but it's limited and redirected to specifics. That will allow her to escape the barrier. She's now under the limiting threshold of power. As to Chicago—did you know they actually *produce* all those wonderful pink flamingos in one large factory near Chicago?"

"Oh" was all Marge could manage.

"We will take care of me later," Tiana said impatiently. "Let us see to Joe."

They went over to the door leading into the far bedroom, and Marge, who got there first, let out a gasp and then shouted, "He's gone! And the door's wide open!"

She and Macore rushed out to the patio and looked around. There were the sights and sounds of a lot of activity, but no Joe and no way to tell where he'd gone.

"He's wandering around here now as an air-headed nymph!" Marge exclaimed. "And going entirely on instinct!" She looked around. "At least there aren't any trees around here."

"But there are lots of men around, and that's what a nymph does when she's not in her tree," Tiana puffed, hauling herself out onto the patio.

Ruddygore thought a moment. "Well, I wouldn't be too upset. We know he's not far, so he's well within range of the Lamp if we act now, no matter if he's physically present or not. I'd say we'd better do this quickly, though, just in case he wanders away and gets out of range."

Tiana accepted his assistance into a patio chair, and then he gave her the Lamp. "Consider well your wording," the sorcerer warned. "Whatever it is, you're stuck with it and so's he."

She thought frantically, then said, "I cannot put it into the right words! I cannot be *sure*!"

Marge decided to help out in the spirit of emergency. "How about this, then? You say that we can't word it properly enough to make him look like he did, but maybe we can. What about wishing his *original* body back, the one he had before he became a barbarian? As I remember he wasn't *that* bad looking, just a little old."

"Yes, yes! That's a sure thing!" Ruddygore cried. "I should have thought of it. Tiana, try something like this: I wish that Joe was no longer of the faërie, but mortal once more, and in the body he had when he was twenty, but with his full memories, mind, and personality restored as it was the day he became a fairy. Can you remember that and do it exactly? Be cautious. Don't clearly end the sentence until it's all there."

Tiana looked at him with interest. "So, if it is all about one person, I can string together as much as all that?"

"You can. Just be precise."

"All right, then. Uh—does not the genie have to appear, or something like that?"

"Oh, no. If you rub the Lamp, he's compelled to, but why bother him now? Plenty of time for introductions later on. Just hold it and look at it and wish. Do it now—before we might lose Joe!"

She took a deep breath. "Uh—I wish that Joe should be no longer a nymph but a mortal man once more, and that he be in the body he had when he was twenty, and that he has the mind, personality, and memories he did before he became one of the fairy folk, and that he be in the peak of physical condition and the ideal lover for my mermaid body and will make love to me this night. There!"

"Done!" came a voice from the Lamp.

Marge looked at Tiana. "You added a little bit there."

The mermaid shrugged. "There was no extra cost for the call," she noted, and handed the Lamp back to Ruddygore.

Far off on the other side of the hotel could be heard

the sounds of men yelling and screaming. It sounded like a real fight was going on.

"I have a suspicion that it worked," Throckmorton P. Ruddygore said.

CHAPTER 11

RETURN TO EARTH

From too much love of living,
From hope and fear set free,
We thank with brief thanksgiving
Whatever gods may be
That no life lives forever;
That dead men rise up never;
That even the weariest river
Winds somewhere safe to sea.
—Algernon Charles Swinburne

THEY HAD COME OVER ON A FERRYBOAT AND NOW THEY returned on what looked like a miniature *Mayflower*. All sails were set, of course, and out of the gunwales great oars protruded and pushed the ship on. Whoever or whatever rowed below was something none of them wanted to see, and, indeed, all but the deck and upper cabins were closed to them. Inside quarters were quite cramped, but well-stocked with food, water, wines, and the rest of the best. Macore had one small beaten-looking Earth-type suitcase which he'd gotten from Ruddygore, and they had brought Irving, but otherwise they were going over cold. The sorcerer had promised that all they would need they would get at the other end.

There was also a small medical kit, with which Tiana

continued to treat Joe. He had a number of bruises, what looked like a black eye, and several superficial but painful cuts.

"Damn it, *ouch!*" he started to say when she dabbed a particularly painful small cut. "At least you could have wished me to appear immediately in front of you!"

Tiana couldn't suppress a smile. The idea of a party of businessmen all seduced by a voluptuous nymph suddenly finding that nymph turning into a tall, dark, husky-looking man was pretty funny, considering how easily he'd managed to overcome mutual confusion, then mutual embarrassment and outrage, and fight his way out of there. Only slightly worse was the wound to his pride in having to march down to the front desk stark naked and demand to know if a Kauri and a mermaid were staying there, and angrily get into another fight when they hesitated to tell him.

Better for him was the fact that he had no memory of anything after being taken by the Master and no memory of the nymph experience at all. It hadn't been intended that way, but that had been the way the wish had been worded. He accepted the story, of course, because they were all there and confirmed it, and it certainly explained the changes in him; but if either Marge or Tiana said what a cute, sexy nymph he'd been one more time, he was going to slug somebody.

He really didn't look all that different. At six two he was a bit shorter than his barbarian form, but still a tall man; and at a fairly muscular two twenty, he was actually in pretty good shape. He looked a bit more Mexican and a bit less Amerindian than he had, and certainly his body was no longer the Mr. Universe machine it had been before, but he really wasn't changed radically. He'd been in good shape when he was twenty, after all. He'd been in the Marines at the time. Sexually, though, he was enormous—far better endowed than he had been at twenty, the size disproportionately large for the body. Tiana had many strings on her wish.

Now dry, Tiana looked remarkably different, although it wasn't hard to see that there were unusual things about her. She was still tall; but without the flipperlike fins, she was closer to five ten than over six feet. She was thin and quite shapely, with very long, straight, black hair reaching down almost to her waist. While only her coloration was changed, she would now be perceived as a young black woman by the America to which they traveled. Although she knew French, German, and, of course, her native tongue from Husaquahr, Ruddygore had to use a spell to give her a working knowledge of English. It was more than adequate, but she still had to translate from one of her other tongues, so it came out a bit garbled at times and without good pronunciation. Macore had the same spell and the same problem, but he had a genius for languages and was certain he'd pick it up quickly when actually using it. Marge and Joe, of course, needed no language help, although it was difficult for them sometimes to remember which language they were speaking, English or the Husaquahrian commercial language they normally used, and both found they had to concentrate or they would slip quickly out of English.

Joe surveyed the close quarters, still in a rotten mood. "At least he could have given us a bigger ship. What the hell *is* this thing, anyway?"

"Ruddygore said it was a scale replica of a Spanish galleon built for some pageant in Spain," Marge told him. "He picked it up when it was just about junked and headed for rot."

"Scale is right!" He got up, stretched, and flexed his muscles. "Not all I was used to. Ti, are you up to a walk around the deck?"

"Of course," she responded. "Let us go out and see what sort of strange place this Sea of Dreams truly is."

She clearly had some problems walking, a little of it a balance problem but much of it simply legs supported by bones and muscle not really designed to bear the weight of a body.

He helped her down the small stairs to the main deck, and they walked forward and to the rail. It was quite dark, and there was no sign of moon or stars. For a while, they stared out into the void.

"I think I hear voices," she commented. "And noises like great machines. I look down and see little flashes, like meteors below."

"You've been across once more than I have," Joe noted. "I wonder just what's out there?"

"Ruddygore once said it was the mind of God. I wonder if it's true?"

They stood there a while longer, staring out into the void they knew was not a void. Finally Tiana asked, "Joe? Do you still love me?"

He put his arm around her and squeezed. "Why do you ask? You know I do."

"Even though I've changed?"

"I've changed, too. I'm not the ideal barbarian anymore."

"You look beautiful to me. I was just . . . wondering."

"Wondering what?"

"If it is proper to make love amid the mind of God."

He looked at her, then pulled her to him and kissed her. "I can't think of a more appropriate place," he replied.

Ruddygore's ships always "made port" on Earth in the early morning hours, and in remote and mostly uninhabited locations, because they were, after all, rather conspicuous. The Company didn't really know where they were being set down, nor did it really matter. Poquah knew, and was supposed to be waiting for them with supplies and information.

Wherever it was, it was warm, clear, and dry, and certainly remote—the stars had faded in as they had entered the Earth's plane of reality and they were stunning, without much of any interference from nearby lights or cities.

Marge stared out at the darkness and sighed. "Well, we're home."

"Yeah," Joe responded, a little disbelievingly. "Home. Well I'll be damned. You know, I never expected to be here again. Oh, I know I talked about it and bellyached about it in the old days, but I never really did."

"Me, neither," Marge replied. "If you remember, I had already decided to leave it for good before I knew there was another place to go."

"Umph. Be interesting sometime to find out what happened after we left. I don't mean who's president or where the Marines have landed this time—I mean about that night. I always wondered—are we dead? Did they pick up our bodies off that super slab and scrape up the truck, or did we just sort of disappear into nothing?"

"You joined the legion of those who vanish forever every day," a familiar voice said behind them. They turned and saw Poquah standing there. The Imir looked rather funny to them, dressed as he was in a black button-down shirt, jeans, cowboy boots, and Stetson. As usual, they had not heard him come aboard. Imirs were only noticed when they wanted to be, which made them occasionally irritating friends but terrible enemies. "I assume it is just the two of you?"

"No—oh, I guess you hadn't had a chance to be told. We have two others, at Ruddygore's direction," Marge told him.

He looked up at the upper cabin in time to see Macore appear, followed by Tiana.

"I can see there have been some changes made," the Imir noted. "I had not expected *him* to get out of the Lamp for a century or so, and I do not know the lady, except that she is a mermaid with some land adaptation spells and is from a clan I have never heard of before."

"That's Tiana," Joe told him. "It's a long story. You might have noticed that I've changed, too."

"All human barbarians look alike to me," the Imir responded calmly. "As for the long story, it is interesting,

I am sure, but irrelevant. We must be on the move. This ship cannot remain here."

A small gangplank extended from the side, but it didn't have much of a downward slope. The ship was still not quite in Earthly space, nor were they until they got off. Marge tested her flying and found it as normal as usual; Joe helped Tiana get down, as she was still unused to her weak legs, and Macore brought up the rear, lugging the suitcase he'd been given by the wizard.

A queer-looking vehicle awaited them, motor running. "Just what the hell is *that*?" Joe wanted to know.

"A coach which has no horses!" Macore said, awe-struck. "How convenient!"

"It is called a mini-van, and it will comfortably seat us all," Poquah told him. "Joe—do you think you could drive this? I need to test your driving skills after so long a hiatus, and it is difficult to run into too much out here."

"Yeah, I think I can. I might be rough and rusty for a few miles, but I'll bet I can get back into it real fast. After all, I drove bigger rigs than this for more than fifteen years."

They got in, discovering that the van had three rows of seats and was more than big enough to accommodate them all comfortably. Poquah took the front passenger seat, since he had to navigate.

Joe spent some time adjusting things, then pulled out and promptly stalled. "Damn! Rustier than I thought," he mumbled, slightly embarrassed. He finally got it in gear; although his shifting and clutching were fairly jerky, he really did seem to get it back quickly.

"On the other hand, once you are a skilled rider, you don't get yourself so bumped up," Macore noted, mostly to himself. He was the only one among them who'd never been on Earth before.

They pulled onto an interstate that was mostly deserted, and Poquah directed him to proceed east.

"Hey!" Marge shouted excitedly. "This is old I-10! We're in Texas!"

"Yes, we are south and west of Midland," the Imir told her.

"Well I'll be damned! This is where we came in!"

"It is convenient in that it meets all the requirements. We'll be staying in a motel this evening, still south of the city, and we'll prepare to remain there at least one day. I will have to go out and get some suitable clothing and other things for you all. The small amount of clothing I have for Joe will obviously not fit, and I did not expect the other two of you. You, Kauri, will have to keep in mind that you must keep your powers of disguise constant at all times. And *do* remember not to fly while you are in danger of being seen doing so. Even if they do not see you as a Kauri, these Earth folk might get a bit upset at seeing a young woman suddenly rise off into the air."

"Don't worry," she assured him. "Protection and defense are built into me. Joe's the only one without danger, though. Ti needs water and she takes some time to get land-adapted again; and, if I remember, Macore has a little problem, too."

The thief nodded. "I don't reflect or cast shadows. It's a pain in the ass for shaving—if that is still a problem. By the gods! How fast does this thing *go*?"

"Then do not shave. If you can manage some growth, it will help disguise you. Our quarry knows you, remember. The fairy folk do not reflect, either, which can cause problems, Kauri, no matter what the spell, and our shadows are often inconsistent. As for speed, Joe is proceeding at seventy right now and probably should slow down. We cannot afford a police check right now, I wouldn't think."

"What you're saying is that a group portrait of us would be rather odd," Tiana put in. "Joe and I would show up, and perhaps two distorted shadows. Handy if you're a bank robber."

"Oh, really?" Macore responded, forgetting for a moment his frightened grip on the seat and the speed at which the surroundings were going past and sounding very interested in this new world. Poquah gave him a withering look. The little thief shrugged innocently. "Hey—it's only professional curiosity."

By the time they'd exited the interstate and began driving up to Midland, the sun was coming up. "I'm going to stick with the goggles for now," Marge told them. "I guess we'll all be in and ready to sleep in another hour or two."

Poquah had selected a motel that had only one story but was rather large and spread out, so that none of them would have to go through a lobby to get in and out. Right now, they were neither dressed nor in any condition to meet the west Texas public. The Imir, however, did have to arrange for another room, but he had no problem getting one that adjoined and had an interconnecting door. He did seem to be spending an inordinate amount of time in the office, though, and they grew concerned. The sun was up now, and they felt quite conspicuous. Finally he returned and handed Joe one key and Macore the other.

"Any problems?" Joe asked him.

"No. It is the same everywhere I go in this insane country. Everyone seems to believe I am someone named Nimoy, or occasionally someone named Spock." They drove off, following his directions, and reached the two rooms. Quickly and nervously, they made their way from the van into the rooms. Macore still had on his gray jerkin and boots, which were a bit out of place here, but Joe and Tiana were literally without a stitch.

"I informed the woman at the desk that you had just flown in and were dead tired, and not to give you any disturbance or perform any maid service today," Poquah told them, "but you never know with these places. Keep all the locks and chains on, and put out the 'Do Not Disturb' signs. Problems might develop before we could correct them with spells, and we do not need problems right now."

"Small bathtubs." Tiana sniffed. "Still, I suppose this will do."

"It will have to. I will return later on." The Imir looked at his wrist, which sported a fancy digital watch. "It is now almost seven-thirty. I shall return by three this afternoon with what is needed and the information to brief you. Until then, I suggest that you get some rest. We will keep to a nocturnal schedule for the time being, both for security's sake and until you get accustomed to acting on your own in this environment."

Macore was in the other room, looking around. He had a childish joy in the light switches and spent a couple of minutes just turning them on and off. He was even more delighted with the small air-conditioning console. To be told about such things academically was one thing; actually to see them was something else. Macore's world was a world of magic, demons, and spells which he took entirely for granted. *This* was truly a Husaquahrian child's magical dream.

"Shall I bring something to eat or drink before I go into the city?" the Imir asked them.

"No, we had plenty on the boat," Joe replied. "You might bring something back when you return, though."

"I'll do what I can," the Imir assured them, and left.

Macore, in the other room, went over to the television and stared at it. "This is a window of some kind?"

Marge laughed. "That's TV. Look—I'll show you." She switched it on, suddenly aware that her position was the direct opposite of her early life in Husaquahr. There she learned the language by spell and was illiterate. Now Macore was in that spot, although at the moment it didn't seem to bother him.

He was fascinated by the images on the television and had to be assured that they could not see him. The major networks all had their morning news shows on, and some of the cable channels were showing things like Wheeler and Wollsey "B" pictures from the thirties, while the sports channel was showing the curling finals on tape delay from Halifax. There were several apparently all-religious channels, and four other channels were showing different episodes of *Gilligan's Island*.

"Same old junk," Marge commented sourly.

"Oh, I kind of like it," the little thief commented. "Particularly the ones with the little short fellow and the fat one on the island."

"Yeah," Marge told him. "Wait till you've seen the same rerun half a dozen times!"

"Huh? You mean they are not acting companies all performing this as we watch?"

"I'll explain film and tape to you later," she said tiredly. "I'm going to sleep."

"So am I," Joe called from the other room. The sound of water filling a tub almost drowned him out. He was a bit distressed to discover that from now on, his wife would have to sleep nights in the bathtub. It simply hadn't occurred to him in all this.

Macore bade them a good rest and closed the door between. It wasn't completely soundproofed, but Marge told him that it wouldn't bother her a bit if he kept the TV on, although he'd best do it softly to avoid waking Joe. "Okay—great!" he responded. "I caught a nap on the way over, and I'm not very tired right now."

She removed the goggles and was soon comatose. From the other room came snores louder than Macore's television. He just sat there, curled up in front of it, watching one thing after the other, often changing channels.

Poquah's hefty tip seemed to keep the maids away; but close on to noon, Macore, who was still sitting there, got irritated when the same episode of *Gilligan's Island* he'd just watched on one channel began on another and he turned the dial. He caught a slight glimpse of something as he turned it, then frowned, stopped, turned it back, and stared at the screen.

He pressed his face right up to it, then stood back. "Oh, my god!" he breathed. There was no mistake. There couldn't be that much of a mistake.

It was some sort of talk show or forum, and apparently it was before a huge live audience. He wouldn't have even noticed it—he'd found seven minutes of David Hartman intolerable and could take about forty seconds of Jim

Bakker—and this, certainly, was the same format. The speaker seemed to be some kind of preacher, and he was dressed in a finely tailored, dark blue suit, had short hair, and wore round, apparently rimless glasses; but still he knew that face, which had been looking into his only a few weeks before.

Dacaro had sure as hell come a long way on Earth in only a few weeks!

"What are these little round things?" Joe asked. "Potato puffs?"

"They are supposedly chicken," Poquah informed him. "You dip them in the little sauce cups, I'm told." He rummaged in the two bags, took out another wrapped package, then handed it to Tiana, who was still very much a mermaid but slowly drying out.

"That's all right," Tiana assured him, unwrapping the package and finding two raw whole fish and a package of raw shrimp still in the shell. "They probably won't taste like much, but they'll probably be better than whatever it is you gave Joe to eat."

Poquah walked over to the connecting double-doors, opened them, then peered in. Marge, of course, was still out cold, and Macore was now curled up, sound asleep in front of the television which was still on. The Imir decided not to awaken them, but went in and turned off the set, then returned to Joe and Tiana and quietly shut the doors again. "Forgive me, but I simply cannot abide that drivel. It has made the civilized part of this world into a mass of illiterate morons." He paused a moment, then added, "Of course, it also appeals to those already in that condition as well, no matter what their origins."

Joe managed to polish off two Big Macs, the nuggets, and a lot more that Poquah had brought along. He was still hungry, but it would do. His only complaint was that the Imir had brought no coffee; the in-room stuff the motel provided was hardly worth the name even on Earth.

Still, Poquah was anxious to get down to his business. "You have the text of the prophecies, I hope?"

"Well, we weren't exactly there for them, and we didn't exactly have pockets," Joe replied. "Macore's got the text, though. You got some clothes for us?"

"Yes. I had to guess on the lady, of course, but I think it will do until she can find some of her own more to her liking." He had, of course, taken the measurements of all three mortals before leaving, so he was actually dead on. He either had a keen eye or an uncanny ability to know just what was required, although he did leave it practical.

Joe's outfit was pretty much an upsized version of what Poquah was wearing—jeans, boots, a flannel shirt, and even socks and underwear, two items of clothing he'd not really been used to wearing for many years. For Tiana, Poquah had selected equally practical clothing—but with women's undergarments, of course, even a bra if she wanted one—and with a long woman's yellow T-shirt. "I decided that you would find boots more problem than asset, so I found you some sandals. I regret the higher heel but they don't seem to come any other way here. I know you will probably wish to remain barefoot most of the time, but there are establishments all over that will not admit you without shoes."

Her lower body had already split but was still more fishlike than human, giving her a really unusual appearance. "I am sure they will be fine," she assured him. "I will try them as soon as I can."

"I procured a very comfortable motorized wheelchair that folds rather nicely," Poquah told her proudly, "and I also found a pair of ingenious folding aluminum crutches for when that is more practical. I think that will take care of your needs."

He was emotionless and officious, but she was touched. "You are very kind. It is more than I expected," she told him sincerely.

Poquah went out and came back with a small object, which he gave to Joe. The big man removed the top of the box and found a wallet, and inside were a number of major credit cards in the name of "Joseph Romero." He looked at Poquah. "That me?"

"Yes. We established the accounts after closing out the stolen one for Ruddygore. They are good, and the best part is that the bill will not have to be paid by you. Do not, I pray, abuse them, though. They are for business and survival. When you return to Husaquahr, none of you will be allowed to take anything from this world with you, anyway."

"Yeah, well I—hey! This is a Class-G chauffeur's license!" Joe exclaimed, then frowned. "But it doesn't have my picture!"

"Not necessary in that state, which is why we chose it. The particulars are a bit off, but I doubt if anyone will really notice."

"You want me to drive a rig, then?"

"Yes. You'll find the permits in order, and we've used a few spells to make it impervious to inspectors. I am having it modified somewhat today but the company we are dealing with here is quite interested in money and assures me that my modification will be ready tomorrow."

"All five of us are gonna fit in a cab?" Joe said dubiously.

"It won't be necessary. You'll see."

The sound of the conversation apparently awakened Macore, who came through the doors and into the other room, not exactly wide awake but definitely excited. "Sorry I fell asleep," he apologized needlessly. "Man! I wanted so bad to wake somebody up earlier! I saw him!"

"Who?" Tiana asked, puzzled. They all turned to look at the little thief.

"Dacaro! That's who!"

"Dacaro!" Joe exclaimed. "Here?"

"No—on the TV thing in there! He was on a show. You know, on one of those religious channels."

Poquah seemed suddenly very interested. "Indeed? Are you certain?"

"Yeah, sure—I'm not gonna forget *him* any time soon!

Oh, he was wearing one of those funny suits it seems like they make men wear here, and he had short hair and, believe it or not, pink eyeglasses, but it was him. His voice, too. Silky smooth, you know? His English is perfect—at least, it's not much different from what the other TV people speak—but he's *some* speaker. Really stirring up the crowds. You could feel the emotion right through the TV."

The Imir frowned. "I had not expected him to get so far so soon. I thought we had weeks, perhaps even months or a year. This changes everything. On national television within a month of his arrival! Oh, my!"

"You act like you expected it sooner or later," Joe noted. "You know where he is, then?"

"Of course. It's been rather easy to find both him and the Baron; they are not exactly engaged in secretive activity." He paused for a moment, as if making a decision, then said, "I was going to wait until Marge was up, but I suppose this can be done twice."

Macore came in, sat on a corner of Tiana's bed, then got up again fast. "That's *wet*!" he complained, then sat down on the floor. They were all ears.

When the Baron had been exiled from Husaquahr, Macore explained, he'd been sent first to the center of Ruddygore's Earth operations, which was in Basel, Switzerland. He had remained there for more than three months, getting to know the new world in which he'd found himself and checking out his place in it. He had been very comfortable, living in a villa owned by Ruddygore just across the Rhine in France, and had spent the first month doing nothing but reading everything in French, German, and English that he could get his hands on. He needed no spells or courses in language or literacy; he proved himself unexpectedly adept at both. The Demon Prince with whom he'd made his alliances in Husaquahr had been a good teacher and supplier of certain books and reading materials from Earth.

He was, of course, a genius with a finely tuned analytical mind; he had been the best theoretician of magic in the history of Husaquahr, far beyond anyone else, no matter what their power. Being stripped of his powers had not made him any less brilliant or knowledgeable.

He spent another six weeks or so on a sort of European grand tour, using a liberal stipend from Ruddygore's company, visiting Rome and much of Germany, France, and England, using falsified Swiss papers that looked genuine enough to stand almost any challenge. Ruddygore's European organization even got them in his own name.

Agents reported him both fascinated by the wonders of technology and appalled by the contrasts such technology created. Still, it was hard to pin down just what real interests he had, since he was fascinated by the ideologies and tensions of the modern world with its omnipresent threat of nuclear holocaust and with the imbalances of wealth, yet he was also apparently fascinated by computers, space science, and technology, and even the misfits and oddballs of society.

The computer, though, had particularly fascinated him; as he was getting warnings that his funds were going to dry up if he didn't decide to do something useful, he enrolled first in a quick and intensive course in how to type, then in a London computer school. For all of its inanities, magic was mathematical and he seemed to find in computer programming the same sort of relationship. He dropped the year-long course after only three months, not because he had lost interest but because he had already progressed, not only beyond the brightest pupil at the school, but beyond the brightest instructors as well.

And then, quite suddenly, he informed his benefactors that he no longer required any of their help or support and that he had obtained sufficient funds to live on. They were baffled by this, but, a few days later, Esmilio Boquillas vanished from their surveillance and they found no sign of him for almost three years.

Exactly what he was doing at that time was a mystery, although he seemed to have spent some time with English and Welsh mystics, mostly cult and lunatic-fringe people, the sort of professional characters that Britain seemed to grow best in all the world. Then he came to the United States, partly to the south, then to the San Francisco-San Jose, California, area, where he emerged once again in public view—*very* public view—as a faith healer.

"He's a *what*?" Joe asked incredulously.

"A faith healer. It appears now that he spent some time looking for Earth individuals with some of the magical talents. There are some—more than you would think—but most have no knowledge of their abilities and thus are undetected even by themselves. Others, when the powers come out involuntarily, believe they have had profound religious experiences, or been involved with alien civilizations, or things like that. He wanted people with sufficient power to handle at least minimal spells, but they had to be people who really believed they could do sorcery—hence his interest in cults, witches, and the like. Apparently he discovered one woman at some Satanist group in southern California who had some real powers. A hostess of a television collection of old horror movies, I believe, who went under the stage name of—pardon—Shockarilla, I think it was. He was at that time employed as a programmer in the San Francisco area, but abruptly both she and he resigned their positions and she went to join him. Soon after, they began doing guest appearances at local churches of no real denomination—there are quite a number of rather bizarre yet still mainstream churches in the area—and their reputation for truly curing really caught on."

"The old boy's very charismatic," Joe admitted. "A lot of folks carry off that faith-healing business with no real chance at success—just people believing so hard they sometimes cure themselves. Just enough of 'em to keep 'em going and keep their credibility up. But the Baron, now—if he had somebody with the power, he could really do it, couldn't he? I mean, restore a lost limb, make blind eyes see, all that."

"He could indeed, as you well know. There really aren't any physicians in Husaquahr as such; the healers are magicians who specialize in healing potions and spells. Boquillas is a genius with a photographic memory, who might well know just about every spell ever written down; and those he couldn't remember, his fine mathematical mind could create," Poquah admitted.

Joe sat back against the headboard, looking a little dazed. "A guy who could really do healing miracles—he could write his own ticket! They'd *flock* to him to be cured! And if he told them they had to stand on their heads and recite 'Mary had a little lamb' three times backwards for the cure to work, they'd do it! Oh, man!"

"And it would not take much of an additional string on those healing spells to make them devoted worshipers," Tiana added. "They would already be most of the way there, out of sheer gratitude and physical proof."

"That is the way of it," the Imir admitted, "although I am not certain that his female adept really has the ability to do much more, even with the spells he supplies."

"And that's where Dacaro comes in, I bet," Macore put in. "If you already have a good scam going, then sticking in a world-class wizard at the right moment is the smart thing to do."

"The computers," Joe said, still thinking of the implications. "I just can't figure—or can I? I don't know much about computers, and I don't know just how easy to get they are, but I'll bet you he's got one *hell* of a computer somewhere that's not only got all the spells but all the formulas to make whatever he wants. Maybe he's rigged one back where he used to work. I know the dispatcher before we left always had a computer terminal in front of him, and so did the one when we arrived at the other end, and both were connected to the same computer someplace over the phone."

"I fear it is far easier than that today," the Imir told him. "Today you can purchase a computer with enormous memory and power for about half the price of an automobile, as rugged as a typewriter and not much larger. If he had enough capacity to store his programs, he would need no more space than it takes for that television set over there. And, of course, spells here are mathematically quite different from spells where we come from. The computer would automatically be able to translate one complex spell into another. The only thing he did not have was someone with sufficient power and training actually to cast complex spells. Now he does."

"What did he want the gold for, then?" Macore asked Poquah. "I mean, it sounds as if he's got a hell of a scam running just where he is."

"He required it, apparently, to purchase a large block of land in a very rugged section of northern California. It was owned by a lumber company that was stopped by the actions of some nature lovers from doing any more tree cutting in the whole area. They were faced with having it taken over by the government and were happy to sell it for what Boquillas could offer upfront, particularly in gold. He and his lady friend incorporated a nonprofit religious foundation to own it—a very easy task in California, it seems. They are, of course, the head of that foundation. Although the land is heavily restricted from any public access, he apparently mollified the nature organization and guaranteed preservation of the land. Everyone is delighted with him, even the country, for while he pays no taxes as a religious institution and retreat, they would have received none from the government condemnation, either—and now they receive substantial contributions to public welfare. The Baron is also a good politician."

"Yeah, okay, so he's got a cult, a following, and a little kingdom of his own. So far I can follow that. But what goes with Dacaro on television?"

"The Baron is quite—in English I believe the slang word is 'slick'—with his theology. It is particularly insipid, bland, and nondenominational. Although he's associated himself up to now primarily with offshoots of Christian religions, he seldom if ever mentions anything beyond 'God' and 'the Lord.' His charm or charisma, as some call it, is sufficient that almost every authentic pastor he meets seems not only charmed by him but convinced that his theology and theirs is a near-perfect match. He knows the truth of oratory—it is not what you say but how you say it that counts for everything. Consider just how little a politician actually says, as compared to what his or her listeners believe about that politician. And because so many of the sincere and legitimate broadcasting preachers here are so affluent and so conspicuous in their success that they are the target of many attacks by cynics and government, they are likely to rally around *any* preacher they feel is being persecuted, even if that individual is clearly a fraud. The Baron's Open Path movement has already been the target of many such attacks, which has won him notoriety beyond California and a great deal of sympathy from those who see themselves, wrongly, in him."

Macore nodded sympathetically. "Yeah, it's always that way. You get some sincere people with good ideas making a real go at it and the con artists and the charlatans aren't far behind."

"You should know," Poquah responded acidly.

Macore grinned sheepishly. "Hey! I only go for the rewards! I don't want the end of the world!"

The Imir frowned. "What is this about the end of the world?"

Macore repeated to him the first verse of the oracle.

"Then it *is* Armageddon at the end! I wonder what those sincere men and women of religion who defend him would say if they knew?"

"They always used to tell us the end was close at hand," Joe noted. "I don't know if they believed it, but somehow I don't think they'd be surprised if it came. I knew a preacher once, one of the hellfire-and-brimstone types, who dropped dead right in the pulpit while preaching a sermon. Heart attack. It wasn't instant, but they said that, just before he died, he didn't look sad or angry or upset—more like *disappointed* it was just him."

"Hmmm . . . well, give me the second prophecy, then, thief, and we will see if we can put the two together."

"Yeah, sure. It's lousy poetry." He recited the longer, more complex verse on how to avert the doom.

"The early part is clear enough," the Imir noted, "and now you three are here, so we've gone that far. Unfortunately, the rest is still unclear to me. The way to solve the problem is there—but unless we can solve the prophecy itself, we will not know the way. Still, this is not a one-sided conflict, or it would be unnecessary. The indications are there that Heaven will aid us as Hell is aiding the Baron."

"You mean angels for the demons and like that?" Joe was interested in the prospect.

"No. It never works that way, particularly not here. Providence will guide the elements we need into place for us. If we take those elements and then apply them in the pattern established by the verse, we will win. If we do not, then the Baron will win and we will all die."

"*Whew!*" Macore said nervously. "It sounds like it's real easy for them and nearly impossible for us. We get one right way to play the hand, and a crazy poem as our only clue, and *they* get a stacked deck!"

"Evil wins out much of the time because it is so easy," Poquah noted. "Good wins because it is earned and deserves to. That is the test, don't you see? Every once in a while an individual or group must face the ultimate evil. A test, as it were. This time it is we who are chosen to do so. Heaven and Hell are betting on our outcome. If we prevail, we prove that good is still superior to evil and the stronger of the two. If we lose, then we prove that the time for Armageddon is indeed nigh."

Macore looked at the faces of the others in the room. "Who? *Us*?"

CHAPTER 12

PROVIDENCE, GHOSTS, AND PETER PAN

Those who insist on living in the past have no future.
—Message found in a Chinese fortune cookie

ALTHOUGH THEY TRIED TO TALK MARGE OUT OF IT, SHE would not be restrained from going out that evening and visiting some of the old places where she'd lived much of her life. She was quite confident of herself and won out when she argued that she'd better find out now if she couldn't fool the people of her old world when it would just be an incident and not a deadly blunder.

In fact, it was useful to allow them all out for a while in Earth society, if only to get accustomed to a new and different world. Joe and Tiana, who was now human-appearing once more, decided on some evening shopping to fill out their wardrobes; Poquah took Macore in tow, although the little thief somewhat protested, to get him oriented to the basic rules of survival on Earth. Macore, after all, had never seen a stoplight, didn't know from which direction traffic came in this world, and had to get used to this funny worthless paper being treated as if it were something of value.

For Marge, it was a matter of flying over the area and seeing how much had changed and how much had stayed the same over the years. She had been born and raised in the area and knew it and the nearby town of Odessa like the back of her hand. It did, of course, look different from the air, and the sights, sounds, and even odors seemed more chaotic, more irritating, than she remembered. This was the true Texas, though; flat and dry, with an economy based on oil, gas, and cows, now pretty much in that order.

Her grammar and high school were still there, but they'd torn down the old junior high and the neighborhood in which she'd been born and raised seemed less tranquil and dirtier than she remembered it.

The feelings and the sensations of the people below were almost overpowering to her. If this place was typical of Earth, the amount of misery, guilt, and anger radiating from the relatively peaceful city below would keep a thousand Kauris busy for the next century. She would have no trouble feeding here; indeed, the problem would be not taking on such a load that it weighed her down and made her ponderous and depressed, for she could not cleanse herself of any excess.

Her thoughts turned to Roger, and she couldn't help wondering if her ex-husband still lived in the same mobile home and the same trailer park outside of town. He wasn't given to taking chances or doing anything without being forced to—she had even had to propose to him—so it was quite likely. She circled around and headed southwest.

She landed just outside the trailer park and took on the guise of her old self. She'd been plain and rather unattractive most of her adult life, or so at least she had always thought, and she took a little time to adjust the image here and there. A bit more of a bust, tight clothing that was well-styled, a nice hairdo, good makeup, that sort of thing. It was very easy to do—she just wished it, and saw it in her mind's eye, and it was so. It was all illusion, but of a broadcasting sort. Any who saw her, even if she didn't know they were there, would see her as she intended to be seen. Only changelings, ones with the power, and those of fairy blood could see, hear, and know her as she really was. The Kauri were somewhat like method actresses, who literally became their parts, yet never lost touch with their true natures.

If indeed he still lived in the old place, he'd bought a new pickup, but that was to be expected. She stood there, looking at the place, and the memories came back, both the good and the painful ones. All of a sudden she didn't really understand why she had come here or what she expected to see. All the real love and affection had gone out of this relationship long before she'd taken that long walk to nowhere up the interstate, and she certainly neither wanted, nor was it possible, to have a resumption of their relationship. The Kauri nature, which was her nature, made that impossible. Or was it, perhaps, some inner desire for revenge? Kauris were generally above all that, or so she'd thought; they sought revenge only for things done to themselves or their sisters, and she had been someone else back then. The place was lighted, though, and from the windows came the blaring sound of baseball play-by-play.

Suddenly the door banged open and Roger came out, a beer in one hand and a plastic trash bag in the other, dressed in shorts and T-shirt. He'd grown much older in the few years separating them; his hair seemed flecked with gray, his muscular body had gone somewhat to flab, and he had a definite potbelly. He opened a trash can over to one side, stuffed the bag in, closed it again, then turned and caught sight of her. He smiled first, as if acknowledging a neighbor, then frowned; his mouth dropped. "My lord, Marge! Is that *you*?"

She sighed. "Hello, Roger," she said.

He came over to her, still disbelieving his senses. "Good God Almighty! Where'n hell you *been* all this while?"

"Away. Other places. Places I never even knew existed."

"Well, wherever it was, it sure as hell was good for you! Jesus! You look as fine as the day we got married!" He paused a moment. "You want to come in and sit a while?"

Without really replying, she followed him into the trailer, still not really knowing what she was going to do or why. This had already gone much further than she'd intended.

The place was a mess, with stuff all over. A small color TV in the combined living and dining room blared into the darkness and there were lots of empty beer bottles around. Aside from being messy as hell and from the very well-worn upholstery she remembered as new or nearly so, it looked pretty much the same.

Roger seemed a little at a loss but also happy. She could read the deep guilt within him that her reappearance had brought to the surface once more, although it was never very deeply suppressed. "Can I get you a beer or a pop or something?"

"No, nothing, thanks." She took a seat in the old chair she'd bought years ago at a flea market in Odessa. It had always been her favorite chair. He turned a kitchen chair around and sat on it, just looking at her for a while. Finally he asked, "Why'd you come back, Marge?"

"I really don't know, Roger. I was just coming through this way for the first time since—well, *since*—and I just wanted to see how you were making out. I can't stay very long. I'm meeting some people in Midland in a little while."

He seemed crestfallen at that, and for the first time she realized that he had really thought, or at least hoped, that she had come back to him. She felt suddenly very awkward, and the situation seemed more wrong than before.

"What sort of people? What you been doin' all this time, anyway?"

"Oh, I've been pretty much of a free spirit," she responded evasively. "I travel light and make enough to get by and see to all my needs." She decided to change the subject. "I see that you didn't remarry."

"Oh, after you left I played the superstud for a while, I guess, and even had a girl or two live here now and again, but didn't none of 'em hold a candle to you, Marge, and that's God's honest truth. The ones with the bodies didn't have no brains, and the ones with the brains had better sense than to take up with me. After three days we found out we didn't have nothing to talk about. Jesus! I missed you, Marge!"

"I didn't miss you, Roger," she said coldly.

That hit him where it hurt, but he was too happy to see her to get mad. Instead he asked, "If that's true, why didn't you just keep goin' past this little piss-ant piece of nowhere?"

She shrugged. "I don't really know. Curiosity, mostly, I think, and maybe some nostalgia. I had some good times here, at the start, before it got all bad."

He stared straight into her eyes. "And now you're a whore, huh? A traveling whore that ain't got nothing to her name. Is that what the girl I married's become? A damned whore. A damned college-educated whore!" His anger was now masking his guilt, and doing a very good job of it. He would either break into violent action, or, she sensed, he would break into pieces. Although he couldn't see it or sense it, her Kauri wings were spread wide now, not for flight but as sensory organs. And suddenly she knew why she'd been impelled to come here, and what she had to do. So much guilt, anger, hurt, and pain. There was an illness in Roger that could only eventually destroy, perhaps others first and then, fast or slow, Roger himself. It was her function, and her power, to treat such things.

The wings spread wide, and she held him suspended in her powers. She kicked off imaginary shoes, and then began to shed imaginary clothing.

Joe had become worried at the sight and sound of an approaching thunderstorm. They tried to hail several taxis, but discovered that the white drivers seemed to ignore them. Some things still hadn't changed. Finally one dropped off a fare near the entrance to the mall and proved to be driven by an elderly black man, and he invited them in.

They had no luck. The storm hit, suddenly bathing the

cab in a torrent of water. The sound of the storm beating on the taxi's roof masked the sound of ripping jeans as Tiana's spell was negated and her lower half was restored to its natural form. It had not been necessary actually to be out in the storm; she was literally surrounded by water and that was all it took. Tiana had a strange mixture of relief at being comfortable again and anxiety at her current condition; Joe had only the anxiety to deal with.

They finally pulled into the motel and directed the driver to their room. When they got there, the storm had already abated and, in fact, was almost over, no help to Tiana.

"Let me open the door first," Joe said hurriedly. "My wife has real bad arthritis and this storm's left her unable to walk."

"Okay," the driver said, sounding friendly and concerned. "Want me to help?"

"Oh, no! I can handle it." Joe got out and opened the door with his key, propping it wide with a chair, then quickly returned. The cabbie was getting out and making for the trunk, which held most of their boxes. Joe looked at Tiana, who shrugged, and waited for the trunk to open, then quickly scooped her up, took her out, bumping her head in the process, and carried her quickly into the motel room. Their beds, of course, were still unmade, and he put her on one and she quickly pulled the covers up an appropriate length and sat up, watching them.

The driver was in a moment later with about half the packages. He seemed a bit surprised to see her already in bed, but he didn't comment. He and Joe went out to get the rest of the stuff. "Just set it here. I'll get it in," he told the cabbie.

The old man did it, then stood there, scratching his head for a minute, and it was clear that he'd seen, or thought he'd seen, something odd when Joe carried her in. He started to say something, then thought better of it, and accepted his fare and a sizable tip. He said goodbye, got into his cab, and slowly drove off, thinking, *I been working too hard. Even if there was such things as that they wouldn't be in this country. And they sure as hell wouldn't be black.*

Joe returned and took the chair away, closing the door. "Close," he muttered. "Too close."

"I suppose I should not have come after all," Tiana moped. "I am far more of a burden here than any help. And this is dry country! What will happen when we get to places where this happens all the time?"

He came over, sat on the bed beside her, put his arm around her, and kissed her. "We've all got our problems. *I* need you here. Leaving you alone back in Husaquahr with that Master-of-the-Dead creep still on the loose would have worried me so much I couldn't have thought straight here anyway."

"I was also pretty upset tonight, not just with the taxis, but with some of the places and people. Nothing was restricted or segregated or anything like that, but I still often *felt* hostility here and there. And for no reason!"

He chuckled. "Honey, don't you worry about that stuff. I know you're second class in these parts, but don't think all that was directed at you. There's a class around here down at the bottom real far below whites, blacks, Mexicans, and anybody else. That's Indian—and I'm it."

Roger had not seen her come, and he was sleeping peacefully when she left, so she walked back out after turning off the lights and turning off the TV. It was late, later than she'd expected to be here, but still early enough to see a bit more. She was certainly no longer hungry, and would not be perhaps for several days, but she knew she'd lifted two burdens tonight and buried her last personal ghost as well.

There was no one apparently around, so she flew into the night, circled one last time around the trailer park, and headed back toward Midland.

There were several thunderstorms in the area and she grew worried about Tiana. She knew she should go back immediately, but she was overly full and needed to work some of it off, changing it to energy, or she might be nasty or mean as hell when she didn't intend to be.

The storms attracted her childish inner nature. There was nothing quite like a west Texas thunderstorm in late spring, one whose violence and power was enormous but whose boundaries one could see from a great distance. She had been in awe of them as a girl and in fear of them as an adult in a trailer park, but she'd never before seen them with fairy eyes, in which their power was tangible and somewhat mystical.

Now the lightning was no threat to one who swam in volcanic fires, and the tremendous updrafts and downdrafts were like a super roller coaster. She knew that she could be slammed to the ground, but she was confident of her abilities to recover before that time. For now, she played at dodging the lightning bolts and rode the violence she could not merely sense but see, and it worked off a lot of excess energy.

It was while doing this that she suddenly had a strong stabbing sensation. It was brief, and not painful, more as if some great invisible lance vibrated through her midsection. Play stopped, and she tried to find the sensation once again. She knew it, although she had never expected to sense it on Earth, and particularly not here, so close to home.

It was a universal, racial call for help. It was the sensation you got when a fairy was hurt and needed help—not just Kauri, any kind.

With two or three of her sisters, it would have taken no time at all to locate the source, even in the storm; but, although the storm passed quickly, it took her the better part of an hour to find that strong pulsing vibration once again, and even longer to be able to hold onto it and follow it down. It was not a strong signal, which could mean many things, one of which was that one of faërie was dying.

She came down, at last, on the grimy tar and cinder roof of a building, now awash in deep puddles. Her only thought was that perhaps something terrible had happened to Poquah, but the Imir would be easy to spot up here on this roof, and it definitely was coming from on the roof rather than inside the building.

She extended her wings and followed the signal's intensity, weak even here, to its source. There was nothing evident on the roof at all, and she grew puzzled, when suddenly she heard a tiny sound from over near the roof edge. She walked over and saw the creature, so small that at first she'd taken the glow to be just reflection on a puddle.

It was the figure of a slender, athletic-looking girl, almost snow white in color but with very short blond hair. From her back extended a set of proportionately large transparent wings, like those of a dragonfly, and she had the shell-like, pointed ears of most fairy folk. She was nude, as were virtually all the flying kinds, and, Marge saw, her body gave off a weak but definite self-luminescence that seemed to pulse with regularity.

She was also perhaps four inches from head to foot.

There were many such creatures in Husaquahr, including a fair number in Mohr Jerahl, but they were usually as territorial as wood nymphs. Unless this one had stowed away on the ship coming over, there was no way to explain finding a pixie on an urban rooftop.

The tiny creature stirred, then managed to open her eyes and bring herself to a sitting position. She was instantly aware that she had company and looked up at Marge in surprise. Her voice was as tiny as she was, and, like that of all pixies, was pitched far too high for human ears, so that only the overtones could be heard as a high, ringing sound by those with good hearing, like children. Marge, of course, could hear it fine, although there were the usual city noises and the rumblings of the storms in the distance that made her bend low to catch it all.

"So what da hell are *you*?" asked the pixie, in what sounded like fluent Brooklynese. "And wud'dya starin' at, anyways?"

"I'm a Kauri. I heard your distress cry and came to help if I could."

"A *what*? Man, oh man! Dey grow deir fairies as big and mean as deir thunderstorms in dis sucking state of Texas!"

Suddenly Marge was struck by a memory chord: *with Peter Pan's glow*. . . . "Of course!" she muttered to herself. "Tinker Bell!"

"Don't give me none of dat Tinker Bell shit!" the pixie retorted angrily. "Ain't been no end of grief since dat Limey wrote dat play da foist time!"

"You're—a native of Earth, then?"

"Sure! Born 'n bred in Prospect Pock. Dat's in Brooklyn, you know."

"I would never have guessed."

"Been dere since da Limeys shot up da place. Made a mess, but we couldn't complain. Because of dat dey left it as a pock. Prob'ly da only big slice o' green left around dere."

"I've never been there, but I'm more interested in how you happened to wind up *here*."

"Yeah, well, I ain't too sure on dat, neither. Fact is, I was dumb, dat's all. I mean, dere ain't no place worth livin' outside o' Brooklyn, 'cept maybe New Yawk and dey even mug da fairies dere dese days. Dat's why most of us up and left a long time ago. Me'n a few udders, we stayed on. I mean, if you can't live in Brooklyn, why live at all?"

"But you left."

"Obviously! I din't have no choice. Dey been takin' little bits and pieces of da pock for yeahs and yeahs, and finally it just got so dere was no way to live no more. We need flowers 'n trees 'n all, and 'cause it's so urban, like, the stuff'd die no matter what *we* did 'less the city came in and helped out. So dey cut the pocks budget again and again until dere was nothin' really left 'cept for trimmin' the battle monument. Dey sent *clods* out wit' no feelin' for growin' tings, you know? Not only did dey not do da job, dey screwed the place up so much it'll take yeahs to get it goin' again. I was da last—maybe da last fairy in Brooklyn.

"Now, what was I supposed to do? Go live in *Joisy*, for cryin' out loud? So I says, 'Gimlet old goil, you either gotta get planted forever in dear old Brooklyn or make it over to da udder side somehow.' Now, dere's only six places dat even *used* to be ways over and out, you know? One's in da Swiss Alps, one's in China, one's in da Amazon, one's in da deserts of Australia, one's somewheres between da Nile 'n da Congo, and one's someplace in Texas. Maybe I got da right spot, since you're here and I don't even ever hear of your kind before, but maybe I'm wrong. That Texas accent of yours is somethin' else."

"Your accent's pretty thick itself," Marge noted.

"What accent? I ain't got no accent. You must t'ink I'm from New Yawk or maybe da Bronx. *Dey* got accents!"

"Out here, *you're* the one with the accent and you better hadn't forget it. What happened to you, anyway? Are you hurt?"

"Got a bruised wing is all. I ain't gonna be able to fly noplace for a day or two but I'll be okay. Two hundred yeahs of dodgin' storms wit' no sweat at all, and I run into dat baby here and lose my traction! It just tore me loose and spun me around and I come to here. I been t'ru almost as bad but never woist."

"Lucky it did happen, if you're not seriously hurt. I'm with a group from the other side. We're over here doing work, but one of our party can get you over there if he wants to."

"Is he one o' us?"

"Yes, but don't count on that meaning anything. Still, I have a suspicion that you're going to have to be with us a while if you're going over at all. I sense another hand bringing you to us at this time. Come on—you game for a little ride?"

The pixie looked disgustedly around the roof. "Well, I sure could use a better neighborhood."

* * *

"And now the company numbers six," Poquah noted. The Imir seemed far more relaxed than previously and much more self-confident. He even seemed slightly better disposed toward Macore, making the rest of them wonder if the little thief had slipped the elf something when they were out. "Providence will send us the seventh in due course. Then it will be up to us to finish this matter."

"I thought the Rules didn't apply here," Joe noted. "I mean, why do we need seven?"

"The Rules in general do not apply, except to us personally of course," the Imir continued. "But seven is a mystical number with some power, as you must know. Seven would be good, even if we are not limited to that number."

"It can be at the crap tables, yeah, but you can crap out with that same seven, too," the pixie added.

"Is that so unlike life?" the Imir asked.

The pixie was standing on the top of the television set eyeing Poquah critically. She wasn't used to seeing other fairy races any more than the humans of Earth were. "He looks like Leonard Nimoy," she commented.

"Too short," Marge responded in a whisper.

"I should know from short?"

It was a good point, well beyond argument. Poquah, if he heard the exchange, ignored it, but turned to the pixie. "You understand that there will be no transportation until, and unless, we complete our mission? All travels have stopped until then."

"Yeah, I get it. I ain't got nothin' better to do anyways, so I might as well string along. Besoides, if dis really is de end of de woild t'ing, what's the difference anyhow?"

"I admire practicality," the Imir commented.

Joe and Macore looked blank as they found themselves cut out of the pixie's end of the conversation. Tiana, to her surprise, discovered that she could hear the pixie, although the accent was bad enough she couldn't make a lot of sense out of the dialogue.

With all of them now present, though, Poquah thought that this was a good time for a general briefing, and they sat around Joe's room and listened to him.

"It was expected that we would eventually have to transport a number of people and equipment, and we did not wish to be dependent on motels and other such public places. As a result, we had shipped here a purchase Master Ruddygore made some time ago for his own personal convenience when in this country. It is a masterpiece of comfort and practicality and is very well disguised. It will serve not only as accommodations but as a mobile headquarters."

"This why you need a truck driver?" Joe asked him.

"Yes. I, too, am capable of driving it in a pinch, but I would rather not do so unless there is some compelling reason for it. I am comfortable with its operation but not comfortable on and around the highways of this place. It will be quite effective, with the van, in which I am much more comfortable, being used for local transport when needed."

"Why go from here, though?" Marge asked him. "I assume our destination is California."

"It is indeed. However, as the pixie told you, this is the only safe and secure landing spot in North America with an access to good roads and modern conveniences, for a variety of complex reasons not worth going into right now. Also, the truck is on record with a real interstate trucking line, and so any checks run on it will show that it is legitimate and has reason to be in the areas it will be. This is more credible if we actually make a run from some distant point.

"We will be entering a hostile area in more ways than one. The Baron already has a substantial following, including many of the wealthy and influential. Politicians and corporate presidents get as gravely ill as the common folk, after all, and as desperate. It is a mistake to think of this as a month-old operation that began with Dacaro's arrival. It is not. The Baron has been building this up for over two and a half years now, and that is a lot of time in a media-oriented society."

"I understand the dangers from the Baron and his lackeys," Tiana said, "but you seem to indicate it's not as simple as all that."

"It is not. In addition to his followers and supporters, public and private, he has been very good to a county that is economically one of the most depressed in the West since the logging boom ended. A lot of money is being dropped there—enough so that, even with his backers, he needed the gold from the Master's vaults to pay off the balance of his mortgage. He has, however, adopted a clever, even fiendish, method of assuming control. His substantial following that is on and around the land all registered to vote, and those politicians who did not accept his authority were then recalled and thrown from office, to be replaced with the Baron's people. His cult controls the political levers of the towns nearest his holdings, and some of county government as well."

"Surely he can't be *that* pervasive," Marge said disbelievingly. "I mean, maybe it's not a heavily populated county, but it hasn't been a long time, either."

"There is opposition, yes, but this technique has worked before with other religious cults and it works now. It is a flaw in the American system which can be exploited by ones with the following and resources to do so. Local governments control power, water, sewage, police, fire, and all the other services people depend on. They set the tax standards and the tax rates. An irate citizen might have his well inspected and condemned by the county, making his land worthless. There is condemnation and eminent domain. A business picketed by and not patronized by a large mass of people will fail. It is immoral, unethical, and absolutely legal. He is doing nothing that others have not accomplished before him, only he is doing it far faster and far more efficiently. The Baron does his homework well and he is brilliant and analytical. The attempt at foreclosing on him was our doing, of course, and our last legal gasp, as it were, although he'll be tied up in court for years."

Joe couldn't help smiling in admiration. "So your folks put the squeeze on him and he paid off with gold stolen from Ruddygore's own vaults. He must have loved that touch." He paused a moment. "Lord! Is this man incredible!"

The pixie, following all this, looked around the room. "And a group of bums like dose in dis room is gonna take on and beat dis guy? You're all *nuts*!"

The Imir repeated the comment verbatim for the benefit of the humans, who only nodded somewhat in agreement. Poquah, however, was not about to grant the point.

"We are not as insane as we might seem, madam," he replied. "First, the magic powers that Boquillas depends upon and which awe his followers and associates are nothing strange to us, nor are we without some such powers ourselves. Second, be reminded that Boquillas himself has great knowledge but no powers of his own—those were stripped from him. The rest around him, with one exception, are Earth psychics of limited abilities and almost no training. I could dispense with them one on one without even straining, and probably even Marge could do so if they tried anything against her. No, Dacaro is the only real threat, the only one we cannot match. Remove Dacaro and *we*, not they, have the balance of power."

"Yeah, but that's the trick, isn't it?" Joe noted. "I mean, Ruddygore could take him out, and so could most real powerful wizards, but he's blocked any of them from coming. He is, on Earth, what Ruddygore or one of the Council would be in Husaquahr. The most powerful with no real competition."

"Let us assume, for the moment, that we *could* take out Dacaro," Marge put in. "It still isn't any piece of cake. Sure, we'd have the power, assuming old gloomy here survives the battle, but there's more kinds of power than magic. What are we talking about? A hundred people? A thousand? Ten thousand?"

"I fear your last estimate is closer to the mark," Poquah told them.

"Okay—ten thousand, plus a government in his hip pocket, right? The cops with their guns, the followers with who knows what? And demons—the verse said something about demons, too. Even Ruddygore had to run from a demon and got pretty banged up in the process if I remember." She looked over at the little thief. "You've been pretty silent on this, Macore. I'd expect you to be the first one to object to all this."

The thief shrugged. "There's a plan. *He* knows most of it, I know most of it, and you all don't know any of it. It isn't perfect, but it's good, very good. Some little details we have yet to figure out, but they'll come. Look—forget Dacaro for now. Otherwise, it's the same kind of problems I face all the time as a master thief. We have to case the joint, as it were, until we know all its ins-and-outs and all its little quirks and traps. In the end, it's a puzzle, just as Ruddygore's vault was a puzzle. Before we act, I'm going to solve most of that puzzle." He looked sheepishly at Poquah. "*We* are going to solve most of that puzzle. You never get a hundred percent solution, but that's what makes a master thief different from a puzzle fan—or a dead thief. A little improvisation as you go. We're being handed the elements; we'll put 'em together. See, that was why Ruddygore was so insistent that we get to the Oracle."

"But we do not understand the messages," Tiana pointed out.

"I think we will, now that I've seen our pixie and had the rhyme explained to me, but that wasn't the point. See, what the Oracle told us was that this was a test, as Poquah said. It's not the inevitable end, just a *possible* end of the world. *The big point of the Oracle's verse was that this was a puzzle that could be solved.* I think we can do it. We've beaten the Baron twice before."

"Yeah, with Ruddygore," Joe commented sourly. "Not on our own. Seems to me that Dacaro made mincemeat of all of us all by himself."

"*No!*" said Poquah sharply. "*You* and *Marge* got the idea for escaping from the demon with the Lamp and made it happen. It was Macore who freed you from Esmerada's prisons, and Joe who managed, with Marge's help, to figure a way to escape from the Baron's prisons and contact us. It was Joe's quick thinking that ruined the Baron's takeover plans for Morikay. We have beaten the Baron before when he had full powers—and that meant the Master to finish him off. Now he is without powers even we possess. His brilliance remains, but so do the basic elements that defeated him in the past, his overconfidence and his arrogance. I have no knowledge of the future, but in the end I will wager that his personality is the key to his undoing."

"Well." Joe sighed. "You're betting all our lives on it."

"And all the lives in both this world and the other," Marge added.

CHAPTER 13

OF POWER, PRIMITIVES, AND PARTIAL PLANNING

> *If I had heard that as many devils would set on me in Worms as there are tiles on the roofs, I should nonetheless have ridden there.*
>
> —Martin Luther

THE TRUCK WAS EVERYTHING POQUAH HAD SAID IT WAS and more. Outside, it looked like any other transcontinental eighteen-wheeler, complete with a sleeper in the cab, and it was the latest in large truck technology. The ubiquitous CB radio, however, had an additional channel that was not a broadcast channel at all, but rode the power lines back from the cab to the trailer and served as an effective two-way intercom which would override any signals the radio was receiving or putting out.

Anyone who opened the back of the trailer and looked inside would see a large number of stacked cartons of nicely labeled products. Indeed, you could take down a box at random and open it and remove its contents—if you liked tacky plaster statues and pink flamingoes, that is. The truck appeared packed all the way to the back, but it was not. The effect was not created by any wizard's spell, to tip off anyone who might have the power, but by a classy stage magician's device that was purely mechanical and purely mathematics and physics, but it was convincing and effective.

One entered or left the soundproofed inner sanctum only by a concealed trapdoor with small steps that came down from the bottom or from an emergency exit reached by ladder through the top. Neither was obvious, even when staring straight at them.

Once inside, even though it was a crawl for them all to get underneath, there was an air-conditioned and effective small apartment, with a master bedroom and associated smaller bedroom with bunk beds, and a combined living and dining room area with kitchenette and minor conveniences, including a refrigerator and a microwave. Water was supplied by a tank on top and was the only thing that needed refilling at regular intervals. The power source was self-contained and apparently did not need refilling or maintenance, but it was not obvious and they did not inquire much about it. Joe guessed it was nuclear, and he really didn't want to know for sure.

The trailer had the logo of Maximillian Express on it, which was a well-known and quite standard cross-country hauler. The logo was bannerlike, gold on blue and rectangular, and proved to be an ingenious one-way mirror. Those inside could see out as if it were dark glass, but it looked like painted metal to anyone outside, even right up close—and it was high enough to discourage anyone getting that close.

All iron and steel sources had been replaced, shielded, or covered. The larder was well stocked, and everything worked. There was one addition of which Poquah was particularly proud. It was over near the smaller bedroom entrance, but had a full view of the main area. It was, in effect, a long but thin marble bathtub, although it had only an interconnection to an outside fixture for a water source.

"I realized that Tiana would have unique needs," the Imir explained. "We cannot, of course, carry that much water, but with a length of hose and the small hand-cranked pump we have aboard we can fill it from any tap or even a river, lake, or stream. It empties onto the roadway, as, I fear, does the water closet."

"I think it is wonderful!" Tiana cried, and kissed the Imir. Poquah, looking both embarrassed and uncomfortable, turned to Joe.

"Do you think you can drive it?"

"Oh, sure. It's easier than what I'm used to and that was pretty good. Give me ten miles and I'll take it down an alley with two inches clearance."

"Very well. All of the permits have been secured, and the weight has been calculated to match the manifest and be within all legal limits."

"They still on that stupid fifty-five speed limit?"

"I'm afraid so, but you have detection devices there and much of our travel will be through areas of light enforcement. Just don't get carried away. I will follow in the van, matching your speed. Communicate with me by radio only when you must, as there is no way to know who is listening. I prefer, when we are going, that one of the two ladies ride in the cab, so that there will always be reports of a male and a female up there. Anyone inside the trailer should enter or exit only when cleared to do so by the driver over the intercom. Macore will ride with me in the van, and we will share the facilities inside. Clear?"

Marge saluted. "Clear, *mon capitan*! Let us march or die!"

At approximately nine o'clock in the evening, with everything including the route and plan squared away, they left the motel for the last time and Joe pulled the rig out onto the highway.

It was far easier than the van, he found, almost as if he'd never quit driving. There was some special set of reflexes you developed as a trucker that never seemed to fade, like riding a bicycle. Through double clutching and sixteen gears, what was a complex mystery to most drivers was second nature to him.

It occurred to him that the first part of the journey was almost a ritual completion of the run he'd been on when Ruddygore had intervened, westbound late at night on I-10 heading toward El Paso—only this time he'd make it, and beyond.

He tried to determine just where that mysterious cutoff was, but he couldn't do it. This country all looked alike, even more so at night, and he was well past the point before he finally gave up. Somewhere along here, too, he was supposed to have smashed up and died in the wreck. He still didn't know if the accident had been allowed to happen, or, if not, just what had happened to his old truck.

Joe stopped once just outside El Paso while he and Macore went into a carryout place that was open all night and bought some dinner for themselves and Poquah, whose diet was not that far off from that of humans'. Inside the trailer, it was a matter of thawing, but not cooking, some fish and other such stuff for Tiana. Gimlet seemed perfectly happy gorging on some jar honey, which would last her a year at her size and weight, and Marge took only occasional fruit juices, having eaten well of the stuff only Kauris consumed and needing no more for a while.

It was, of course, pretty boring, but that was only to be expected. At least Tiana, dried out, could ride for a time with Joe, and Marge then took advantage of the view if nothing else when the mermaid grew tired or had a need for water. Gimlet had little desire to come out, even though she was able to ride almost anywhere, keeping to her instinctual requirement to stay very close to her food supply.

They made good time and Joe really enjoyed it; but, at about an hour after sunrise, he made for a truck-stop lot, pulled in a little away from any other trucks, and decided to call it a day—or night, as the case might be. Marge was already asleep, and those who ate normal food used the truck-stop restaurant. Tiana went, too, finding that she had no trouble with salads. Although cooked food didn't really appeal to her, she had decided to eat with them occasionally, just for the company. There was nothing in her constitution that prevented cooked food from going down and doing the job; it was just that she had somewhat the same reaction to it that her companions did to seeing her eat a raw fish, head and all.

Joe took advantage of the trucker's store to buy himself a new hat, not much different from the trucker's hat he'd had made for him in the days back in Husaquahr—only a bit better quality.

It was difficult for him to explain his childlike joy at sitting there at what was basically a boring and tiring job hour after hour, particularly since he, himself, hardly had such glee when he'd climbed into rigs for a living and pushed them from Nowhere to Anywhere without even really seeing or enjoying the places in between, but it was a simple thing to him. He'd been an adventurer, a warrior, and even something of a god, but always there was a dispatcher there controlling his movements and scheduling his appointments. Even though he was still on assignment, here he was, behind the wheel, with no worry about load limits or schedules or bills that had to be paid, a somewhat free knight of the road, the way all the songs said it was and the way it never was before.

They went up I-25 and then over I-40, not because it

was quicker but because, while a bit out of the way, it avoided most of the major cities and also much of the congestion. They had no problems and, from all appearances, were little noticed by anyone at all, let alone anyone hostile to them. There was something of a sweat at what Joe called *Arizona Customs and Immigration*, the inspection station where all trucks had to stop and have their permits checked and stand an agricultural inspection, but the dummy load and the rear seals helped get them through with no problems. As with customs between countries, very few trucks had their cargoes fully inspected; to do so would create a bottleneck forty miles long.

California was tougher and nastier at their inspection, even stopping all private cars, but when they opened a few of the boxes and saw the contents they were more than satisfied that no dangerous insects were lurking inside, or could stand to live with forty thousand plaster Buddhas and nine thousand lawn jockeys, which were among the more outstanding items on the cargo manifest.

They had no problems keeping Tiana's tub full and reasonably fresh, although they had traveled through mostly very dry country. There had been one thunderstorm, but she had been in the tub at the time and so it didn't matter that the land adaptation was cancelled. It wasn't this part of the ride that worried Joe. Now, however, they made a slight jog south to I-5, then proceeded due north. The Baron's holdings were in the northern part of California, above San Francisco and above the wine country, more in the land of the redwoods, but it was a marine climate, perennially shrouded in fog and mist and quite wet the year around—and particularly so in the middle of spring.

Although Ruddygore's organization on Earth was based in Europe, it had some connections and much in the way of assets in the United States. Poquah regularly phoned north to teams of private detectives employed to work with and provide much information to them before they arrived—and, hopefully, to provide backup, when and if needed.

"A tremendous amount of work is going on inside the compound," he told them. "Trucks and skilled workmen have been going in and out all the time, and the Baron has a substantial amount of free labor in his resident followers, who appear to live mostly in tent cities in clearings created by the old logging operations."

"If he only had a castle, he'd feel right at home," Joe remarked. "I mean, here are his serfs toiling for him while his heart bleeds for them."

"He has his castle—of sorts," Poquah said, pulling out a small packet of photographs. "These were taken at great risk by operatives with special equipment." The photographs showed various views of a huge old Victorian-style mansion surrounded by redwood trees and somewhat shrouded in mist. The house, nonetheless, was impressive.

"Where in hell did he find *that*?" Marge asked.

"It was there, although not in that good shape, when he bought the land two and a half years ago," the Imir replied. "There is still a great demand for redwood, but there was always money in the logging business—quite a lot if you imagine the house when new. It was built by and for one of the early California lumber barons, a man named Stockman Mills, before the turn of the century. It has, however, a tragic history. He was killed in a logging accident while out looking over his operations—by accident, it was claimed, although it was suspected that it was actually murder by a rival baron. His new bride, a San Francisco society matron, and he hadn't even moved in yet when it happened, and she never did move in, although she paid to keep the house up for many years. It was finally sold to a large lumber conglomerate who used it as a base of operations; then later it was sublet to the government for something called the Civilian Conservation Corps, I believe. It then fell into disuse and disrepair until a large number of young people discovered it in the sixties and founded a commune of some kind there."

"I think I know the type," Marge remarked.

"They seemed to have repaired the house and kept it up. Indeed, they seemed to have a good deal of money for it—enough so that eventually they attracted attention. It was found they were engaged in the growing of some narcotic or the other, and it was broken up years ago. Until the Baron purchased the land, it was boarded up and again, I assume, falling apart, but people seem to have known how to build houses in those days. We don't know its interior configuration now; but when it was built, it had a deep cellar and a total of twenty-four rooms on top. We know the Baron installed running water and indoor plumbing, but it is not connected to the county system and so must be by well and septic tank. It had no electric when the Baron purchased it, but if you see these trailers and that odd operation over to the side and in the back of the house, you'll see that he now has his own small generating station, sufficient for his needs. He may have been spoiled in the past few years, but one suspects he does not need a fully electrified home, considering his background."

"Electricity again," Macore muttered. "I like what it can do here, but I hate to see it involved in a problem. I had a hell of a time with that one electrical alarm in Ruddygore's vault."

The Imir looked up at the thief. "How, indeed, *did* you get around that one?"

"Spells are nothing but energy in a controlled field, and so is electricity. They're used, controlled, generated, transmitted, and the like in totally different ways, but they're really two sides of the same coin. I just treated the electrical current as if it were a spell and diverted it. Even *I* have enough power to do *that*."

It was obvious that Poquah had never thought of it that way—and, in fact, neither had Marge. If electricity could be treated as a particular kind of spell energy, and if spells traveled along electrical lines.... There was something there, but neither could yet see it.

The Baron had spent much time with his magical knowledge and his powerful computers. What problems had he posed to those computers, and what had the computers solved for him? What, in fact, could a mind like Boquillas come up with if, instead of laboriously having to work out each complex mathematical formula for a spell by hand, he could do so with the speed and ease of a computer?

"Now that we are getting close, there is something else I'd better tell you," the Imir added. "We are not the first party hostile to him to go to his lair, and we are not the first to wish to do him harm. Some, including some of our detectives, have become his strongest converts, particularly in the last month. Others have simply vanished."

That sobered them. Up until now, it had been something of an adventure, an exotic or nostalgic visit to new places, depending on which of the band you were. Now the fun was coming to an end. Now they were coming close to their old and treacherous foes, and, unlike the experience on the River of Dancing Gods, they could not even bluff a backup by a higher power.

"It's only three days until the full moon," Tiana reminded them. "We must make allowances for other strange powers as well."

"Oh, yes—the were business," Poquah said, nodding. "That's mostly a physical spell, I thought, yet it persists."

Joe sighed. "It's a long story, even though you heard most of it, but when I wasn't myself and the original mermaid wasn't herself I bit her, and it carried over. Since—well, I've been bitten again. Let's leave it at that." He seemed a bit embarrassed by that, and was surprised at Poquah's response.

"For our purposes, it will be a very handy thing. The Baron's followers, who call themselves the Elect, have among them two groups that are a potential nonmagical danger. One group, called the Elders, is an elite all-male security force. Most are or have been violent criminals, or combat soldiers, or law officers, and all are tough, nasty, and ruthless. They are his security force and they are quite good at what they do. The other group, the Ministering Angels, is under the command of his nominal wife and actual adept, the former Lynn Syzmanski, usually now called the Baroness by their followers."

"That's the former horror movie hostess?" Joe asked.

"Indeed. She began with pornographic movies, had aspirations to be a real star, but never made it past the late movie. A self-administered spell provided by the Baron has restored her to her youthful prime. Her Ministering Angels are her stunning supporting cast now, but don't underestimate them. Beneath their beauty, they have been given body-building and other extensive training, and have learned every deadly art, including all of the martial arts. They are many things, but to us they are deceptive and quite effective bodyguards for the top echelon. Even stark naked, it is said that they could defeat professional combat troops. I repeat: Do not underestimate them. They are designed to be underestimated—until it is too late."

"Neat system," Marge noted. "The guys guard the property and external dangers; the girls guard the people."

"Yes," the Imir agreed. "So, you see, being a were is not necessarily a liability. We have timed this well enough so that both you, Joe, and you, Tiana, will be able to do some infiltrating more effectively than anyone else. And, of course, you are impervious to anything except silver, which includes the sort of bullets they use here."

Joe nodded. "I figured as much. That saved me from the Baron once before, remember."

"Yes, I *do* remember. Only do not be complacent. Rest assured that the Baron remembers quite well, too. He expects you, and has a particular score to settle with you, so don't get too cocky. Let *him* be the one with the overconfidence."

"We'll remember," Joe assured him. "Now what's our

first move? We'll be in his backyard tomorrow night, unless you want me to keep going today."

"No, that will not be necessary. We need immediate facts and a layout. I need to know what that manor house looks like now, and I need to know what has been added or subtracted since. Tomorrow, we will split up into temporary teams. Marge, you and Gimlet can fly and both of you have exceptional night vision. You will take Gimlet with you and do a general flyover, getting an idea of the terrain and the situation within. If you are undetected and in the clear, then Gimlet is well suited actually to enter the house and check it out."

"Dis goi's a big shot wizard and you t'ink he won't know me?" The pixie sounded worried.

"He will not expect a pixie in particular. You don't reflect or trip optical alarms, and your hearing is more than adequate to avoid sonic alarms. You can see spells, even if you can't read them at his level, and avoid them. No risks—see what you can see and get back out to Marge."

"Yeah. Easy fer *you* to say, hot shot. And wudd'l *you* be doing while we got our necks stuck in it?"

"Macore and I will be checking with our operatives. Joe—you and Tiana will have a different mission. You'll be traveling a bit, and can leave early if you're up to it. We have located a long-time resident of that commune I spoke of, living just over the county line. We want to know what changes they might have made—particularly hidden areas, which would be logical for ones in their business to create."

"Yeah, I see," Macore put in, his professional thief's mind working. "They were doing something illegal and they had to be always afraid that the law would sneak up on them, so they had to think of all the ways and guard against them. They'd know the lay of the land pretty good."

"Just as interesting," Poquah responded, "is how the

law managed to get inside in spite of all that forethought and catch them with incriminating goods."

"I am a little concerned about going so far," Tiana said. "If it is as wet a climate as is indicated, I might well be unable to use the adaptation at all, or I might change at any moment."

The Imir shrugged. "Believe me, if this person even noticed it at all, she would think it an asset."

The place clearly had once been a church, in older, better times. It now was a pale shadow of itself, with paint peeling off its stucco walls and obvious gaps where parts of the exterior had split, fallen, and splintered to the ground. There was no cross atop the small steeple anymore, nor any other signs of its former life in the dingy small town that had been bypassed by all the highways and by life itself.

A hand-painted, crude sign over the entrance read: THE NEO-PRIMITIVE HAWAIIAN CHURCH.

Tiana had worn one of her overly long dresses and was using the wheelchair, although she still had her legs for now. The dampness was already creeping in, and it was only a question of time until the air struck the inner ridges of the coastal range and was lifted high enough to give up its moisture.

Joe stared blankly at the door as he helped Tiana out of the van. "Now what are we supposed to do?"

"Knock?" she suggested.

He did, but there was no response. Finally he decided just to open the door, an old wooden two-part barrier that formed an entry arch. It opened, and he helped Tiana up the steps and then back into the chair, and they went inside.

It seemed foggier inside than out, with a thick mist curling around the floor of the old structure, but the mist was definitely not of natural origin. The air was thick with an incredible mixture of incense scents as well. The whole of the interior appeared to have been cleared of pews and other structures and thickly woven straw matting had been placed over the entire floor. On all sides were enormous images of Hawaiian gods and totems, some quite realistic, others very crudely painted and decorated in garish colors. Ahead was the altar, upon which stood a gigantic and very impressive wooden carving of a Hawaiian deity, flanked by others in descending order of size and, possibly, rank. In front of the deity was a sculpted horizontal redwood platform, decorated with flowered garlands, and on it, stretched out, was the still figure of a dark-skinned female body, stark naked except for a lei and flowers in her black hair. Somewhere, from cheap speakers, Hawaiian chants came forth in a monotonous drum-accompanied performance. The needle definitely needed cleaning or changing.

Both of them were shocked and thought much the same thing. Tiana looked up at Joe. "Do you think she is a sacrifice?"

"I—I don't know."

"Joe—I'm changing. The rain must be here."

"Just sit tight. I'm going to see if she's still alive." He approached slowly, warily. He would not have been at all surprised to find a horde of Polynesian savages suddenly rise from the thick mist of the floors and attack him with spears.

He walked up to the altar and heard Tiana's wheelchair follow close, the same tenseness in her as in himself. He looked down at the girl and was relieved to see a very slight rise and fall, indicating breathing. She was certainly of Polynesian ancestry from her looks, but not as young as she'd appeared from a distance—perhaps early thirties. It was hard to tell.

He stood there a moment, wondering what to do, when her eyes opened and she looked up and saw him standing there. Suddenly she sat up and swiveled around so she was sitting, facing them, and she smiled. "Oh, hi!" she said.

Joe was so taken aback that he was at a loss for words

for a moment. Finally he managed, "Uh—I'm sorry if we disturbed you."

"Oh, you didn't disturb me. I always meditate for two hours after dinner. It helps clear the head and combats food allergies. I'm Mahalo McMahon. And you are?"

"Uh—I'm Joe Romero, and this is my wife Tiana."

The mist covered the wheelchair up to the spokes, further masking any sign of fins, already difficult to see in the eerie light of the old church.

"You folks here for the services, just passing through and got curious, or are you something else?"

"Something else," he told her.

She suddenly froze up. "We don't talk to narcs. You caused us enough trouble."

"We're not narcs. We don't care about that at all. We *are* interested if you were one of the folks who used to live at the Mills place, though."

She looked suspiciously at the two of them. "You're not wearing yellow, but I don't talk to Pathies no matter what."

"What has yellow to do with them?" Tiana asked her.

"They all wear something yellow. I don't think it means anything, just a uniform or something, you know."

They filed that one away under *useful things Poquah forgot to mention* and got on with it.

"If that's your attitude, I think we *can* be friendly. You see, we knew the Baron long ago. This isn't the first time he's tried to become powerful and subjugate lots of people."

"Lots of people don't like him, but he's got real power. If you're for real, you're not long for this world."

"We are for real," Tiana assured her. "The Baron once commanded armies with a demon as an ally, and still we defeated him. We know who and what he is and how he does what he does."

Mahalo McMahon was unconvinced. "You sound German, and you, big boy, sound like a truck driver with too much education. Where the hell could he have commanded armies? He ain't old enough to have been a Nazi."

"Not in Europe," Joe told her. "Not anyplace you've ever heard of. He's from a different place—than here. So are we."

"Yeah? Like where?"

Joe heard a noise behind him, turned, and saw that Tiana was removing her dress. When she finished, she said, "Joe—pick me up so she can see me."

He was hesitant. "You're sure?"

"Just do it."

He went down to her, not feeling good about this, as McMahon, still nude except for flowers and lei, watched in a mixture of suspicion and fascination.

Joe lifted Tiana up, and there was no mistaking what sort of creature she was. The eyes of the woman on the altar went wide, and her mouth dropped a bit.

"From a place where races like mine live," said Tiana. "From a place that took in the fairies when they were run off this world. From a place where good and evil men do battle with sorcery and with swords. Can you accept that?" Joe put her back down into the chair.

For a few moments Mahalo McMahon said nothing. Then, finally, she whispered, "Wow! Like in *Dungeons and Dragons*." She thought for a moment, then said, a little more confidently, "Okay, I believe you, at least for tonight. Tomorrow I'll decide if you got a real bad disease or if this was the best hash I ever smoked, but for now I'll believe you. All right, Conan, what do you want to know?"

Once she got into the spirit of the thing, Mahalo McMahon was a wealth of information, not only on the house and grounds but also on the True Path itself, although this information was often punctuated with digressions on just about anything.

That night she was alone in her little church, testing out what she called the atmosphere, but usually there were between half a dozen and a dozen regulars, most, like her, "forcibly removed from agriculture," and a couple who were very young and had a nostalgia thing for the days of communes. All were women, some with small children, and the church seemed to be something of a feminist commune. They'd picked it because the Hawaiian religions were generally close to nature, and also because she had read that no woman was ever sacrificed to a volcano—only men. Of course, women in the old Hawaiian culture were strictly subordinate; that was why it was the "Neo-Primitive" church. As a church with a physical building, they generally avoided taxes and had a certain freedom in what they did.

As for the Baron, she thought of him as a "creepy kind of preacher; you know, like Jim Jones used to be," but handsome and charming on TV or in the few early times before he'd sealed himself off from all but the media, which he carefully controlled. His cultist group, which perhaps numbered several thousand, was totally dedicated and quite dangerous and ruthless, but beyond his small domain, she thought he was overestimated.

"In two or three years he might be powerful enough to influence some votes in the legislature or go national, but right now, even as these things go in the West, he's strictly small potatoes," she assured them. "Now, that don't mean that he's not strong—that new preacher he's got is supposed to be dynamite—but just that his strength don't even extend to outside the county, like here. Folks around here don't like or trust him, and there's enough people and towns in *this* county that he won't find it as easy to take over."

Finally, there was some time for her to satisfy her own curiosity. "This place you come from—this somewhere else? It's like in the books, huh? Dragons and unicorns and all that?"

"Yes, all that," Tiana assured her. "But no machines, no electricity, none of the modern conveniences. It sounds romantic, but actually can be quite dull, or quite dangerous, or back-breaking work, depending on who and where you are."

"Yeah, well, ain't that just like anyplace else?" She paused a moment. "If you get by the Baron and go back, can you take passengers?"

"Not really," Joe told her. "It's not up to us or anything we control. But if anybody would like it over there, I think you might. I'll put in a good word for you, but don't get your hopes up."

That seemed to satisfy her, and they left the little church and walked into a cold, damp, misty rain. They got into the van and started off.

"Joe—I like her. She seems more of Husaquahr than of Earth."

He chuckled. "Maybe, but I'd like to see her when she's straight first. If she's ever straight."

"Uh—it is still early and it is not far to the ocean, is it?"

"About ten miles. Why?"

"If we are about to go full into the Baron's lair, I would like one chance to swim in the ocean. I do not know if I will get another chance."

"You're thinking of the 'pickled fish' line." He tried to sound casual, but he'd been thinking of it as well and he couldn't see a good outcome. "It's pretty messy out—the ocean will be choppy and the shoreline around here is pretty rough with sharp rocks and the like."

"Joe—it is this body's natural element. I will be all right."

He hesitated, weighing anxiety now versus never hearing the end of this later, and finally gave in. When they came out on US-101, he went down a bit and then took a road toward the sea.

The weather was bad enough, and his concern over Tiana real enough, that he never gave a thought that the two small headlights far in back of him might be following him.

* * *

The compound was smaller than even the smallest of landed estates in Husaquahr, but it was fairly large nevertheless. With Gimlet riding in her pouch, peering out at the terrain below, Marge did as complete a survey of the place as she could.

Poquah had certainly overestimated the number of permanent followers, at least those on the land. Although it was impossible really to tell, with the wetness driving most indoors, she doubted if more than seven or eight hundred actually lived in the tents that dotted the clearings, and certainly no more than a thousand. That was certainly bad enough, but it was no legion. In a sense, it was comforting, since it was a large enough group that most were likely strangers to one another, while it was small enough to keep track of.

There were not only guards and patrols, but spells as well on this land. She had no trouble in diverting them around her, but they clearly were effective against ordinary Earth people, causing tremendous disorientation. You could break into the place with little trouble, but you'd wander around and never find your way out again. It was clever and effective—the Elders and their dogs would certainly find you after awhile.

The great mansion looked less impressive in person than in pictures. Clearly the place needed painting, and there were still rough patches on the roof and even some broken windows just boarded up on the upper floors. This was indeed the very early stages of the Baron's plans, and what money and resources he had were obviously going into other efforts.

There were two large trailers with noisy electrical generators, one powering lights around the grounds and some remote security outposts, the other leading to the house itself. Some plumbing and other work had been done; an old outside well was now capped and had a complex of pipes leading from it into the house. Marge guessed that there were two wells, one there and one probably under the old kitchen itself, but there was no way to be sure without going in there.

It was certain that the house was a place of magic—dark, powerful magic. Both Marge and Gimlet felt it as well as saw it, and for the Kauri it was the strongest sense of pure evil since she'd come face to face with the Demon Prince Hiccarph himself. It was not a feeling the pixie was accustomed to at all, and certainly not one she enjoyed.

"You expect *me* to go in *dere*?"

"I think you'll be safe, if you're careful," Marge assured her. "I'd do it myself, but I suspect that there are defenses in there for Kauris. He knows I'll be one of those coming, and he knows me pretty well. These spells will be designed against those of Husaquahr; you're of Earth, and he won't be expecting that. If you feel anything demonic, get out of there *fast* though. Those demons won't have trouble with the Earth-born, and that's both of us."

Marge found a window high up on the third floor that had been weakly repaired and set down on a sill in front of it.

"Looks like it could be a trap for flying folks," the pixie said worriedly. "Dat opening's just big enough for somebody like me."

"That's why I think it's safe. He'll be expecting somebody more my size, and it might be rigged so if the opening were enlarged it would trigger a trap, but not otherwise. You've got power and speed and guts. Go on."

"I beg to dispute," the pixie responded worriedly, but she went to the opening and peered in.

It looked deserted, and, surprisingly, appeared to have no spells. There were bat droppings around the place, but nobody was home right at this hour. Taking a deep breath, Gimlet crawled through and inspected the room.

At first she thought it was a dead end; there seemed no way out and it was certainly unused, perhaps since the original owners, but then she found an old dumbwaiter. It effectively blocked the shaft, as, perhaps, it was intended to do, but pixies, as Marge said, had some power to compensate for their size. She flew in, then excreted a small bit of a shiny, powdery substance, and the dumbwaiter rose slowly, just enough to allow for a gap beneath.

The shaft proved to go all the way to the basement, although Gimlet was in no mood to experiment more than she had to. The doors to the dumbwaiter were all shut, of course, but since at least one had to have been opened in order to raise the little car to its blocking position on the third floor, she managed to find one, right at ground level, that slid back a bit with what little weight she could put on it. She decided to risk leaving it open for a quick getaway. The gap was small enough that it probably wouldn't be noticed anyway, and the place was drafty as it was.

Methodically, she began to explore the house.

Joe had spent some time going over the information and drawings McMahon had provided; but as the time wore on, he just settled back, listening to a country station on the radio, and began to snooze.

Suddenly he awoke with a start as both doors to the van were jerked open with force. He started to make a move, but the two men, one at each door, had pretty large guns.

"Just step out of the van and make no funny moves," the one closest to him warned. Both were dressed in dark business suits soaked through from the rain, but both also had on yellow shirts and yellow ties.

He did as instructed. "All right, boys. What's this all about? I have about twenty bucks you're welcome to but, other than that and the van, there's not much here."

The other man slid into the van and picked up the drawings and diagrams, looked them over, then stuck them in his suit coat.

"Don't be funny," the first man said. "We're not robbers, and I think you know it. Now, where's your lady friend?"

Joe gestured in the direction of the pounding surf. "Out there. She had a sudden urge for a swim."

The man struck him—hard. "Don't be funny, I said! What do you take us for, anyway?"

"I take you for the Baron's men. I take you for what he calls his Elders. A little out of your jurisdiction, aren't you?"

"Aw, skip it," said the other. "She's a cripple and won't be hard to find. Even if we don't, what's she gonna do on her own out *here*?"

Being covered by the other one, the first was cocky, and stuck his pistol almost up Joe's nose. "Listen, smart guy. We ask, you answer. If we like your answer, you might live through this. If we don't, you're gonna be pretty sore."

"I've been pretty sore before, but asking questions is free."

They didn't like his attitude, but they were here on business first. Joe longed for his old, perfect body now, which could have disarmed and made mincemeat out of both of them in a series of moves, but he decided not to risk anything until he also found out a little.

"Okay, big guy—why were you pressing that bubble-brain back there?"

"We wanted good directions to the beach and some pineapple."

The man hit him again. The other said, "You have a lot of plans about the castle here. What were you trying to do?"

"Find out all I could about your happy little heaven."

That was better. "Why?" the first one asked. "Who are you working for?"

Joe thought fast. "The Sierra Club," he told them.

That brought both of them up short. "The *Sierra* Club?"

"Your boss made a deal to get the land and keep it out of the hands of the government. Now he's moving in hordes of people, generators, lots of equipment—we think he violated his agreement. We think he's preparing to make so many changes he'll damage the land beyond repair. Since you've refused to let us in, we're getting information where we can. And that's the truth."

The first man stared past Joe to the second. "What do you think?"

"I think we ought to take him in and let the Master talk to him."

"Yeah, I—"

Joe moved with sudden swiftness against the first man. He was not in the condition that he once was, but he knew all the moves and he wasn't in bad shape. He was not about to desert Tiana and be hauled before Dacaro or Boquillas right now.

Both he and the man outside the van went down, and the gun flew into the darkness. Ignoring the man down, he turned and kicked the van door hard before the first man could react, catching his arm between the door and the post. He then flung the door open and pulled the man from the van violently, adrenaline and mental training replacing what he'd lost.

The gunman recovered, though, and was no pushover, suddenly coming to life and pushing Joe off, then launching himself on the big man. They struggled and fought for what seemed several minutes, but finally Joe seemed to prevail.

There were three sharp explosions, and Joe felt terrible, tearing pain in his back. The first man had found his pistol and had panicked. Joe cried out in agony and released his own opponent, then rolled onto the ground.

The first man helped the second man up, and they looked at Joe. "What'll we do now?"

"Get back to the castle and report. We can ditch the van on the way so his lady friend can't find it, even if she can drive."

"What about him?"

"Forget about him. Can't you see with your own eyes? He's dead."

CHAPTER 14

INTO THE DRAGON'S LAIR

. . . For I well believe
Thou wilt not utter what thou dost not know . . .
—William Shakespeare, *King Henry IV, Part I*

IT WAS A BRIGHT AND SUNNY MORNING, ATYPICALLY warm and clear for this part of the country in this season of the year. Poquah wished to take full advantage of it, but he first had to arrange for a car to be sent over by some of the detectives on retainer.

It had been well after six when one of the special trouble numbers had rung and the call had been relayed to the Imir. He knew something had happened when Joe and Marge had failed to return or call in the previous evening and he already had people out at McMahon's place checking on things. What they had discovered had not been encouraging. McMahon had apparently not returned from the church and there was no sign of her anywhere. The tape recorder was still on and the small fog machines were still hissing and overheating, although long out of the chemicals that made them go, but of the high priestess of the Neo-Primitives there was no sign.

The Imir was relieved, then, when he heard Joe's voice on the line.

"Yeah, three shots right in the back at point-blank range. Really screwed up my shirt. I'll tell you, that were stuff really paid off for me last night. Good thing they weren't using silver bullets, anyway. I figured the best thing to do was to play dead, though—the shock knocked me out for a couple of minutes, and when I came to I had the choice of lying there or killing them. I figured I was better dead. No sense in the Baron learning that somebody got up after taking those kinds of slugs. He'd know in a minute it was me."

"I agree. But why did you take so long to call?"

"Hell, Poquah! It was the middle of nowhere, and I still had to wait for Tiana, although she was nearby and saw most of it. I cleaned off as best I could, but a guy walking or hitchhiking up the road with a blood-stained back would be about as obvious as a mermaid jumping up on a pier and making a phone call. It took some time, and I still feel really conspicuous here."

"I will be down to pick you up as soon as possible."

It was about a fifty minute drive along less than perfect roads, but Poquah had no trouble finding the spot and picking Joe up by the side of the road. The Imir had brought along clean clothes, which Joe needed badly, and the big man changed while they went back to pick up Tiana. She was glad to see them, although almost reluctant to leave the sea. She alone had not suffered at all during the period.

"They didn't make us, so they must have had the church staked out," Joe told him. "What I can't figure out is why they let her loose in the first place if she was a threat to them."

"She probably wasn't," Poquah replied. "At least, they did not believe she had any information that couldn't be gleaned elsewhere. They allowed her to be bait unknowingly, I suspect, since she's an obvious source for anyone looking into the Baron's affairs. That is why her abduction now worries me. If it was just after you left, then we might weep for her but not worry very much, since they might simply have decided that she was of no further use. However, if they went *back* for her after their encounter with you, then they wanted to pump her for information on you, and, as I gather from your preliminary account, she knows quite a bit."

"It was the only way to get her to open up," Tiana explained. "It did not seem much of a risk."

"Yeah, considering she was higher than a kite at the time," Joe added.

"Most would dismiss her story, but Dacaro and the Baron will not. We must assume that they will put the Elders' account together with hers and come up with the correct assumptions. They will assume that it was you, Joe, and that means they will not assume that you are dead, and they will also now assume that Marge is here as well. We must accelerate our timetable, even though the evidence shows that the Baron is not yet as strong as we believed. There is not only increasing danger to us, but also the danger that he will accelerate whatever plans he has in operation. I want you both to get a good night's sleep because you'll have to be ready to go while it's still light. Tonight is the first night of the full moon; if we lose it, we lose one opportunity."

"So you want us to go in tonight?"

"Yes. This will be an exploratory foray at ground level, but it may give us the last few pieces of the puzzle. Late this afternoon, if the weather holds, I'd like to go into town and pick some likely prospects. I spotted the van, off the road a few miles ahead. But since it will be recognized now, we'll leave it and stick to this car. We can always pick it up later, if we need it."

"The demonic force behind all this resides below," Poquah told them in a briefing before they were to go into town. "Gimlet and even Marge felt it and knew that it was there, although it does seem somewhat under control by the proper spells and restrictions. Do not underestimate it."

"Still only one demon, though," Tiana remarked. "Can it be Hiccarph again?"

"It is doubtful. The demotion seemed plain, and they

wouldn't trust a known blunderer and insubordinate on an Earth project. It will be one of the majors, though—count on that. We will have to find some way to deal with it. I am still not clear why they need it this close to the Earthly plane of existence. Dacaro has more than enough power for this sort of operation." He thought a moment. "Unless Dacaro himself is being prepared merely as a conduit through which the demonic power can flow. Yes, that must be it, but what could the Baron have dreamed up that would require that much raw power?"

"Great, so we got a demon in the cellar—" Joe began, but Poquah cut him off.

"No, beneath the cellar and not quite in this plane of reality, but real enough."

"So, all right, that gives us still more of a blank. Did Gimlet get down to the cellar at all?"

"No, the tremendous force of evil made her quite naturally too afraid to do so. The first floor, however, has been redone so that there is a single long room along the left side, here, terminating in a standard altar and having a few hundred folding chairs. This is obviously the chapel where they conduct services for the locals. On the other side, there is a large and comfortably furnished reception room and in back of that is the kitchen. On the second floor is a suite of offices, still in the unfinished stages, used by Dacaro and the Baroness, and also headquarters and quarters for the chief Elders and the heads of the Ministering Angels. The third floor is only partially used, apparently as communal quarters for more of the enforcement personnel, and is partly sealed off. The fourth floor is boarded up and not used at all."

"Hmmm..." Tiana studied the drawings made from Gimlet's observations. "So where are the Baron's offices?"

"In the cellar, we must assume. The Baron and Baroness use the master bedroom on the second floor, while Dacaro is currently sleeping in a small area behind the altar downstairs until they finish up his own complex. The exterior is well patrolled by the Elders; the interior has a Ministering Angel or two in each of the rooms. Gimlet says that all of the Angels are totally enslaved by spells, and are specifically assigned to a task—a room, a person, and so on. The Elders have more freedom and individuality and less clearly defined tasks, but are no less bound. She also states that there is a lot of equipment of various sorts piled up all over the place, and that technicians seem to be working there day and night. Just what's up, though, is unclear, although I have some suspicions. Come. Let's go into town."

"Aren't you afraid they'll recognize me?" Joe asked him.

"It is unlikely that those Elders will be around, and I wouldn't worry about them in any event. The Baron, if he doesn't already know, will know soon enough."

The day remained fairly clear and warm, giving Tiana some help, and the three drove the car from the old industry siding where the truck was parked and into the town.

It was in fact a quite attractive little place, not very large but with all the requisites—a general store, a small café, a couple of tiny old churches, a sheriff's office—but no jail—a gas station, a tiny branch bank, a Wards catalog store, and nine places selling redwood burl. There were mostly pickups parked diagonally up and down the lone main street, but not a lot of people or traffic. The place looked unnaturally, antiseptically clean, though, and, while the people they did see were all dressed pretty normally for this place and the time of the year, almost all of them seemed to have something yellow on—a shirt, a skirt, or perhaps a kerchief. Even Joe, Tiana, and Poquah wore yellow shirts this time; in Stockman Mills, even those who weren't members of the True Path found it better to show solidarity.

It looked peaceful, orderly, and friendly enough, but there was something intangible in the air that they could nonetheless all feel.

"You can almost smell the fear," Tiana remarked.

Poquah nodded. "It is a strong stench, like being in one of the towns after the Baron's soldiers had taken it."

"But—can't all those legitimate religious figures smell it, too?" Joe asked him. "I mean, here was Dacaro guest-preaching on some guy's TV show a few days ago, and you tell me he's gotten support."

"People see what they wish to see," the Imir responded. "In just recent Earth history, we find Hitler the social reformer, Pol Pot the democratic liberator of Cambodia, and Khomeni the democratic liberal. In this very state, they hailed the Reverend Jones as a liberal reformer and even appointed him to government office. Humans are very much oriented to the surface, rather than what is within, both here and back home."

"But he can't fool all of the people all of the time," Joe noted. "Eventually he has to come out into the open."

"Perhaps. Probably. They all did, didn't they? But how much innocent blood was spilled to stop the cancers that should have been obvious? How many dead, maimed, and ruined in Husaquahr to block the Baron's visions of social reform? That is why we must stop him here and now, while the toll is still relatively small."

The plans and the passwords were set. Tonight, a few more people would attend the services.

Shortly after dark, Marge joined them. She had no need for transformations and disguises, being well able to manufacture her own. In fact, she just wanted to test things out a bit while it was easier to escape, and went into the general store on the pretext of buying a small can of orange juice. She used pretty much the same appearance she'd worn back in Texas, but without makeup and wearing plain-looking clothes. It was an easy, natural illusion to maintain, although she decided to forgo glasses as a follower of a faith healer.

"Peace be unto you, sister," said the young, clean-cut-looking man behind the counter who was dressed all in yellow.

"And to you, brother," she responded, having been

briefed on the conventions they used. There weren't many; the Baron wanted loyalty and he really didn't want to work at a wholesale transformation of individual personalities—yet. She got the juice, gave him some coins, and, smiling, left the store. It was both easy—and disturbing. There had been a small TV camera of the kind usual in store security on them at all times, and, since no one had challenged her, they were going to have a real problem if and when they reviewed that tape, for she'd neither show up on it visually or vocally. Of course, the store would also be eighty cents short for the day. Her money was as illusory as her appearance.

She would have to avoid close interaction with others where such cameras were likely to be, and alter her appearance and clothing each time. She walked down the street, smiling and nodding to those she met, and walked past the small church at one end of town. It was unusual for a town this small to have two churches, although they both were clearly closed, possibly from lack of interest. The one church, an old Protestant one, was being fixed up, possibly to handle overflow, but this one was left vacant, although it did look cared for. The old, weathered sign out front read: ST. DIONYSIUS ROMAN CATHOLIC CHURCH.

Curious, she walked up the path and saw someone tending to what appeared to be a small garden on the side of the tiny church building. He was humming a tune and seemed to be in fairly good spirits, although it was rather odd to be tending a garden after dark, all things considered. He was dressed all in black; for a moment she wasn't certain he wasn't some kind of specter, a trap of the Baron's. This was, after all, enemy territory in spades.

The man heard her, or sensed something, turned, looked over at her, and an expression of total amazement was on his face. It was a kindly face, with rimless glasses, rosy cheeks, and blue eyes. He was perhaps fifty, graying, and looking far more weathered than his years. He was also, by his dress and collar, a priest, and by his manner and his odor, quite drunk.

"Faith! What sort of fairy vision is this?" he managed, using a not very authentic-sounding Irish brogue.

She was certain that her illusory powers were on and fully working, so she decided he was just being pleasant. "You are a priest? Here?"

"Aye, that I am. And what, pray tell, might you be, all orange and with crimson wings?"

That settled it! *The man could see through her disguise!* For some reason, her illusory projection, which could fool whole cities, had no effect on this man. "You can see me with wings?"

"Aye, sure I can! Are ya some demon from the heathens yonder come to close me down at last?"

"I'm no demon, Father. They are my enemies as much as yours."

He stood up and waved the trowel. "Then let's have at the beggars!"

She tried to quiet him and finally managed it. "It won't work—that way. This evil is the kind you preach about, and that your liberal theologians claim doesn't even exist."

He sank back down and sat on the grass. "Used to preach about, you mean. Hasn't been anybody come to these services in months." He sighed, and tears welled up in his eyes. "It never was much of a congregation, understand—just twenty or thirty people—but adequate for an old man who couldn't get along in the big city churches after bein' an army chaplain for twenty-five years." He reached into his coat for a flask, opened it, took a good slug, then carefully recapped it and put it back. "Now there's none that come, even for baptism. He took the whole of the Church of the Woods on the other side of town, too, including Bob Moody, the pastor."

"I'm surprised he didn't come directly for you. A Catholic priest on his side would have been something interesting."

"No. He wants no deaths, not even accidents, around

here. It might attract attention. He hoped that, without a church, my superiors would simply declare this and me a loss and send me away, but I've no place to go and no place to stay except here, and I have my army pension, so I'm officially retired anyway. He can't have me, for I know him for what he is and who he represents, and he wants me nowhere near his little compound." He hiccupped and then looked sheepish, but continued. "You see, his master knows I've performed exorcisms." He sighed, and took another slug from the flask. "I don't know why I stay, but that's just the way it's been. Too old or too stubborn, I guess."

She was certainly interested now, even though the man was becoming increasingly drunk. She doubted if he could stand up right now, yet, oddly, the more he drank the less accent he had and his conversation remained lucid.

Exorcisms! Few even in his own church, let alone others, still believed in it at all. If he had not only a belief in demons but knowledge of how to control or send them back, that was in itself magic of a very high art. It was too bad he was so pickled now that he was starting to lean to one side. Clearly it wouldn't be more than a few minutes before he passed out completely. She thought he was out cold now, but suddenly he perked up.

"It's my fate to be ground into the ground here and now," he wailed, stifling a sob. "Do you know what my name is? Francis Xavier O'Grady. I had it legally changed because I was in awe of Barry Fitzgerald." He raised the flask unsteadily. "Here's to old Barry, the greatest priest of all times!"

"Then you're not really Irish?"

"No, actually I was born Casimir Wyczalek. In those days, in Boston, you didn't have priests named Casimir Wyczalek, and nobody would confess to a priest whose name they could neither spell nor pronounce. So I had it legally changed—and they went and elected a Polish Pope!" He broke down in deep sobs.

"Uh—Father, about those exorcisms. Were they real?"

He stopped for a moment and nodded. "Indeed. Otherwise I would never have tried, in spite of all those Georgetown psychiatrists saying as how it was because their mothers talked mean to them when they were still in the womb. But devils can be controlled. Their power is limited, lass, to those who fear or worship them. With the right words and the right symbols and with God's power, they can be stopped." He tried to get up, but couldn't quite manage it. She went over and offered him a hand, although she was far shorter and much slighter than he.

He took it, but did not rise. "Such a strange hand," he said, marveling. "There is an unnatural warmth and power in you. I can feel it, but I do not feel the evil such power usually accompanies. Are you an angel, then?"

"I'm no angel, but I am of the fairy folk. The Baron is a man of great evil who came from our world to this when he failed there. We—what is that little pin in your lapel?" It was a strange, abstract design of some gold or gold-plated material.

"Why, 'tis the fish, the ancient symbol of Christianity. Surely you should know that."

She felt an eerie shock, the same sort of shock she felt when she'd discovered the injured Gimlet on the Midland rooftop.

While the demons are stopped by a pickled fish. . . .

"I must go now," she told him. "Will you be all right?"

"Aye, I'll be fine, don't worry. As fine as you can be when you're alone in the seat of Hell on Earth."

"You are not alone, Father," she told him. "In fact, some time tomorrow you can expect a visit from other friends."

The True Path leaders didn't want the identifying marks too attractive or too distinctive; the believers should seem just average-looking people going up to the services. Ordinary nonbelievers who tried to walk in were caught by the spell; that had been what had frustrated the detectives. Still, none of the believers had spells themselves, or at least not spells of any similarity not otherwise accounted for, so the way through the spell had to be physical. If so, Joe and Tiana, as weres, were home free. Marge would not go in as a parishioner, but would instead join the throng after flying over the barrier.

The true faithful donned yellow robes before going in, which was handy, since a were transformation didn't include clothing and might have been embarrassing. There was no way to time the change accurately, and no sure way that Joe and Marge would keep together without merely changing into each other, which wouldn't have been much help, so they just donned the robes Poquah had procured and then joined the throng near sunset. Although they had a password system, neither expected to be with or know the other until it was all over; inside, they would be strictly on their own.

Joe tried to angle himself so he stood along the side of the path near where a couple of men roughly his size were talking, but he knew the folly of trying to get what he wanted at random on a curse like this from bitter experience. The men, it turned out, were waiting for their wives, and Joe found himself, not for the first time, turned into a woman by virtue of perhaps three seconds and five inches. He didn't mind that so much—he'd had it happen often enough he almost expected it—but the woman had been a good five inches shorter than he, and now the robe, which had been deliberately tailored a bit short on him, was baggy and dragged on the ground. She was also fat and not at all in good physical shape, which made the long trek into the compound and up to the mansion a real effort. He had no trouble in distancing himself from the real person whose body he now perfectly imitated.

It grew damp and chilly in these parts at night, too, and most people had on their clothes and shoes under their robes. Because of the problems involved, he found himself barefoot and wearing only the robe, and that only increased his misery.

Still, he made it, and found himself in a sea of yellow. The grounds in front of the house had been fully lighted by the perimeter lamps, and the big front porch was also all bright. Before the front door was a lectern, and on either side of the porch and on slim poles in the back were loudspeakers. It was clearly the only way these people could be accommodated.

Whatever the physical mark was that got you in, it was on the body, for he'd had no problems. Now he just took a position about halfway back and waited for it all to begin. For such a large throng, there was little or no talking and much meditation. He liked it that way, boring as it was. He didn't want to have to get friendly with anyone and make any slips here.

Finally the front door opened and a darkly handsome man in a yellow suit walked out, flanked by four beautiful yellow-robed women: his Ministering Angels. Even here he wasn't taking any chances.

Dacaro appeared very sleek and very Earth modern, but otherwise he hadn't changed a bit. He looked out at the crowd and seemed to smile cockily at the power represented there. Then, after a moment, he began to speak.

"Peace be unto you, my brothers and sisters following the True Path." His voice was the same silky, mellow voice it had been so long before, but his English was flawless and about as devoid of accent as any could get. He might have been from Kansas or Nebraska.

"And to you and all the Lord's works," responded the crowd reverently.

"Brothers and sisters, we meet here tonight at a crucial turning point in our divine mission," he continued. "You are the leaders who will not only see the great revolution we will make, but will lead it and guide it in our Lord's name." His voice began rising now, and he took on a really good preacher's tone.

"You have seen the hand of the Lord in how far we've

come in so short a time. Less than three years ago we were unheard of. Then the Master came, with the power of the Lord in his hands and mind, and walked among many of you and healed you of what science could not. He cured your cancers, made sick hearts healthy, and even regrew and restored limbs that had been severed from you, or made useless. This was his *sign* to you, and those of you who understood came to him to serve! Together, we have built this place. Together, we are building the capital of a new tomorrow for ourselves and our children and our children's children!"

There were many spontaneous "Amens" and other such comments from the crowd.

"Together, we will reform this wicked land, where the rich live off the sweat of the poor and consider unemployment of nine percent to be just fine and ten percent below the poverty level to be *acceptable*. Where none can walk down the streets of a major city at night without fear, and probably not without being mugged or raped or shot. Our courts are courts of law but seldom of justice. In much of our land the color of your skin or the nation of your ancestry determines what job you can get or who you can marry or where you can live. The conservative churches preach that affluence is divine will and poverty is punishment, and want to limit even more any freedom of action. The liberal churches fund faroff violent revolutions and argue whether God and the devil really exist."

His voice dropped again to a conversational tone. "And so we must play by the old rules. We must pretend to be like them, self-righteous hypocrites who, like the ancient Pharisees, are so sure of their own infallability that they allow no freedom, allow no divergence from their views, and build million-dollar temples, not to God, but to themselves, while the evils of the world proliferate.

"Well, we're going to put a stop to that.

"If affluence is the mark of divine will, we must first be affluent. I know the sacrifices that you all have made—that we all have made—to come this far, but we can only give so much. They smile and they chuckle at us and they call us a 'cult'—just another crazy California cult. But two nights from tonight, at about this time, right here on this porch, we will show them who is on God's side. Most of the equipment is already installed. Tomorrow we will work like beavers to establish the rest. It has cost almost all of our resources, but it won't matter.

"Two nights from tonight, over there to one side, will sit a trailer with a giant electronic dish. And from that dish, what goes on here will be beamed to twenty million homes across the country, live by satellite. The Blessed Art Thou network, which reaches all those homes, has reacted to our persecutions by granting us four solid hours. Those four hours will revolutionize the world! At the end of that time, we shall have our money and we shall be, in one sweep, a national force and movement!" His voice began to rise once more. "The power of *God* through me will reach out through that dish and flow into space and down into the living rooms of America. All who see shall become in one night our sisters and brothers.

"And it is only the beginning! Within months, we will have our own channel, available free and live to all, and broadcasting continuously. We will sweep this nation—and we will sweep the old clean, and with the new we will then bring the entire world to the glories of God's true kingdom!"

There was much joy and applause at this. Joe joined in, secretly wondering just what in the world the man was talking about. He'd seen the religious channels now and again. Sometimes they were interesting, sometimes dull, but they hardly had the kind of effect Dacaro was not only talking about but basically guaranteeing. Money, sure—put some slick show-business personalities on for an hour's telethon to buy cough medicine for giraffes with sore throats and you'd haul in a million bucks. But real conversions? A national movement in one night? What the hell was he talking about?

The services went on for another two hours, sometimes

with Dacaro, sometimes with others, including the Baroness herself, looking very much the radiant porn queen she once had been, despite the unflattering robe.

The theology seemed remarkably bland in some ways. Not once was Christ, or Allah, or any other specific deity even mentioned, only God or the Lord and the Devil, of course. The believers here were the holy people, the ones chosen by God to cleanse and sweep the nation and the world. Anything done in the name of the True Path was holy, including, although this was never spelled out, lying, cheating, stealing, or anything else. *Even murder*, Joe thought, remembering the previous night.

Anything done with, or between, the Elect, as they were called, was holy as well. Apparently this included sex of any kind, since "the Lord's beautiful gift of animal nature" was alluded to. It certainly wasn't the kind of message that would make the Blessed Art Thou network donate four hours of its time, but this was the Elect speaking to the Elect from a very secure area. It certainly wasn't the message Dacaro preached as a guest on the show Macore had caught, nor was it likely to be the message he broadcast two nights hence. This was the real stuff.

The Baron did not put in an appearance and apparently rarely did so. He was, however, the One True Prophet of God, sent by God to Earth to remove all of the old false, mistaken, and perverted messages that came before, and give the true will of God to the world. A return to the Garden of Eden was promised, and to imitate Eden was the goal of them all; for, once they joined the Elect, all their past sins were forgiven and even original sin was washed away.

It was still not any different at its core from a thousand other California—and other—cults, and Joe couldn't see how it could do much better than the more successful of the rest. Many had become quite large, quite rich, and even respectable, but none had ever really attained the kind of power Dacaro was talking about. It was easy to dismiss his promises on that alone, if it hadn't been for the fact that Dacaro was a master sorcerer, backed and supported by the greatest mind in sorcery of two worlds.

Dacaro had been right about one thing—they'd come very far very fast. It was hard to believe that it was only a Lunar month since the man who now made these bold claims had been a prisoner in a magic Lamp in Ruddygore's vaults and had never heard of television and satellites and even business suits.

Many remained after the service, but Joe, damp and cold, decided to leave with the early crowd. He felt a great deal of relief at not tripping over his own robe, and even more when he exited the compound perimeter without challenge. There was still the chance that someone might mistake him for the woman he'd twinned, and he wanted security and safety, if at all possible, and quickly.

Almost at the town, he hung back a bit, then went off into the woods toward the prearranged but out-of-the-way meeting place. It had been decided to rendezvous there to be met by Poquah and taken to transportation, rather than risk a pickup in town, just in case one of them ran into trouble.

Joe was the first to arrive, and had enough time to begin to worry that perhaps the others had indeed run into trouble. Finally there was a crackling in the brush, and he took refuge behind a tree.

"Forty gross of pink flamingos," whispered an unfamiliar voice. He sighed and whispered back, "Thirty-six gross of Buddhas with clock in stomach," and stepped out.

"Oh, nuts, it's a woman again," said the unfamiliar newcomer. She was small, slightly built, certainly no more than fourteen or fifteen, and her robe was much too big.

"Yeah, what else? Murphy's Law—whatever can go wrong will go wrong. I assume that's you, Ti?"

"Yes, it's me. You know, it's nice to have secure legs and no pain, but I'd really forgotten what it was like to feel the damp and chill."

More sounds, another newcomer, and this one had a

robe that fitted. Still, the passwords were exchanged and Marge relaxed and became her Kauri self once more.

She eagerly told them about her encounter with Father O'Grady, and hoped that it meant what she thought it did. Tiana seemed slightly disappointed to discover that she really didn't figure in the rhyme at all, but it was still heartening to find the elements coming together.

"Well, as Macore says, we now have the puzzle in place," Marge noted. "The trick is to solve it in just the right order."

"That is less a trick than it seems," Poquah said, suddenly appearing in the midst of them and making them all jump. He had one hell of a power when he cared to use it.

"Damn! Don't *do* that!" Joe gulped, catching his breath. "I assume you heard Marge's story?"

"Indeed, yes. A practiced demonologist improbably and implausibly set down in our midst, just when we need one. This is the hand that Providence has now specifically provided us. Come—let us go back to the trailer and compare notes on tonight. Perhaps, with the help of our thief, we can now assemble our plan and perhaps understand theirs."

Macore listened with intense concentration as each of the three told what he or she had seen and heard and about Father O'Grady as well. Then he thought long and hard and made notes in a small notebook he'd bought, occasionally asking esoteric-sounding questions on things like computers and television transmissions.

Finally he said, "Okay, I think I got what they're going to try. Let me float it past you and see if there's anything fundamentally wrong with my thinking."

"Shoot," Joe invited him.

"Okay, now as I understand it, we've got a demonic presence, at least Hiccarph grade, plugged into the house. Right? And we've got a world-class sorcerer in Dacaro sort of as a bridge between the demon and audience. Now remember my trick with the electric gadget in Ruddygore's vault? Put them together and it's obvious."

"I'm afraid it is not obvious to me," Tiana told him, and the others nodded.

He sighed. "You're real suckers, you know that? You gotta think like *them* to get inside them. Okay, at its heart, its lowest common denominator, what's a spell? Energy, right?"

"I'm with you so far," Marge said. "Go on."

"So where does the energy for a spell come from? It doesn't come from nowhere—it comes from the energy that's all around us. Heat, light, you name it. We convert a tiny part of that into another form, like that microwave oven over there or the TV. We do it by sheer will, by a talent or power we're born with to varying degrees, and they do it with transformers and all that other mechanical stuff, but it's all the same in the end. Now, you undo a spell basically by converting the spell energy back into its original form. Got me?"

"You make it sound so simple," Tiana said acidly.

"Well, no matter, that's what happens. You want a doctor's thesis or something with three syllables or less? Okay, now this might not be a hundred percent right, or even close, but it's as right as what I just said about spells. This television thing. It takes light energy from what's reflected off its source and turns it into some other kind of energy in the camera. Then it's sent in little jiggles to this sender, which changes it again and shoots it up to this man-made moon. Am I right so far?"

"An oversimplification, but, yes," Poquah agreed.

"So, it gets bounced back down to any receiver that's tuned to it, changed back into its previous form, then back into the form before that, and finally, in the TV, changes back to light that hits the viewer. Never mind if that's really right, the point is energy at the source is transformed just like a spell and directed by machines until it not only hits someplace else but can be infinitely duplicated—and exactly duplicated—at every receiver and finally at every TV that turns to that channel. Don't you see that's what he's gonna do? *He's gonna broadcast a spell that'll take on anybody who tunes in, even for a minute!*"

"It's not possible," Poquah objected. "For one thing, the energy is quite weak when received, compared to what is transmitted."

"Oh, yeah? But the signal, the mathematics of energy, is still complete and intact. So how do they get it back to strength for all those TVs?"

"They—they amplify it at the receiver and again at the set," Poquah responded, and for the first time he seemed to betray some emotion. "Good heavens! It's so insane it just might work!"

"It's going to have to be a pretty simple spell," Marge noted, "if he's going to get them in the middle of changing channels."

"Two spells, then, overlaid," Tiana suggested. "One so brief that it might take hold in a single second and have but a single command—stop and watch. And a second, a long and complex spell that would deliver those viewers to the Baron's hands. An instant conversion which might also compel them to call in. Once identified, the Elect would be sent out to give them all the instructions, theology, and orders. If what Macore suggests is really possible, they could even get follow-up spells one by one over the telephone."

Joe shivered, although he now felt warm and dry. "So that's where he gets his figure. All those cable viewers switching around randomly during the four-hour time slot; hit 'em for a second and you got them. Maybe not twenty million, but over a million sure, maybe lots more. Lots of money immediately, the conversions of family members and friends later—maybe even by just calling them to the phone. Wow! It's a hell of a plot!"

"But such a spell would have to take into account line fluctuations, differing power levels, and means of transforming the energy, all sorts of things," Poquah noted, trying to find a way to prove they were wrong. "A spell that could automatically adjust to that would be so infinitely complex that no human mind could grasp the figures, let alone play with them to get it right."

"Computers," Joe reminded him. "First Boquillas learned computers. *Then* he researched cults. I bet he had the idea from the first time he ever watched TV back in the first days in Switzerland. He studied computers, knowing that only they could do this kind of math—and even then he'd have to program them himself. They don't come with Wizardcalc."

"He must have worked it all out with his usual mathematical precision," Marge added. "He came here because this place is most tolerant of religions and most tolerant even of aberrant ones. You said he traveled through the south, where the most famous television preachers are located, then came here and got a job in the computer industry. That must have given him a computer big and powerful enough to solve his final problems."

"Yeah, but he couldn't practice the spells. He got his local power, the Satanist, but he needed more. He needed Dacaro and he needed to block Ruddygore to make it all work, so he went to his old allies in Hell to get their cooperation. I'm sure he wasn't any too popular down there, but this plan probably knocked their little demonic socks off," Joe agreed. "They were the bridge between home and here. Hell decided on this Master of the Dead and got him all the best magic spells in exchange for a little help—never mind what it's for, old boy—it doesn't concern Husaquahr, only Earth. You can *have* Husaquahr. It would never even cross his mind that, if they take Earth, it means the final battle and the end of both worlds."

"So now we have it," the Imir said cautiously. "The total picture. We know exactly what they are going to do, and how, and when, and even where. We now also have all the elements of our own puzzle guide—the Oracle's rhyme—in place. We will talk to this priest tomorrow when he's sobered up—if he *ever* sobers up. Macore?"

"Marge? Or Gimlet? What about this porch? Is it solid or does it have a crawlspace underneath?" the thief asked.

Marge looked at the pixie, who shrugged.

"Joe—didn't your Hawaiian priestess say something about trapdoors rigged in the porch?"

"Uh—yeah. Come to think of it, she did. I'd forgotten."

"All right, then. I've got a potential solution to the puzzle, but it's gonna be pretty damned hard on some folks, I'm afraid."

They all leaned eagerly forward. "What is it?"

"I can't tell you. Even when it's happening, I can't tell you, because it's possible, even likely, that it will require some of you to get caught. Poquah, I'll need a way around that barrier spell."

"That is not too difficult. It will be even easier if we can examine both of our were friends here while still weres and find the point of commonality."

It turned out that the only thing the two bodies seemed to have in common that could not be explained as normal was a small polyp inside the left armpit. Poquah was satisfied. "Behold the sign of the true Elect," he told them. "A very nice touch. Who would notice?" He turned to Macore. "It is not even truly sorcerous in nature, only in origin. It will be rather simple to give you one, even right now."

"Okay, then do it," Macore said. "Tomorrow, I'm going to have to ask you to erase any knowledge or memory of my very existence in this world from Joe and Tiana's minds."

"Huh? Why?" Joe wanted to know.

"I told you—no clues. If they catch you, the less they know the better. As for why not do the same to the fairy folk, it's because their minds can't be as easily dissected by Pathies as yours, and also because it's damned near impossible to do on you all without it being noticed, or am I wrong?"

"That is correct," Poquah agreed.

"Wait a minute," Tiana put in. "Do you mean that only you will know this plan in full? And if anything happens to you, the plan fails?"

"No. Poquah already knows the added elements you don't, although I'm gonna have to explain it all to him to show him how it puts itself together. I think he'll deal quickly with any fairy folk to avoid any chance of them using their power against him. Why not? He only needs to keep you all on ice until he broadcasts and then it won't make any difference."

"You are certain you can get in there?" the Imir asked him.

"Why not? I got into Ruddygore's vaults. Compared to that, this is a piece of cake."

"You are sure this will work?" Marge asked worriedly.

"Of course not. Nothing's ever a hundred percent. But it all fits in and clicks with the people we have and the rhyme we got, not to mention the other information we've acquired. I do, however, have one backup, if it all falls down. It's not a sure thing, either, and it's sure not part of the Oracle's script; but since I got the idea from Dacaro, it should work."

"From *Dacaro*!" Marge exclaimed.

"Yeah, but don't worry about it. I doubt if I'll need it. The important thing is this—you're all gonna have specific jobs to do. Every one of you. They'll all be dangerous, but so will mine. I usually work solo, but the Baron's expecting a mob and some specific characters as well, and we have to provide them. Sorry about that, but that's why some of you might get caught. If so, don't worry what happens to you, so long as you don't go and get yourselves killed. Given a choice, surrender. Either we'll bail you out or it won't matter anyway."

"Sounds like a cheery thought," Marge noted. "Still, you don't think they don't know about the porch and the trapdoors, do you, Macore? I mean, they'll probably have people under there and run the dogs through and everything."

"Yeah, they probably will, on Monday night. But I won't be there on Monday night." He clapped his hands together in anticipation. "We'll all start this tomorrow night," he told them, then looked over at the pixie. "Gimlet, old goil, I don't even understand the contraption, but can you type?"

CHAPTER 15

ONE HELL OF A MESS

It did not last: the Devil howling, "Ho!
Let Einstein be!" restored the status quo.
—Sir John Collings Squire

"YOU REMEMBER NOTHING OF LAST NIGHT, FATHER?" Joe asked, a little frustrated and wondering whether he, the priest, or Marge was crazy.

"No, I'm afraid I—well, I was in no shape to remember things last night, I fear. It's the pressure of all this going on around me."

The priest that Joe and Poquah faced was quite a different sort of person from the one Marge chanced on the previous evening. He was tall, military in his bearing, and quite cold sober.

"You're not Irish, though, in spite of your name?"

The priest sighed. "No, I'm not, although I don't know how you know that. It was one of the stupider things I did in my youth. I'm afraid that I've always had a taste for the grape, or worse, but I never could really handle it. I was on the wagon for years, went through AA, and was a fine example—until this business happened here."

"We are here, we hope, to end this business, Father," Poquah said. "If what we've heard is true, we may need your help to do so. We have battled this evil man before and won when all others had been defeated. We know him and respect, rather than fear him—but this is our gravest challenge."

"What do you need done, then?"

"You have, we understand, performed exorcisms?"

The priest sighed. "Yes. Unfortunately, those were mostly in my off-the-wagon days. I have some memory of the subjects, but little memory of the actual exorcisms. Those for whom I performed them seemed comforted and pleased."

It was becoming increasingly clear to both of them that Father O'Grady was really two people, one drunk and one sober. The drunk saw Fairies as they were and had at least one foot in the supernatural world, while the sober one was the coldly rational and somewhat distant intellectual they faced.

"Tell me, Father—do you believe in the Devil?" Joe asked. "I mean it, I'm not just kidding around."

The priest thought a moment. "Yes, son, I believe in the Devil and in Hell. I've been partly there. I was in Vietnam for quite a long time, and I was later in Beirut. I've also stood in the preserved remains of concentration camps in Germany, where you can still feel the evil. I believe that God exists and I have come face-to-face with evil, and so I have no choice but to believe in the Devil as well."

Joe nodded. "The Devil's here, Father—and not in an abstract sense. He's over there, in that compound, in that old house."

"The Baron has opened a pathway between Hell and the house," the Imir added. "It is there and it is real and tangible. He draws his power from it. The Baron and

Dacaro are evil men. Dacaro has more sheer temporal power than the Baron, but it is the Baron's intellect and will which guide him. Something monstrous is going to be loosed tomorrow night. We are going to attempt to stop it from happening, even at the cost of our lives. We will attempt it with or without you, but we need your help, your expertise."

"But you can't even get in!"

"We can get in—any time we wish. The trick isn't getting in, it's accomplishing what we must accomplish. The Baron fears us so much that the Elders attempted to kill my companion here the other night, using pistols. It may require violent action, even killing some of them, but it must be done."

Oddly, the priest seemed more fascinated than put off by this. It was very clear that he was so afraid of the True Path and so disgusted with it that he would leap at striking a blow against it, and his combat experience certainly didn't hurt. Chaplains didn't fight, but bullets never respected their rank or position.

"Assuming we could get in at all, what would you have me do? You're not talking about some demented man who is, or thinks he is, possessed by spirits. I admit I'm having trouble even accepting the idea, but you are saying that there is a demon, evil incarnate, in there. That's not an exorcism."

"It isn't exorcism that we need," the Imir told him, "nor could it be very effective in any case. Somewhere in the cellar of that old house is the gateway, the way through. We need to get into that cellar, which also contains the Baron's offices, find that gateway, and seal it shut. Cut it off or contain it. Even Hell is constrained by laws and agreements that it made. But it will take no simple pentagram drawn in chalk. There is too much power there for that."

Father O'Grady thought for a moment. "What is needed, then, is a Seal of Solomon. It resembles the Star of David, but in addition has various legends and symbols written in the created triangles. Activated by the proper liturgy, it is supposed to prevail against the Devil himself."

"Then that's what we must do. Seal it off. Once sealed, how much trouble would it be to undo it?" Poquah asked him.

"I've never done any of this, but I've read up on it. If properly done, it could not be broken from either side. That gateway would be closed, the Seal set within the very Earth itself and guarded by the power of God. Even broken or erased, it would exist."

"Then that is what we need. I'm not minimizing the risks for the impossibility of the task, though, Father. We may well have to fight our way in there. We may face forces beyond our control. And, if we *do* make it and locate the place and even seal it, we may not be able to get back out again, for it will do nothing to those, some with power themselves, who will be after us."

"Are you trying to talk me out of it?" The priest sighed. "You realize, gentlemen, that you would be thrown out of here or be taken out to the nearest asylum under normal circumstances. Had I not seen this power of evil you speak about in operation here, I would not even have given you the time of day. They've left me here as a poor, old, retired drunk of a priest, not only to be a permanent bad example, but also because they felt I would eventually pack up and leave. I'm angry and I'm frustrated. I haven't felt this way since I stood in front of the Marines' demolished barracks in Beirut and helped them haul out the bodies of more than two hundred fine young men. When you meet and look into the eyes of fanatical young men who are perfectly willing to drive a truck full of explosives into a place and detonate it, even though they, too, will die, all because some so-called religious leader, for his own ends, told them God wanted them to do so, and you turn around, in your own small, peaceful village here in the United States, and see the same look and the same devotion on those who once were your friends and neighbors . . ." He paused a moment, trying to force down his fury.

Finally he said, "Gentlemen, I still think this is madness, but perhaps even my death or disappearance will cause some ripples elsewhere. I have no family, my friends are my enemies, and I have no future. Perhaps I am driven by this to be as deluded as that fanatic who drove that truck into the barracks. And yet—I will go with you. I must believe that God has placed me here for some reason, in this situation. When do we go?"

"Tonight, Father," Joe told him. "That's when you'll also get a few new lessons in the supernatural."

The little church seemed the ideal place to meet at sundown, and Joe and Poquah left and went back to their car. Both were preoccupied with the coming night's work and got in without even thinking about it. Suddenly they froze as someone's head came up in the back seat, and both whirled and halted themselves only at the last moment.

"Mahalo McMahon!" Joe exclaimed. "What the *hell* is *this*?"

She was still wearing the flowers and the lei and nothing else.

"Hi ya, Conan! Geez, I'm sorry I scared you like that, but there didn't seem to be any other way. They're all over the place."

Joe looked at Poquah, who checked her out for spells. She had one, but it wasn't in the nature of a controlling threat. She was definitely not working involuntarily for the Baron, although that didn't mean she wasn't working for him freely.

Poquah started the car, and they drove off, not toward the trailer but just around, while they evaluated what she said. Poquah had the power to know truth from fiction.

"It was real late, y'know, long after you left. I got some more of that good stuff out and started to refill the pipe when they suddenly came busting in the front door. I mean, geez, I was alone in there! Luckily I got lots of exits out of there, since you never know who or what's gonna come around to maybe bust you. I rolled back and hit the trip that dropped me under the altar and really put me under the church, you know what I mean? Well, I'm scared to move, like maybe they got the whole place surrounded, you know? So I wait there and I hear 'em walking all over and like that; finally I hear this woman's voice say, 'We could be here all night in this cold and rain,' and this guy's voice says, 'Yeah, but she can't get away.' So she says, 'We don't have time to waste on turning over every slab in this joint. Put a watch on her house and her friends and let's go.' And then she pauses and adds, 'Mahalo McMahon, I am the Baroness de Boquillas! If you are within the sound of my voice, *as you are now, so will you remain*, until you come to me along the True Path.' And all of a sudden I get kind of tingly, you know, and then I hear 'em leave."

She'd huddled there under the church for hours, then managed to sneak out, avoiding the two men set to watch the place, but she was cold and stark naked. Her house and the houses of her friends were all covered—she spotted the watchers, but there was no way around them—and so she'd spent a cold and miserable night in an old woodshed. In the morning, she had the idea to steal some wash off somebody's line so she could at least get out of there—a sari from a sheet or something—and she had the opportunity, but she could not do it.

"I mean, like, it's *creepy*, but I can't stand the thought of putting anything *on*. Nothin' but these flowers, anyway. I got to admit I never much liked wearing any more clothes than I had to, but this is different. The idea of putting something on is like—well, like the idea of eating shit or something."

"It is a conditional curse," Poquah told her. "The Baroness is the Baroness because she has some power and the intellect to use it. If she had been patient and well practiced, she would have searched for something containing your body cells and summoned you to appear, but they don't seem to be that concerned with you. Lacking that and the power of a Dacaro, she could only cast a simple, elemental curse. You would either have to live as a wild animal, be locked up in an institution for compulsive nudity, or come to her. You appear to have come to the same conclusion yourself."

"Yeah, well, what else could I do? I mean, I'm *starving* I don't know how those deer and bears do it. So, anyway, this morning they loaded up this pickup with crates of apples and oranges and stuff like that, and I saw that the guy driving was one of *them*, so I managed to sneak into the back of the truck, figuring I could eat on them. He got in and drove off up here, so I ate a few apples and had to kind of tag along for the ride. When he stopped for the stop sign back there, just before coming into town here, I jumped out and ran for the woods. I was just trying to figure out what to do next when I saw you two drive up, and I recognized Conan, here, so I figure, what the hell, I'll try for something and I sneaked into the back of the car and that's it." She paused a moment. "You know, it's funny. These flowers are still fresh, too. Should'a dried out yesterday."

"She's telling the truth," Poquah told Joe, turning the car around and heading back toward the trailer.

"Yeah, but what are we going to do with her?"

"I've given her spell a cursory once-over, and I find it very much the Baron's trademark in these things. It's simple, but it would take a great deal of time for me to undo. Conditionals, in particular, usually have bad little traps for those undoing them. No problem, if I had two or three hours to spare, but I do not."

"Hey! You can't leave me stuck like this!" she protested.

"All in good time. Stuck for a while, that's all. Get her into the trailer. I'll drive up and park the car, then work back down to you."

Tiana was the only one awake there when they got in,

and was startled to see the self-styled Neo-Primitive Hawaiian priestess and equally fascinated by her story. As for McMahon, she wasted no time in going through much of the fruits and vegetables she could find, although she did not touch meat. Only then was she relaxed enough to look over and really appreciate the hideout in plain sight, and she was impressed.

It took Poquah a good half hour to return, but this was mostly because he wanted no signs around the trailer that it just wasn't parked there until needed. Nobody ever looked twice at trailers like this, which was the beauty of the thing, although lots of cars parked around it would certainly draw immediate attention.

"We will be active tonight," Poquah told them, when at last he felt safe enough to enter, "but we cannot fully spring our trap until tomorrow, almost at the last moment. You will just have to trust that Master Ruddygore has mapped this out and knows what he is doing."

"He has always come through in the end for us," Tiana noted.

"Yeah—after getting us in trouble in the first place," Joe grumped.

"This is the second night of the full moon," the Imir reminded them. "Now that we know how to bypass their security spells, we don't require one of them for you two. We can arrange our own pattern to our advantage."

"Sounds good to me," Joe noted.

"Anybody mind telling me what you're talking about?" Mahalo put in.

"Our part of the operation tonight is to sneak into the Baron's compound, seal off the doorway to Hell he's created, and then do what damage we can to him, his transmission equipment—anything. Getting in is no problem. Getting to the objective will be a terrible problem. Getting out—well, we must depend on others to allow that."

"It's a bigger organization than it looks," Joe explained to the newcomer. "A lot more than just us here." Actually, he had only Poquah's word for that, but he felt pretty certain it was true. "Each of us has a job to do."

Mahalo looked at them and frowned. "Now, wait a minute. You, Spock, are the only guy here who can cure me of this curse, right? And you're going in *there* tonight?"

"Yes. You can remain here until it is finished. It is safe here, and if anything happens to us, you will be looked after by others."

"And can these others lift this thing?"

"No. But they'll eventually be able to get in touch with someone who can."

"Uh-uh. I'm not going to stay cooped up in here and then have a lot of strange guys have me at their mercy. If you go, I go."

"I'm afraid there is no real provision in the plans for you. Besides, it is likely we will get caught, even if we succeed."

"Then you need me all the more. I know that house. I lived there for six years. There's passages, entrances, and exits in there I bet even the Baron hasn't found yet." She paused a moment. "Hey, look—you guys think you're gonna *win*, right? I mean, caught or not, if it all comes together, the Baron's finished? The cavalry can march in and rescue the widows and orphans?"

"I believe I understand your question. Yes. The most important thing to do is to get the mission accomplished tonight. That may get us killed, or it may not. If we succeed, the next most important thing is not to get killed, even if it means surrendering. Once our missions are accomplished, it's up to others to see it through."

"Okay. I'll take care of the not-getting-killed part. You take care of the job. Just make sure the cavalry remembers *this* captive when it comes, huh?" She frowned and stared at Poquah for a moment, then reached out and pushed back his hair on one side. "You got real weird ears. I knew there was something funny about you. You some kind of warrior elf or something?"

"Why, yes, in fact I am. How did you know that?"

"Geez, I'm not *ignorant*! I read Tolkien twelve times!"

Father O'Grady was sober, and therefore not quite prepared for the assembled crew. He also, it seemed, could not penetrate Marge's illusion as a sober man, but she could drop the illusion for him. He crossed himself when he saw his first Kauri without a haze of booze, but he was certainly convinced. He wore one of his black suits, but he'd removed the white collar and also added lamp black to his face and hands. He had been in hostile territory before and he knew his business.

A little more unsettling for him than seeing a Kauri was seeing Mahalo McMahon, undressed as she was. The only thing more unsettling than one Mahalo McMahon was *two* Mahalo McMahons, which is what they got. It had not been intentional, but at sundown Mahalo, inside the trailer, had been a fraction closer to Tiana than the woman detective Poquah had arranged for. Tiana was not completely put off by the turn of events; McMahon was in superior physical condition, it seemed, in spite of all the junk she smoked. If anything, it was Mahalo who was a bit taken aback by the change, which suddenly gave her a near twin sister. The flowers, of course, had not duplicated, but the curse had, until sunup at least. Tiana was forcibly as naked as Mahalo.

This time, Joe had been luckier. The man he'd duplicated was about his size and build and in fine shape. He was also a black man; Poquah had thought it convenient for a night operation, as he needed no lamp black at all.

Although unclothed, both Mahalo and Tiana could carry guns, and Poquah gave them small but deadly hand guns. McMahon was a bit nervous about it, but she decided to take it anyway. Tiana was just as bad a shot, but felt better with some reassurance. Joe, outfitted in camouflage fatigues, carried a semiautomatic rifle and, in a sheath, the great sword Irving, which hummed softly in anticipation of battle. It had been a long time. Poquah preferred the dagger and the short sword. His job was more to counter or cast spells than to fight; if he needed to, he wanted it to be fast and quiet, with no iron in the weapons.

Gimlet, it seemed, was involved in another operation entirely complementing theirs, and had vanished. Marge would fly lookout for them until they entered, then hang loose to create diversions when needed outside the place. Mahalo was the guide; Joe and Tiana were to guard against physical threats, and Poquah against those of sorcery. Once O'Grady sealed the opening, they would try and find the Baron, if they could, or get out fast, if they could not. A small force of agents paid for the purpose waited, heavily armed and ready, on the opposite side of the holdings, but were not to try anything until they either heard shots from the mansion or got the go-ahead from Marge. If the Baron was upstairs in his bed, and all were fast asleep, he would be beyond Joe's reach, and so there was no sense in waking him, Dacaro, or the followers in the tents if it could be avoided.

As they were set to go in, Joe looked over at Tiana and whispered, "You remember all that stuff I said about being bored and wanting adventure? If I ever say anything like that again, drive a silver stake through my heart or something." She smiled, kissed him, and they were off.

Mahalo brought them to the house by a route so complex they couldn't even follow it, but it seemed to be one designed by somebody—an escape route, it appeared, well planned, only enacted in reverse. Because of its use of the terrain and even a couple of small streams, it was quite effective in masking their movements and always providing both cover and a measure of isolation from the settled areas. It was a good route; so good, in fact, that when an informer had given it to the narcs in exchange for probation later, the narcs had used it quite effectively to sneak up on and surround the house.

There were heavy patrols, usually with Dobermans, but the dogs could not be let loose except under the tight control of their Elder masters, since Dobermans had real trouble figuring out friend from foe and were color blind. Several times men with dogs came quite close to them, but, with Marge's warnings from above and a few very casual little spells from Poquah, they seemed either to lose interest or charge off, pulling their masters in other directions.

Joe and the others finally emerged about twenty feet from the house, but then they were stopped for a while. There were nasty-looking guards everywhere, all armed with weapons and looking very much like soldiers on guard duty. The floodlights, too, remained on, leaving any approach to the house open, well lighted, and within sight of a guard or patrol.

Poquah seemed more concerned for some reason that there was the sound of dogs underneath the front porch, and a clear indication that they were just about living there. He dismissed that worry almost immediately. Any thief who couldn't get around mere vicious guard dogs wouldn't have lasted long anyway.

"Wait here. I will be back," the Imir instructed them, and pulled his dagger. He seemed to vanish, worrying both O'Grady and Mahalo.

"Where'd he go?" she whispered to Joe.

"He's like that. Just hold on."

They waited tensely for several minutes, and then the warrior elf was back in their midst. "Of the three secret entrances you describe, they have found two of them," he told McMahon. "The third is well concealed, but may or may not open, and probably not without noise. The generators should mask it for most, but there are two Elders there whom we cannot get around. Forgive me, Father, but I haven't time to freeze them, solve their own spells, or turn them into toads. Joe—we need silence on this. You come with me. I'll need you to get rid of the bodies."

It was over very quickly. From nowhere, the Imir appeared and with perfect timing cut one's throat using his short sword. When the other turned around and froze for a moment before giving the alarm, he, too, suddenly had a blade in his throat. Joe came out, keeping low, and quickly dragged the bodies into the brush. Using magic, Poquah was able to undo the two bolts that held the small panel on from inside, and he slid it away. It did creak, but no one came running, so the generators had done their masking job.

Now, quickly, at Marge's commands from the treetops just above, they darted one by one across the open space to the rectangular hole, a tight squeeze for all except Poquah. Joe brought up the rear, and got stuck for a moment. They pulled him in finally, just as a birdlike song carried a warning that someone was coming. Poquah reached back up and pulled the plate on, securing it again by the bolts. It would be an unlikely means of exit, once the guards were found missing.

They all wound up in a small area not much better than a crawlspace, but one no one would have expected was there. McMahon had explained that her friends had actually built up the floor in what was then the dining room above so that this passage could exist. There were no entrances from above; it was assumed that these would not be very practical in a raid, anyway. It led to an opening behind the woodpile in the cellar, which was just where they wanted to be.

They could feel the evil presence in the crawlway. Even Joe and Mahalo, who had no real power, seemed to sense it; to O'Grady, it was nearly overpowering. The priest had almost had a sense of being in a dream through all this, of being a detached third party who didn't quite believe what he was saying or doing, or even if he was doing God's work. Now, though, in the presence of that terrible power, all doubts fled. This was indeed the enemy, the same enemy he had felt in war, the same enemy he had felt standing in the center of Buchenwald, the same enemy whose presence nearly overpowered him at the ruins of the Marines' compound in Beirut. There was no longer any doubt. *Oh, Jesus, Mary, and Joseph. God the Father,*

God the Son, God the Holy Spirit, be with me and make me up to this task!

Poquah pushed out the panel as best he could and cautiously peered out. This part of the cellar, this room, was lighted with but a single bare bulb, but it was sufficient. It appeared to be used as a storeroom, with all sorts of junk around. There was no spell inside the room, but there was one, a good one, on the door. Poquah let them all come out, quietly, while he studied the spell and prepared to disengage it. He had expected it; in fact, looking at the spell, he had expected worse.

Still, it took him about twenty minutes to get it off, twenty minutes in which almost certainly the guards had been discovered missing, and perhaps their bodies found. There would be, most certainly, an alert all over the place, but that was also expected. The plan had been entirely directed at getting them in, and it had done so. Getting them out was left to improvisation—with, it was hoped, a little divertive help from their friends outside.

Once the spell was off the door, they cautiously opened it. It led into a main chamber that was rather well lighted, although by a combination of fluorescent lights rigged up overhead and some quite nonelectrical, large, free-standing candles. It was clear what the room was for, and there was no guessing the spot in the center.

The old stone floor had been carefully cleaned and scrubbed, and then, on top, an elaborate set of painted signs and symbols had been laid in some sort of shiny gold substance. The whole design was flanked by a pentagram painted in a solid white that seemed raised, as if to distance it from the stone; at each point of the pentagram there was a huge and ornate free-standing candlestick with an enormous candle, lighted and burning. It was an awesome and frightening sight, and one that left no doubt that it was the source of the evil of this place.

"No one, but no one, is to break that pentagram or touch those candles," Poquah warned. "Any breach, and the demon will be free to come out—and nothing can save us. Father?"

The priest suddenly felt the urge for a very strong drink—no, a *lot* of very strong drinks. He had been under fire, had shrapnel wounds, and had gone through a lot, but this was the first time he was scared before, rather than after, the danger. Still, shaking like a leaf, he removed a small box of children's colored chalk and began to draw an elaborate design on the floor outside of the pentagram. When he was through, he looked at it and shook his head. "It's crude, and there's barely enough room in here to get the entire pentagram inside the center of the Seal of Solomon."

"We'll use builder's line, then," Poquah told him, reaching into his small pack. The line was thick and prechalked, and when laid out straight—using pieces of junk as weights and the crude Seal, which at the moment looked exactly like a Star of David, two triangles superimposed, one upside down—was a general guide to clear the candlesticks. It still didn't look impressive, but it was correct. The angles were all equal and the sides were straight. With red chalk, the priest then drew in various characters in what might have been Hebrew along each inner wall of the design.

Something went *click*! in back of them, and they all turned. What had appeared a solid stone wall now was shown to be an impressive mirrorlike device that perfectly reflected the wall to its right and did not appear to reflect any inhabitants in the room. With lighting now on in back of the mirror, the rest of the room became clear.

"That is very impressive," remarked Dacaro. "Don't you agree, Baron?"

"I do indeed," replied a familiar voice. "Oh, please don't move! I see you all bringing up your weapons. The shield is quite bullet proof, I assure you, where we stand. If you look to the left and the right of us, you will see figures with weapons of their own, and they will shoot without thinking, I fear, at any sign of hostile action. Their bullets have an iron and silver content, I might mention, so please don't try anything. They are *quite* expensive and difficult to come by."

Joe looked at Poquah, who shrugged. "What can we do?"

"Drop all your weapons where they are and line up against that far wall there," Dacaro ordered them. "Quickly, please. And don't disturb the candles or the pentagram. It would be unpleasant for us, but even worse for you and the whole world if anything did, as I'm sure you understand."

They did as instructed, feeling helpless and frustrated. Joe, hands up and standing next to Father O'Grady, whispered out of the corner of his mouth, "Can't you say your liturgy now? You drew the damned thing."

"No. There's one symbol missing. They let us get this close just to toy with us."

"Now, don't think of anything rash," Dacaro told them. "There are only two exits—this way and the way you came in. I assure you that the way you came isn't much use anymore."

"You *did* know about that entrance," Joe said accusingly. "You left it deliberately untouched so we'd be sure to take it!"

"Very astute. We figured what the game was when we saw you talking with O'Grady, and that seemed the easiest solution. We were curious to see if it could be done, and, if so, how. The Seal is quite impressive. It will make effective blackmail against our friend down there when he decides to get too ambitious. As you might expect, we are not totally in accord with his aims," the Baron said calmly. "Now, we are sliding back a portion of the panel near you. Poquah—you first. Ah. Now you, Father. Yes, that's fine. And now the two lovely ladies, one after the other. And, last but not least, you, Joe."

Joe did as instructed and found that merely being "covered" wasn't the word for it. The room on the other side of the mirror of illusion, which Poquah had not detected, since it was a variation of an illusionist's apparatus and not magical in the real sense, was fully as large as the other. Covering them with semiautomatic rifles were five of the most beautiful women he had ever seen, all wearing high-heeled leather boots, gold tassels hanging from a chainlike belt hung on their hips, and not much else. Each rifle was on a different one of them. By the way the women held them and the looks on their faces, there was no question that they would shoot and shoot straight, if given even the slightest provocation.

The Baron wore slippers and a pair of lounging pajamas; Dacaro had on a pair of jeans, a flannel shirt, and regular slip-on moccasins.

Esmilio Boquillas was still the same, the sort of man who continued to improve in attractiveness and magnetism as he grew older. He looked tan and fit, despite spending little apparent time outdoors, and much as Joe remembered him. "You haven't changed a lot, Baron," he noted.

"Why, thank you, Joe. You have changed, certainly. I assume this is a convenient form you took for this operation. And the ladies—I assume that one of these is the lovely Tiana and the one with the flowers in her hair is Mahalo McMahon. I am quite impressed, Ms. McMahon. We had dismissed you as a drug-brained airhead. No, no, Poquah! Don't pull that vanishing act on us! Your friends will die immediately, and it won't work on us anyway."

"You are still very sharp for one who was stripped of his powers," the Imir noted coldly.

"There is an almost infinite variety of kinds of power, Poquah. I was stripped of only one of them."

"Do you want to call me out, Imir?" Dacaro asked, almost taunting the elf. "Want to go head-to-head down here after they've gone upstairs?"

"It is quite tempting," Poquah admitted, "but I perceive us as being close to equal in power and experience, and you have the advantage of the Baron's newest spells. I assume that the Lamp would never have permitted me through if I were able to be even your equal. Such a duel is pointless."

Dacaro grinned, but Joe thought he detected some sign of relief behind that confident exterior. The only time the old adept had ever faced power head-to-head that Joe knew of, he'd run—back into the Lamp. "Seems to me that fellow you left behind in Husaquahr would have been a better overall wizard for you, Baron," he said dryly. Dacaro gave him a withering stare, but the Baron held him back.

"That's probably true overall, but unfortunately Sugasto wasn't in the Lamp, which was the only way to get anyone here and block pursuit."

"Sugasto! So *that's* why he seemed so familiar!" Joe remembered Sugasto, briefly. The ancient adept who'd stolen the Lamp more than a thousand years ago and had wound up imprisoned in it for all that time by his own greed. "The last I remember of Sugasto, he was stuck in the body of a horse going downriver with Dacaro."

"He managed to make himself known to me. He was in intensive training at my northern retreat as one of my adepts when we had our unfortunate defeat. He's quite talented, though, and very ambitious—as you'd expect from spending a thousand years among the djinn. Dacaro, though, is good enough, and he's bound by the Lamp to my service."

"It wouldn't matter about the wish, Baron," Dacaro assured him. "What more could I want than I'm getting now? And I could never come up with those spells or this whole plan. You know that."

"Yes, I do, Dacaro. However, it is getting very late and we have a busy time tomorrow, as you might all know. I hadn't known who exactly would appear, although I certainly expected Joe and Poquah, so we'll have to put off any final arrangements until tomorrow. We have prepared a secure set of storage areas for you all until then."

Poquah was led off with Dacaro and his beautiful but deadly Ministering Angel, and placed in an iron cage suspended from the cellar ceiling. He had some immunity to iron, but being suspended completely enclosed and surrounded by it made him weak as a kitten.

No matter what the obvious differences, the Baron was not about to be fooled by any were tricks again, so he ordered both Mahalo McMahons and Joe, who was stripped naked as were the others not already nude, imprisoned together in what appeared to be some kind of a large vault. Everything in it had been moved out, but its walls were sheer metal. There was a small ventilation area near the top, but it wasn't even large enough for a pixie to get through. It wouldn't kill them, but, weres or not, Joe and Tiana weren't about to escape from the thing.

That left O'Grady, who was feeling frustrated and humiliated, standing there stark naked and covered by beautiful women with nasty rifles. "Take him upstairs and lock him in a secure room," the Baron ordered. "And—give him three or four bottles from the liquor cabinet. Our friendly lush will take himself out of the game, I think."

"I'm still a little uneasy," Dacaro noted. "That Kauri's got to be around someplace, and she's got real power until dawn."

"So what? Why do you think I made certain that all the household guards were women? Kauris have no power over women, and they have no power over you or me, thanks to our own protective spells. I expect she's hovering about right outside now, or perhaps perched atop the building." He suddenly brightened. "Why, yes! I believe we can come up with a spell for that." He walked back, past the iron cage and the vault. In his small office, he switched on the light. He sat down in his office chair and turned on his computer, then played with it for about five minutes. Dacaro saw a lot of numbers, then watched as the screen transformed itself into a multicolored pattern of enormous complexity. "There!" said the Baron. "Think you can cast that on the house in a couple of minutes?"

"Yeah, I think so, but I don't understand it."

"If she is either on the house or touches it while this

is in force, she'll stick to it like glue. She and no one else—it's attuned to Kauris only, and she's probably the only one on Earth. Do it and then go to bed. Tomorrow is a big day, and some time this morning we'll pick her stuck and comatose body off the house and take care of her, too."

"I'll do it, but I still smell something else going on. Even if they had that seal in place, they wouldn't have stopped us, just slowed us down. And I'll bet you a fortune that only the fairy folk in this mob know what else is going on—and we can't selectively drag it out of them before they die."

"I know. We'll have to be on alert, but cast that spell first—now. It will give us one less thing to worry about, and we can deal with the rest comfortably, knowing it's our only problem."

Joe and the two women had had a miserable night, but they managed to drift into sleep off and on, huddled together for warmth in the cold and antiseptic vault. They were even more miserable when they awoke, however, hungry, thirsty, stiff, and, as Mahalo pointed out, with no place to go to the bathroom.

Joe began to suspect they'd been forgotten, but finally the vault door opened and both Dacaro and the Baron were there, looking very dapper in suits, ties, and patent leather shoes. With them was a tall and strikingly beautiful blond bombshell, dressed quite well but not too revealingly. Joe guessed that she would change later, hooking on sex appeal those that Dacaro couldn't.

"Good afternoon," the Baron said cheerfully. "May I introduce the Baroness de Boquillas?"

Joe had the sudden urge to rush them, but he knew it was futile. Dacaro had the power to stop him with a wave of the hand, and behind them were the Ministering Angels, now wearing nice powder blue robes but otherwise just as well armed and determined. He remembered Poquah's command that they were to stay alive at any cost and hope that whatever was being worked by others was going to save them.

Boquillas pointed to Mahalo McMahon. "That one is yours, my dear. I'm sure we can make her into a wonderful Ministering Angel."

The woman smiled evilly and beckoned to the Polynesian to come out. "Perhaps so. If not, we can always give her as a gift to old fang-mouth in there," the Baroness said. "Come." It was said simply, but there was no question that it had the force of a spell behind it from Mahalo's look and her instant obedience.

The Baron snapped his fingers, and two Ministering Angels appeared with handcuffs and leggings. "I had these prepared a week or two ago, just in case," Boquillas told Joe and Tiana. "They are ordinary, but are silver-plated. I would not suggest struggling in them, because they will cause permanent damage, even to you."

Dacaro took them and fastened the cuffs on behind their backs, then snapped on the leg irons, which were essentially handcuffs for the feet. Even the handcuffs were really manacles, with a few inches of chain—enough to allow some movement, but hardly very much. Neither of them was likely to hit anyone or run very fast, that was for sure.

Joe looked up at the iron cage and saw it was empty. "What did you do with Poquah?"

Dacaro grinned. "Wish I could take you up and show you the upstairs entrance hall. Got two beautiful marble statues up there, facing each other. One's a nude of an elf warrior, the other's a beautiful female winged fairy creature. Got 'em cheap, too."

Joe struggled in his rage but to no avail. Finally he calmed down. "So you got Marge, too, huh? So where's the souls?"

"For all the good it will do you, the only thing Dacaro had available were two of Father O'Grady's used whiskey bottles," the wizard said, chuckling.

"How can one man be so despicable?" Tiana wanted to know.

The Baron looked at Joe. "Follow me into my little office, Joe. I wish to speak with you alone for a moment." He saw the alarm on Dacaro and the Angels, but quieted them. "It's all right. Tiana's out here with you, and he's quite encumbered. Come."

With some difficulty, Joe managed to follow him, then stood there while the Baron closed the door. Joe just stared at him for a moment. "Just what kind of a creature are you, anyway, Baron? How can a man be so charmingly evil without showing signs of total insanity?"

"I appreciate the vote of confidence in my sanity," Boquillas replied, sitting on a corner of his desk. "You see, Joe, all my life has been devoted to mathematics. It sounds dull and ridiculous, but it's really the most practical of all things because *everything* is mathematics. Not just spells, not just dry and abstract formulae, but real. You are mathematics, Joe, and so am I. The beauty of a leaf, the falling rain—all mathematics. That's how spells work—by altering the mathematics in some way to achieve a new balance. The more I studied, the more I looked at the world, the more I realized that there was but a single great random factor that kept human society from also being mathematically balanced. Human societies—all of them—were somehow structured in a nonlogical, nonmathematical way. *That's* the true punishment of original sin, you see. Eve, in perfection, was not perfect. She made a single irrational, illogical decision, and Adam went along with it. Don't you see, Joe? This all-wise, all-knowing, all-powerful, omnipotent Creator *blew* it. Adam and Eve were both imperfect from the start, yet they were regarded as perfect creations.

"And that, of course, was Satan's point of view. Either the Creator intended perfection and failed, or he wanted all this misery to happen and is therefore punishing human beings for no reason at all except his own perverse pleasure. He created Satan and the others, too, don't forget.

It is a terrifying vision to a mathematician, yet the conclusion is inescapable on the face of it. *The Creator is insane!* We have a root random variable at the core of our being that comes from that insanity."

"Ever think your problem was in thinking of Him as human, as natural? That maybe He's so far beyond anything we can comprehend that He's beyond our understanding at all?"

"I considered it, but it is actually an irrelevant point. What isn't mathematically balanced is insanity. Such a being is, therefore, insane, and I refuse to be a party to serving one who is not the heart of all logic and mathematics."

"And the Devil is?"

"Well, the Devil's got his own problems, I admit, considering the record; but taking the long view, Satan's fight is my fight because he is battling the Creator, and for the same reasons. Look at this world! I thought ours was bad, but it pales by comparison to the Creator's chosen and personally created own! The world is a madhouse in which the bulk of the population at any time is in slavery or subjugation, starving or in other miseries, and Hell is allowed to run roughshod while all the good and saintly of this world are killed. A world that worships martyrdom above all else, that equates good with dying for a good cause, is a world that is so mad it is unbelievable. Out of this, I have the means to create a single, worldwide, mathematically balanced society. I have the tools. I might well fail; if I do, the world will be destroyed. But if that happens, it will be because it *deserves* to happen. Better to end it than to bring into being generations yet to be born to suffer all the more!"

"I'm no priest, Baron, or theologian. I can't give you the answers, if there are the kind of answers either of us will understand. All I understand is that, by the prophecies of the Oracle of Mylox, your plan will lead to Armageddon, unless it is stopped, and I think these people should have the right to blow themselves up without your interference."

Esmilio Boquillas smiled wanly. "Joe, what can I do with you? I like you, but you and I will always be enemies. Marge and Poquah are in two whiskey bottles on my bedroom mantel. On Tuesday our drunken priest may go his own way—I'll even have some of his superiors under my control. He is headed for the madhouse and we both know it. He is no threat. But you are a threat. Something watches over you, Joe. Something protects you. I can't put my hand on it or find it, but it's true. All the others, including Tiana, I can handle, but you always seem somehow to slip out of every total and absolute trap that is laid and cross me up."

"What do you plan to do with Tiana?"

"I will remove her from that odd mermaid's body that Sugasto somehow stuck her with and place her soul in the body of one of the Angels. That will rid me of the were curse, and restore the undisciplined power that the mermaid condition suppresses. She will be under my control, but a good mate for Dacaro."

"You mean your surrogate and life insurance. You don't trust Dacaro, once this is too far along, anymore than I would. She's stronger than he is—if she's fed the spells."

"Exactly. But, you see, Joe, I can't do the same for you. No matter where I stuck your soul, somehow it would go wrong for me. If I transformed you into a monkey or a toad and removed all your memory, it would somehow be brought back. I stab you through the heart, my men shoot you three times in the back with a .44 Magnum, and here you stand, healthy as a horse. You were even a horse yourself once, and that didn't stop you."

"So if you're going to kill me, let's get it over with. One of those silver bullets ought to do it."

"That would be quick, easy, and relatively painless. I'll certainly give you that option. Quick and painless, or very drawn out and very ugly. It is your choice."

"What the hell are you talking about?"

"Dacaro rightly pointed out that your actions wouldn't stop us, just badly inconvenience us. There's something else afoot, something more serious and permanent going on, and I want to know what it is. I want the text of what the Oracle told you, and I want to know your interpretation. You know what I'm doing here. Somehow, you've all figured it out. I want to know what counters are being taken by others."

Joe chuckled. "I don't know them, Baron. They wouldn't tell me or Ti and you understand why. A wave of Dacaro's hand and I'd spill my guts. What little I did know was erased by a spell so complicated it would be tomorrow morning before you could solve it and then dismantle it."

"I don't have any proof of that, Joe. All right—we'll go the hard way."

It proved to be a big cellar. Joe was suspended in a small room with a high ceiling, the chain of his hand manacles secured by iron bolts to an overhead beam, so he dangled in the air. It was painful and somewhat dizzying at the same time.

Beneath him, perhaps three feet below, was a small tub in which had been placed a very large number of nasty-looking snakes. They were not, however, ordinary snakes, but ones modified by spell.

"The snakes' venom is a compound of silver nitrate," the Baron explained. "It is almost five now, and sundown is at six thirty-three today. No one will disturb you, Joe, but at sundown the only thing close is going to be those snakes. You'll turn into one of them and drop, as you did with the rats in my old dungeon. They cannot climb beyond the slanted screen barrier, so neither will you. If they don't bite you repeatedly when you drop in, they will all bite when you change back at dawn after a thrilling evening as a snake. Angels will be armed with silver bullets outside the door, and someone will keep an eye on you from time to time. If you get any good ideas, just yell the information and someone will shoot you, if it's of value to us. Otherwise, the snake pit. Believe me, Joe—the door cannot be opened from this side, and there are no windows or other exits big enough to admit anything of value or to use as an escape. No matter what, they'll shoot you, in whatever form, if you try that." He sighed. "Good-bye, Joe. I go to my destiny. Too bad you couldn't come along."

He exited and the door closed with an unnerving finality. He twisted slowly, his arms aching like hell, and all he could think was, *Damn you, Poquah! Your cavalry better come in time!*

CHAPTER 16

SPELLING OUT THE BIG BROADCAST

And, as that Theban monster that proposed
Her riddle, and him who solved it not devoured;
That once found out and solved, for grief and spite
Cast herself headlong from th' Ismenian steep,
So strook with dread and anguish fell the Fiend...

—Milton

GIMLET ONLY SUCCEEDED IN HER MISSION BECAUSE Dacaro was paranoid enough that he wanted no one, not even Ministering Angels under his spell, to be in his small office when he worked. Being a wizard, no one had even bothered to investigate when occasional sounds of typing had issued from the office after he'd gone to eat. She was pretty well satisfied; she just hoped she hadn't misspelled anything.

After completing that part, she was on her own in the big house. She didn't worry about the guards, since any pixie that could remain unnoticed in Brooklyn had no worry about being unnoticed here. She was aware that she alone held a real advantage; unless the other team was captured and had talked or had been asked the right questions, not a single one of the enemy even knew she existed.

It was late in the afternoon when she completed the task and was satisfied, though she moved on out to see what else she could do. She was met almost immediately by the two marble statues newly placed in the hall, and she had no question in her mind, considering what Joe and Tiana had told her, that these were no artist's copies and that the team below had met with failure.

She checked in all the rooms up and down the hall, including those with the enforcement arms in them, and even the Baron's bedroom, but found no one else familiar until the last door, more a closet really. She almost skipped it, but slipped under the sill by flattening herself and found Father O'Grady inside. There were several whiskey bottles around, and the priest, stark naked, was sitting there looking forlorn in a corner.

Something seemed to attract his attention, though, and he looked up and saw her. His expression became instantly friendly and childlike. "If only you could hear me," she sighed.

"But, faith, I hear ye fine, little fairy," the priest responded in a whisper.

She was startled. Certainly he wasn't hearing on the usual level. The only thing she could figure was that this guy had real wizard's power—but only when he was drunk.

"Tell me what happened," she asked him.

"They caught us, that was all. They were layin' for us all the time. They aren't sure they can control their beastie, y'see, and they wanted me to show 'em how. I drew it all but one small character. 'Tis a shame indeed."

"Listen—if I can get you out of here, do you think you could get down dere somehow and finish it?"

He thought a moment. "How? They've got their damnable security in every room and in every hall."

She thought a moment. "Dat's downstairs. Hey—listen. Do ya t'ink you could shimmy down a long rope in your condition?"

He got up unsteadily. "To vanquish the foe I would shimmy 'til it hurt!"

She flew to the lock, then seemed to back her tiny rump into it. There was a little glow when she left, and he was croggled by the idea. "Pixie dust!" he breathed. "Uh—it's your *excrement*?"

She stood in midair and shrugged. "Dem fairy stories was for kids. What can I say about the real t'ing?"

He went over and tried the door. It slid open noiselessly and he peered cautiously outside. "Coast clear. Lead on!"

"Yeah, well, wait'll you see de dumbwaiter."

"Almost sundown," Dacaro said. "It's a big night. In an hour and a half we'll own a little part of this world." He and the Baron walked onto the porch and looked out at the grounds and the equipment. New temporary lighting had been installed just to flood the front porch, and over to their left sat the great satellite dish on its trailer, wires going to a separate truck trailer with the control room in it. The three cameras were in place, and being checked by their technicians, which were provided by the cable network. A thousand folding chairs were set out behind them on the lawn. Tonight those who attended would wear no yellow robes, but their finest and fanciest clothing, and look damned respectable, as did those within the house.

The night was atypically clear and relatively warm. Dacaro, thanks to the Baron's computer, had arranged it that way.

A fancy lectern with a banner over it reading TRUE PATH CRUSADE was set up in front, and the microphone was in place and could be detached so Dacaro could walk out from behind it if necessary. Two boom mikes, out of camera frame, supplemented it, and all were tied together in the base of the lectern by a mass of switching and other electronic gear that almost filled it.

The Baron intended that he and the Baroness would watch the proceedings from chairs in the front row center of the audience; Dacaro had to carry the talkathon ball, of course. He would have assistance, but he'd be on as part of it for the entire time, and, by doing so, act as a carrier for the more subliminal but vitally more important spells being transmitted at the same time. Dacaro, or even himself in his prime, would have been incapable of broadcasting that steady level of power for more than a few minutes, but Dacaro merely had to be on. The power would come from below.

Boquillas took a moment to appreciate his own brilliance. The sun would be down in a moment, and that would finally be the end of Joe. He had beaten them all, including Ruddygore's best, and he'd killed, imprisoned, or enslaved all those who had cost him dearly in the past. This was indeed a night to remember.

Gimlet had gone ahead of the priest, who had a very tight fit and was also very tight. Moving the panel in the basement back just enough to get through, she looked over the place. As she expected, it was empty—no, it wasn't. Two of the Ministering Angels with their nasty rifles stood near a small door over to one side. She knew they would have to be taken out before the priest made it down this far.

She lowered her glow to the minimum and shot from the opening. In a flash, she was hovering over the two guards, one on each side of the door. They hadn't noticed her, obviously. Now, she flew back and forth over each in turn and a twinkling substance settled down and came to rest in each of the guard's hair. They did not seem to notice, but odd smiles suddenly crept out on their faces and they seemed to relax a bit. One giggled.

It was a bit noisier when the priest got down and pushed the door all the way back. He hardly made it, feet first, out of the opening, and only his condition kept him from feeling the pain.

He looked around, saw the two Angels, and froze. They looked at him, started giggling uncontrollably, and began pointing and gesturing, but the last thing they seemed to want to do was shoot him.

He felt suddenly a bit insulted. "What's with them?"

"I peed on dem. Dey're pixilated, y'know. Forget 'em." They both looked through the glass, which was darkly transparent from this side, and saw only the deserted entry point with the candles burning. The priest stared.

"They didn't even erase what I drew!" he said. "The Seal's intact!" He turned excitedly. "Quickly—find me a piece of chalk. Red's best, but any will do."

She went off and looked through Boquillas's office. The pack they'd taken from the priest was still there, and she shed a tiny bit of her essence on it and it levitated out and followed her to the priest, who took it and smiled. "I'll finish the Seal," he told her. "You go see if you can help some of the others."

Gimlet turned and looked at the hysterical guards. "I wonder what dey're guardin'?" she muttered, and flew to the door. One of the laughing and giggling guards obligingly opened it for her.

She flew immediately to Joe, knowing he could see but not hear her. He seemed happy to see her, or anybody, but puzzled. Suddenly, through his pain-wracked mind, he managed to say, "Stay with me! Sit on me if you have to! Sit on me until . . ."

It was six thirty-three, and he suddenly found himself free and falling through the air, and barely had the presence of mind to pull up. The move was instinctive; he was now an exact twin of Gimlet, and had all of her instincts, drives, powers, and limitations. Everything but her accent.

"What's happening?" he asked her.

"Gee—dis is neat," Gimlet commented. "Been a long toime since I had a sister."

"Can the comedy—you know what happened, and thanks for arriving in time. Close, though." He sighed. "It's always so damned close."

"I freed da priest. He's drunk as a skunk but he's in dere now finishin' up da drawing or whatever." They quickly exchanged what information they had.

"I'd say let 'em go ahead with the show for now," he told her. "We can't do anything about it. Let's try and free any we can. I know where the souls of the fairies are kept—the Baron told me."

They used the dumbwaiter route up and out into the second floor. Thanks to Gimlet's room by room search earlier, she knew exactly where the bedroom was.

Joe looked around, enjoying how effortlessly gravity seemed not to exist for him. It was as easy to go at any speed in any direction as it was to walk it. The only trouble was, everything looked so *huge*.

The bottles were just sitting there on the mantel of the bedroom fireplace, but they were a good case in point. He and Gimlet were both no more than four inches high—not more than half the height of the whiskey bottles. Both had corks in them apparently from old wine bottles, but Joe found himself able to stand comfortably on the cork.

"Can't we just uncork 'em here and hope for da best?" Gimlet asked hopefully. "I mean, dey're fairy souls."

"They could still wander and never find their bodies," he replied. "Our best bet would be to uncork them next to the statues."

She sighed. "Well, I guess we can manage it, but after dis, we're both gonna be too pooped out to do any more."

He found out that she wasn't speaking metaphorically, either. Still, once the stuff was on the bottles—as opposed to the corks—Joe found he could lift his as if it were attached to his tiny body by ropes. Even the empty bottles were terribly heavy, but barely manageable.

They had just gotten the bottles to the door when the Baroness walked in to the room. They both froze, the bottles as high as they could maintain them. Joe thanked Providence that they liked high ceilings at the turn of the century.

The lady of the manor was not alone, but was followed by two Ministering Angels, neither as yet out of their apparently normal household uniform of high boots, tassels, jewelry, and nothing else. Neither was armed, and they helped the Baroness undress and get newly fixed up, then brushed her hair and checked her makeup.

"Gimlet!" Joe whispered, although his voice, like hers, wasn't within the realm of normal human hearing. "One of them is Mahalo!"

Mahalo McMahon finished brushing the Baroness's hair. "Thank you, Mahalo," the lady of the manor said. "Tiana, bring me the Chanel from the cabinet over there."

"At once, Mistress," the other answered and went to get it.

Joe stared at the other woman. If that was where they'd put Tiana, they'd never chosen a more different body for her. The woman was small, almost petite, with one hell of an athletic body and small, firm breasts. She was tanned and had a playfully cute kind of face, set off by long, straight, light brown hair.

"I can't hold dis much longer," Gimlet noted. "Let's try'n sneak outta da room wit' dese t'ings before dey kill us. Dey're bewitched. We need the Imir."

She was right, of course. Slowly, carefully, and nervously, they each made their way down and out the door. No one was in the hall, but there were the sounds of loud voices downstairs, perhaps a small crowd, and some other voices from rooms down the hall. This had to be fast.

"Which one's which?" Gimlet wanted to know. "Best we put dem next to each statue."

"No matter what, we'll probably get the wrong ones,"

Joe muttered. "All we can do is trust to the luck that's got us this far." He wasn't sure about Marge, but he had a feeling that Poquah in a Kauri body would hardly be a thrilling love goddess.

They set their bottles down and, as Gimlet warned, neither had much reserve. The corks moved a bit, but wouldn't come all the way out. Each of them grabbed what they could and tugged.

Joe's came suddenly free with a force that almost knocked him down the stairs. Gimlet's came a few seconds later. Then they held their breaths. Both souls had gone into the bodies nearest them, but which was which?

It took about a minute, a very nervous minute when it seemed as if someone was going to come by at any moment, before the fixtures turned back into living, breathing beings. Marge, for one, looked puzzled, but seemed to realize quickly the position and danger she was in.

Joe flew down to Marge's shoulder. "Is that you, Marge? Or did we mix it up again?"

"Joe?" she whispered. "Is that really *you*?"

"Until sunup, anyway. Come on—we got to move it. They're going on the air in maybe a half hour, forty minutes. We got to be away."

Poquah looked less surprised, and there was no question that, this time, things had worked out right. At least they'd had a fifty-fifty chance for them. "Where are the others?" the Imir whispered.

"The Baroness is in there with Mahalo and another we think is Tiana, soul-transferred. O'Grady's drunk but he's down in the demon's room with his chalk."

"Are they alone?"

"Yes. But we can get them later!"

"Is either woman armed?"

"Not that I saw, but we don't have the time!"

"Yes we do," Poquah said and walked boldly into the bedroom. Marge decided she might as well follow, although there was almost nothing she could do to help, and the pixies joined in as well.

The Baroness was being worked on by the two women and looking into her mirror. Although four creatures entered, there was nothing reflected in it except the three humans and the door, although suddenly the Baroness noted that it had suddenly closed on them. She turned, as did the two others, and gaped at the duo she saw. She didn't even notice the pixies.

"You!" she called out. "How—"

The two Angels immediately stepped in front of their mistress and took up fighting positions.

Poquah put out his hand and from it issued a series of sparkling yellow bands. They wrapped around the two Angels and held them. The Angels moved meekly out of the way.

The Imir looked at her and his eyes seemed aflame. "Now you will know what it feels like to be on the other end of such sorcery," he said darkly.

A bit later, the Baroness, with no memory of the incident, walked out the door, summoned two blue-robed Angels, and went downstairs to greet her guests. Poquah took the time to lift the rather basic spells placed on Mahalo and Tiana. The Baroness was crude with spells, lacking finesse, although she got the results she wanted.

"Oh, wow!" said Mahalo McMahon. "I guess the cavalry arrived, huh?"

"No, not quite," Poquah told her, "but it is close. Some of us must see to Father O'Grady. The rest of you should clear out—now. Dacaro's down greeting guests—I can feel him—so we can't go that way. Gimlet, you got O'Grady down there somehow. Can you show me how?"

"Yeah, sure. You'll fit a lot better dan he did."

"I can go out the window, if he's lifted that damned sticky spell," Marge told them. "You want me to fly out and get a raid in here."

"No!" Poquah said sharply. "We must not interfere. The broadcast must go on as scheduled!"

"Huh?" they all managed.

"You'll see. Kauri, I'll open the window here and you fly out. Don't touch the exterior and you should be all right. Just take a good perch in a tree someplace and watch what happens."

Tiana looked at the two pixies. "Joe? Is one of those *you*?" she managed, chuckling.

He nodded and waved.

"You don't look much like a fish either, honey," Mahalo noted. "They put you in a new package."

"I wonder what they did with the poor girl whose body this was and who is now a mermaid?"

"Impossible to know, at least until dawn," Poquah pointed out. "She would be a were, remember. We must go. O'Grady may well need help and a lot depends on him."

"Hey! What about us? How do *we* get out?" Mahalo wanted to know.

"You don't. Too many people, lights, guards, and spells about. You'll have to stay here until it's finished."

"We will miss whatever fun you have planned!" Tiana objected. "It is not fair!"

"No choice. I haven't time to give you a spell effective enough to get you by."

"But what if the Baron returns?"

"He'll have far too much on his mind to come to the bedroom," the Imir promised. "If he does, he'll find two servile Ministering Angels. Just act the part and remember that he doesn't have as much power as you do, Tiana."

She frowned. "That spell you put on the Baroness—what did it do?"

"Gave her a case of what Master Ruddygore once called *Beavercleaveritus*. She'll be so sickeningly sweet and good you'll want to throw up. She can't do *anything* even remotely bad. Maybe you'll see. They'll take it for an act downstairs until it's too late, but she's out of it. Now—I must go."

With that he opened the door a bit—and seemed to

vanish. The pixies followed in the air, keeping close to the ceiling where possible.

A couple of other Angels were in the hall and should have seen Poquah, but appeared not to notice him, even giving way without a second glance when he passed. It was the first time Joe had been able to see Poquah when he was in this phase, and it was fascinating. It would not, however, get him past Dacaro or into the cellar, whose entrance was much too public from the first floor.

The old dumbwaiter, however, served one more time.

Until now, there had been nothing from the pentagram, but now that O'Grady had completed it, after fifteen tries, and started to say the words that would activate it, something happened.

It was at first just a feeling, a *presence* growing somehow in the midst of the five-sided figure, but the sensation of overpowering evil was beyond anything he had ever experienced, even beyond belief.

If he had been the least bit sober, it would have stopped him completely. Even so, he stumbled over some of the words and had to back up. He did not want to look ahead as he prayed, did not want to see what was forming there, but he did, and the figure he saw was beyond words to describe. Raw power it was, at once the most horrible and loathsome thing he'd seen and also one of the grandest. It was a sight far worse than his nightmares, a vision so terrifying there was an intense feeling to stop this work and fall down and worship the thing.

"Stop, priest!" the thing thundered, its voice the voice of a million Auschwitz camps and billions of innocent dead. "I will crush you if you continue!"

Suddenly the panel in the back rolled back and Poquah entered. The two pixies tried, but could not penetrate the force of evil there. Through the one-way glass, they could see the priest and Poquah clearly, but only a shimmering shape in the center of the pentagram.

"It can't get at you, Father!" Poquah yelled to the

kneeling naked figure. "It can't cross that pentagram and those candle sticks! Seal this one bastard away from this place it profanes!"

The demon prince roared defiance, but turned toward Poquah. "Silence, elf shit! You are not your master, and even him could I devour, if I chose!"

The change of focus took some of the pressure off O'Grady, who continued. That and the booze gave him barely enough insulation to finish the long and complex passage. He was still amazed he remembered it. It had been years since he'd studied it, and the text almost seemed to be coming from—somewhere else.

Suddenly his spirit soared, and he stood up and grinned at the terror beyond description. "Begone, ye demon! Your better has bested you! In the name of the Lord God, Creator of the Universe, *this place is sealed*!"

Suddenly the demon howled, and where the strings were, forming the Seal, was now a mass of fire forming the great seal and spelling out letters. Slowly, the six lines began to converge on their center at the pentagram.

"It's *shrinking*!" a shaken Joe managed from behind the screen. "Well, I'll be damned!"

"Probably!" roared the creature, but it was definitely in agony. It, too, seemed to be shrinking, losing substance and power. The lines of fire continued their march, passing the candlesticks and consuming them in a nearly electrical fire, then consuming the pentagram itself, which was no longer needed.

There was a sudden burst of pure bright light that seemed to blind them, and then all was still and quiet except for the buzz from the untouched fluorescent light fixture. On the floor, the great Seal of Solomon was etched into the very stone itself, about the size of the inner area of the pentagram. The aura of evil, the terror that the room had held, was gone. It just felt suddenly cold and damp down there.

"Well, I'll be—darned," Father O'Grady said. "The thing actually worked! Praise be to God!" He turned to

Poquah. "This calls for a drink!" he proclaimed and collapsed on the floor.

The Imir rushed to him and checked him, and the two pixies flew in immediately to see for themselves.

"Passed out cold," the Imir told them. "Might as well leave him here and make him comfortable. Right now this is the safest place in the area."

"You do that," said Joe. "You still won't tell us a damned thing, so Gimlet and I are going to go up and watch the show."

"Be careful," the Imir warned. "Dacaro is still dangerous as hell; there are no guarantees our plans will work, and that audience and most of the people in this house are still the enemy."

"We'll remember. Just call if you need us."

"You can do no more. Now—go. It's almost time. I can feel Dacaro's spell reaching down to connect with his nibs in here at this moment, and I'll have to give him a reasonable facsimile of a connection so he feels secure. Not that he could do anything but go through with it, anyway."

The Baron and Baroness had taken their seats and the last checks were in. Dacaro brought his script up to the lectern, although it was a scant ten pages of giant-sized double-spaced type, just enough for the introduction. He'd wing it after that.

The connection to below felt a bit odd, but he put it down to nervous excitement. This night was everything—and more—that he ever dreamed when he'd decided on the black side of the arts.

The Baroness leaned over and whispered to the Baron, "Golly gee whillikers! I'm so *excited*!"

He sighed. "Enough of that, my dear. We are secure. Just look pretty and watch the show. I don't know what's gotten into you, anyway."

"Oh, okay, honey. But, *golly*! Everybody looks so *nice*!"

He stared at her for a moment and a hint of suspicion

crossed his mind, but he finally dismissed it as just excitement. He didn't feel himself tonight, either, although he put it down to tiredness and pressure. Even though this was a big moment for him, he still wished it was all over and done with. There! The recorded gospel music was already going out! They were on the air!

A ghostly, disembodied voice that was actually pretaped said, "The Blessed Art Thou Network proudly presents, from Stockman Mills, California, live, the Reverend Richard Dacaro and the True Path Crusade for the Lord!"

There was a lot of applause. As that was going on, the pixies spotted Marge back in the trees and went to her.

"Everything squared away?" the Kauri asked.

"Okay below," Gimlet responded. "Ain't nothin' goin' out of here tonight 'cept what we're seeing now."

"Yeah, I'm real curious as to this other part. What did they have planned? An air strike?" Joe wondered. "I mean, they're still on top. Their gimmick just won't fly tonight."

"Oh, I got an idea. My feet are still sore," the real pixie said.

"Your feet?"

"From typing dose extra lines in da script."

The applause died down, and Dacaro, looking really splendid, began. As had been anticipated, he was more than a little nervous at this, despite his earlier hour-long stint, and so he kept pretty close to his script.

"Brothers and sisters," he began, "we welcome the rest of you across this great land of ours to our glorious crusade. Here, in this natural setting, we can feel the presence of God around us, and I hope some of that communicates to those of you out there."

He went on leading a group prayer, then launched into his keynote sermon. It was a typical sort of nondenominational sermon, except that it wasn't very long.

"We must rid our beautiful nation, one nation indivisible, of those elements that corrupt our young. We declare war tonight on the evil that spreads over this land! Why, in this very spot, in the midst of God's most wondrous nature, at one time not long ago they grew the noxious weed that rots the minds and steals the souls of our young! Well, we have liberated this land for God, and they shall not have it back!"

There was great applause, and Marge commented, "He's really pretty good. I almost feel like phoning in a donation myself."

"Brothers and sisters here and across this great nation, we can here, now, today, make a start at a true revolution for our country! Not one that will burn or loot or pillage, but one based on God and scripture, one that drives the evil drugs and pornography and booze and filth from our land and our young! I wish all of you out there could see, could feel, could *know* what this country would be like if *we* were in charge!"

"DONE!" cried a voice that went over the microphones and out to the satellites.

Dacaro stopped, as if it were the voice of God, but he had no choice in the matter and no time really to reflect on it. He grew suddenly transparent, and seemed to be sucked as if by a vacuum cleaner into the lectern itself. But the podium was not deserted, for in a simultaneous reversal another oozed out and solidified, a huge man in formal clothes and top hat with a big white beard.

Both Marge's and Joe's jaws dropped. Finally Marge managed, "The Lamp! *Macore hid the Lamp in the podium!*"

The crowd, however, hardly noticed Ruddygore up there. They were, as were at least a million people tuning in across the country, in a state of absolute shock and horror, for the Lamp had granted Dacaro's unintended wish.

They knew *exactly* what the country would be like if the True Path were in charge.

It broke through spells, and it broke through all manner of faith and belief. It just *was*. Down there, some people were so nauseated they were throwing up all over their nice clean suits.

Ruddygore had seemed dazed for a moment, but now he suddenly seemed to see the lights and the cameras and he brightened like a small child discovering a new toy. He grabbed the microphone and began singing, "*I am the very model of a modern Major General. . . .*"

A technician had had the presence of mind to shut down transmission, but there were still all those people out there. Ruddygore continued to sing.

Joe looked forward and grew alarmed. "Boquillas has split!" He looked at the other two. "You check this side of the crowd, and you, Gimlet, check the other. I'm going back into the house. He may try some sort of slicker getaway there, and Tiana's trapped in there!"

He did not try to see or make contact with Ruddygore, who was just standing there for a while like a joyous Santa having the time of his life, but went up and flew in the bedroom's open window.

The two women were still there, listening to the commotion but not yet fully understanding it.

Joe suddenly realized he couldn't communicate directly with either one. Or—could he? Tiana had the power, she might barely be able to make him out in the fairy speech.

"Ti!" he cried, going right up to her. "Dacaro's gone and Ruddygore's here, but the Baron's escaped!"

She looked at him strangely for a moment, then seemed to hear. "Okay. If I get it, the Baron's escaped but we won. Come on, Mahalo! If he goes anywhere he'll head for that exit-laden basement of yours!"

There were people screaming and running all about, but they ignored them and pushed their way through, to be ignored in turn. The cellar door was definitely ajar, and first Mahalo, who was the larger, and then Tiana made it, Joe flying right on top.

Joe looked over and saw the reclining priest, but no Poquah. He must have left to get to Ruddygore. There was, however, someone in the Baron's small office, rummaging around for something.

Tiana walked boldly to the open door and saw Boquillas

just sitting there in his office chair in front of his computer looking dazed and confused. It was unlike him, but she knew he wouldn't go quietly.

"You're done, Baron," she said. "We've taken you again."

He looked up at her and seemed very confused and disoriented, and then he got up and looked at the pair of crossed sabers mounted on the wall. In a single motion he grabbed one and wrenched it free of its mount.

Joe had been ignored and did a fast survey of the office. He found that Irving was in fact still in its scabbard by the side of Boquillas's desk.

"Irving! To the woman and fight as if it were me!" he commanded.

The sword suddenly shot from its scabbard and went right through the computer terminal. It caught them all by surprise, but Tiana grabbed it by reflex and felt its heft and balance. "All right, Baron, this was meant to be," she said. "I will step outside, but not stand aside."

The Baron stared at her a moment, then reached up and took the other saber down, so that he had one in each hand. He then walked tiredly out of the office and faced the woman with the broadsword. "I will leave now," he said woodenly.

Tiana did not have the size and strength she was used to, but Irving was not merely a broadsword but a semi-living creature with a mind and powers of its own. It could not help her strength, but it needed little skill or direction to be effective, for it was forged with dwarf magic in the fires under the mountains.

She thought about that. "Baron, if you will throw one of those sabers down at my feet I will give you a fair fight. Otherwise, I kill you where you stand."

"Ti! No!" Joe screamed. "He's a monster with nothing more to lose! Kill him now!" He ached to be the one with the sword instead of her. He owed Boquillas one.

The Baron knelt down and slid the saber over to Tiana. She reached down, picked it up, then put down Irving.

The Baron did not take advantage of her at this, and let her start the fight.

There was the sudden clang of steel against steel, but the Baron seemed to be fighting without any will or reserve left. In seconds, Tiana had pressed him to the wall and then methodically disarmed him, although she was unused to her new body and he had by far the advantage in size and reach. He stared at her, showing no fear, only resignation. "You must kill me," he told her, sounding very tired indeed.

Tiana paused a moment, then lowered her saber and shook her head. "I cannot kill this poor, miserable wretch like this." She half turned away from him in disgust. "Let Ruddygore deal with him."

At that moment a shot rang out and reverberated through the cellar. She was shocked and stunned for a moment, then turned to see the Baron slowly sinking to the floor, a bloody wound in his chest. She looked over near the stairs and saw Mahalo McMahon there, holding one of the rifles abandoned by the pixilated guards. She looked a little shocked and stunned herself. "I—I couldn't help it. I saw it there and was covering you, and you turned away and he made a move for the sword and I just—shot, that's all." She dropped the rifle and seemed to be more than a little bit in shock herself.

Poquah suddenly came down the stairs in a rush. "You must all get out of here quickly!" he shouted. "The audience has become a mob and they have set fire to the mansion! Stand away from the far wall and Marge will set off a charge that will blow the old door off, spells and all!"

Tiana went over and checked the Baron. "He is still alive!" She looked around and saw the limp, naked body of Father O'Grady on the other side of the glass. "Mahalo! Snap out of it! You are no murderer yet! See if you can get O'Grady on his feet and help him when they blow up the door! Poquah! I will need help with the Baron!"

The Imir looked at the bloodstained form and frowned,

as if debating whether to help the Baron or not, but finally he said, "You go help the other get the priest out. I will use a spell to levitate that carrion out after you."

At that moment there was a tremendous explosion inside the room in which Joe had been held captive and strung up. He flew to Poquah. "The snakes! There are venomous snakes in that room!"

The Imir ran over, threw the door open, and looked around. "They are there, but they are all dead. They could not survive their own mutated venom when Dacaro's influence was removed. Come! There is a hole in here that even our Master could fit through—but hurry! I can see smoke from here and it is getting very, very warm!"

The two women were able to get O'Grady to a more or less standing position, but he was definitely still not of this or any other world except perhaps his own. With one on each arm, they managed with several slips to get him into the room where hands from outside could help ease the women's burden.

Smoke now filled the cellar area, and flames began to be seen along the ceiling, helped by the sudden blowing open of the door. Poquah finished his spells and, very slowly, the Baron's limp form lifted a few inches off the floor and followed the Imir to the room and then to the door itself. Joe shot out into the open air, stopped, then turned to watch.

Ruddygore and a number of stern-faced men helped lift the Baron out the rest of the way just as the ceiling fell in with a crash and a roar. They barely made it back to the well area before the flames shot for a moment straight through the opening and into the light as if from a flamethrower.

The unfamiliar men took Boquillas's limp form and hustled it away with a speed and professionalism that was impressive; the rest stood there for a while, watching the old mansion go up like a flaming torch, until the heat, which grew hot enough to begin to ripple the paint on the generator trailers and melt the big satellite dish, became so great that they were forced to turn and walk back into the cool woods. Fire sirens sounded in the distance, but they would be useful only in keeping the conflagration to what it was already consuming and prevent, if they were lucky, a major forest fire.

Tiana, in fact, voiced that fear to Ruddygore, but he was unconcerned. "I managed a spell sufficient to keep the fire contained within its current boundaries, which will last until the inevitable rains rush in. I wouldn't worry so much. I personally wouldn't be upset if it consumed that entire stupid town, but I would not like to lose those redwoods."

The whole forest was a madhouse, with crowds ranging from the virtually undressed to the formally dressed running every which way in panic. Elder, Ministering Angel, Elect, technicians, special guests—all were the same now. The True Path was in ashes, and would not be followed again by any who were there or by any watching the initial broadcast.

Ruddygore's organization was quite prepared for them, although the agents had not known exactly what would happen until it did. A few small vans awaited the wizard's party, and they were guided through and quickly whisked away. There was even an ambulance to receive the Baron, although it had not been thought at the time that he might be the one to make use of it.

Even so, it took some wizard's spells and over an hour to clear the town and the county.

CHAPTER 17

EXPLANATIONS AND RESOLUTIONS

Evil monsters must be killed more than once. The more evil the monster, the more times it must die before it is sent to Hell or oblivion.

—Rules, XIV, 303(a)

"LET'S GO BACK TO THE ORACLE'S VERSE ONCE AGAIN and you'll see my thinking on all this," Throckmorton P. Ruddygore said, relaxing in a hotel suite in San Francisco and facing the company.

"The first three lines obviously meant Joe and Marge," he continued, sipping champagne between comments. "The 'thief' part undoubtedly meant Macore, although I was hesitant to let an absolute greenhorn on Earth. He seems to have adapted well, though."

"If you consider a fanatic addiction to *Gilligan's Island* adapting, then I guess you're right," Marge agreed.

"Well, if it wasn't an addictive thing, I suppose it wouldn't have run that long. At any rate, it was clear that the thief, Macore, had to go under something—it appeared to be underground, though it turned out to be under the porch and up through a trapdoor, but that difference was minor. I could not, of course, understand the 'pickled fish' reference, and thought it might refer to Tiana, particularly since conditions barring her were removed by that body switch, so I raised no objections to her going, despite the obvious inconvenience."

"I, too, thought it was me, although I did not like the reference to being 'pickled,'" Tiana agreed.

The wizard nodded and wolfed down a croissant. "This left me with a few questions that needed to be resolved here—the pixie business, for example. The real problem was that we had to give a treasure freely to the villains and Macore had to sneak it in. What sort of treasure? It seemed obvious from the fact that the word 'wish' was used three times in the verse that it had to be the Lamp. I, of course, was more hesitant to have Macore transport it here, particularly with the risk that it would fall into the Baron's hands—one chance at it and he might have been able to wish his powers back—but clearly its presence was mandated. I told Macore to inform no one except Poquah that it was even here, and to use it or otherwise risk it only if he felt the meaning of the verse was perfectly clear in his own mind."

"You put a lot of trust in Macore, considering the vault episode," Joe noted.

"But that was at least part of it! His explanation of how he solved all of the fatal traps of my vaults, which no one, not even the Baron, had been able to do, convinced me that no one else could adequately solve the riddle of the verse and put it all together. He is rather—limited—in many things, but in the solution of real puzzles with genuine dangers he is a genius. He looked everything over, assembled all his information, put it against the basic puzzle—the verse—and the true puzzle—how to stop the Baron and Dacaro—and he did it! The use of our pixie friend here to type that extra sentence, that very clever and direct wish, into Dacaro's script while it was still in the typewriter was absolute genius."

"Just where *is* Macore, anyway?" Marge asked. "We haven't seen him since the night we all went into the house."

"After waiting and planting the Lamp, masking it in a metallic box that looked like it connected to all that other apparatus inside the lectern, he got away and fast. Poquah had arranged for memories of him to be erased from Joe and Tiana, so it was unlikely that the Baron or Dacaro knew he was part of the group. If they'd seen him, they might have put two and two together. If they'd caught him, there was no way to keep him from being forced to spill the whole plot. As soon as he was out, we got him well away, although he really did want to be in on things at the end. I understand he is enjoying Disneyland enormously. If he's not in jail, he will join us later, when we fly back to Texas for our return voyage."

"How'd he get past those dogs?" Joe asked. "They just about lived under that porch."

"But they were still just dogs. Macore is a professional thief. He runs into guard dogs all the time. I don't know the exact method, and whether he used a spell or drugs or a combination, but anyone who couldn't be stopped by the traps in my vault would hardly be concerned with four Dobermans."

"What I can't figure out is how *you* got there," Marge said. "I mean, didn't the wish Macore made bar you from crossing?"

"It did indeed—only I didn't come that way. Think back to the hotel in Marahbar, and remember that, after you all left to come on the voyage here, Macore lingered a few moments. I had already prearranged this with Jinner, who was in the Lamp, so I simply made a wish and changed places with Jinner. At that point I resided not in Husaquahr but in the land of the djinn. I traveled nowhere, including across the Sea of Dreams. The land of the djinn is contiguous only with the location of the Lamp. Thus, the Lamp crossed, not me, and when Dacaro made his unintended wish, having had his own quota of wishes fulfilled, he both freed and replaced me. I was here, but I had not violated the barrier. Before we return, with the aid of associates here and in my own way, I will deal with Mr. Dacaro."

"I understand you're some kind of wizard and all that,"

Mahalo McMahon interjected. "You gonna kill him or turn him into a toad or what?"

"I think everyone is better off not knowing," he responded carefully. "It is a most unpleasant business, you understand, for he's a rascal but no worse than many in Husaquahr—or here, for that matter. He cannot, however, be left on Earth with his power, nor can I trust him under any conditions back home, which is almost certainly a real mess right now. I can only assure you that you will never see or hear from him again unless you wind up in Hell."

That seemed definite enough. "I still do not understand why you just did not have someone make the wishes and come out at the start of all this," Tiana commented.

"I couldn't afford to. Oh, Macore and Poquah had instructions to get me out of there if things went sour, but otherwise I was better off hidden. If I were on Earth, Dacaro would have known it, would have felt the power. And, so long as they had the demon prince Astaroth with them, I could not have defeated them, and this time I had no place to run."

"What about the Baron?" Joe asked.

"The Baron suffered enormous damage to his spinal column and had a great loss of blood, some internally. He's being kept alive now only on a life-support machine at a private hospital under my control. He has never regained consciousness and may not."

"Then why not just pull the plug and be done with him?" Tiana wanted to know.

"There are some questions I wish to ask him. Most particularly I wish to ask him just what spell he worked out that enabled Dacaro so quickly and efficiently to remove souls from bodies and imprison them, or switch them around. It is a routine task for any competent sorcerer, but it involves demons and much ceremony and preparation and usually takes several hours. He not only did it in what appears to be minutes, but did it without the aid of a demon or any ritual, almost like changing coats. It was something Boquillas did not work out here—clearly this was the price our friend Sugasto, the Master of the Dead, got for going after you—but something his fine mind had worked out while still in Husaquahr. Sugasto apparently was given access to the Baron's private files of proprietary spells, of which this is the most sophisticated, and he is using them."

"Even if the Baron regains consciousness, why should he tell you?" Tiana wanted to know. "He seemed only to want to die after this defeat. He hardly fought me at all, although he is a skilled swordsman and might well have won. He has no reason to tell you."

"It's very doubtful he ever will be able to tell, but if he can, there are things that might be offered. If he dies, his torment in Hell will far exceed anything the usual evil one would get, for he failed Hell over and over again. If I have the formula, there is a way out. You remember, Joe, what happened to your mind when you became a wood nymph?"

"I've been told," he responded irritatedly. "I don't remember it for sure."

"Oh, I see!" Tiana exclaimed. "You can offer to use his own process to place him in the body of such a nymph. Eventually, perhaps quickly, his entire memory and personality would be suppressed and he would become the creature of instinct Joe almost did. But he would put off punishment until Judgment, if he was lucky and found a nice tree, and he could argue his own case then based on his idealism."

"Very good," Ruddygore replied, nodding. "It is a price I believe he would be willing to pay. And if I know the process, I can make things very uncomfortable for Sugasto."

"I—I guess I shouldn't have shot him," Mahalo said sadly. "I'm real sorry, but, like, it seemed like the only thing to do at the time."

"So when do we go home?" Marge asked the wizard. "And who all goes?"

Ruddygore looked around the room. "Ms. McMahon—is it your wish to go with us? I promise you that, once over, you may never return, and it's not the romantic place you might think. It's full of war and death and it has no televisions, transistor radios, electric lights, central heating, or air conditioning; and I'm afraid it's going to be even more of a mess, now that Sugasto's had a month without me to consolidate his position. It will not be an easy road, and, as Marge can attest, you cannot even tell now what might happen to you or what you might become."

"I been thinking a lot about that," the former cult priestess said, "and I got to admit it's kind of scary. But then I think of what I done with my life here and what's been goin' on. I mean, I never was much good at school and I dropped out when I was real young and became a hippie. I've never really had any other life. I'm still a hippie when everybody I knew or was close to is over forty, in jail, or a has-been hippie in a time of tanning booths and polyester suits. I don't know if this place you come from is really better or worse or not, but, you see, it's *different*. When going's better than staying, it's better to go, I guess."

"Fair enough. We owe you that much, I think. And we owe you more than that, Gimlet. In fact, we owe the whole game to you."

"Well, it ain't Brooklyn, but if you gois is like most of da folks dere, I think I'll get along okay."

"Marge?"

"I'm ready. I was always out of place here, and I'm even more out of place here now. I burned my last bridge on this trip. I'll go tomorrow."

Ruddygore nodded. "What about you, Joe? And you, Tiana? Neither of you look the way you used to, and you aren't likely to. And, of course, Sugasto is there, and there'll be a big fight."

Joe squeezed Tiana's hand. "I didn't think we had a choice, but we're certainly going back. Oh, I admit I wouldn't mind a vacation here once in a while, but I kind of like it back there, even with all the crazy stuff. And since Ti and I aren't gods anymore, maybe we can finally get a chance to see some of the place and be ourselves. As for Sugasto—well, we beat the Baron and the demons of Hell, didn't we? Now that I know who I'm facing and just what's what, Sugasto seems like a pantywaist."

"There is always a Sugasto." Ruddygore sighed. "Always another evil threat, always more evil armies with new variations on the march. Peace is very transitory in either world, but particularly so in Husaquahr." He paused a moment and lighted a cigar. "I'm afraid it's in the Rules."

"Thanks to Ti's quick thinking, I've still got Irving, and the poor thing hasn't had a whole hell of a lot of use," Joe noted. "Actually, Ti's got more of a change than I have. What about it?"

She looked at Joe, then at the others. "I admit it is taking some real adjustment being so much smaller, but this body is in excellent shape and is not so bad. I have the power still, and I will be a were again before long, I think."

"You'll go back under the Rules," the wizard reminded her. "This body is more suited to a courtesan or entertainer or something like that than a barbarian priestess or warrior."

She shrugged. "I have been that and a mermaid and a goddess. Perhaps it is time for some variety. I am of Husaquahr. I wish to go home."

Ruddygore sighed again. "Well, that settles it, then. In one week, we'll take one of the company jets from Oakland to Midland, and the next night we'll leave. Poquah will remain here for a while, checking on the Baron's condition and aiding with sorcery if he can, but that will be that. I, of course, must return as soon as we use the Lamp to clear the barrier. Otherwise, I'd have to continue using the inconvenient method to go between, which I would find very irritating. There's still a villain to track down and beat, and I don't think he'll be any easier than this one was." He paused a moment. "I visited Father O'Grady last evening. He was straight and sober, and there was a real fire in his eyes. I'm not sure if he'll ever believe his memories or believe that the fairies helped, but he's got his faith back, that's for sure."

"He isn't the only one," Marge noted. "I looked at the papers the last couple of days. It's still big news what happened out there, but they're already explaining away its effects. I bet a hundred Ph.D.s in psychiatry, psychology, and sociology will be awarded for explaining away the mass hallucinations and hysteria we caused across the country and proving clearly and scientifically why what they thought they saw, heard, and felt just couldn't be real."

Ruddygore chuckled. "However, the churches of the nation will have record turnouts this Sunday, I bet. I don't know how many were actually watching the abbreviated broadcast, but I understand the Reverend Pike, who heads the Blessed Art Thou network, is taking a year off and sticking all his money into missions to feed the poor in Latin America. As for the rest—boy! Have they got religion!" He roared with laughter.

Joe seemed not to hear. "Well, if we've got a week, then I've got one favor to ask you. It's a personal one, but it's important to me. I might need the help of your detectives, though."

"Ask away, Joe," the wizard replied. "I suspect it's a last bridge of your own, is it not?"

"More or less," he admitted. "You know I have to go—if I can find him."

They all looked at the two with puzzled expressions.

"How old would he be now, Joe?" Ruddygore asked.

"Eleven—no, twelve. Oh, hell, he probably doesn't even remember me!"

"Still, I understand what must be done. Okay, Joe. Get a plane and charge it all to the accounts. Just be sure to be back in Midland in a week. I'll give you the name of the hotel. And I've already anticipated you in the other regard. You'll find the report in my briefcase over there."

Tiana now understood, as did Marge. "Do you wish me to go with you, Joe?" Ti asked him.

"No, not this time. This is one thing I have to do myself."

"I tell you, I am certain," Tiana whispered to Ruddygore. "For five days now we have lived together, and she is not who she says she is. At first I put it down as her odd life or my cultural differences, but any woman her age who has to read the directions in a box of tampons is not someone born and raised in this world. Finally, I could stand it no longer, and I asked her if she was sure she wanted to leave her new lover, Brian, back in California for this new world, because she was hot for him when we spoke back in her temple. She answered that it was only a passing thing. A passing thing! She mentioned no lover by any name to us back there. This whoever or whatever pretending to be Mahalo McMahon is not!"

"I know," Ruddygore responded softly. "I wasn't—quite—truthful with you all in San Francisco. Poquah removed all the spells from the Baron in order to see to his condition and to see if magical healing could help. It could and it did, but as a side-effect it freed the bound spirit inside. You see, the Baron was always a cautious man, a paranoid with good reason to be. When Joe, Marge, and Dacaro were in his clutches, he sent the demon Hiccarph instead of dealing with them himself. He must have brooded all night about his capture of the lot of you. Too easy, and if you succeeded, too inconsequential to his long-range plans, but he had no real way of finding out what else was going on, because none of you knew. As a cautious man, he would never even consider that I would risk the Lamp, let alone myself."

She gasped. "You mean—"

"Yes. After leaving Joe over the snake pit—a touch I'm afraid he could not really avoid because he, like us, was still bound by the Rules personally even here—he sought out McMahon and, through this process and probably with the aid of the demon himself, so that not even Dacaro would know, he switched bodies with Mahalo. He even added the Ministering Angel spell, although there was certainly a way to break it. The demon then cast a spell on Mahalo that made her act, and perhaps believe, she was the Baron. It would not have held up in the long term, but for that crowded and confused few hours it was simple. If anything went wrong, Mahalo was commanded to allow herself to be killed. When you couldn't do it, the Baron shot her. He is a very good actor, after all, and I doubt if he counted on this long a delay."

"Then—Mahalo is the Baron? He expects to be taken back across so he can link up with Sugasto?"

"That's right. And once we are aboard ship and off across the Sea of Dreams, we will have a little session, the Baron and I, and I will learn what I must, because I've had the time to analyze his protective spells and solve them. He will have no defense. And then I'm going to send him on, with no memory of our little chat and a few additional spells. I'm going to let him lead me right to Sugasto. He will serve a new master, for once, and he will serve me well, until I send him to Hell."

She stared at Ruddygore, but could find nothing else to say. Her thoughts went to the other victim instead. "Poor Mahalo, then."

"No, she was lucky. The Baron failed to kill her, although the shot was true, a last little touch of divine Providence, I think. We'll find her a body, perhaps among the evil or condemned, that's twenty years younger and perhaps with more beauty than she had. I can do what *they* can, even now—just not as quickly or as easily. By the end of the voyage, I'll know their way, and how to undo it as well. Sugasto will not be easy to fell, but he's in for a horrible shock, nevertheless—and a number of conniving and faithless Council members as well, don't you worry. We've beaten the ultimate evil itself this time. The Rules almost mandate a happy ending."

"I wonder much about that 'almost,'" she said, thinking of Joe.

It was well after dark, and the neighborhood, so crappy looking by day, looked even more sinister and fearsome by night. It had the smell of garbage about it mixed with the sulfurous air from the nearby refineries, and there was trash all over the place. Here and there among the blocks of rowhouses, flanking long, narrow streets better suited to horses than cars, were places deserted, abandoned, boarded up, and covered with graffiti.

The government and the times had changed, but it still looked like home to him. Legions of the unemployed, uneducated, and dispossessed of society, many because of their dark-skinned heritage were locked in ghetto neighborhoods like this, forgotten and ignored except by the dope dealers and the welfare agencies.

The slum was a self-perpetuating environment, each generation breeding the next at the bottom of the ladder because there was no clear way out for most of them. The environment was in itself an evil as tangible as any bred by sorcery and demons, and it worked its evil well. In its own way, this place, and the places like it in urban centers across America, were also openings to Hell, ones not so easily plugged up by a Seal of Solomon.

There was no real way to get to the boy at home without all sorts of a fuss, and his mother's current live-in was, according to the reports, a real nasty sort whose business was extortion and whose business associates were always around. He didn't have time to chance seeking him going to and from school; Irving wasn't exactly known for showing up very much in any event. That left now, when he was usually hanging out on the street with a gang of punks who had already gone to hell and were seeking to increase their numbers.

He turned a corner and saw them, sitting around the

front steps, radios blaring, just as the detectives had said they would be. He even knew who they were by name and photograph, and what some of the older ones were as well. The three older teens—Alvy, Clarence, and Charlie—would be the problem, showing off for the younger ones.

They sat there and eyed his approach as jewelers eyed diamonds at the start of an appraisal. He went up to them, stopped, and eyed them coldly. He was under no illusions, but he'd taken better punks than these.

"You lookin' for something, Geronimo?" Clarence asked snidely. All three of the bigger ones got up, leaving the younger foursome seated, all eyes and snickering smiles. "Hey, my man! I'm talkin' to you!"

"I'm looking for a boy named Irving de Oro," he responded, aware that the other two were slowly going to either side of him and slightly in back. The reports said they all carried knives but no guns on the street. He hoped the reports were correct. He looked at one of the younger boys on the steps and pointed. "You him?"

"What's it to ya, slick?" the boy answered back.

"We ain't used to suckers comin' by after dark in our territory," Clarence said coldly. "When one do, he dance to *our* tune and answer *our* question. You da *fuzz* or something?"

"I'm a something," Joe responded coolly. "I'm something that's gonna have to have real self-control to keep from killing all three of you if you don't take off in the next five seconds." He tensed, knowing where each was and judging their relative speed and positions. Out of the corner of one eye he saw Alvy's knife come out, and it was a real pig sticker, too. "Then, again, maybe if I just take that knife away and cut that dude's balls off it'll make you think a little."

"Kill that sucker!" Clarence ordered, sharp and angry, and they moved, but Joe moved much faster, so fast it was almost a blur. He reeled and grabbed Alvy's knife arm and, as they watched, actually lifted the husky teen by that arm. There was a *crack* and then Alvy was tossed into Charlie, who was just making his move. The two bodies collided, and Alvy pushed Charlie down and the second boy's head hit the street with a real nasty sound. Clarence was suddenly backed up only by four suddenly scared kids of twelve and under and he looked nervous. He glanced over at the foursome and screamed, "Get 'im! Get 'im!"

The four froze, mouths open, as they watched the stranger demolish their heroes like some kind of superman.

Realizing he wasn't going to get much help, Clarence started to back off. "Hey, man! Keep it cool! We just kiddin'!"

Joe slowly revealed Alvy's knife in his right hand. "I'm not," he responded coldly. Clarence's eyes bugged, and his right hand went into his jacket pocket and there was no mistaking the threat. The leader did in fact have a gun. "Use that—even let that hand get in there, and you'll die here," the big man warned. "You got two choices, punk. You take that jacket off nice and slow and then get out of here or you go for that gun." He heard the four younger boys stir and get ready to run. "You boys stay where you are! I don't want to hurt anybody if I can help it, and not any of you, unless you give me cause!"

Clarence took that as an opening and went for the gun. The knife seemed to fly from Joe's hand as if launched by a rocket and penetrated the boy's side all the way. He gasped in pain and fell backward, trying to reach the knife and screaming, "You stab me! You stab me, you son of a bitch! Help! Get me a doctor!"

The kids took that as a cue to run, and in their own territory they would have had no trouble in vanishing, but he had two advantages. He only wanted one of them, and this had been his old neighborhood, too.

The small boy ducked into a nearly invisible passageway between two blocks of rowhouses and ran down the narrow cement walkway and into the alley behind as if the devil was chasing him. Dogs started barking all over the place, but, true to the neighborhood's nature, nobody came out to interfere or see what the commotion was about. Joe was certain, though, that someone was even now calling the cops.

The boy made the alleyway and turned right—and suddenly felt himself held in an incredibly strong grip. He struggled in fear but could not break the hold.

"Irv! Calm down and shut up! I'm your father!" Joe yelled.

"You ain't! You ain't! My father's dead!"

"I'm not dead and neither are your friends out there if they get to a hospital! Now stop this and calm down. I been through a lot just to see you and by God I'm gonna see you!"

The boy stopped struggling and looked up at the stranger. There was suddenly some doubt in his mind, and you could see the wheels turning in his head. "You really my old man?"

"No, I'm your father. There's more of me in you, it seems, than your mother. Look at me and think of when you look in a mirror." He moved over to where some light from a house shed a little light on the alley.

"You *is* him! I seen your picture once."

They could hear the sound of sirens now. "Let's go where we can talk without company," Joe suggested. The boy looked hesitant, but he was still both too scared and too curious to run now. They made their way to a well lighted street about four blocks back and got into Joe's car. He started it and drove out toward the airport.

The kid hadn't had much of a life, that was for sure. The bastard his wife had left him for had walked out on her when Joe's payments stopped and it became clear, because no body was found in or near the wrecked truck, that the insurance companies and union weren't going to pay off.

She had never wanted nor liked the child; she'd kept him only because it would hurt Joe more for her to do so, and because it would bring her in more money in child support. He had vigorously contested custody, of course, but the judge had proclaimed that a child was better off with his mother and particularly if the father was an interstate truck driver. She had denied him any visitation rights, although he was fully entitled to them. Courts didn't do much about enforcing the father's rights in child custody cases, although there were now laws protecting the wife's rights under the same agreement.

She'd wound up on welfare, taking on menial jobs when she could, and she'd vented her frustrations and hatred of Joe on the kid. Lately he'd been hooking school more than attending it, and taking to the streets with the big guys. Twice the school had flagged him as a potential child abuse victim, but he'd clammed up when pressed; and when they talked to his Mom, she was all sweetness and light—and then she beat the living hell out of him after they were gone.

She'd taken a succession of men into the house at various times as live-in lovers, but none had been too thrilled about the kid being around, either. Irving was already learning the street business as a lookout for Clarence's robberies of corner stores and other such places across town, and he'd been picked up once and was now on probation.

She'd told him that his father had deserted them, but he'd always known that it wasn't true. In fact, Irving had a somewhat idealized vision of his father, but his father was dead someplace out west in Texas, and he'd had no hope that the kind, gentle man who'd doted on him and played with him and took him all sorts of places when they lived in a nice neighborhood long ago would ever return.

"I didn't die, Irv," he said gently. "Your Mom wouldn't let me see you or talk to you. I sent you all sorts of presents and letters, but I guess she never let you see them."

The boy was close to tears but didn't want to show

weakness. "No. She say you never once even asked for me—but I know it was a lie."

"It was. I thought a lot about you. I hoped, one day, to come back and see you, but until now I haven't been able to. I've been away. Far away in another land. This is the first time, maybe the only time, they let me come back."

The boy looked at him. "You was somethin' else with them dudes! I never saw nobody could move that fast!"

"You have to, where I'm living now."

"You—you ain't stayin', then." The same twelve-year-old who not an hour earlier had been scared to death of this man now already seemed stricken at the thought that this was just a visit. "You say—the only time."

He nodded. "I'm afraid so." He felt suddenly very angry. *Damn it*! he told himself. *I can't leave him here! I can't consign my only son to Hell!* "Irv—this is sudden, and you have to take a lot on trust from me. If you want, you can come with me. Right now—it has to be now. No going home, no saying good-bye, no leaving notes or picking up favorite things. Right now."

The boy hesitated. "Where?"

"To someplace far away. Someplace where nobody we know will ever find us. Someplace—*magical*."

The boy looked up at his father, trying to decide what to do. It wasn't much of an existence, but it had some good points and was the only one he'd ever known.

"This place—it like in South America or Africa or something?"

Joe shook his head and smiled slightly. "No, it's much farther than that. It's a place with good guys and bad guys and other stuff, too. The fairy-tale kind of stuff. Witches and wizards and strange kind of creatures. Dragons and unicorns and other things." He decided not to mention the fact that there was also no television. Why risk losing the war?

"Ain't no such place. You just connin' me?"

"No con. There *is* such a place, always has been, and

that's where I wound up. If it's not at least that, I'll get you back. Deal?"

The boy still hesitated, wondering if this strange man who seemed really to be his father wasn't cracked in the head and escaped from some looney bin someplace. And then he thought of Alvy and Charlie and Clarence. They'd heal up, sooner or later, and they'd remember who that big dude was looking for.

"Well, I guess I should," Irving said nervously. "At least I'll see if you really nuts or not."

"*That* has nothing to do with where we're going. You're sure? It's now or never. I can drop you back near your home, or you come now."

"I'll come."

Joe let out a blood-curdling war whoop that would have awakened his ancestors. He stepped on it and made the exit for rental car return at the airport in record time. "Okay, son! We're off and running now!" he almost yelled. "We got dragons to slay and damsels to save and whole armies of bad guys to face down with guts and a magic sword! We got wizards and witches and zombies and elves and we got the *magic*!"

Irving stared at his father, and for a fleeting second he almost believed the words.

ABOUT THE AUTHOR

JACK L. CHALKER was born in Norfolk, Virginia, on December 17, 1944, but was raised and has spent most of his life in Baltimore, Maryland. He learned to read almost from the moment of entering school, and by working odd jobs amassed a large book collection by the time he was in junior high school, a collection now too large for containment in his quarters. Science fiction, history, and geography all fascinated him early on, interests that continue.

Chalker joined the Washington Science Fiction Association in 1958 and began publishing an amateur SF journal, *Mirage*, in 1960. After high school he decided to be a trial lawyer, but money problems and the lack of a firm caused him to switch to teaching. He holds bachelor degrees in history and English, and an M.L.A. from Johns Hopkins University. He taught history and geography in the Baltimore public schools between 1966 and 1978, and now makes his living as a freelance writer. Additionally, out of the amateur journals he founded a publishing house, The Mirage Press, Ltd., devoted to nonfiction and bibliographic works on science fiction and fantasy. This company has produced more than twenty books in the last nine years. His hobbies include esoteric audio, travel, working on science-fiction convention committees, and guest lecturing on SF to institutions such as the Smithsonian. He is an active conservationist and National Parks supporter, and he has an intense love of ferryboats, with the avowed goal of riding every ferry in the world. In fact, in 1978 he was married to Eva Whitley on an ancient ferryboat in mid-river. They live in the Catoctin Mountain region of western Maryland with their son David.